Praise for Phoebe Conn's
Defy the World Tomatoes

"If you're looking for something different, passionate, romantic, and adventurous, then I recommend this book for you. There's passion to be found and control to be given up in order for two uniquely opposing characters to find love!"

~ *Among the Muses*

"Defy The World Tomatoes is overflowing with action, suspense, drama and love. It's like ordering the supreme pizza, you get a little bit of everything. Enjoy!"

~ *The Romance Reviews*

Look for these titles by
Phoebe Conn

Now Available:

Defy the World Tomatoes
Where Dreams Begin

Defy the World
Tomatoes

Phoebe Conn

Samhain Publishing, Ltd.
11821 Mason Montgomery Road, 4B
Cincinnati, OH 45249
www.samhainpublishing.com

Defy the World Tomatoes

Print ISBN: 978-1-60928-294-3
Digital ISBN: 978-1-60928-242-4

Editing by Linda Ingmanson
Cover by Kanaxa

First Samhain Publishing, Ltd. electronic publication: November 2010
First Samhain Publishing, Ltd. print publication: October 2011

Dedication

Defy the World Tomatoes is for my father,who brought the joy of music into our lives.

Prologue

The Ritz, Barcelona, Spain, Present Day

"I won't kill for you," Griffin swore. "I'll gather whatever useful intelligence comes my way, and gladly pass it on to Interpol, but I draw the line at murder, even with a despicable sort like Lyman Vaughn, who most certainly deserves it."

Lucien LeGran remained silent while Griffin punched diamond studs into his pleated tuxedo shirt. Then the Frenchman nodded thoughtfully. "I must say I'm surprised that someone of your passions hasn't already killed a man or two."

"I pour my passions into my music, Lucien, and that's all you need to know." Griffin slipped on his shirt, fastened the studs and tied his bow tie with the same deft elegance he displayed at a grand piano. He turned as he picked up his jacket. "It's time I left for the concert hall."

His visitor rose and followed him to the door of the luxurious suite. "Lyman Vaughn is too devoted a fan not to surface at one of your concerts soon, and you need only let us know. Your service is greatly appreciated, Griffin. Don't ever doubt Interpol's commitment to you."

Griffin shot him a cynical glance. "You needn't repeat your speech about the benefit to humanity outweighing the personal risk, because I'll never be your assassin."

"What you do is more than enough," Lucien emphasized, but he could not help but hope that if the time ever came for such decisive action, Griffin Moore would not fail them.

Chapter One

Darcy yanked the hose past a tiered cluster of succulents in hand-thrown terracotta pots and continued spraying off the cement walkways. The paths' lazy curves lured tourists deep into the heart of the Defy the World Tomatoes' nursery, and few left without buying at least one unusual plant and filling a green shopping bag with the charming collectibles carried in the adjacent gift shop.

It was early spring, and during the week business was often slow, but even if the paths had been teeming with the usual swarm of weekend tourists, Darcy still would have noticed the tall, dark-haired man standing at the entrance of the pottery shed.

Like most of their customers, he had paused to admire the large iron goldfish suspended from the overhead beam. The separate sections of the striking sculpture formed a dramatic blend of sharp angles and flaring curves and drew a constant stream of compliments.

Darcy assumed the morning's lone customer garnered effusive praise of his own. He was over six feet in height and broad shouldered. His thick black hair was without the slightest curl and, while superbly cut, brushed the collar of his chambray shirt. He wore scuffed loafers with faded Levi's slung low on his narrow hips, so clearly he hadn't sailed into Monarch Bay on his own yacht. Or if he had, he'd changed clothes before leaving the docks for a stroll down Embarcadero.

Despite his casual attire, as he examined the iron fish his gestures held a wealthy man's confident elegance. Darcy felt assured that, while it was an expensive piece, the cost would be well within his reach. Inspired to promote the charming work rather than simply gawk at the handsome stranger, she quickly retraced her steps, turned off the water and coiled the hose around the frog-topped spigot.

A sunflower appliqué adorned the bib pocket of her forest green overalls, and she adjusted the angle of her matching baseball cap as she approached him.

"Good morning," she called out. "That sculpture is by Toby McClure, a talented Los Angeles artist. All his work has that same irresistible whimsy."

The man's expression held only mild interest as he stepped back and continued to assess the piece. After an uncomfortably long silence, he finally nodded. "I'll grant you that it's whimsical, but I just might be able to resist it."

His deep voice held a delicious hint of an accent Darcy couldn't place and, up close, he was even better looking than he had been at first glance. A golden tan graced his finely chiseled features. Darcy wished the color of his eyes wasn't hidden by wire-rimmed sunglasses.

With hair that dark, she feared his eyes were as deep a brown as her own. Unfortunately, she'd never had a bit of luck with brown-eyed men. It wasn't that she didn't find them attractive, for she most certainly did, but somehow they never asked her out more than once or twice.

She tried to recall the last time she'd actually been out on a date; then, ashamed of the romantic drift of her thoughts, she licked her lips and made an effort to come up with a witty defense of Toby's work, but to her dismay, none came to her. She just wanted the man to remove his dark glasses so she would know whether or not he was a hopeless cause. Inspired, she hoped to lure him inside.

"If you find Toby's work appealing, perhaps you'd care to look at some other samples. I have photographs of his most recent pieces in my office."

The man glanced at the slim gold watch on his right wrist. "Sorry. I like the fish well enough, but I don't have anywhere to display it. Your sign lists custom landscape design. Do I need an appointment to speak with your landscaper, or is he available now?"

There'd been a time when such a presumptuous question would have prompted a bitterly sarcastic response from Darcy, but as one of the Tomatoes intent upon defying the world, she could ill-afford to lose a customer, even a blatantly chauvinistic one. She forced a smile and doffed her cap with an exaggerated flourish.

"You're looking at her, but you needn't apologize. Most people assume all landscape architects are male, but I've earned the appropriate college degree and first-hand experience to handle whatever you require."

As Darcy continued to regard him closely, the man failed to react with either surprise or, God forbid, annoyed disappointment, but she was sorry he hadn't responded with an encouraging smile. It was unusual to find such an attractive man without a statuesque blonde by his side, but Darcy doubted he would be good company if his mood were always this preoccupied or, perhaps, downright melancholy. A quick glance at his left hand revealed no wedding band, but he hadn't come seeking a dating service, and she again hauled her wandering thoughts back to business.

"If you have any doubts about my ability," she stressed, "you're welcome to view my portfolio." She gestured toward the building that housed the gift shop. The two-story structure resembled a random collection of upended boxes with long narrow windows cut in the sides, but Darcy's elegant landscaping softened the sharp angles while the salty sea breeze had aged the wooden siding to the lush, smoky patina of driftwood.

When he still appeared to be hesitant to respond, Darcy drew herself up to her full five feet two inches. He was a good foot taller, but she'd never been intimidated by height. She fought to hang on to her temper, but a peppery edge crept into her voice.

"Are you objecting to me personally, or is it women in general who bother you?"

A faint smile lent a slight curl to the man's lips. "Women have always bothered me," he confided in a softly suggestive whisper, "but that's as it should be. I didn't mean to offend you. I was simply searching for the best way to describe the job. I just bought the old Hadley place up on Ridgecrest. Do you know it?"

Darcy recognized the name of the exclusive street, if not the particular house. Ridgecrest curved through the mountain slopes encircling Monarch Bay and provided access to a great many beautiful homes. Somehow she doubted "the old Hadley place" was anything less than a tastefully appointed mansion. That meant she definitely wanted any landscaping job he might offer.

She relaxed her stance and softened her voice to its former cordial level. "I'm sorry, but I moved here less than a year ago to open Defy the World with a college friend. I haven't had much time for sightseeing."

"That's all right. You can't see anything but the gate from the road anyway."

"You must have a marvelous view of the sea," she replied. Now certain his home had to be a palatial estate, Darcy sent a mental command for him to yank off his dark glasses, but he stubbornly resisted doing so.

"Yes, the terrace faces the bay. It's why I bought the place. What I have in mind is a Zen garden overlooking the sea. Have you any experience landscaping those?"

"A Zen garden?" Darcy repeated numbly. Her specialty was the exuberant use of colorful flowering plants and, unfortunately, that was not what was required.

"Of course," she replied confidently, which was a bald-faced lie. "You'll want an expanse of white sand carefully raked to suggest ocean waves, a few boulders to conjure up a mountain range, perhaps a wind-tortured cypress or two and a comfortable wooden bench from which to contemplate it all."

Clearly delighted by her evocative description, the man flashed a wide grin. His teeth were very white and, against his dark skin, the expression had an immediate high-voltage impact. "That's exactly what I had in mind. How soon can you begin?"

Stunned by his unexpected show of warmth, Darcy had to glance away. She quickly reassessed her opinion of his melancholy bent and wondered how many women had been the object of a similar rakish grin and fainted dead away.

Damn! she cursed silently. It had definitely been too long since she'd been out on a date, and now it was nearly impossible to confine her thoughts to the relevant aspects of their conversation.

Still, she made the attempt. It was Tuesday morning, and she wondered if he had a formal party planned for Saturday night. On more than one occasion, she'd been asked to rip out every sprig of greenery from a yard and, as if by magic, produce the most splendid of gardens by the weekend. At least he'd come by early in the week so the task, while formidable, could be accomplished.

She gathered her resolve and looked him in the eye, or at least the sunglasses. "I'll need to come up to your house and survey the site, then draw up plans for your approval. If you'll be home this afternoon, I can come by around two o'clock."

"I'll make it a point to be there. You'll need my address." He pulled a business card from his shirt pocket, but it held only his name and telephone number. "Do you have a pen?"

Darcy plucked a green ballpoint from her bib pocket. "Here you are." Defy the World was printed on the side and a small red silk rose sprouted from the top. She'd never considered the pens ridiculously feminine, but as he reached for it with his left hand, it looked impossibly fragile.

He made a quick note of his address and, after handing the card and pen to Darcy, extended his right hand. "I'm Griffin Moore."

As her tiny hand disappeared into his, Darcy's breath left her throat in a hoarse gasp. Griffin's fingers were long and slim, his grasp firm, but the heat of his touch matched the fiery intensity of his smile and sent a sizzling thrill clear to her rubber-soled boots. At almost the same instant, the outdoor garden was filled with the lively rhythms of native flutes and drums. The lilting tune swirled around them with the grace of animated butterflies and, for a terrible moment, Darcy was so lost in Griffin's smile that she completely forgot her own name.

"Darcy MacLeod," she finally blurted, but she couldn't bear to withdraw her hand and felt a painful tear of separation as Griffin released his hold.

He immediately glanced toward the outdoor speakers mounted on the gift shop. "What charming music. Do you know what it is?"

Darcy's business partner, Christy Joy, selected the CDs and tapes they played and sold. Darcy told herself she wasn't afraid to introduce Griffin to her and ask for the title, but she was enormously relieved it wasn't necessary.

"That's Otavalomanta. They're Indians from Ecuador who claim to be descendants of the Inca. We've sold quite a few of their CDs. I believe the plants enjoy their high-spirited music as much as people do."

Another hint of a smile crossed Griffin's lips. "Yes, I'm sure they do. Bring one of their CDs with you this afternoon."

He turned away and walked out of the nursery before Darcy found her voice to say good-bye. He hadn't made a polite request for a CD. He'd spoken a command with the ease of a man accustomed to being obeyed, and she hadn't even blinked. She drew in a deep breath and released it in an anguished sigh.

He probably had half a dozen leggy blondes at home, along with a gorgeous redhead or two, but she'd never been so deeply affected by any man. That she'd obviously had no such dramatic effect on him was humiliating.

"Brown-eyed for sure," she swore softly and reluctantly got to work tending the plants.

In what Darcy felt certain was a cowardly move, she merely announced an afternoon appointment and left Defy the World without describing Griffin Moore to Christy Joy. As she drove from the coastal village toward the mountains, she tried to justify that shocking omission of such a significant detail, but the only possible explanation was a deplorable suspicion that Griffin might prefer the pretty blonde to her. She was appalled that a single meeting had prompted a jealous streak she hadn't previously suspected she possessed.

Just who was Griffin Moore to come striding into Defy the World and make her feel so inadequate? She caught sight of her reflection in her truck's rearview mirror and hoped a triple coat of mascara had enhanced her eyes sufficiently to make him take a second look. Everyone always said her eyes were her best feature, and she wore her hair pixie-short with fringed bangs to frame them attractively.

As for her outfit, she flat-out loved the comfort of overalls, and the ones Christy Joy designed for Defy the World were colorful and fit well. The only problem was that a man with Griffin's obvious sophistication probably hadn't taken a second look at a girl in overalls since he left preschool. She could have gone home and put on a pair of tight Levi's and a sweater, but this was, after all, a professional visit, not a seduction. As if she could seduce someone like Griffin!

The thought made her laugh, and she sat up straighter and

turned off the thoroughfare onto Ridgecrest still wearing a smile. She'd been through the area a time or two simply to enjoy the pine-scented route and the sparkling view of the bay in the distance. Most of the beautiful estates lining Ridgecrest had been built in the 1920s, when wealthy families from back East had flocked to the Pacific Ocean for the summer.

Set back from the road and screened by oak and fragrant eucalyptus, many of the estates had changed hands numerous times, but, like the quaint town of Monarch Bay, had endured. Now modernized and redecorated, they were showplaces once again.

Darcy had memorized Griffin's address the moment he'd handed her his card, but she had to continually scan the long stone walls and impressive iron gates for the numbers to chart her progress up the hill. She finally found Griffin's address near the summit. He'd left the gate open for her, and she drove slowly up the curving driveway.

Even expecting something grand, Darcy was stunned by the beauty of the Mediterranean-style villa. Freshly painted in a rich terracotta shade which nearly matched the red tile roof, its arched entrance and high Palladian windows promised an interior of classical perfection.

The landscaping, however, consisted of scattered clumps of badly trimmed camellias. Darcy couldn't imagine why Griffin wished to begin at the rear of the house when the front cried out for attention, but she was elated to discover so much work needed to be done.

She swung her Chevy truck around the circular drive and parked by the front door. She'd brought the requested Otavalomanta CD and picked it up along with her clipboard. "This is just a job like any other," she whispered as she moved up the brick walk, but her wildly beating heart failed to agree. As she raised her hand to the bell, she prayed the door wouldn't be opened by a pair of stunning twins in skimpy fuchsia bikinis.

The bell rang with a faraway echo, and Darcy strained to hear the click of high heels across what would surely be a tiled entryway. The thickness of the carved wooden door blocked the sound of Griffin's approach, and Darcy was startled when he suddenly swung it open.

Much to her delight, his sunglasses were tucked in his

shirt pocket, for without their shadow his eyes shone with a lively intelligence and wit, and she envied him his dark sweep of thick lashes.

His large, expressive eyes were definitely as handsome as the rest of him, but as deep a brown as dark chocolate, and with that knowledge came a sharp sting of disappointment. Darcy had to swallow a revealing moan, but even knowing the likelihood of his ever caring for her was extremely slight, she felt a real sense of loss.

"Good afternoon," she managed in a breathless rush. "Here's your CD." She thrust it into his hands, then silently scolded herself for not having done it with more grace.

Griffin, meanwhile, began studying the musicians pictured on the CD. They wore blue ponchos, long braids, worn fedoras, and looked convincingly like modern-day Incas.

"Thanks. Do you want to just add this to my bill, or would you rather I paid you now?"

"I don't really care, but our bookkeeper insists that we keep the landscaping commissions separate from the gift shop sales."

Griffin reached into his pocket, withdrew a gold money clip and peeled off a twenty-dollar bill. "Will this cover it?"

"Yes. Just a minute, I think I have change."

"No, keep it as a delivery charge." He stepped back to allow her to precede him into the house. "I hope the scent of fresh paint doesn't bother you, and you'll have to excuse the lack of furnishings. I haven't had time to move in more than a bed and my piano."

The high, beamed ceiling caught Darcy's notice first, then the wide staircase which curved up to the second floor. The interior had been painted a rich ivory which glowed against the dark wood but cried out for colorful paintings and tables to display huge bouquets of fresh flowers. On their left, she caught a glimpse of what appeared by the level of the chandelier to be the dining room, and on the right, a spacious living room.

The highly polished dark hardwood floor was covered by a magnificent Oriental carpet with a navy blue background setting off a writhing pattern of gold and terracotta flowers. The stylized design was so intricate, Darcy thought she would have to crawl over it on her hands and knees for hours to truly appreciate its beauty.

When her gaze finally reached the far end of the room, she

found not simply a piano, but a concert grand in gleaming ebony wood. Amazed by the impressive instrument, she turned back to Griffin.

"Do you play the piano, or is it merely for show?"

A faint air of puzzlement filled Griffin's expression, but, after a strained moment, he shrugged. "I enjoy playing it upon occasion. Let's go out through the french doors."

He led the way through the living room to the three sets of french doors which opened out onto the terrace. He unlocked the center set and again waited for Darcy to precede him.

The house was built in an L shape and, as they stepped outside, the kitchen and maid's quarters were to their left. The brick terrace was bordered by an expanse of parched grass which Darcy agreed would be improved by the addition of a Zen garden. Beyond, the hillside sloped away to provide a panoramic view of Monarch Bay. The afternoon sun danced on the Pacific Ocean with a shimmering sparkle, and Darcy drank it in for a long moment before glancing up at Griffin.

He appeared to be equally lost in the splendid view, and the seriousness of his expression again hinted at melancholy while his posture remained proud. Darcy had known several men with his height who had adopted a stoop-shouldered slouch, perhaps in an effort to reduce the distance between themselves and others. She'd always thought it a shame that they hadn't stood up straight and had even told a couple to do so. From what little she'd observed of Griffin, however, she doubted he ever walked with a dejected slump, regardless of his mood.

She wondered if he'd come there alone willingly, or perhaps had chosen a solitary exile at the end of a painful love affair. Who would leave him? she scoffed silently, but she knew only too well that love did not always guarantee happiness. Griffin glanced down at her, caught her observing him rather than the proposed site of the Zen garden and, embarrassed, she quickly directed her attention to the overgrown plot.

"I bought the house from the daughter of the original owner," Griffin explained. "She's in her eighties, hasn't lived here in half a century and was elated to find someone who'd restore the beauty, rather than merely throw together a careless remodel of her childhood home.

"The interior renovations were all completed before I moved in last week, but I wasn't certain what I wanted to do with the grounds until I got here. What do you think of my idea?"

Had he asked for her suggestion before offering his own, Darcy would have proposed replanting the lawn and surrounding it with a flowering border that would provide color without obstructing the magnificent view. Now she believed the stark beauty of raked sand suited him.

"This is an enchanting spot for a Zen garden," she responded. "It should provide the perfect respite from the cares of the day."

Griffin shoved his hands into his hip pockets. "That's the idea. The sunset is well worth watching. I'd almost forgotten how beautiful it can be."

Intrigued, Darcy waited for him to expand upon that wistful statement, but he failed to elaborate. Because he'd impressed her as being an intensely private man, she refrained from asking him to clarify his comment.

"It'll take me a few minutes to measure the area, and then I'll work up a sketch and quick estimate."

Griffin shook his head. "I don't care what it costs."

Darcy glanced back toward the sparsely furnished house. It was clear evidence of his wealth, but she'd learned the hard way that a landscaper with only a verbal contract had nothing to hang on to but air.

"That's good to know, but I can't operate that way. You'll have to approve and sign my estimate, or I won't be able to take the job."

When Griffin looked down at her this time, she saw something new in his gaze and recognized it as a flash of anger. Apparently he didn't like to be crossed, and she'd just refused to do things his way. That meant a life with him would be wildly exciting, but it would be lived solely on his terms. Some women would accept that onerous condition as the price of love, but she was not among them.

She'd left his address posted on her appointment board, so the police would come calling if he flew into a murderous rage and flung her off the cliff. Buoyed by that thought, she discounted the fact he probably outweighed her by a hundred pounds and raised her chin proudly.

"One of the first commissions I had here was from a woman who wanted me to plant a rose garden that would be the envy of all her friends in the garden club. I told her it would be expensive to include the rarest varieties, but she swore she didn't care a fig about the expense. She just wanted spectacular results and, while we conferred on the selection of roses, we never discussed the cost.

"When the work was finished, she was absolutely thrilled with her new garden, and I mean ecstatic, until I presented her with the bill." Darcy shifted her gaze toward the sea. "In an instant, she was completely transformed into a foaming-mouthed shrew who spewed out some of the raunchiest insults imaginable. Sailors would have blushed, or maybe paid her for such inventive slurs. I mean it was really ugly."

Now that had been frightening, she recalled. Hoping she'd aroused Griffin's curiosity, she paused and made him wait for more. They were standing within a few feet of each other, and she could actually feel him watching her. Even if she didn't get this job, she hoped he would shake her hand so she would have an excuse to touch him again. Her palm began to itch just thinking about it, and she wiped her hand on her overalls.

"Well," Griffin prompted, "what did you do?"

Darcy risked a quick peek at his eyes and was relieved the fiery light had dimmed to a mere glow. She faced him squarely and continued. "I just stood there and waited for her to run out of breath, then I told her I'd have my crew back within the hour and that we'd yank out every last rose. I said I'd still have to charge her for the labor, but without the roses, her bill would be a modest one."

"But without the roses, all she would have had was dirt."

Darcy nodded. "That's right. It looked like a simple choice to me, and we hadn't pulled up more than half a dozen bushes when she calmed down enough to discuss a payment plan. Now that's an afternoon I'll never forget, and the whole nasty scene could have been avoided if I'd just insisted that she read and approve my estimate. Only fools don't learn from their mistakes, Mr. Moore, and I don't repeat mine."

Griffin gave a grudging nod to concede the point. "I'll not ask you to compromise your principles, Ms. MacLeod, but please be assured I'll okay whatever figure you select."

"Darcy," she reminded him.

"Darcy." His faint accent caressed her name obligingly, but he turned away without asking to be called Griffin.

Insulted, Darcy couldn't draw a deep breath until he'd

returned to the house, and even then she wasn't certain who had actually won that exchange. Deciding it'd probably been a draw, she took comfort in the familiar, made some quick measurements of the scruffy lawn, then sat on the terrace steps to create a sketch. Knowing what was required, she'd prepared some rough figures before leaving the nursery and was about to complete her written estimate when Griffin began to play the piano.

She'd once dated a man who could produce a passable version of "Memories" from CATS, and a few Beatles tunes. That's all she'd expected from Griffin, but he was playing an intricate classical piece whose lofty strains soared to the living room's twenty-foot ceiling and then rolled out over the terrace in thunderous waves. The only classical selections she could name were the "1812 Overture" and Ravel's "Bolero", and it was neither of those.

She quickly added the costs entailed in constructing the Zen garden, then got up and crossed the terrace to stand at the french doors Griffin had left ajar. She hesitated to enter the living room for fear of disturbing him even more than she already had, and so simply propped her shoulder against the jamb and waited for him to finish whatever it was he was playing and look up.

The piece was a lengthy one, however, and Griffin demonstrated far more than mere technical brilliance. He played with the very same passionate fire she'd glimpsed in his dark eyes. The music washed through her in a sensuous rush and, far from being annoyed at having to wait, she stood transfixed, caught up in the melody Griffin coaxed from the keys with a fury that would surely have reduced a lesser instrument to a heap of kindling.

Other than the sticks Darcy had tapped together in the rhythm band in kindergarten, she had no experience in creating music. She'd been to a couple of rock concerts, even seen the Grateful Dead once in San Francisco, but she'd never attended a symphony performance. Still, even a novice such as she would have recognized Griffin's genius.

When he finally drew the piece to a crescendo of pulse-pounding chords, she couldn't help but shout, "Bravo! That was fantastic."

Griffin glanced up and for a terrible moment appeared not

to recall who she was. Afraid she'd disturbed him after all, Darcy approached the piano with a cautious step. "I'm sorry if I interrupted you, but I thought you were finished. I've never heard anyone play so well."

She remembered hearing the Russians were passionate and mentioned the only composer who came to mind, praying she didn't sound as ignorant as she truly was. "Was that Tchaikovsky?"

Griffin left the piano bench with an easy stretch. "Franz Liszt. I'm glad you enjoyed it."

He came forward with a slow, smooth stride, and Darcy couldn't seem to make her feet take a step backward even after he'd invaded her personal space by several inches. He came to a halt so close she had to crane her neck to look up at him. She thrust her clipboard into his solar plexus to jolt him into stepping back and create more distance between them.

"At the top of the form, I've made a drawing to show the placement of the cypress and boulders. My total is at the bottom. If you'd like to get other bids, please go right ahead. I'll not be offended, and you'll find my prices are competitive."

Griffin took hold of her clipboard and, after a quick glance at the form, reached toward her. "Do you mind?" he asked.

Darcy was too shocked to object when he plucked the rose-topped pen from her bib pocket, but his fingertips grazed her breast to coil an electric charge around her ribcage. With an almost painful sweetness, lingering sparks drifted downward to leave her moist with desire. She shook her head, but it wasn't simply to offer the pen.

Griffin's slightest touch brought such a heart-stopping thrill that she couldn't help but wonder if she would survive should he ever show her the same unbridled passion he'd just lavished on his piano.

Then, with a slight tremble, she wondered how she could bear to exist if he didn't.

Chapter Two

Darcy pulled into her parking space behind the Defy the World Tomatoes nursery, but she was uncertain how she'd made it down the winding mountain road. She hadn't had a crush on a man in years—if fascination this intense could even be defined as such—while the hypnotically attractive Griffin Moore was clearly immune to her charms.

Yet that morning he had slyly admitted that women had always bothered him. His voice had taken on a breathless edge that had made her ache to hear far more intimate confessions. That proved to be his most revealing remark of the day, however, and she knew little more about him than when he'd sauntered into Defy the World shortly after she'd rolled open the gate.

His dark good looks stirred a real physical hunger, but his voice held an elusive quality that made her cling to his every word. Clearly he was American, but his faint accent made her suspect he might have spent his formative years in Europe, or some exotic isle in the South Pacific where French was the principal language.

She relaxed her grip on the steering wheel and sat back to draw a deep breath. An army brat, she'd been an only child. Her family had moved so often she couldn't really say where she'd grown up. She'd been born in Georgia while her father was stationed at Fort Benning, but her only memory of the state was a blur of green. They'd spent three years in Germany when she was in grammar school, and she'd been to Paris, London and Rome before she was old enough to understand what a privilege being able to travel truly was.

Now she liked staying home and, with that marvelous

house, perhaps that was also Griffin's desire. Unfortunately, as self-contained as he was, he was going to have to stay put for a very long time for them to become friends.

"Not bloody likely," she mumbled to herself. Finally leaving her truck, she entered the nursery through the rear gate.

She was pleased to find half a dozen people strolling the paths, and there were even more in the gift shop. She had to wait for Mary Beth, the clerk who also did their bookkeeping, to ring up a sale before she caught her attention.

"I gave my client a receipt," she assured Mary Beth and then handed over the office copy of Griffin's estimate along with five crisp one hundred-dollar bills, and the twenty for the CD.

Mary Beth wore her long, curly brown hair tied neatly at her nape. She preferred tailored clothes, and her one concession to the garden theme of Defy the World Tomatoes was a floral print vest worn over her oxford cloth shirt and denim skirt.

Dipping her head, Mary Beth sent Darcy a frantic glance over her gold-rimmed glasses. "I can't recall the last time someone paid you in cash. Could he be a drug dealer?"

In action-adventure films, the South American drug lords were always dark and dashing. Griffin Moore definitely fit the part, but Darcy doubted he was involved in anything illegal. "I didn't ask what he did for a living, but he struck me as an honest man. Do you actually expect some drug kingpin to turn up here in Monarch Bay, or have you just been reading too many thrillers lately?"

Mary Beth set the estimate aside to enter into the computer later, but quickly slipped the cash into the register. "I know the difference between fiction and reality," she protested smugly, "but since you mention it, it wouldn't hurt you to spend more of your spare time reading."

"What spare time?" Darcy scoffed. "I haven't had more than five minutes to call my own since Christy Joy invited me to become her partner."

After moving to Monarch Bay, she'd bought a kayak and paddled around the bay a time or two, but that had been her single diversion. It was no wonder the sight of Griffin Moore had made her drool. Then she began to wonder if he'd ever been kayaking.

A woman approached the desk with a question about the

orchids on display near the small ceramic fountains, and Darcy left the counter with her. Spare time, she fumed silently, but she smiled sweetly as she extolled the ease with which orchids could be grown.

Although Darcy was preoccupied, her customer brought a gorgeous cymbidium with a half-dozen blooms and, as Darcy went on out into the nursery, she heard Christy Joy exclaim over the plant's beauty.

Christy Joy's personality was as exuberant as her blond curls, and she had a talent for displaying a sincere interest in every customer, which did wonders to stimulate repeat business. She and Darcy had met their freshman year in college. Darcy never would have predicted how close they would become, but it was impossible not to love someone as genuinely sweet as Christy Joy Jennings.

Darcy's talents lay with horticulture and, while everyone responded to the nursery's varied selection of cacti and well-tended plants, its success was due to her professional competence rather than her somewhat reserved manner. She bent to tighten a grouping of bright red potted geraniums and felt a lingering sense of wonder that she was a co-owner in such a remarkable venture.

She looked up to find Christy Joy's four-year-old daughter playing hopscotch across a set of scallop-shell-shaped stepping stones set in a gravel border. Her name was Catherine, but everyone called her Twink. Darcy made her way around the circular path to reach her.

"How are you doing this afternoon, Twinkle Toes?" she asked.

Twink raised her arms above her head as she twirled around on the last stone. Dressed like her mother in a bright yellow-and-blue-print pinafore and ruffled white blouse, she had the porcelain prettiness of an expensive doll. There were ribbon laces on her pale blue tennis shoes, but she'd never been able to sit still and was a tomboy at heart.

"Okay, I guess," the little girl responded.

"Just okay? How did things go at preschool?"

Twink hopped back across the stones. "Angela threw up and got sent home."

"Oh dear, was she embarrassed?"

Twink paused on one foot and caught her balance with

outstretched arms. "No. Throwing up's not like wetting your pants."

"Of course, I'd forgotten." Darcy extended her hand. "Come help me count the little stone frogs. I want to see if anyone bought one this afternoon while I was away."

Twink took Darcy's hand and skipped along beside her. "Let's get some real frogs and let them swim in the fountains and hop all around."

"Like you do, Twink?" Darcy laughed at the mayhem live frogs would surely create. "Our customers might be terrified if one came leaping out at them, and we can't have that."

Disappointed, Twink pursed her lips. "It would be fun though, wouldn't it, Darcy?"

"Yes, baby, it sure would."

With Twink's chatty company, the afternoon passed quickly. At six o'clock, Darcy rolled the gate across the nursery entrance and locked it. Then she went inside to check the day's receipts. It was a nightly ritual the partners had begun on opening day, and charting the slow, steady growth in business provided constant reassurance to them both.

Mary Beth made a quick tally and announced the sum proudly. "Not bad for a weekday, and with Darcy's new landscaping commission, it'll be a good week."

Christy Joy wiped off the counter and straightened the selection of tiny gift books displayed beside the register. Her daughter was coloring at the little child's table nearby, allowing her a minute to talk. "Is it something exciting, Darcy?"

Darcy provided only a brief summary of the Zen garden, and not a word about Griffin Moore. "Looks like the gift shop was busy all afternoon."

Christy Joy smoothed a curl back into the cluster atop her head. "It sure was, but I don't want to forget to tell you the landlord's attorney called."

"Jess Stevens? What's he want?"

"It seems the elusive owner of the Ivory Corporation is in town and wants to meet with us tomorrow at nine."

"Here or at Stevens' office?"

"Here. I'll bake rolls and serve coffee, you know, make a little party of it."

Darcy leaned against the counter. "This is a business

meeting. We really don't have to entertain. The shop and nursery are doing well, and we make the lease payments on time. That's any landlord's dream. Did Stevens mention his name?"

"Yes, Griffin Moore."

Mary Beth appeared puzzled. "Where have I heard that name?"

It took a moment for Darcy to recover from the shock. "Griffin Moore's the man who ordered the Zen garden," she reminded Mary Beth. "His name is on the estimate. He was here this morning, and I was out at his home on Ridgecrest this afternoon. I don't understand why he didn't mention a significant fact like being our landlord."

"Maybe he wanted to see how we operate first," Christy Joy suggested.

"He was working undercover," Mary Beth interjected.

"You have definitely been reading too many thrillers," Darcy warned. "The man's a hunk, and there's no way he could disappear into a crowd and work undercover."

"Really?" Christy Joy's expression brightened. "Is he nice?"

Darcy shrugged. "He plays the piano beautifully, but he's rather distant. I can't swear that he's nice."

"Now I'm worried," Christy Joy admitted.

So was Darcy, but for an entirely different reason.

Griffin strolled into the Defy the World Tomatoes gift shop the next morning smartly dressed in a gray suit, white shirt and maroon tie. His attorney, the silver-haired Jess Stevens, was by his side.

"Good morning," Griffin greeted them. He nodded to Darcy and then smiled at Christy Joy. "I'm Griffin Moore."

"Christy Joy Jennings," she responded and offered homemade caramel rolls and freshly brewed coffee. Mr. Stevens appeared to be delighted by her hospitality and accepted both, while Griffin declined politely and began a slow tour of the shop.

Darcy watched him examine everything from the scented candles to the lacy crocheted sweaters. When he reached the orchids, she finally felt justified in joining him. She'd worn a form-fitting pair of Levi's and a pale lavender sweater, but, next to a man in a thousand-dollar suit, she felt as though she were dressed in rags.

"We've done very well with our orchids," she remarked.

"Do the two of you run this whole enterprise alone?" he asked.

He'd dropped his voice to a husky whisper, and Darcy feared Christy Joy and Jess Stevens would assume they were exchanging secrets. She wished they were. "No, Christy Joy manages the gift shop and supervises the clerks, who will arrive at ten. I run the nursery, but I have help from George Kimble, a retired science teacher, who knows as much about plants as I do. A couple of high school students come in after school.

"When we have a landscaping job, like yours..." She tried not to bare her teeth, "...I hire a crew to handle the labor. We're very proud of how well we've done, which I'm sure you can see."

Griffin nodded. "I apologize for not being more forthcoming yesterday, but I was sincere in my request for the Zen garden. Go ahead and deposit my payment."

"I already have," Darcy assured him.

"Good. It's important to keep a close eye on finances." Griffin called over to his attorney. "Jess, why don't you explain my plans? It was nice meeting you, Mrs. Jennings. Good day, ladies."

Darcy stared after him as he walked out with the same self-assured grace that marked all his actions. She'd considered him distant, but that morning he'd been positively glacial. He was certainly a master of the abrupt departure, but she felt unsettled, as though nothing positive had been accomplished by their brief meeting.

She walked back to the counter where Jess Stevens was wiping crumbs from his mouth on a floral napkin. "What plans?" she prompted. "After all, we have a year's lease, and he can't raise our rent."

"No, of course not," Stevens assured them. "That was delicious, Mrs. Jennings. I'm surprised you haven't included a bakery here."

"Thank you, but I'm as anxious as Darcy to hear Mr. Moore's plans."

Stevens fortified himself with another gulp of coffee. "Yes, let me get to that. Now, as obviously you were unaware, Ms.

MacLeod, Mr. Moore is a well-respected concert pianist. He began winning prestigious competitions in his teens and has been touring many years. He owns property in several cities, but he's especially fond of Monarch Bay. Now that he's made his home here, his plans are to turn this facility into a private recording studio."

Darcy and Christy Joy shrieked in unison, "What?"

"Please, there's no need to become alarmed. Your lease doesn't expire until the end of September, so you'll have plenty of time to relocate."

Christy Joy's eyes filled with tears. "Where does he expect us to go?"

"That's really not his concern, Mrs. Jennings."

Darcy couldn't help but take this disaster personally. "Is he pissed that I failed to recognize his name?"

"I doubt Mr. Moore ever becomes pissed, Ms. MacLeod, but he's not a vindictive man, I assure you."

Darcy just shook her head. "Son-of-a-bitch. Why doesn't he build a recording studio in that mausoleum he calls home? Why does it have to be here?"

Jess Stevens straightened. He wore a navy blue suit and brushed a crumb he'd missed from his lapel. "That's his privilege, Ms. MacLeod. Now, I suggest that you and Mrs. Jennings begin making plans to relocate."

"This isn't a shoe store where we can load up the boxes and cart them down the street," Darcy shot right back at him. "We've created a whole world here."

"It's a beautiful world at that," Stevens added. "My wife loves to shop here."

"Well, that's a comfort," Christy Joy sobbed. "What are we going to do, Darcy?"

"First, we're going to tell Mr. Stevens good-bye. Why don't you take a couple of rolls home for your wife? Christy, will you wrap them up, please?"

"Why, thank you." Stevens shifted his weight from foot to foot while he waited, then took the green bag and, with an apologetic smile, hurried away.

Darcy sank onto the floor. "Maybe we ought to hire our own attorney."

Christy Joy wiped her eyes on the lace hanky she kept in

her pinafore pocket. "I was married to J. Lyle long enough to know there would be no point in that. If only we'd been able to buy the property last fall before Mr. Moore decided to move here. He might have sold it to us."

"He doesn't strike me as the reasonable sort," Darcy fumed. "You sew. Can you make a voodoo doll? We could stick pins in its hands and ruin his career."

"That doesn't make any sense, Darcy. Then he'd stay here in Monarch Bay rather than tour, and I want him out of town permanently."

Darcy propped her elbows on her knees and rested her head in her hands. "We're doing better every month, but there's no way we can save enough to lease another building, completely redecorate and move. We can't use just any building, anyway. We need outdoor space for the nursery. We're screwed."

Christy Joy leaned over the counter to look down at Darcy. "Maybe not. We have nearly six months to come up with a plan."

"It's not a plan we need. It's money," Darcy argued.

"Moore's rich, isn't he?"

"What do you want to do, guilt him into paying for our move?"

Darcy had used all her savings, while Christy Joy had spent her divorce settlement to go into business. Things had been going so well, and now she felt as though they'd run full tilt into a brick wall.

She struggled to push herself up off the floor. "We didn't call ourselves the Defy the World Tomatoes for nothing, but I'll be damned if I know what to do."

"I can't work any harder," Christy Joy complained. "I'm already exhausted. It's a good thing Twink and I live upstairs, or I'd never get into work on time."

"Let's play Scarlett O'Hara and worry about this tomorrow," Darcy said. "Then at least we'll be able to get through today."

Christy Joy began nibbling on a caramel roll. "Did you have breakfast?"

"Yes, and it's a good thing too, because I sure couldn't eat now."

For the rest of the morning, Darcy smiled until her cheeks

ached, but none of that forced sunshine reached her heart. For a few months, she'd had the job of her dreams, but now she could feel it slipping through her fingers.

George Kimble prided himself on his ability to read a face. It was a skill he'd refined over his teaching career, but that day a stranger could have glanced at Darcy's goofy smile and known something had gone wrong. He eased himself down onto the tall stool behind the nursery cash register and nudged her with his elbow.

"Want to tell me about it?" he asked.

Darcy's shoulders slumped sadly. "I suppose there's no point in hiding it," she began, and hurriedly explained their impending disaster. "I keep telling myself that we'll cope somehow, but right now, I don't see how."

George shook his head in dismay. "At least the bastard will be able to sit in his Zen garden and contemplate the havoc he's created."

"Are you trying to put a positive spin on this?"

"Hell, no." George raised his drooping hat to scratch the remaining fringe of gray hair above his right ear. "But you could use a boyfriend. Do you like him?"

Darcy's gaze raked the sky. "That's really not the issue, and believe me, he's way out of my league."

"That wasn't my question," George insisted.

Darcy backed away. "I need to make some telephone calls. I can haul the cypress, bench and rolls of plastic in my truck, but I want to make certain the sand and boulders are delivered in the right place."

Certain he had his answer in her abrupt change of subject, George chuckled to himself. "Don't forget to sell him a new rake."

"I've got the deluxe wooden model all ready to go," Darcy replied.

Darcy didn't know how she was going to face Griffin, but when she arrived at his house the next day, he wasn't home. It was her experience that homeowners usually stuck around. The worst argued about the placement of every flower and shrub.

The best merely peered out their windows and waved.

She set her crew to work leveling the ground and spreading out the plastic liner that would keep weeds from sprouting up through the sand. Once the sand and boulders were delivered, the men spread the pale white sand evenly and shoved the boulders into place. Then they planted the cypress and moved the bench to the edge of the sand.

As far as landscaping jobs went, this had been an easy one. Darcy dismissed the crew and began raking the sand into a wavy pattern on her own. When she paused to survey the result, she noticed Griffin leaning against the corner of his house. Startled, she wondered how long he'd been watching her.

He was casually dressed in gray sweats and running shoes. He wasn't smiling and, as he came toward her, she had to fight the urge to hide behind the largest of the new boulders.

"Good afternoon, Mr. Moore. Is this what you had in mind?"

"I think so, but let's sit on the bench and give it a try." He took the special rake from her and slid it under the bench, out of their way.

She'd brought a bench large enough to suit his proportions and, when she sat, her feet dangled off the ground. With no hope of achieving any measure of tranquility, she glanced up at him.

"You been working out?" she asked.

"I try to get to the gym every day. Now that I'm thirty-six, it's not as easy to stay in shape."

Darcy assumed he must be joking, because if there was an ounce of fat on him, it sure wasn't noticeable. She tried to concentrate on the sparkling ocean in the distance, but Griffin was simply impossible to ignore. His hair was damp, and he smelled of spicy soap. His breathing was slow and regular, as though he was enjoying the quiet moment, but she squirmed unhappily.

"Tell me why you chose to become a landscape architect."

He'd used that soft, inviting tone Darcy was sure must capture everyone's attention, but she feared she was particularly susceptible to his resonant baritone. "Have you ever been to the Hotel Del Coronado just south of San Diego?"

"Yes, it's a remarkable place. I understand Thomas Edison

strung the lights."

"That's what they say. A woman named Kate Sessions did the landscaping. She was born before the Civil War and was way ahead of her time in her regard for ecology. She traveled the world to import plants which would thrive alongside those native to California.

"I must have been about twelve when I visited the hotel with my parents. We took a tour, and the minute the docent described Miss Sessions' work, I knew what I wanted to be. I went to Cal Poly San Luis Obispo to study. That's where I met Christy Joy. Now, you tell me something."

Griffin turned toward her and smiled. "Anything," he promised.

His smile, his husky voice and his darkly compelling gaze were mesmerizing, and the question she'd meant to ask fled her mind. "Are you a vampire?"

Greatly amused, Griffin responded with a rich, rolling laugh. "Vampires don't exist, and even if they did, I'm sitting out here in the afternoon sun, and it hasn't turned me to ashes."

Somehow Darcy didn't find his proof all that convincing. "Well, there's something damn odd about you," she blurted.

Griffin sighed. "Yes, I know, but perhaps it's merely the European influence. Tell me, do you find me lacking in warmth?"

"Right at this moment, no, but..."

"So the answer is yes," Griffin posed thoughtfully. "I'm working on it."

He didn't appear to be inviting her sympathy, which Darcy would have regarded as ridiculous, but his poignant comment touched her nevertheless. "I'm sorry I knew nothing about your career. I suppose I should have known when I heard you play."

"You needn't apologize. No one knows everything. I can't name a single quarterback with the NFL."

Darcy conceded that point readily enough, but she hated to waste what could be her only opportunity to find him in a congenial mood. "I can understand why you'd want your own recording studio, but why does it have to be in our building?"

"It's not your building. It's mine."

His voice now rang with unmistakable authority, and Darcy

had nothing more to say. "I think I better go."

"No, stay and watch the sunset with me, and then we'll talk about the rest of the grounds. They're in desperate need of your talents, wouldn't you say?"

He'd offered a tempting lure to keep her there and, instinctively, Darcy recognized a danger that, with tantalizing steps, he might make her bargain away her very soul. If he weren't an actual blood-sucking vampire, he seemed fully capable of sucking away her last ounce of free will. It was a terrifying thought, and yet she stayed put and watched the sun slowly slip beneath the waves.

As the dusk darkened, Griffin reached for her hand, then stood and lifted her easily to her feet. "This garden is perfect. Thank you. Let me give you the final payment before we make anymore plans."

Darcy pulled her hand from his before the delicious tingle of his touch overwhelmed her reason. "It might be better if you hired another firm."

Without touching her again, Griffin drew her along toward the house. "I don't want another firm, and you can't afford to turn down lucrative commissions when you'll need the money to relocate."

That piece of logic annoyed Darcy no end. "That may be true, however..."

"However what? Would you feel as though you were sleeping with the enemy?"

"Mr. Moore, really, if you think my services will include more than plants, you're badly mistaken."

Griffin unlocked the kitchen door, reached in to turn on the lights and ushered her inside. "It's merely a figure of speech."

He flashed a wicked grin, and she wondered if any woman had ever found the strength to climb out of his bed. She'd never met anyone like him. A part of her longed to just go for it, but a taunting inner voice whispered, *Don't you dare.*

"I'll be away several months a year," Griffin confided. "Could you landscape the grounds as your idol would have in native plants that will survive the inevitable neglect?"

"Yes, I'd love to do that, but won't you have someone here, a housekeeper, butler, some sort of staff to maintain your home?"

He nodded thoughtfully. "I suppose I should hire someone."

He leaned back against the center island and crossed his arms over his chest.

The remodeled kitchen was aglow in white enamel and stainless steel. There was a commercial-size gas stove, a huge new refrigerator and a complete array of the latest small appliances. There was no sign their owner had made so much as a slice of toast there, however.

Darcy was surprised he'd given such little thought to the lovely home. "What do you usually do?" she asked.

"This is the first house I've ever owned. I've always lived in hotels, where everything was provided."

Darcy rested a hip against the counter opposite him. "You've never been on your own?"

"Oh, hell, yes. I've been on my own for twenty years, but I lived in hotels even when I was married."

Darcy found that an especially painful bit of news. He was in his mid-thirties, clearly a celebrity in some circles, probably very rich ones, and he'd had plenty of time to marry and divorce. Still, it hurt to think he'd once been another woman's beloved husband.

"What happened?" she inquired softly.

"With my marriage?" He looked down at the glossy marble floor and paused as though he were weighing how much to reveal. Finally he glanced up.

"Carla and I met at Juilliard. She was also a very fine pianist and, at the time, it seemed a perfect match. But she was even more fiercely competitive than I am. It drove her crazy not to play as well as I do, regardless of how many hours she practiced. Her anger poisoned the relationship. Then, a year after we split up, she married a German conductor and retired to have his babies." He smiled, but it failed to reach his eyes. "So it all worked out for the best."

Darcy appreciated knowing the facts, but he'd included only his ex-wife's emotions rather than his own. "Not if Carla broke your heart."

"It was a long time ago. I'm not carrying a torch for her, or anyone. What about you? Are you seeing someone?"

Because Darcy had blatantly pried into his past, there was no way she could avoid his question. "With a new business, there's been no time. I do like men, though," she added and then blushed.

"That's good. Now, I'm not completely inept in the kitchen. I've figured out how to broil a steak. Why don't you stay for dinner?"

Startled by the unexpected invitation, Darcy hauled herself back to reality. "You realize you're trashing my life, don't you?"

Griffin discounted her complaint. "That's business, it's not personal. Besides, I'm sick of eating alone."

Darcy ran her hands down her dusty overalls. "Sorry, but I'm a mess."

"That's easily solved. I've half a dozen bathrooms. Choose one and shower, or soak in the tub, and I'll lend you a robe."

Darcy imagined a black silk robe and, custom-tailored for his impressive size, it would conveniently fall open to provide a provocative glimpse of her petite figure. Embarrassed just thinking about it, she straightened and rested her hand on her hip.

"Does that line actually work for you?"

"What? You've lost me."

"You know damn well what I mean." Darcy didn't even try to mimic his accent, but she succeeded in producing a seductive tone. "Come on in, I'll broil you a steak. Just slip into my robe and get comfortable."

Griffin raked his hand through his hair. "Granted, you'd not be the first woman to wear my robe, but all I'm talking about here is dinner."

"How flattering."

"Flattery had nothing to do with it," Griffin insisted.

His glance had turned to ice, and Darcy wasn't even tempted to stay. "Mr. Moore, you are drop-dead gorgeous, but we're on very dangerous ground here, and I'm going to leave before one of us says something she'll regret."

She stepped to the backdoor and rested her hand on the doorknob. "Let's talk about the grounds tomorrow morning. How's nine o'clock for you? If you still want me to handle the job, that is."

Griffin frowned slightly. "Has no one ever told you that you're drop-dead gorgeous too?"

"Oh, please. On a good day, I'm cute, nothing more."

Griffin closed the space between them and dropped his voice to a haunting whisper. "Beauty, Darcy, is in the eye of the beholder."

Darcy watched him lean down and, even knowing what he meant to do, she couldn't make her feet carry her out the door. He placed his fingertips under her chin to tilt her face up to his and then kissed her so gently, so softly, so sweetly, that it took her breath away.

It was all she could do not to grab hold of his sweatshirt and yank him back down to her level. "I'm out of here," she cried, and she forced herself right on out the door. She hurried around to the side of the house where she'd parked her truck, but Griffin was right on her heels.

The motion-sensitive exterior lighting blinked on, and she was in no danger of tripping or becoming lost. "I can find my way."

"I know, but I'm coming with you anyway. A gentleman always escorts a lady to her car."

He might have excellent manners, but Darcy wondered if anyone ever dared to tell him what to do. As they passed by the four-car garage, she was surprised to find a Land Rover parked outside.

"I thought you'd drive a Porsche," she shot over her shoulder.

"I got over fast cars in my twenties."

"I'm sorry I missed that." Darcy nearly leapt into her truck, then had to fish her keys from her pocket.

"Wait a minute. I owe you some money."

"I'll pick it up in the morning. Good-night."

Griffin shook his head as she drove away, then he began to laugh. Darcy had such lovely, delicate features, and a shapely if petite figure, but clearly she'd picked the right name for her business.

It'd been a long while since a defiant woman had presented him with a challenge and, relishing the prospect, he returned to his kitchen bent on eating his steak rare.

Chapter Three

Christy Joy looked up from a stack of invoices to greet Darcy. "Good morning. I thought you'd be back last night before closing."

"So did I, but I was so dirty I just went on home." Dressed in pale blue overalls appliquéd with sweet peas and a pink T-shirt, Darcy looked sparkling clean, now.

"I assume Mr. Moore was thrilled with your work."

"Thrilled might be an exaggeration. He did seem pleased, though. I'll pick up the final payment this morning. There's a lot of work to be done up there. It'll be like landscaping a small hotel, but I'm not certain the money will be worth it."

Darcy's downcast expression puzzled Christy Joy. "Need I remind you that we can't afford to be choosy?"

"That's what Griffin said, but I don't like being around him."

"Look, if his behavior is out of line—"

"No, he's exceedingly polite." Darcy regarded Christy Joy as her closest friend, but she was reluctant to confide that Griffin gave her that same dizzying, foot-tingling feeling she got standing atop a tall building and looking down at the tiny ant-sized people below. It was the primal fear of falling, and a gut-wrenching warning that falling for him posed as terrible a threat.

"Then what's the matter? If you cultivated his friendship, you might be able to influence him to put his recording studio elsewhere."

"Prostitute myself, is that what you mean? Why don't you sleep with him?"

"Darcy! What's gotten into you? You know I've got Twink to

consider. If Lyle thought I was sleeping around, he'd sue me for sole custody. I won't take that risk."

Darcy propped her elbow on the counter. "Is that your only reason?"

Christy Joy smiled as though she were actually considering an affair with the handsome man. "I'll bet he's got great hands, but no, I prefer heart to technique. From what little I've seen of Griffin Moore, he appears to confine his emotion to the piano. Still, it can't hurt to be nice to him."

The thought wasn't lost on Darcy. In fact, she'd gotten damn little sleep because of it. "It works both ways, though. He might flirt with me in hopes of winning me over to his side."

Christy Joy laughed. "When a man looks that good, I doubt he bothers to flirt."

Unable to dispute that insightful observation, Darcy grabbed her clipboard. "Wish me luck."

"You know I do," Christy Joy called after her. "Give my love to Griffin."

Even with luck, Darcy felt as though she'd already gotten herself in too deep, and as she drove up Ridgecrest, she wished Griffin were a dairy farmer who didn't mind getting his boots muddy rather than a concert pianist accustomed to being pampered by the doting staffs of exclusive hotels.

He was just bored. That had to be why he'd been coming on to her. Either that, or he came on to anything female, which was an even more distressing thought. She dreaded their next meeting, but as she rolled up his driveway, she found a brand new silver Beamer parked in front of the house.

She checked her watch and, while it was a few minutes to nine, she feared she'd come at a bad time. Maybe the car belonged to Jess Stevens, and he and Griffin were plotting ways to move Defy the World Tomatoes out of their building early. Or the beautiful car could belong to an equally attractive woman who had shown up last night after Darcy had left.

That possibility really rankled, and she used her flower-tipped pen to begin making diagonal slashes along the edge of the worksheet attached to her clipboard. When the front door swung open, she was almost afraid to look, then risked a peek.

The woman was tall, slender, blonde and dressed in a

bright red suit with matching stiletto heels. She carried a black leather briefcase and appeared to be furious while Griffin leaned against the doorjamb, his arms folded lazily across his chest.

He let her rant uninterrupted and, while Darcy's window was down, she caught only snatches of the one-sided argument. The irate blonde seemed to be accusing Griffin of disappointing someone, but obviously he wasn't overly concerned. Embarrassed to be eavesdropping, Darcy slumped down in her seat, but Griffin had already spotted her and waved.

He took his guest's elbow, walked her around her car, opened the driver's door and eased her inside. She was still sputtering angrily when she drove away.

Darcy climbed out of her truck and met Griffin in the middle of the wide, circular driveway. "I don't even want to hear it," she cautioned.

"It's quite an interesting story," Griffin insisted.

"I'm sure it is, but irrelevant. Now, if I describe the plants I want to use, will you recognize any of the names?"

"Probably not, but the camellias have survived since the 1920s, so I'd like to keep them."

Darcy made that notation on her worksheet. "Fine, we'll prune them so they're more attractive."

"Darcy," Griffin confided, "that was my former agent Karen Randolph. We parted company because I've insisted upon cutting back on my concert schedule. She warned it would ruin my career, to say nothing of what it would do to her income, and threatened I'd probably end up performing on cruise ships or in Las Vegas lounges."

Darcy was enormously relieved to learn she hadn't just observed a lovers' quarrel, but she remained flippant. "Whatever. It really doesn't matter to me."

"Of course it does. I don't throw beautiful women out of my house for no reason. Although sometimes, as you well know, they walk out on their own."

Darcy shot him a harshly disapproving glance, but he wore an expression of such tender concern that she instantly regretted it. The infuriating man continually played on her emotions, and she feared she might soon become powerless to resist.

"Look, I'm wise to you, buddy, so give it up."

"You're wise to what?"

Darcy propped her clipboard on her hip. "You're amusing yourself by distracting me, and you are definitely a distraction. But why don't you just go on inside and practice scales? I'll make my sketches on my own. I'll show them to you when I finish and pick up that payment you owe us."

Griffin's glance narrowed menacingly. "This is strictly business. Is that what you mean?"

Darcy knew he couldn't possibly be that dense. "You just came out of nowhere and—"

"No, that's not true. I've been to Monarch Bay a dozen times in the last five years."

"Be that as it may—"

"I like it here," he continued. "The seaside scenery is spectacular. The people, with few exceptions, are friendly. Best of all, no one has any idea who I am."

"Is that right?" A fiendish possibility took shape in Darcy's mind. If he craved anonymity, she would post his address on the Internet.

"There's something dangerous about your smile," Griffin observed slyly. "What are you thinking?"

"Nothing much," Darcy nearly purred. "I was just considering how hard Christy Joy and I have worked to attract the very tourists you wish to avoid."

"Don't try selling maps to my house. I'm not a rock star, so you'd not make any money."

"I don't know. San Francisco is filled with sophisticated symphony patrons. They might all love to join you for afternoon tea."

Griffin glanced away, but he appeared to be more amused than insulted. "Actually, that's not a bad idea. I could probably raise funds for some worthwhile charity hosting tea parties here. I could play a couple of tunes, pass a tray with cute little tea sandwiches and convince everyone I'm a lot of fun to know. Perhaps you could wear a French maid's outfit and serve the tea."

"That'll be the day!" Darcy was tempted to hit him with her clipboard.

Griffin took note of the murderous gleam in her eye and backed away. "I'm only kidding, Darcy, but perhaps I should go work on my scales."

Darcy was more angry with herself than him. When he turned everything she said to his own advantage, she should have been smart enough to keep her mouth shut. Then again, a glimpse of his smile was almost worth the cost to her pride.

Forcing her mind back to work, she stepped off the front yard and made a note of the dimensions. She also checked out the side yards and then paused on her way to the rear to listen, but the house was silent. It wasn't until she reached the terrace that she found Griffin seated on the new bench.

She'd gloated upon discovering his desire for privacy created an unsuspected vulnerability, but watching him now, all alone, his thick black hair ruffled by the breeze off the ocean, she lost all interest in harming him. Instead, she sat on the terrace steps and made some quick sketches. When Griffin hadn't moved by the time she'd finished, she took care to rap lightly on the bench before she joined him.

"I hope I'm not disturbing you."

"No, I was just remembering how delicious my steak was last night. I'm sorry you missed it."

"I avoid red meat." She tapped her clipboard to focus his attention on her drawings. "In creating a natural landscape, I combine open spaces with carefully arranged groupings of plants so there's a variety of colors, shapes and textures that appeals to the eye."

"Fragrances are important too, aren't they?"

"Yes, of course, I should have mentioned them. Are you allergic to anything?"

"Poison ivy, like everyone else, but you wouldn't do that to me, would you?"

Darcy was truly amazed by how easily Griffin turned even the most innocuous of subjects into a personal comment. "That would be unethical," she answered.

Griffin began to chuckle. "I admire a woman with principles. The *Architectural Digest* would like to do a feature on my house. I'd insist that they include the grounds. That would help your business, wouldn't it?"

Darcy's heart leapt to her throat. "Are you serious?"

Griffin shrugged. "I'd not tease you about something so important."

"Well, it would be phenomenal publicity, of course, but I imagine you'd have to purchase some furniture."

"Yes, I thought of that. A decorator from San Francisco has handled everything thus far, so the color scheme is set, and the kitchen and bathrooms have all been redone. Well, not redone, really. I insisted upon keeping the original art deco tile work in the baths. Would you like to see them?"

"You're inviting me to tour your bathrooms?"

"That does sound rather odd, doesn't it? Still, I might be able to convince the *Architectural Digest* to do a feature on art deco tile, and then I'd not have to bother with purchasing more furniture."

Darcy was unable to tell if he were simply pulling her leg. He appeared to be completely serious, but she still found it difficult to trust anything he said.

"I thought we were talking about landscaping," she reminded him.

"We are. I like your ideas. Go ahead and prepare your written estimate, and I'll sign it. Now, let's go." He stood and offered his hand.

Darcy ignored the gentlemanly gesture, scooted forward and stood on her own. "If there's a possibility my work might appear in *Architectural Digest*, then I'm going to go ahead and make watercolor versions of the sketches. Not that I wouldn't have gone all out for you before, but I'd like to be thoroughly professional."

"For the magazine's benefit?"

"For yours, actually," Darcy explained. "I haven't had a project this large, and I want to do it right."

"I'm sure you will. Now, I've been sitting here thinking this would be a good place to fly a kite. Do you know where I might buy one?"

Had he mentioned a hot air balloon or a blimp, Darcy couldn't have been any more surprised. "As a matter of fact, I do. There's a shop in Monarch Bay called Fun in the Sun that carries big, colorful nylon kites. Most people take advantage of the breeze off the ocean and fly them on the beach, but you could certainly fly one up here. You'd just have to watch your step so that you wouldn't fall off the bluff."

"Obviously. Come with me. Let's go buy a kite."

"Really, Mr. Moore, I have work to do. The Fun in the Sun is just up the street from Defy the World. They hang windsocks out front. You can't miss it."

"You complained about not having time to date. Take off an hour now. You'll not regret it."

His sly smile made her wonder just what flying a kite with him would entail. All too easily, she imagined him wrapping himself around her to guide the string. She began to fan herself with her clipboard.

"As you so cleverly informed me yesterday, I can't afford to turn down commissions. Neither can I afford to neglect the ones I already have. I also need to be down at the nursery pushing cacti."

"Yes, I noticed you have a remarkably diverse collection. Let's put some around somewhere. There, you just sold several dozen. Now you can fly kites with me."

Darcy couldn't help but laugh. "Mr. Moore, clearly you're used to women eagerly accepting your invitations, but I really do have work to do."

"Another time, then."

Darcy opened her mouth to tell him not to hold his breath, but he appeared to be so sincerely disappointed, she thought better of it. That he could offer such outrageous invitations and then leave her feeling guilty when she refused confused her completely.

"Didn't we agree to stick to business?" she asked. "I'll need to bring in a bulldozer to grade the yard. I don't want to disturb your practice schedule. Would it be better for us to work in the morning, or the afternoon?"

Griffin jammed his hands in his hip pockets. "I've stopped rehearsing. Work whenever you please."

"Can you just stop like that? I mean, don't you have to play every day to keep your edge?"

"Now you sound like Karen. I fired one agent today, and I sure as hell don't need another. Good-bye, Ms. MacLeod."

"Oh, no you don't." Darcy stepped in front of him to block his way. "You owe us some money. A check will be fine."

Griffin pulled his money clip from his Levi's pocket and peeled off hundred-dollar bills. "Here you are. I'll expect a receipt."

"You really ought not to carry such big wads of money," Darcy warned. "It makes you an attractive target to muggers."

Griffin flashed a mocking grin. "Why, Darcy, I'd no idea

that you cared."

"Mr. Moore, really." Darcy had his receipt ready and removed it from her clipboard. "Here you are." Embarrassed by his constant teasing, she felt a bright blush fill her cheeks, but as she walked away, he was chuckling to himself.

When Darcy returned to Defy the World, she debated mentioning the *Architectural Digest* feature to Christy Joy, but decided against it. For all she knew, Griffin had merely made it up to inspire her to keep working for him. She was ashamed by how effectively it had worked.

On her lunch break, she hurried down the street to Song and Dance Music to look through their classical CDs. They were arranged by composer and, as she thumbed through them, she found several featuring Griffin as the soloist. Dressed in tails and seated at a grand piano, he looked terrific from every angle.

Each CD included effusive praise from music critics. Darcy's favorite lauded Griffin's spirited passion and unparalleled technical brilliance. She'd recognized how well he played, but clearly she was too ignorant when it came to classical music to appreciate just how extraordinarily gifted he truly was.

That he had stopped rehearsing left her both puzzled and alarmed. She couldn't afford to buy all of his CDs, so she chose the one containing Franz Liszt's *Hungarian Rhapsodies*, hoping that was what she'd heard him play.

She carried the CD up to the counter, where the clerk was an earnest young man with bright red hair and a million freckles. "Good choice," he said. "Moore plays as though he invented the piano."

"You sound like a fan."

"I sure am. I heard him at the Music Center in Los Angeles a couple of years ago. He played three encores, and the whole audience was still standing and applauding wildly ten minutes after he'd left the stage for the last time. The man is phenomenal. I've heard he visits Monarch Bay occasionally, but I've yet to see him."

"Perhaps your luck will change."

"I sure hope so. I'd love to have his autograph."

Griffin had scrawled his signature across her first estimate, but Darcy quickly discounted the thought of reproducing it for his fans. He missed no opportunity to take advantage of her, it seemed, but she wouldn't stoop to taking advantage of him.

She swung by her truck before returning to work and left her new CD there rather than take it into the gift shop to add to their collection. She'd been enthralled by Griffin's performance, but she didn't want the plants jarred into collapse, or their customers, either.

After its initial rocky start, the rest of her day went well, and then, at a quarter to six, Griffin walked into the nursery carrying a long, slim package from Fun in the Sun.

"It won't be dark for another couple of hours," he said. "There's a nice breeze, and you're finished for the day. Come on home with me, and we'll try out my new kite."

George had overheard Griffin's invitation and walked up to Darcy. "I'll lock the gate. You've been working too hard and could use some fun."

Griffin introduced himself and reached out to shake George's hand. "Thanks. I've tried to tell her the same thing, but totally without success."

"Did you remember to buy string?" Darcy asked, grasping for a means to postpone the date.

"Of course. They won't let you out of Fun in the Sun without a big reel. Now, don't give me excuses, let's go."

"All right, but I'll drive my own truck. That way you won't have to bring me back into town later."

"Whatever you'd like."

George gave Griffin a thumbs up sign behind Darcy's back. Certain something significant had passed between the two men, Darcy glanced over her shoulder, but George was merely smiling innocently.

"Have fun," he said.

"If he claims I fell off the bluff, you'll know he's lying," Darcy warned. "Tell the police it was murder."

Griffin quickly discounted her dark prediction. "I think I'm the one who's in danger here, George, but I'll do my best to see no one comes to any harm."

"You just have a good time, kids."

Darcy didn't see any hope of that, but she stopped off to tell Christy Joy a quick good-bye and then went on out to her truck.

Griffin waited for Darcy in his driveway. "I don't mean to shock you, but unlike most men, I actually enjoy reading directions. Let's go on out to the terrace. I'll read the notes with the diagrams, and you can assemble the kite. It's shaped like a dragon with a long, notched tail. It's very colorful. I hope you like it."

"It's your kite," Darcy reminded him, but when he pulled it out of the package, she couldn't help but be impressed. "Start reading, I want to see this thing in the air."

"First we have to unroll it."

"All right, I'll hold the tip of the tail while you walk backwards, and that ought to do it."

"Hey, I thought I was giving the directions here."

"Sorry. I'll keep my mouth shut," Darcy promised.

"Well, not all the time, I hope." Griffin soon had the dragon stretched out across the terrace. He checked the directions again and sorted through the accompanying dowels. "These go in the head and wings. Do you see the slots that hold them?"

"Slots?" The dragon was red and breathing orange flames. Darcy felt along the sides. "They've got to be here somewhere. This is your kite, after all. Why don't I read the directions while you attach the dowels?"

"Don't complicate things. Just get busy."

Darcy raised a hand. "Let me see that diagram."

Griffin stepped beyond her reach and hid it behind his back. "Come and get it."

"No way. You're the one who wants to build the kite, remember?"

"An excellent point." Giving in, Griffin knelt beside her. "Maybe they didn't sew this one together correctly at the factory."

He was mere inches away and studying the kite's construction rather than tormenting her. His lashes made shadows on his cheeks, and he was quite appealing when he was in a playful mood, but none of it seemed real to her. It was all just a trick, and he probably wouldn't stop until he'd convinced her that she actually wanted to move Defy the World clear out of town.

Then she grew curious. "Why do you need a recording studio if you've stopped rehearsing?"

"Later. Here we are, the slots open on the other side. Hand me the first dowel."

Darcy slapped it into his hand. "Tell me."

"Let's get the kite in the air first." Griffin slid in the dowels, then attached the string. He stood and shook out the kite, then looked up at the cloudless sky.

"Is there some trick to getting this thing in the air?" he asked.

"You've never flown a kite?" Darcy stood and moved out of his way.

"I began playing the piano at five and just looked up a couple of months ago. There's a whole lot I've missed, including the art of kite flying."

Darcy didn't know whether to laugh or cry, but she imagined he must have been a very serious little boy indeed. "You need to run while you let out the string, and the wind will carry it aloft for you."

Griffin looked around to judge the distance. "If I stay on the terrace, I shouldn't be in any danger of falling off the bluff."

"Go for it," Darcy encouraged. She watched him cross the terrace in an easy lope and when he turned back into the breeze, the kite bounced upward. "That's it, just let out the string."

Griffin fumbled with the reel, then caught it and laughed when the kite rose steadily into the air. The wind whipped the dragon's long tail and serrated wings, pushing it higher. "Wow, it looks like a real dragon, doesn't it?" he shouted.

"It sure does. Now just move back a little and keep letting out more string." She raised her hand to shade her eyes, then walked across the terrace to where she could observe Griffin as well as the brightly colored kite.

She remembered the kids who had played in the high school band as being rather nerdy. Not that she'd been Miss Popularity, but at least she hadn't always had her nose in a book. With Griffin's looks, no one would have ever called him a nerd, but it saddened her to think he must have missed out on a lot of the fun of growing up.

"Is this all there is to it?" he asked.

"Not really. The wind can shift and send a kite right into the ground, or into a tree. The power lines are buried underground up here, but usually they pose a threat too. Then, if there are others flying kites, your string can become tangled in theirs and send both kites plunging to earth.

"Depending on the wind conditions, flying a kite can be frustrating, or like today, just plain fun. Let it go up as high as you'd like, but remember you'll have to rewind all the string when you bring it down."

"I'll keep it in mind. Why don't you come here and try it?"

Here we go, Darcy thought, but the prospect of having him wrapped around her wasn't all that unappealing. She moved to his side and gradually took control of the string. To her infinite dismay, however, he stepped back out of her way.

"Now, tell me why you need a studio," she prompted, as much to distract herself as to discover his intentions.

Griffin moved up behind her and began to rub her shoulders. "You look rather stiff. Does this feel good?"

His touch was light but sure and incredibly soothing. "Christy Joy said you'd have great hands."

"Did she?" Griffin chuckled.

Darcy hadn't meant to pay the compliment out loud. "Please don't tell her I said that."

"I'm going to be tempted, but maybe we can work out something."

"Do you expect a bribe?" Darcy felt a strong tug on the string and released a bit more. The kite was way out over the bluff now and dancing against the sun.

Griffin leaned down and nibbled her right ear. "Stay for dinner. I bought a roasted chicken. You eat those, don't you?"

Darcy felt his breath on her cheek and couldn't recall his question. "Chicken?" she mumbled numbly.

Griffin kissed her left ear lightly. "Yes, do you like them?"

He was wrapped around her now, and as snugly as she had imagined—no, hoped. She relaxed against him, and he began to trace teasing circles around the tip of her left breast with his right hand, while his left crept slowly down her stomach toward the sweet spot between her legs. His hips were pressed against her back, and there was no mistaking the intensity of his desire.

"This is what you had in mind all along, isn't it?" she nearly moaned.

"Do you blame me?"

Darcy dipped her head. She supposed this was simply his usual routine. He would be in town for a few days to give a concert, and if he wanted to connect with a woman, he would waste no time in going about it. Even better than a sailor with a girl in every port, she bet he had women all around the world eagerly awaiting his return.

"Darcy? What was his name?"

Startled, Darcy turned to look up at him. "Whose name?"

"The man who broke your heart."

Enfolded in his embrace, Darcy could not recall any of the other men she'd known. "Griffin Moore," she breathed out softly.

Griffin released her to reach for the kite string. "Do I frighten you that badly?"

She'd blurted the truth, and there was no way to take it back now. Instead, she sat on the terrace steps and waited for him to reel in the dragon kite. When he sat beside her, she kept hugging her knees, but she knew exactly what she wanted to say.

"Now do you see why we ought to stick to business?" she asked.

"No, things were just getting interesting." He reached for her hand and rubbed his thumb across her palm.

Darcy pulled her hand away and laced her fingers together in her lap. "You're not only famous, you're amazingly talented. Why would you hole up here and stop playing?"

"You believe I owe you an explanation for some reason?"

"Yes, you just had your hands all over me."

"And everything has its price?"

Darcy would have slapped him, but he caught her wrist in mid-air. "I'm not for sale," she swore through clenched teeth.

"Calm down, Darcy. I don't pay for sex. Now, I'm getting hungry. Let's go inside and have dinner."

He'd drawn her to her feet before she could break free of his grasp, but she was still angry. "Is it impossible for you to provide a straight answer?"

"On an empty stomach it is." He slid his fingers from her wrist to her hand and led her into the kitchen. "I hope you won't mind eating at the counter."

Astonished by his audacity, Darcy had no interest in food. "I don't think I can eat."

She washed her hands at the sink and splashed water on her face to cool down. Griffin might have switched off his passion, but she could barely control hers. She didn't even want to wonder what really making love with him would be like when she doubted she would survive. She grabbed a stool, sat and knotted her hands in her lap.

Griffin washed his hands then yanked open the cavernous refrigerator. "What would you like to drink? I have wine, soda, tea. There might even be a couple of cans of beer in here."

"I'll stick with water."

Griffin got out a glass, plunked in some ice cubes and filled it with water. She accepted the glass with shaky hands and then dribbled the water down her chin. "Hey, I thought you were enjoying yourself out there," he said.

"I was," Darcy admitted, "but a little too much."

"That's impossible." He returned to the refrigerator to hide his smile and quickly removed a roasted chicken and several containers of salad. "We may not have much in the way of ambiance here, but the food should be good."

Darcy didn't think she could take a bite, but Griffin served her plate and after she had taken a tiny nibble of chicken, she felt surprisingly hungry. "Thank you. I can't remember the last time a man made dinner for me."

"Have I finally done something right?"

The man did everything right, as far as she was concerned, but that would remain her secret. "I'm going to ignore that question until you answer mine."

Turning serious, Griffin laid his fork across his plate. "The problem is, I'm not sure I can trust you."

"Then we're even," Darcy assured him.

After a long pause, Griffin nodded. "Fair enough. I'm playing as well as I ever have, probably better, but there are no challenges left to me now. I can keep touring until I snap and fly apart in a thousand directions, or I can slow down now to free up the time to compose my own music. If no one likes it, then so be it, but at least I will have given some meaning to my life.

"Now if you really want to hurt me, you'll tell anyone who'll listen that I'm suffering from a mid-life crisis and can't even play chopsticks anymore."

Darcy swallowed hard, but when she looked at him, it was awfully difficult to concentrate on what she did want. "I won't tell a soul, but if we lose Defy the World, then Christy Joy and I will be the ones to disintegrate, and nothing you record in our building will be any good."

"What are you doing, putting a curse on the place?" A slow smile twitched at the corner of Griffin's mouth.

"Curses, like vampires, probably don't exist, but if you destroy us, you'll surely have very bad karma."

"You're getting spooky, Darcy."

Darcy slid off her stool and set her half-eaten dinner in the sink. "I'm going home. It'll take me a couple of days to work up the watercolor sketches, and then I'll give you a call. You needn't walk me out to my truck."

"Oh yes, I will," Griffin insisted.

Darcy took her keys from her pocket as they circled the house. She just wanted to get out of there before the evening got any wilder, but she'd no sooner closed her truck's door than Griffin reached through the window to grab hold of her hair.

Then he leaned in to kiss her.

It wasn't anything like the tender kiss he'd given her last night. It was long, slow, deep and utterly delicious. When he finally broke away and stalked off to walk in his front door, she needed a full five minutes to get control of her breathing. Everything about the man was magic, but heaven help her, if either of them were cursed, it was she.

Chapter Four

It wasn't until Darcy got home and put on the new CD that she realized how ridiculous her threats must have sounded to Griffin. Listening to his music was like having him in the room, and she could easily visualize the intensity of his expression and the ease with which his fingers sped over the keys. The man was a musical genius, and she'd warned him to avoid bad karma.

She could still feel the lingering tingle of his touch through her clothes and, as his music swept through her, she stretched out on her bed to savor the delicious sensation. His magnificent performance deserved a standing ovation, but should she ever attend one of his concerts, she didn't know where she would find the strength to leave her seat.

The man overwhelmed her senses. She tried to convince herself it was a good thing, but it was awfully difficult to believe.

Griffin ran through the most difficult passages of half a dozen of his favorite pieces before he began to work on one of his own. The melody was haunting, and the variations were so intricate they challenged him as his usual repertoire no longer could.

When he glanced at his watch, it was past midnight. He was tired, but not nearly tired enough to welcome sleep. What he wanted was to lose himself in Darcy's delicate beauty, but she was maddeningly disinclined to spend more than a minimal amount of time with him, and none of it in his bed.

He'd never been drawn to petite women, but Darcy had more attitude than an Amazon leather-clad biker chick. Their kind had never appealed to him, either, but he was convinced Darcy's tough façade hid a touching vulnerability. He smiled whenever he thought of her, which was quite often.

That she apparently liked him not at all was merely a minor problem he was confident he would eventually overcome. It would be exactly like learning a new piece of music and, one day soon, he would master her just as easily.

Christy Joy took Twink to a babysitter on Saturdays, but that morning she was running behind schedule and rushed in the back door without a minute to spare before it was time to unlock the front. She took a deep breath and reminded herself how much she loved her colorful shop, but on stressful mornings like these, she feared it was taking too great a toll on her and her darling daughter.

The clerks always straightened up before they went home for the day, but Christy Joy stopped to refold a couple of sweaters before she opened the register. When the bell at the front door rang, she expected one of the clerks, but it was Jeremy Linden, a sport fishing boat captain, who had entered.

Jeremy removed his white cap and raked the sun-streaked tips of his light brown hair off his forehead. He stood just under six feet, but even dressed in a loose-fitting denim shirt and khaki pants, his slim build made him appear taller.

"Good morning, Christy Joy. Is Mary Beth coming in today?"

"Yes, she'll be here in a minute. I see you have the latest Tom Clancy book. I think it's wonderful that you and Mary Beth read so many bestsellers. I wish I had time to read something other than children's books for Twink, but I'm afraid after our bedtime stories, I fall asleep nearly as quickly as she does."

"You're working too hard, but I guess it keeps you out of mischief."

Christy Joy laughed as though straying into mischief were even a possibility. "Twink loves that little boat you gave her. It's just the right size to float in our fountains. It was a very thoughtful gift."

Shrugging off the compliment, Jeremy adjusted the fit of the Clancy book's colorful paper jacket. "Twink's an awful cute little girl."

"Thank you. Like any mother, I'm very proud of her."

Christy Joy did not know quite what to make of Jeremy Linden. He hired his boat out for charters, and he'd begun strolling through Defy the World Tomatoes even before they'd opened their doors to the public. From the day she and Darcy had leased the property, they'd welcomed whatever interest the townspeople had shown, but Jeremy had never come in to chat like the others. Instead, he'd simply wandered around taking everything in without ever offering an opinion.

She'd noticed him first because he was attractive, with the wind-toughened appearance of a man who spent his life at sea. Then, gradually, she'd become intrigued by his silence and had gone out of her way to speak with him just to see if he would respond. He always had, but more often with shy smiles and obliging nods than complete sentences.

While he apologized for not being able to use any of their merchandise on his boat, Christy Joy often saw him fondling their wares as though he were searching for a treasured keepsake. As with all their conversations, this one was punctuated with long pauses, but when Jeremy finally looked up at her, his green eyes sparkled brightly against his deeply tanned skin. Reassured of his interest, she hoped he would stay a while.

"Our business is showing a steady increase," she confided, "and with luck, we'll have a terrific summer. But for now, I refuse to think beyond the end of August. How are things going for you?"

Jeremy inclined his head slightly. "Kinda slow, but sport fishing is always better in the summer. The gray whales begin their migration soon, and usually a few people happen along who want to go out and watch them. I can't offer any guarantees that we'll actually sight a whale, but that's real easy money."

Christy Joy had never found Jeremy in such a talkative mood, and she smiled to encourage him. "When I was in grade school, my class went whale watching. We only saw one whale, but it was so exciting. Do you suppose Twink is old enough to appreciate what a privilege it is to see a whale swimming free?"

Jeremy shifted his feet in an awkward shuffle, but then nodded. "Sure. Maybe someday when you're not too busy, and I don't have a charter, we can take Twink and go out and chase whales."

Had his offer been spontaneous, Christy Joy would have been pleased, but she feared that he'd mistaken her question for a pointed demand. "Oh, Jeremy, please don't misunderstand, I wasn't fishing for an invitation.'

Amused by her breathless apology, as well as her choice of words, Jeremy couldn't help but laugh. "If you want to fish too, that's okay." Mary Beth came through the door then, and, still chuckling, Jeremy turned away to walk with his back to the counter.

Christy Joy was uncertain how she'd gotten herself into such an awkward situation, but this was the first time she'd ever heard Jeremy laugh, and it was a very pleasant sound. Mary Beth was dating Wes Lundberg, a CPA with his own accounting firm, and regarded Jeremy as merely a friend, but Christy Joy still felt as though she'd overstepped her bounds.

She hoped Jeremy would soon have so many charters he'd forget all about providing lessons on marine life for Twink, but he gave her a jaunty salute as he left the shop, and she feared hers was an invitation he would remember. Of course, if she and Twink were to go out on Jeremy's boat, it wouldn't be a date. It would just be whale watching and nothing more.

Maybe they could take Twink's preschool class, she thought for an instant, then realized it would be an even greater imposition than she'd already made. There were women who used their children's needs as an excuse to spend time with a man, and probably an equal number of men who were attentive to a woman's children as a means to impress her, but she would never be a party to either ploy.

Absolutely not. If Jeremy actually followed through on the trip, she would bring snacks and make certain they all had a wonderful time. It was the least she could do, but as she approached Mary Beth, she had the sinking feeling she'd done something wrong.

"Mary Beth, if things don't work out for you and Wes, would you date Jeremy Linden?"

Mary Beth pushed her glasses up her nose. "Whatever makes you think Wes and I aren't a perfect match? Oh, never mind, you needn't explain. Jeremy and I both love to read, but that's not the same as having a romantic interest in someone, that sizzle that makes you turn and look twice at a man. But why are you asking? Did Jeremy say something about me just now?"

"No, apparently he just stopped by to drop off the Clancy book. Has it ever struck you as odd that you and a sea captain have the same tastes in reading?"

Mary Beth slid one of the Defy the World's flower-tipped pens behind her ear. "What's wrong with liking mysteries and thrillers? Jeremy's very good at analyzing and comparing plots, but that just makes him an interesting friend. Haven't you noticed how he looks at you?"

Startled, Christy Joy slipped her hands into the pockets of her blue gingham jumper. "Why no. I thought he just enjoyed perusing our stock."

Mary Beth rolled her eyes. "That's just an excuse, Christy Joy. The man comes in here to see you."

"You're kidding." Christy Joy hadn't noticed Jeremy giving her any special attention. "I imagine he's just lonely."

"Which could very well be, but he looks at you as though you were a delicious glob of cotton candy that he can't wait to wrap around his tongue."

"Mary Beth! You stop right there." Christy Joy was enormously relieved when the arrival of another clerk forced an end to their conversation and she could attend to business rather than Mary Beth's wild imaginings.

Darcy left the watering to George that morning to remain in her office and work up some dazzling sketches for Griffin, but she just couldn't concentrate. Every job she did provided an advertisement for the next, and if she could post a discreet sign on Ridgecrest, she might receive several more lucrative commissions. Unfortunately, at the rate she was progressing, she wouldn't have a single impressively detailed sketch ready to show him in a week, let alone the couple of days she'd promised.

Unable to sit a minute longer, she went out to find George. "I'm going to walk over to the post office and check on the flowers. There might be some that need replanting."

"Good plan," George replied. "Everyone in town goes in at least once a month for stamps, and it pays to keep it looking sharp."

"Right." Darcy put on her cap, carried her clipboard to make notes and went striding on down Embarcadero. She turned inland at Monarch Bay Boulevard and went up two blocks to the post office. Even with her critical eye, the landscaping was a panorama of colorful perfection, but she pinched off a fading blossom here and a brown leaf there to justify her visit.

She heard footsteps on the walk and, without turning around, knew exactly who it would be. Her chest tightened in anticipation, and she had to force herself to turn slowly rather than spin like a prima ballerina.

"Good morning, Mr. Moore, you're out early."

"It's nearly noon, Darcy, and I've been up for hours. After all, it's no fun staying in bed alone." He was wearing sunglasses, but they scarcely disguised his taunting gaze. "I had no idea you did the landscaping here. Do you come by each morning to pull weeds?"

"No, once a week or so will do." He'd walked right by the sign for Defy the World Tomatoes at the edge of the flowerbed, and Darcy doubted that he'd missed it.

"I have to pick up my mail, and then, if you're finished, I'll walk you back to your nursery." He started up the post office steps, then turned back. "Do you know if there's a music store in town that sells manuscript paper? I've several compositions in my head that I ought to write down before they blur into a single hideous wail."

Darcy had to crane her neck to look up at him. "You came here to write music and neglected to bring the proper paper to transcribe it?" she inquired skeptically.

"Obviously a terrible oversight," Griffin admitted. "Now, answer my question."

Darcy's glance shot down the row of bright yellow daffodils. From what she'd seen of Griffin Moore, he was not the type of man to overlook such a significant detail, and his answer didn't ring true. It was disturbing, but then everything about the man was.

"I'm not sure, but Song and Dance might have your paper. The clerk is a big fan of yours, by the way, and I'm sure the store will place a special order for you if they don't carry anything you need."

Clearly astonished she would possess such knowledge,

Griffin came back down the steps. "How did you happen to discover this remarkable clerk's preference in music?"

Caught, Darcy mumbled under her breath, "I bought one of your CDs."

"I beg your pardon?" Griffin stepped closer.

Thoroughly embarrassed, Darcy nearly shouted, "I bought one of your CDs."

"I would have given you a dozen, had you asked," Griffin confided softly. "If there's ever anything I can do for you, just say so."

Darcy clamped her jaws shut rather than tell him to keep his hands off their building, but the effort made her cheeks ache. "Better grab your mail. I've got to be going."

"I think you'll wait." Griffin took the post office steps two at a time and returned in a matter of seconds with a handful of letters which he jammed into the hip pocket of his Levi's. "How long have we known each other? Has it even been a week?"

"Not quite."

"You're counting the days?" Griffin reached out to hug her and nearly lifted her off her feet. "Sorry." He carefully set her down and took her hand to continue their walk. "There's something in the air here that I find most inspiring. Now if I can only capture it in music, I could end up famous."

"You're already famous," Darcy reminded him.

"Perhaps, but that's no reason not to set goals."

"My goal is to make a tremendous success of Defy the World Tomatoes," Darcy countered.

"You appear to be well on your way."

"Yes, unless we're stepped upon by an evil giant."

"Is that how you see me?"

Every time Darcy glanced up at him, she got the same fluttering sensation in her stomach. Half of her wanted to grab him and never let go. The other half cursed her for having such a terrible weakness for such an impossible man.

"You confuse me completely, and that's not good," she confessed.

"I'll not apologize for being who I am."

"Nor should you." His hand was warm, the pressure of his fingers comforting on hers, and she wished he weren't from an exclusive world where landscapers remained in the yard rather than track leaves inside beautifully appointed mansions.

"It's Saturday," Griffin suddenly recalled. "Are you free tonight?"

"That all depends on what you have in mind," Darcy responded.

"Dinner, movies. What do people do for fun here?"

"I've really no idea."

"None at all?" Griffin teased. "What's the matter with the men in this town that they aren't pursuing you night and day?"

"Maybe they just have more sense than you do."

Griffin laughed and leaned down to kiss her cheek. "You are an absolute delight, Darcy. I wish we'd met on my first visit here."

Darcy thought it was a damn good thing they hadn't. When they reached Defy the World, she pointed him on down the street toward the music store and went back to staring numbly at her sketchpad. All too soon she heard Griffin speak to George, and he did not sound happy. Before she could leave her desk, Griffin leaned in the doorway.

"Was that your idea of a joke?" he asked in a near snarl.

He sounded furious, but Darcy had no idea what had upset him and reacted with curiosity rather than terror. "I can't even imagine playing a joke on you. What do you mean?"

"The clerk at the Song and Dance is a purple-haired freak with a nose ring who calls herself Isis. I still gave her the benefit of the doubt and introduced myself, but all I got in return was a dismissive shrug, so she was obviously no fan of mine.

"She leaned over the counter and said, 'What can I do for you, dude?' At least I found the paper I need, so the trip wasn't a total waste."

Darcy left her chair in a single hop and pushed her index finger into his broad chest to emphasize her point. "I was straight with you. The clerk I met was a red-haired young man. I'm sorry, I should have described him to you. If the 'purple-haired freak' mentions your name, I'm sure he'll be devastated to have missed you."

Griffin caught her hand and brought it to his lips for a quick kiss before he released her. "He'll survive. Where would you like to go for dinner?"

Darcy stepped back and swept him with a suspicious gaze.

"Did we agree to have dinner together?"

"Yes, we did. There's a French movie at the Monarch Theater which looks pretty good. It starts at seven, but I don't want to rush you."

Darcy loved foreign films, and it had been ages since she'd treated herself to one. She shoved her hands into the pockets of her dark green overalls and rocked back on her heels. "We close at six, so we'll have to go to the movie first and dinner afterwards, if that's all right with you."

"It's fine. Give me your address and I'll pick you up at six forty-five."

He reached for the pen in her bib pocket, but Darcy snatched it first and handed it to him. "I'm right around the corner at 231 Poppy. It's the red house with the yellow trim and green door. You can't miss it."

Griffin made a note of her address on the bag from the music store and handed her back the pen. He leaned down to give her a quick kiss on the cheek. "Until tonight, then."

Darcy closed her eyes as he walked away, unable to keep from thinking how limited her wardrobe was. Of course, a movie and dinner didn't require a ball gown, but she couldn't go in overalls either. She thought she had a couple of dresses hanging in the back of her closet, but she wasn't actually sure.

Giving up all hope of creating sketches, she went out to the nursery. "Go on to lunch, George, I'll handle sales."

George moved out from behind the counter. "You and Mr. Moore going out tonight?"

"We are, if I can find something to wear."

"He seems to like oxford cloth shirts and Levi's," George mused. "I read an article in one of my wife's magazines that suggested a woman ought to dress like the man she wants to impress, sort of mirror his clothes."

"What makes you think I'm trying to impress him?"

"He's good-looking and rich. Why wouldn't you? Now, if I were you, I'd find myself a cute little denim skirt and oxford cloth shirt. He wears loafers, but you needn't go that far. Wear flats and you'll do just fine."

Darcy shook her head in disbelief. "I had no idea you worked as a wardrobe consultant, George. What other talents are you hiding?"

George responded with an enigmatic smile. "That's just between me and my wife. Now I'm going to lunch. When I get back, you can go shopping."

Darcy stared at him as though he'd just suggested she eat bugs, but she thought he just might have the right idea when it came to clothes. She never wore the frilly dresses Christy Joy adored, but a denim skirt and shirt sounded just right. She drew in a deep breath and released it slowly. She hadn't bought a new outfit to please a man in more than a year, so maybe it was time, but she had no idea what to do with the butterflies that cruised her stomach whenever Griffin Moore appeared.

Griffin arrived right on time, but rather than invite him to come in, Darcy stepped out of her colorful house and pulled her door shut behind her. "The Monarch's about a ten-minute walk. Why don't you just leave your car here?"

"That's fine with me." Griffin swept her with an appreciative glance before reaching for her hand. "You have such nice legs, Darcy, why don't you wear shorts to work?"

Darcy had been afraid her denim skirt was too short, and now she was positive of it. "Thank you, I do wear shorts in the summer, but overalls are a lot more practical out on a job. I mean to finish your sketches this weekend, but—"

"My yard isn't going anywhere, and whenever you complete the sketches will be fine. I want you to have fun tonight rather than worry about work."

"That would be a pleasant change." They were both wearing blue oxford cloth shirts and Darcy feared she'd gone too far in mimicking his wardrobe, but if he'd only noticed her legs, she supposed things were going rather well.

She didn't recognize anyone in the line at the theater, but didn't appreciate the admiring glances sent Griffin's way. That he remained focused on their conversation was flattering, however, and she was relieved to discover they shared a preference for the theater's back rows.

Once they were seated, Griffin again took her hand and shocked her by resting it in his lap. He wasn't rubbing her knuckles along his crotch, which she would have put a stop to immediately, but just knowing what lay beneath his button front fly filled her cheeks with a fiery blush.

She'd never encountered another man who had touched her so easily, as though they knew each other well and were accustomed to exchanging affectionate gestures. She liked affectionate men enormously, but knowing it was simply Griffin's manner made her wonder if he really thought of her as anything special.

Then the movie began and the witty romantic farce captured her attention so completely she ceased to obsess over Griffin's motives and lost herself in the fun.

The charming story starred a penniless young man whose poor opinion of modern art inspired him to pose as an artist to romance a series of wealthy art patrons. When he fell in love with the baker's daughter who served him his coffee and croissant each morning, he then had to juggle his generous lovers to keep the innocent lass from discovering the stylish women visiting his studio were getting more than art.

Darcy laughed so hard she missed a great many of the subtitles in the last third of the film, and she was still laughing as she and Griffin exited the theater. "I was too busy watching the action to catch all the words, but the phony artist's paintings actually began to sell to legitimate collectors, didn't they?"

"Yes, and he was forced to fabricate lucid explanations for his work as though he'd actually begun with some lofty purpose. But he did earn the money to marry the baker's daughter by his own goofy efforts and ceased to scam lonely women. I'm glad you enjoyed it."

"I noticed you laughed before the subtitles explained the whole joke, so obviously you speak French fluently."

"*Oui,* but I've heard you speak Spanish to your crew, so you could pick up French rather easily."

"In my spare time?"

Griffin dropped his arm around her shoulders to offer a comforting hug. "You need to cultivate not only healthy plants, but a better balance between work and leisure, for your own well-being."

"Have you succeeded in that regard?"

"I'm working on it. It's the primary reason I moved here. Where would you like to eat dinner?"

"Let's walk up to the Wild Thyme. It has the best food in town."

The other theater patrons had dispersed around them, another couple was walking their way ahead of them, but with the shops closed on Saturday night, there was no other foot traffic on the sidewalk. The slight fog off the sea gave the streetlights a misty glow, and Darcy thought it a wonderfully romantic atmosphere until Griffin suddenly pulled her into a recessed doorway.

"Quiet," he whispered. "Someone is following us."

Darcy listened for footsteps and heard them slow, stop for a moment, and then speed up. As they drew near, Griffin raised his arm as though he meant to deliver a vicious karate chop, but as soon as the man stepped into the soft ray of the street lamp, Darcy caught sight of his red hair and grabbed Griffin's sleeve.

"Wait! That's the clerk from the Song and Dance."

The startled young man noted the murderous gleam in Griffin's eye and took a frantic backward step. "I'm sorry, Mr. Moore, I wasn't stalking you. I wasn't even sure it was you."

"I have a black belt in karate and could have killed you rather easily," Griffin swore darkly. "Don't follow me again, ever."

The clerk raised his hands. "No, Mr. Moore, I was just trying to get close enough to see if it really was you. I didn't mean to bother you."

"You're close enough now. Am I what you expected?"

"Well, I didn't realize you were so tall." He wiped his sweaty palms on his pants and extended his hand. "I'm Tom Holcomb, and I think you're great."

After a slight hesitation, Griffin shook Tom's hand. "Go home, Mr. Holcomb, before you get yourself in any worse trouble."

"Yes, sir, I'm on my way."

Griffin waited until the hapless clerk had started back toward the theater at a near run before he again reached for Darcy's hand. "I'm sorry. I didn't really believe in your warning about being mugged, but with you here, I didn't want to take any chances."

Darcy blamed herself for putting the threat of muggers in his head, but the swiftness of his reaction to a few footsteps had frightened her badly. "Do you really have a black belt, or were you merely trying to scare him as badly as you did me?"

"No, I do have a black belt, but I've never had to use it to defend myself, or at least not yet. I'm sorry if you were frightened."

Darcy's heart was still thumping wildly, and she took hold of Griffin's arm to steady herself. "I won't be able to enjoy dinner now. We open at ten o'clock on Sundays too, so I really do need to get home."

"If that's what you want."

Griffin walked her home without saying another word, but she could feel his disappointment over the way the evening had ended. She thought she ought to at least invite him to come in for coffee, but as she inserted her key in the lock, he'd already begun to back away.

She'd left a light on and pushed the door open. "I really did enjoy the movie," she told him. "Would you like to come in for a minute?"

Griffin studied her shaky smile and shook his head. "Not if you're afraid of me, or what I might do."

The man had such an expressive face that Darcy didn't doubt his sincerity. She wasn't afraid that he might attack her, but that didn't mean she wasn't wary of her own lack of self-control where he was concerned. She licked her lips and forced a more inviting smile.

"No, really, I'd like you to come in." She walked through her door and waited for him to follow.

The living room was painted a deep terracotta and filled with philodendron whose trailing leaves reached from an assortment of plant stands to the hardwood floor. He could see into the kitchen where she had pots of herbs growing on the sill above the sink, and rows of African violets sat along the sills of the living room windows.

"I like the jungle look," he finally announced and turned back to close the door. "Why don't you slip off your shoes and stand on the coffee table."

"What?" Darcy tossed her purse on the sofa, but she couldn't even imagine why he would make such an outrageous request. "Why would I want to do that?"

"Just try it, and you'll see."

He was smiling now and, persuaded there was no threat involved, she kicked off her flats and stepped up on the low table. "Here I am. Now what's supposed to happen?"

Griffin stepped in front of her. "Now we're nearly the same height. Doesn't it make you feel more comfortable?"

It took Darcy a moment to appreciate the change in her perspective now that they could see eye-to-eye. He was still better-looking than any man had a right to be, but at least he no longer towered above her. "Yes, actually, it does."

He moved closer still, but didn't touch her. "Kiss me."

He had a maddening way of issuing commands, but Darcy didn't mind obeying this one. She rested her hands on his shoulders and slanted her mouth over his to begin a kiss that grew increasingly bold. She wrapped her arms around his neck to hold on while he kissed her as passionately as he had last night. When he drew away, she was too dazed to focus clearly.

Griffin took hold of Darcy's waist and carefully set her down on the floor. "I never take it any further on a first date and, while I could stay and kiss you until dawn, I know you have to be up early. Good-night. I'll let myself out."

Darcy watched the door close behind him, then bent to grab a shoe and hurled it against the varnished wood. She was positive he'd tasted how eager she was for more and had deliberately left with her wanting it. She reached for her other shoe and threw it as well.

"Manipulative bastard!" she fumed. She was used to dating fertilizer salesmen who, while charming, always wanted more than she was ready to give. To find herself on the other side of that dilemma with Griffin annoyed her no end.

"That man will be the death of me yet," she swore, but when she turned on his CD, it was again pure magic.

Chapter Five

Christy Joy took Twink to church on Sundays and then out to brunch, so on those mornings, Darcy opened Defy the World Tomatoes. That Sunday she came in at eight a.m., shut herself in her office and completed the watercolor sketches she hadn't been able to even begin on Saturday.

When George arrived at ten, she'd already opened the shop, bid the clerks good morning and was out watering. "Beautiful day, isn't it, George?"

George bent to angle a potted geranium toward the sun. "Yes, it sure is, and it sounds as though your date went well."

Darcy swallowed a harsh laugh. "The film at the Monarch is hilarious. You ought to take Marge."

"That all you care to say?" George straightened slowly and rubbed the small of his back.

"Pretty much, but thanks for the wardrobe tip. I like the new clothes."

"Good, and I've got another tip for you. Saw this one on TV. Scientists did a study of what scents men respond to best, and they found pumpkin pie spice beats out the most expensive perfumes. You ought to get yourself a little canister in the baking aisle at the market and use it just like dusting powder."

Darcy was tempted to turn the hose on him. "Are you just making up this stuff, George?"

"Absolutely not. Give it a try and see if Griffin doesn't stick to you like glue."

"I'm not sure I even want him stuck on me," Darcy argued.

"Well, then, just do it as an experiment, and you'll know if it works when Mr. Right comes along."

"If he's Mr. Right, won't he notice me without my smelling like a Thanksgiving pie?"

George shook his head. "Sadly, a lot of men need a swift kick in the seat before they realize what a treasure they've found, so it's better to be on the safe side and douse yourself with the spice."

"I'd rather you just kick Griffin around the block a time or two."

"If I were ten years younger, I'd give it a try, but now, darlin', you'll have to rely on your own devices."

"Thanks anyway, George." Darcy seriously doubted Griffin could be enticed with pumpkin pie spice, but the mere possibility of getting the better of him lifted her spirits enormously.

The lovely day brought out tourists as well as residents of Monarch Bay, and Defy the World Tomatoes had their most profitable Sunday ever. As Mary Beth ran the final total, Christy Joy squealed with glee.

"We didn't expect to do this well until summer. What do you think, Darcy? Should we rethink our objectives?"

"No, let's not get too excited just yet. This might be a mere blip rather than a trend."

Mary Beth was quick to agree. "It's always best to err on the conservative side. Besides, just think how excited you'll be to keep exceeding your target."

Darcy waited until Mary Beth had gone home to confide her real worry. "If our sales remain this high, we'll have to reorder stock, but that'll mean using most of the money we should be putting aside to move."

Christy Joy briefly considered their alternatives and suggested a plan. "Let's reorder only what's selling really well. We'll sell that merchandise through the summer, then unload everything else at a gigantic moving sale. That way we'll be able to reopen in our new location with brand new stock."

After all the hard work they'd put in last fall, Darcy didn't understand how Christy Joy could sound so enthusiastic about repeating that ordeal. "We've learned a lot about running a business, but the thought of moving simply exhausts me."

"It does me too, but we'll survive. I'm sorry we've been so busy all day that I haven't had a chance to ask about your date. How did it go?"

Darcy again commented on the amusing film and then shrugged. "Griffin is such a complex individual that I can't figure out what he's really up to, so I'm being real careful."

Christy Joy gestured with a rose-tipped pen. "With Twink and J. Lyle to consider, I'm forced to be cautious, but you don't have to answer to anyone. You ought to do exactly as you please where Griffin is concerned."

Darcy pulled up a stool and sat. "It's not just that he plans to coldly put us out on the street, Christy Joy. The guy's got more layers than an artichoke, and I'm not sure I want to start peeling off leaves and dipping them in butter."

"My God, that sounds decadent, but the better Griffin knows you, the more difficult it'll be for him to screw with Defy the World Tomatoes."

"Oh, he's already screwing with something, but I'm just not sure what." Darcy had thought he might come breezing through there that day with one of his ridiculous requests, but she refused to admit how disappointed she truly was that he hadn't.

Their work completed for the day, Darcy bid her partner and Twink good night, left her truck parked behind the nursery and walked around the corner to her rented house. Preoccupied, she failed to notice Griffin's Range Rover until he climbed out carrying a bag from the Emperor's Palace.

"I had no idea you delivered Chinese food in your spare time," she called to him.

"Only to you. As I see it, I owe you a dinner. If you'd rather have something else, I'll go get it."

Darcy paused on her front steps. "Did you bring their walnut shrimp?"

"Of course. It's the best thing on their menu."

"Damn straight," Darcy swore. "Come on in."

She wished she had time for a quick shower, but she didn't trust Griffin not to pick the bathroom lock and climb in with her. With his gorgeous bod all slippery wet, she would drown for sure.

"Just put everything on the table. I'll get the plates."

Darcy hurried into her kitchen, but first opened the

cupboard where she stored her baking supplies and searched for the pumpkin pie spice. She'd actually used some a couple of years ago to bake a pie from scratch for a friend's potluck Thanksgiving dinner. The little jar had been pushed to the back, but once found, she quickly flipped open the sprinkle lid and tossed some inside her T-shirt. She felt utterly ridiculous, but she'd been comfortable in George's choice of clothes, so it was worth a try.

She put the tea kettle on the stove, grabbed plates, napkins and utensils, and carried them out to the round oak table she'd refinished herself. She'd started out in a furnished rental and had bought what she now owned one piece at a time at antique and used-furniture stores. None of it matched, but with so many plants sitting around, she doubted anyone noticed.

"At least I own a table," she mumbled as she set their places.

"And a fine one it is too. I like your furniture. It has character."

"It's a wonder *Architectural Digest* hasn't called."

Griffin slid into a chair. "Perhaps they believe bigger is better."

Darcy watched his sly smile widen. The man had a killer grin, and she was certain he knew it.

"I won't touch that one," she replied.

Griffin laughed. "Yeah, you will. It's just a matter of time."

Darcy couldn't subdue the bright blush flooding her cheeks, so she sat and reached for one of the food cartons. "You want to keep those pretty teeth of yours long enough to eat dinner?"

"I sure do, but Darcy, you're so awfully cute."

She opened the container to find the promised walnut shrimp, and her stomach began to rumble in delighted anticipation. "After I've fashioned a noose from your black belt, you'll rethink your opinion."

"That's quite an image, but let's call a truce while we eat. You can talk dirty to me later."

The whistle of the tea kettle provided Darcy with an excellent excuse to leave the table. "Do the air-headed society chicks you usually date actually get your jokes?" she called from the kitchen.

Griffin waited until she'd brought him a cup of tea to respond. "Like fast cars, I outgrew brainless beauties in my twenties. In the last couple of years, I've dated a museum director and a French Olympic champion. What about you?"

Darcy returned to her chair and savored a bite of shrimp while she searched her mind for someone, anyone, even remotely impressive. Unfortunately, she came up empty. "Let's just say my last couple of boyfriends were employed and leave it at that."

"Having a job is a commendable trait," Griffin remarked between bites of broccoli and beef. "Let's try a more entertaining subject. What would you do if you won the lottery?"

"That's easy—I'd buy our building from you."

"It's not for sale. What else would you do?"

Darcy paused to consider some choices and frowned slightly as she voiced them. "It bothers me that families with small children are homeless. With low-cost housing disappearing, things are only going to get worse, so I'd give the money to Habitat for Humanity."

Griffin stared at her a long moment. "Nothing for yourself?"

Darcy scooped out a second helping of walnut shrimp. "All I want is your building. Now what would you do with the lottery loot?"

"I'd help keep music in the schools with VH1's Save the Music."

"You watch VH1?" Darcy was shocked to learn he was a fan of the popular cable station.

"I'm not a total nerd," Griffin protested.

Darcy licked her fingers, then caught him watching her a bit too intently and used her napkin instead. "I never said you were."

"True, but I'm sure you've called me a lot worse names, and frankly, I'll admit to having a few faults."

"No! I never would have guessed. Oh, I have your sketches ready. I could run back to my office and get them when we finish."

"Don't bother. Just bring them by in the morning."

"Sure," Darcy agreed, but now that she'd taken the edge off her hunger, it was difficult to concentrate on the last of her dinner. It was a delicious surprise, but seeing him was even better. She had a terrible weakness where he was concerned and held the uncomfortable suspicion that he knew it.

Still, she would be a fool to get attached to him when he would surely wake up soon to the fact that she earned her living hauling plants around in a battered truck, while he was accustomed to being wined and dined by royalty.

"Your frown worries me," Griffin remarked. "If you have other plans for the morning, just say so."

Darcy speared a crisp piece of broccoli, but didn't guide it toward her mouth. "No, I can come by around nine."

"Well, if it's not a scheduling conflict, what's wrong?"

Darcy laid her fork across her plate and sat back in her chair. She was reluctant to broadcast her insecurities, but she didn't feel right remaining silent about her misgivings either.

She took a comforting sip of tea and answered as truthfully as she dared. "I'm afraid our lives are too different for us to ever have anything serious, and I'd rather not be your flavor of the month."

"What makes you think you'd last a month?" Griffin shot right back at her.

Appalled by that arrogant rebuff, Darcy came out of her chair to point him toward the door, but he easily caught her arm and pulled her down on his lap. She struggled to rise, but she lacked even a quarter of his strength and couldn't break free.

"Let me go, you bastard!"

Griffin nuzzled her ear. "I was teasing you, sweetheart. I don't treat women like scoops of ice cream, and the truth is, they usually leave me, not the other way around."

"Liar," Darcy insisted through clenched teeth. "You just gave me a sample of your vicious wit, and I'll bet you use it whenever you tire of a woman. She'd be as insulted as I am right now and leave you. Then I'll bet you sit back and congratulate yourself on not having to face a messy breakup."

Griffin slid his lips to the tender hollow behind her ear. "Where do you get this stuff? I'm not into causing pain just to watch women cry."

He dropped his voice to a husky whisper as his lips again grazed her skin. "I love your perfume. When you take the trouble to smell this good, it's difficult to believe you don't care about me. What's it called?"

"It's just something I whipped up in the kitchen," Darcy replied smugly. She wasn't certain how she'd gone from being livid with his lip to snuggling against him, but with his incredible charm, none of her usual defenses proved effective.

"Whatever it is, it suits you." He pressed her close, then relaxed slightly, but not enough to allow her to escape him.

"If I have a vicious wit, as you claim, I've not used it to end relationships. I've traveled a great deal in years past, and if I'm away at Christmas, or miss a girlfriend's birthday, she usually finds someone else to keep her entertained."

"You ought to find a woman with her own business so she'll have plenty to keep her occupied when you're out of town."

Griffin slid his fingers through her hair and then gently mussed it. "I thought I already had." When Darcy failed to respond, he dropped his arms, but she surprised him by remaining seated in a graceful curve across his lap.

"I'm in no rush," he assured her, and he gathered her into a fond embrace. "We have plenty of time to get to know each other."

"I've never met anyone like you," Darcy admitted softly, "and I don't even know where to begin."

"I'm not so different from the next guy. I was born in Atlanta, and my parents still live there. My father's an attorney, and my mother gives piano lessons. If I visit them for more than a week, I begin to sound like a Southerner again rather than the cultured artist I was trained to be."

Darcy refused to admit she'd never been able to resist a Southern accent for fear he would use it to his own advantage, and he already possessed too many. "Did your mother teach you to play the piano?" she asked instead.

"Yes. She thought it was cute that I was so fascinated by the music she played, and she began giving me impromptu lessons. By the time I was five, she realized I was the most talented student she'd ever had. When she'd taught me all that she could, she found me a more accomplished teacher, and then another. I completed the last of my training in Europe, although, of course, there will always be more to learn.

"I could have begun a successful concert career in my teens, but I wanted to meet musicians my own age, rather than totally miss the fun of growing up, and so I came home to attend Juilliard. It proved to be a wise choice, for when I began winning international competitions, I was old enough to handle the pressure and deal with the instant fame."

"You never wanted to do anything else with your life?"

"No. This is what I was born to be. I know it as surely as you knew the day you saw Kate Sessions' work and decided to landscape fabulous gardens."

Darcy turned to look up at him. "How did you remember her name?"

"Why are you surprised? I remember everything about you."

When he inclined his head, Darcy welcomed his kiss, and in the next breath she welcomed whatever his loving might bring. The cost would surely be a broken heart, but not to know such a remarkable man would be an even greater tragedy.

Griffin kissed her until they were both dizzy and then pulled away. "We'll have to do something about your schedule. When you work seven days a week, there isn't much time for us to be together."

Darcy tried not to scream in frustration, but she hadn't even slept with the man, and he was already trying to run her life. She considered his criticism misdirected, and her posture stiffened.

"Christy Joy and I thought once we got the business running well, we'd each be able to take off a couple of days every week. Unfortunately, neither of us owns a crystal ball, and we didn't foresee having to move in the fall. That means there won't be any time off for anyone anytime soon. So before you complain about my frantic schedule, stop to consider why I'm so damn busy."

Griffin moaned in mock pain. "I'd like a truce on that subject too."

"How convenient, but if we avoid the inevitable conflicts, all we'll have is bland co-existence. That won't leave much room for the passion you pour into your music."

"My God, Darcy, are you this tough on all the men you date?"

Darcy bowed her head slightly. "No, only the ones I really care about, and you know I'm right."

Griffin hugged her. "I wish I'd never leased you that damn building."

"Then Christy Joy and I might not have gone into business together. I'd not have moved here from LA, and we'd never have met."

"So you see this real estate disaster as a good thing?"

"Yeah, in some strange twisted sort of way, it is."

With a gentle hold, Griffin picked her up and set her on her feet. "Finish your dinner, and then we can negotiate some ground rules."

Darcy sat in her chair, but left the broccoli untouched. "Everything was delicious, but I'm full."

"Fine, but I'm still hungry." Griffin scraped the carton to slide the last bit of walnut shrimp onto his plate, then added some fried rice. "I was afraid I'd not brought enough, but you didn't eat very much."

"I'm not even half your size, Griffin, it's only natural that I'd eat less." She sipped her tea and watched him eat. He had as fine manners as she'd expected and didn't once lick his fingers.

When Griffin finally finished, he tossed Darcy a fortune cookie. "I hope it says you'll meet a tall, dark and handsome stranger."

"I'd prefer tips on what to do with him." Darcy cracked her cookie in half and pulled out the paper fortune. She scanned it quickly and began to laugh. "Get promises in writing. How apropos. What does yours say?"

"You will get a lucky break," Griffin responded. "I'd say I already have. What if I look for a new building for you? Would that make dating me easier to bear?"

Darcy reached for her tea and took a long swallow. "I wonder if that's one of the promises I should get in writing."

"Probably not. After all, I just offered to look, not to provide a new location."

"True." Darcy watched a sly smile play across his lips and wished he would kiss her again. She knew if she were to return to his lap, he would, but she remained seated in her chair.

"You're used to getting your own way," she cautioned, "and people have noted that I tend to be a bit stubborn."

"Clever observation, but like every couple, we each have flaws." Griffin stood and began clearing the table. "Let's put the leftovers in the frig, and then I'll help you with the dishes."

A man who did dishes. Darcy shook her head in

amazement. "No way. You brought dinner, so I'll handle the clean up."

"Do you want me to leave?"

"I'm not sure what I want," Darcy confessed truthfully.

"Then it's definitely time for me to go." He brushed her cheek with a quick kiss and headed toward the door.

"Wait a minute." Darcy left her chair, but lingered beside the table. "Now I feel as though I've said the wrong thing."

Griffin took a step toward her. "When you compliment the passion in my music, I can forgive you almost anything."

"You can forgive me? Is there no end to your arrogance?"

Griffin crossed the distance between them and looped his arms around her waist. "Probably not," he confessed with a deep chuckle. "Just kiss me good-night, and I'll leave you to the dishes."

It was impossible to argue with a man who acknowledged his faults, and Darcy reached up on her tiptoes to kiss him. She was soon lost in his embrace and, once again, he was the one to end the dozen kisses that had followed the first. She couldn't think clearly with him so near, only long for more, but she refused to beg.

Griffin waited for her dazed gaze to clear and then stepped back. "I can see what you're thinking, but I doubt I'd fit in your bed."

"Your imagination has to be better than that." Darcy struggled to stifle a yawn and failed. "I'm sorry. We had a really busy day."

Griffin caressed her cheek tenderly. "Why don't you come home with me? Then you'd be there tomorrow morning."

Darcy shook her head. "It's too soon."

"Can't be soon enough for me," Griffin whispered against her kiss-swollen lips.

The man always smelled good and tasted better. She slid her arms around his waist and held on as his kisses melted away all thought of resistance. She was dizzy with desire when, with a gentle hug, he briefly lifted her off her feet, while he scarcely seemed affected by her affection.

"Come to my house at eight o'clock, and I'll make breakfast for us. We can eat out on the terrace and pretend we're in Italy."

Darcy tried to breathe deeply enough to form a coherent

reply. "Fine, but the view of the Pacific will be enough for me."

He squeezed her hands and this time made it through the door before he looked back. "Don't stay up too late." He winked and was gone.

Darcy slumped back down in her chair. Griffin turned her insides to jelly, but her head was still telling her to slow down. She knew it was wise to make romantic decisions with her heart and business decisions with her head, but he mixed her up so completely she couldn't separate her emotions from her anxious thoughts.

"It's the damn brown eyes," she finally swore, and it took her a long while to gather the strength to do their few dishes.

Darcy awoke a dozen times during the night. In an attempt to soothe her jangled nerves, she got up and made herself another cup of tea. But when she crawled back into bed and fell asleep, she was awake again within the hour.

It was all Griffin's fault. What he offered was adventure of the most intoxicating sort, but as she lay in her rumpled bed, she longed for a steady soul mate rather than a famed pianist who would surely use her up and spit her out before she'd learned the names of his favorite composers.

By the time her alarm went off at seven, she was relieved to get up. She made her bed, showered and washed her hair, then searched her closet for something Griffin hadn't already seen. At last she found a pale green velour sweater and matching jeans she'd worn last spring and forgotten.

Enormously relieved not to have to visit him in overalls, she pulled on pale lavender lingerie, slipped on the green outfit with bronze flats and thought she looked pretty cute. Unfortunately, as she walked to her office, she felt like unraveled yarn.

She usually loved the stillness of the new day in Monarch Bay, but that morning the seagulls were noisily circling overhead. She picked up the promised sketches and noted the eight o'clock appointment on her wipe-off board. Her hand shook so badly she had to erase the message twice and try again, but the third effort was clearly legible. As she left for Griffin's, she glanced up at the gulls and hoped their raucous din wasn't a dire warning.

She hadn't been so nervous around a man since high

school when she'd had a desperate crush on a popular football player, and her friends had pressured her to invite him to the winter dance. It had taken her a week of stomach-churning torment to work up the nerve to dial his telephone number.

When he'd answered, she'd issued a well-rehearsed but stammering invitation. He'd sounded surprised to hear from her and, as unsophisticated as she, he'd told her how excited he was to be going to the dance with one of the cheerleaders.

The brief conversation had left her thoroughly humiliated, and she hadn't asked another man out on a date from that day to this. She hadn't thought of high school in years, but that morning, she felt as awkward and lost as she had at sixteen.

Griffin answered the door dressed in Levi's and a charcoal gray silk shirt. He looked well-rested, greeted her warmly and quickly drew her inside. "On my way home last night, I began to wonder if you ever consider the view from the house rather than from the street when you make your initial sketches."

"Yes, I do, but with the sea at the back and the mountains at the front, I imagine anyone gazing from your home would find the distant view more appealing than a beautifully landscaped yard."

"They might, but just humor me and come on upstairs."

"Is this another pitch for the bathroom tour?"

"No, but you'll be sorry you put it off when you finally see them. The master bath has wisteria sculpted into the tile work that is especially fine."

"Wisteria? Well, that does it. Let's go." Darcy would have agreed to view anything to avoid looking at him when he was so handsome it hurt.

"Ladies first." Griffin gestured toward the stairs and followed her up. "Turn left at the top. My room is at the end."

Darcy felt him trailing close behind and tried to focus on the beautifully carved handrail. "Even without furniture, there's a real warmth to this house."

"Yes, I felt it the first time I came here."

Darcy paused at the top of the stairs and glanced both ways before turning left. "How many bedrooms are there?"

"Seven up here. There's a maid's room off the kitchen and two full apartments over the garage for additional staff."

His door was closed, and Darcy waited for him to open it.

The room was painted the color of chocolate milk with a bold area rug in chocolate and cream beneath a king-sized bed covered with a cream-colored spread. The furnishings were dark, obviously expensive and starkly modern, as were the paintings. It was a thoroughly masculine room, as though the owner had given no thought to adding a woman's tender influence to his life.

A set of double doors led to a walk-in closet and another to the promised bath. French doors opened out on a balcony overlooking the sea. It was a room as spectacular as its owner, and Darcy forced herself to concentrate on wisteria as Griffin opened the bathroom door for her.

The bathroom was huge, with a tub, separate shower and a glossy black marble floor. A long mirror covered the wall above the black marble counter holding the double sinks and reflected the pale mauve tile trimmed with black. It was a stunning room, and the tile work was indeed superb, but as Griffin's gaze caught hers in the mirror, she saw only him.

He leaned against the doorjamb and crossed his arms over his chest. "The decorator couldn't find towels in an exact match for the tile, so he went with black. He apologized profusely, but frankly, a towel is a towel to me."

Darcy watched a trickle of water left from his morning shower lazily careen down the clear glass enclosure. "Black is good for a man."

She went to the window looking out on the sea and traced the pattern in the tile below. "Maybe we could plant a wisteria at the base of the bedroom balcony to echo this theme."

"See, I told you you ought to tour the bathrooms. They may inspire all sorts of remarkable possibilities."

Darcy glanced at him again in the mirror. She'd once dated a man who couldn't pass a mirror without commenting on his looks, but rather than himself, Griffin was observing her with a fond glance. A sly smile played across his lips, and he appeared to be genuinely interested in her comments.

What she was most interested in, however, was him. He would surely break her heart, but while still whole, her heart thundered his name. She drew in a deep breath and decided to go for it. Giving up any other course as absurd, she went to him and began to unbutton his shirt.

"Let's forget breakfast," she suggested in a provocative

purr, "and take up where we left off last night."

Griffin laughed and straightened to his full height. He grasped her waist and, with two strides, set her on the counter between the sinks. He stepped between her legs and rested his hands lightly on her thighs.

"After I got up at dawn to cook for you, don't you even want to hear the menu?"

"No. Whatever it is can't possibly be better than you." Darcy unbuttoned the last button, and Griffin shrugged off his shirt and tossed it aside. Crisp black curls fanned over his chest, narrowed to a thin strip down his well-defined abs and disappeared beneath his belt. She spread her fingers across his chest and thumbed his nipples.

"I do have feelings," Griffin protested. "I don't just service women on demand."

Darcy zigzagged a fingertip down his crotch and felt his body's eager response. "Just this once, make an exception."

Griffin caught her chin to force her to look up at him. "We were going to agree upon some ground rules last night, but somehow we got distracted."

Darcy barely recalled the mention of rules. "What sort of rules did you have in mind?"

Griffin yanked on her sleeves and eased her sweater off over her head. He tossed it atop his shirt. "We need to agree on what's business and what's personal. I won't mix the two, nor will I allow you to either."

While he slid her bra straps off her shoulders, she unbuckled his belt and began to unbutton his fly. He was wearing black silk boxers, and she eased her fingers under the waistband. "You'll tell me what I'm not allowed to do? That's your idea of agreeing on rules?"

Griffin caught her hands. "You can't sleep your way into a new lease, so if that's your intention, give it up now."

Darcy licked her lips and smiled suggestively. "There's only one thing I'm inclined to give up, and it has nothing to do with buildings."

"Cross your heart?"

Darcy unsnapped her bra, flung it toward the growing pile of clothing and made a cross on her bare breast. "Do you have any other rules?"

Griffin rolled her nipples through his index fingers and thumbs. "Yes, this has to be an exclusive relationship. I won't see other women, and you won't see other men."

The man did indeed have great hands, and Darcy squirmed slightly as she thought of his touching her more intimately. "Better define what you mean by 'see'," she asked.

He increased the pressure on her nipples. "How detailed do you want it? Spend time with alone, date, dine with, sleep with, or any other sexual pastime. Is that clear?"

Darcy finished unbuttoning his fly and reached through the slit in his boxers to grasp his cock. Her hands were small, and her fingers didn't meet as she encircled him. He felt huge. "Fair enough," she agreed. "Anything else?"

"Yes, never lie to me, and I mean that. Don't leave things out. Don't conveniently forget to mention something I ought to know."

Darcy ran her thumb along the underside of his cock to rub the sensitive ridge where the shaft met the head. His breathing quickened slightly, which she considered a point for her side. "If anything, I'm too honest, but you can't lie to me either."

"I won't," he swore.

"Anything else?" Fearing a bizarre request that would be a deal breaker, Darcy held her breath.

"One last thing. I know you and Christy will talk, and I don't care if you tell her the sex is great, but our conversations have to remain private."

"What's your real worry, that I'll tell the *Enquirer* you lie on the beach all day swilling beer in your underwear?"

Griffin leaned in to give her a kiss that demanded her full attention. "Very funny, but fortunately, the tabloids have no interest in classical musicians. Just promise you'll respect my privacy."

"You needn't worry. I won't even admit I know you, let alone brag about what you say. But what do we have here, promises not to mix business and pleasure, and of fidelity, honesty and loyalty? You don't moonlight as a Marine recruiter, do you?"

"Damn it, Darcy, I'm serious."

"You're also half-naked in a bathroom with my hand on your dick. Now either you trust me to protect your heart and your career, or you don't. Which is it?"

Griffin released a groan that bordered a growl, scooped her off the counter and carried her to his bed. He dropped her in the center none too gently, then sprawled out on top of her.

"That mouth is going to get you in a lot of trouble," he warned.

Darcy arched her back to rub her now delightfully sensitive nipples across his hairy chest. "I knew you were trouble the first time I saw you. Just bring it on."

Griffin kissed her deeply rather than reply. Then he began to tease her gently rounded breasts with the tip of his tongue before sucking first one and then the other into his mouth. Propped on an elbow, he used his free hand to unzip her jeans and slid his hand into her lace panties.

Darcy's breath caught in her throat as he slipped two fingers inside her. She was so wet, he stroked her with an easy rhythm, and then rose.

He rolled off the bed to remove her pants with a swift tug, then peeled off her lacy lavender panties. He tossed them over his shoulder and shed the rest of his clothes. He crawled up over the end of his bed, grabbed her ankles and spread her legs wide.

His lean, well-muscled body was the perfection Darcy had known it would be, but she suddenly recalled an important detail. "I sure hope we don't have to send out for condoms."

"They're in the drawer in the nightstand to your left, but we don't need them yet," Griffin assured her. He stretched out to lick her navel, then slid his hands under her bottom to angle her hips toward his mouth. "You smell so good, and I'll bet you taste even better."

Darcy had sprinkled on the pumpkin pie spice liberally, but doubted she would taste like a pie. Then his tongue trailed the length of her cleft, and she ceased to worry over being confused with a dessert. He knew just where to touch her, and when he again slid his fingers inside to caress her in time with his tender lapping, she grabbed hold of his hair to press him closer still.

She remembered her first glimpse of him, but she'd never dreamed a week later she would be shoving him into his bed. As the rush to climax built, she moaned way back in her throat and tilted her hips to lure him deeper. Her whole body throbbed with an aching need for release, but he slowed his pace to prolong the sweet torture, then quickened it again to send her tumbling over the edge.

A wave of heated ecstasy swept through her, warming her clear to her fingertips and toes, but Griffin gave her no time to drift on pleasure. Instead, he grabbed a condom and dipped into her, slowly stretching her until she was completely filled. He spared her the burden of his weight as he thrust deeply, then rolled over to bring her up on top.

His eyes were half-closed, and Darcy loved being able to gauge his reaction as she rolled her hips to ride him. She reached back between his legs to tickle his balls with the tip of her nail and felt him pitch beneath her. She slid her nails up his belly and began a sweet circular dance that swiftly flooded her with renewed desire.

Griffin reached for the spot where their bodies joined and rubbed her in time with her own sensuous rocking. He had amazing control, and thrust up into her until, with a convulsive shudder, he came and pulled her into bliss along with him.

Exhausted by their shared rapture, Darcy lay sprawled across his chest, unable to do more than offer a grateful moan. Joyously relaxed, she fell asleep convinced she'd died and gone to heaven.

Chapter Six

"Darcy," Griffin whispered. When she failed to stir, he set the breakfast tray on the nightstand and shook her shoulder gently.

"Come on, Darcy. It's time to wake up."

Darcy recognized his voice and smiled in her dreams. She rolled over and snuggled down into her pillow.

Griffin sat on the side of the bed and rubbed her back in gentle circles. "I really hate to wake you, but you'll be furious with me if I don't."

His touch felt so good, Darcy twisted slightly to encourage more, but she remained fast asleep. Then Griffin nibbled her ear, and she raised a hand to bat him away.

"Darcy," Griffin called more insistently. "Wake up, sugar. It's time for breakfast."

Darcy yawned sleepily, rolled toward him and opened one eye. "What time is it?" she asked in a sleepy slur.

"One o'clock."

"One!" Darcy sat up and yanked the sheet over her bare breasts. "One o'clock in the afternoon? Why didn't you wake me sooner? I should have been at Defy the World by ten."

Griffin was dressed as he had been earlier, and not a hair was out of place. "Don't panic. I called Christy Joy and told her our meeting was taking longer than you'd anticipated."

Darcy shoved her hands through her hair, leaving it spiked in wild disarray. "Oh great, what did she say?"

Griffin reached for the tray and placed it on her lap. "She said you deserved some time off and to take as long as you need. But I knew you'd not want me to let you sleep until dark."

There was a rose on the tray, half a grapefruit and an avocado omelet that was still steaming. She'd never had a man bring her breakfast in bed, and she had to blink away her tears. She quickly reached for her fork and took a bite of omelet. It melted in her mouth.

"This is delicious. For a man who's always lived in hotels, you've learned to cook with remarkable speed."

Griffin shrugged slightly. "I'll admit the first couple weren't up to that standard, but they tasted just as good."

"You're an absolute marvel, Mr. Moore, but where did you get the rose?"

"I climbed a neighbor's fence."

Darcy's eyes widened. "You didn't!"

"I figured they wouldn't miss it, but you'll not tell on me, will you?"

Darcy shook her head. He'd obviously been awake for hours, but she was so amused by the theft of a rose from his neighbor's yard that she couldn't be angry with him for not waking her.

"Your secret's safe with me. Now, as delicious as this is, I need to get to work."

"Have a few bites of grapefruit first. That one is especially sweet."

Darcy picked up her spoon and scooped up a section. It was as good as promised. "Yes, this is wonderful too, but—"

"You needn't rush off," Griffin assured her. "I've decided to buy that big iron fish. Can you devise some way to hang it in the garden you're planning for me?"

Darcy swallowed the bite of grapefruit with a hasty gulp. "Griffin, you don't have to pay for my time."

"Of course not, that would be prostitution. Is that what you think I'm suggesting?"

"No, I think you're trying to help us earn enough money to move. That's sweet, in a perverse sort of way, but you needn't do it."

"What if I just happen to like that spectacular goldfish?"

He looked hurt, and she wondered if she'd misunderstood his motives. She took another bite of the heavenly omelet. "All right, if you really want the goldfish, we might hang it on the arbor we'll have to build to support the wisteria vine."

Griffin thought for a moment. "Yes, that would work, and then it could be seen from the terrace. What about a fountain?"

"Lined with Spanish tile?"

"Wouldn't that be appropriate?"

"Yes. If you want a fountain, I'll add one. Did you want it at the front or on the terrace?"

"I'll have to think about it. Maybe both."

Darcy reached out to take his hand. "I really like you, Griffin, and it has nothing to do with whatever business you might send my way. Now, we agreed to separate business and pleasure, so I really shouldn't be discussing landscaping from your bed."

Griffin broke into a broad grin. "I didn't consider that when I mentioned the fish. I'll leave so you can get dressed, but I sure hated to wake you when you looked so at home in my bed."

"I'm sorry. I didn't sleep well last night."

Griffin stood, then leaned down to kiss her. "That wasn't a complaint."

Darcy remained in bed for several minutes after he'd left the handsomely decorated room. She glanced around and imagined herself waking up there every morning, but a pup tent would be equally inviting if Griffin shared it.

She took a couple more bites of omelet and grapefruit and, without Griffin to distract her, noticed the sterling silver pattern featured not simply a modern swirl, but a music note. It was attractive, appropriate, and undoubtedly a custom design.

Unwilling to consider what twelve place settings must have cost, she got up and went into the wisteria bathroom to shower for the second time that day. Griffin had folded her clothes so they were unwrinkled. Damp from the shower, her hair fell into place with a brush of her fingertips.

She picked up her breakfast tray to return it to the kitchen, but because his bathroom had indeed proven to be artful perfection, she decided to look in on the others. She carried the tray to the top of the stairs, set it down and went back to explore.

She began with the bedroom next to Griffin's, but when she opened the door, she could only stare, for rather than the empty space he'd led her to expect, there was a haphazard collage of maps tacked to the wall and several tables topped with glowing computers. A printer spewed out a steady stream of documents, but she was too shocked to investigate their source. Frightened that Griffin had failed to mention he was running such an ambitious enterprise, she turned to leave and ran right smack into him.

"Find anything interesting?" he asked.

"I just wanted to see the other bathrooms," Darcy hastened to explain. "But this looks like a war room. What are you doing here, Griffin?" She doubted he could actually be the drug kingpin Mary Beth had imagined, but he was definitely up to something.

"Nothing even remotely sinister," Griffin swore. "The computers are programmed to answer fan mail. It's a sophisticated set-up which allows them to respond to email in the language it was sent. They also keep track of how many times a fan has contacted me, so the same reply is never repeated.

"They provide a suitably grateful response, list my upcoming concert dates and information on ordering CDs. Other computers answer letters in the same warmly appreciative way. A clerk in my agent's office enters the sender's name and address, and the response is printed here so that I can sign it. The mail is still coming through, so apparently Karen didn't believe me when I fired her.

"What did you think I was doing, tracking satellites, or managing an off-shore gambling operation?"

His relaxed explanation made perfect sense, but, glancing toward the maps, Darcy was still alarmed. She'd always relied on her instincts where men were concerned, and she truly felt things weren't nearly as innocent as he insisted they were.

"I suppose you use the maps to keep track of concert tours?"

"Yes. What's the matter, Darcy? Don't you believe me?"

"You told me you'd moved in a bed and your piano. But you actually have an entire bedroom suite, and an office with computers that probably run twenty-four hours a day."

"Yes, they do, but so what? Didn't you realize I'd probably have a fan or two?"

"Don't be flip," Darcy cautioned. She was convinced he'd have a reasonable answer for any question she might pose, but, rather than being relieved, she was growing increasingly uneasy. In so many ways, he was too good to be true, and this eerie room filled with softly humming computers gave her chills.

"I really need to get down the hill," she said as she scooted by him. She picked up her breakfast tray and carried it down the stairs at a near run.

Griffin reached the bottom of the stairs a second behind her, took the tray and again set it aside on the floor. "I didn't mean to spook you, but this isn't Blue Beard's castle. Will you come back tonight?"

"No, let's not overdose on each other." Darcy swung open the heavy front door and dashed through it.

With his long stride, Griffin easily overtook her. "There's no danger of that."

"Let's not take the risk." Darcy made straight for her truck and yanked open the driver's door, but Griffin reached around her to slam it shut.

"What the hell is going on here?" he asked. "Are you sorry you slept with me? Is that what this is all about?"

He looked more confused than angry, but with all her senses tingling, she felt like Spiderman and couldn't wait to get away. "I'm not in the least bit sorry," she exclaimed. "You're an amazing lover, but I need to get to work."

"Women complain men cut and run after sex, but damn it all, Darcy, you look scared to death. Go play with your plants, if you must, but I'll come into town later. We can have a thoroughly civilized talk, and maybe you'll have calmed down enough to be honest with me."

He stepped out of her way, and she drove off without yelling at him for keeping what she feared were gigantic secrets, but she couldn't understand how the day could have begun so well and then spiraled into abject terror.

When she returned to work, she sipped half a bottle of water and took a dozen deep breaths before she peeked into the gift shop and waved to Christy Joy. Then she went into her office, closed the door, sat at her desk and let her forced composure crumble.

All too soon she heard George talking with one of their teenage workers and knew she couldn't avoid him indefinitely. She reached for a tissue and dried her eyes seconds before he rapped lightly at her door.

"We missed you this morning. You want to talk?" he asked.

Darcy glanced through the open doorway to the soothing greens of the nursery and shrugged helplessly. "I don't even know where to begin. Did you ever have a hunch about something, or an uneasy feeling that things just weren't right?"

"Sure, everybody does. I've learned to heed them too. What's got you so jumpy?"

Darcy recalled Griffin's insistence upon secrecy, but she hadn't actually agreed to his demand. Now, with the sun bouncing across her office floor, she was reluctant to describe how frightened she'd been to discover a roomful of coldly efficient computers. It would sound too silly.

"I just got scared," she murmured.

George nodded thoughtfully. "Are you talking about Griffin Moore?"

"Yes and no, but it wasn't anything he did. In fact, he's treated me almost embarrassingly well."

George appeared to be weighing his words carefully before he spoke. "I read an article in one of Marge's magazines that might apply here."

Darcy rolled her eyes. "I can't wait to hear it."

"Don't be so quick to judge, Missy. A noted psychologist, whose name I've forgotten, wrote that some singles, they could be men as well as women, long to meet Ms. or Mr. Right. But when they actually do, they use every barrier they can haul into place to prevent that special person from getting close."

"In other words," Darcy added, "they sabotage the dream relationship for which they've been praying. Is that what you think I'm doing?"

George glanced out at the nursery. "I really can't say. I'm just offering one expert's opinion that made sense to me. You might want to give it some thought."

Darcy shook her head. She'd been fine with Griffin, better than fine, until she'd opened the door to the war room and been scared half out of her wits. "I appreciate the thought, George. Marge is a lucky woman to have such a thoughtful husband."

"Well, I'm sorry to say it wasn't always the case, but she trained me right. You ought to do the same with Griffin Moore."

"I could just as easily teach the Statue of Liberty to polka."

"A bit set in his ways, is he?"

"I don't know him well enough to say for sure, but he's used to getting his own way and obviously likes it."

"Who doesn't?" George asked. "Now, I better get back to work or the boss is liable to dock my pay."

Darcy laughed with him, but once he'd gone, her posture resumed a dejected slump. She folded her arms on her desk to create a passable pillow, laid her head down and closed her eyes. She tried to analyze the way the morning had ended in dispassionate terms, but had nearly dozed off when the telephone rang.

Jarred awake, she didn't answer until the third ring, but then managed a professional tone. The caller proved to be a neighbor of Griffin's who'd seen her truck and wanted an estimate on completely replanting her yard for her daughter's wedding.

Darcy tapped her pen against her clipboard as she ran through her usual questions to gain a better idea of what the woman expected. When the caller mentioned gardenias, azaleas and camellias, she understood.

"You want a wonderfully romantic backdrop for the wedding and reception. I can do something truly lovely for you that will continue to give you pleasure long after the day of the ceremony, but first I'll need to visit your home." She made a note of the address and set up an appointment for the following morning.

She'd hoped working for Griffin would bring her additional commissions on Ridgecrest, but this woman had just seen her truck and been inspired to call. Maybe she should have driven around the exclusive neighborhood a couple of times a week and let everyone assume she was working up there. Of course, she didn't actually have the job yet, but she at least had a good chance of landing it, and that perked up the day considerably.

Needing fresh air, she left her office to walk through the nursery and clear her mind. There were some cacti that needed to either be marked down and sold or repotted, and she debated which would be the smarter move. Because repotting cacti was a chore everyone hated, she marked them down and bid them a hasty farewell.

She was standing by the suspended fish sculpture Griffin had admired when he walked through the gate. He wasn't smiling, and Darcy braced herself for another unfortunate confrontation. She felt her cheeks tremble as she tried to smile.

He responded with a curt nod. "I thought maybe I'd take the fish home today."

"Well, think again," Darcy countered. "It's too heavy to throw in the back of your Land Rover, and even if you got it home, you couldn't carry it yourself."

"I'm a lot tougher than you apparently think I am."

Darcy looked at him askance. "I know you're tough, Griffin, I've seen just how muscular you are, but the fish weighs a ton, or at least it feels like it. I'll hang a big sold sign on it and deliver it just as soon as we get the arbor built."

"I doubt Toby McClure would appreciate your reluctance to collect my money and deliver the work today."

Darcy was amazed he recalled the artist's name. Then the truth hit her with the force of an actual slap. "It isn't just Kate Sessions' name you recall, is it? You remember everything you hear. It must be the auditory version of a photographic memory."

"I don't play by ear," Griffin scoffed. "I actually read music."

The warning gleam had flashed in his eyes before he'd glanced away, but Darcy refused to back off. "You have a phenomenal memory, speak several languages fluently and probably have an I.Q. in the 200 range."

"Sorry, but it was only 177 when I was tested, but I was fourteen, cocky as hell and didn't give it my best effort. But what does any of that have to do with an iron fish?"

Darcy shook her finger at him. "Precisely, and we both know that's not why you're here."

Griffin gave a begrudging nod. "No, it's not. I came to see you. Let's go on down to the beach and talk."

"I work here," Darcy reminded him. "I can't just go flitting off to the beach after I've missed half the day."

"I could help out. What needs to be done?"

Darcy thought of the cacti and immediately discounted the idea. When he had such handsome hands and arms, she didn't want him scratched. "We're doing all right here. Why don't you go to the gym, and I'll meet you later."

"I don't feel like working out. Maybe I'll just go down to the docks and look at the boats, but I'll be back at six."

It was more of a threat than a promise, but Darcy was

trying to make sense of things, not avoid him. "Fine, I'll be right here."

He turned on his heel and left, and only Darcy heard one of the teenagers snickering nearby. "What's so damn funny, Todd? If you have time to stand around laughing at me, get a broom and sweep off the walkways."

Caught, Todd shrugged and went to fetch a broom.

It truly was a lovely afternoon, and Darcy sat on a redwood bench to enjoy it. Unfortunately, she soon had to rise to answer a customer's question about bougainvilleas, but she sold the woman three good-sized plants with peach-toned blossoms and considered the effort worthwhile.

She was checking the day's total on the nursery register when Christy Joy came outside to join her. "Thanks for not throwing a fit about this morning. I really didn't mean to be so late."

"We got along fine, but now you owe me."

Darcy couldn't dispute that. "You need a babysitter?"

"Not today, but I do have a favor to ask. Jeremy wants to take Twink and me out whale watching one morning early, and I want you and Griffin to come along."

"Why, to throw J. Lyle off the scent?"

Christy Joy smoothed her upswept curls. "I know, it's stupid, but I'd feel a whole lot more comfortable if Twink and I didn't have to be alone with Jeremy."

"He seems like a nice guy."

"I think so too, but I'm just hollow. I can manage Defy the World and raise Twink, but that's it. I've nothing left for Jeremy, but I don't want to hurt his feelings and turn him down when I brought up the subject of whale watching in the first place."

Darcy knew what she meant by hollow, as in empty of reserves, but she certainly didn't have that problem with Griffin. "I've got an appointment for an estimate tomorrow at nine which might cut it too close. What about Wednesday?"

"Jeremy said anytime this week, so Wednesday should be fine."

"Good. I can't speak for Griffin, but I'll be there. It's been ages since I've been out on a boat, and it's always fun. I'm very proud of Defy the World, but we aren't having nearly enough fun, Christy Joy."

"Oh, come on. I enjoy the shop and the time I spend with Twink."

"But you're complaining of feeling hollow," Darcy reminded her.

Christy Joy raised her finger to her lips. "Hush. Don't you dare spread that around. I need to get back inside, but tell me first, how was your morning?"

"Indescribable," Darcy exclaimed.

"That good? Well, lucky you."

Darcy let Christy Joy go without expanding upon her appreciative comment, but she was still confused about what had really happened that morning when Griffin returned.

"I still want to go down to the beach," he said. "Do you have a jacket?"

"Sure, I have several hanging in my office. I'll go and get one." She expected him to wait by the gate, but he came along with her and helped her into the dark green windbreaker. When he took her hand, the thrill was still there despite her misgivings.

It was a short walk to the beach, and they took off their shoes and strolled on down past the vacation homes to the tree-lined edge of the bay before Griffin pulled Darcy down beside him in the sand.

"I have a concert in Seattle on Saturday, and I want to take you with me."

The invitation was the last thing Darcy had expected to hear, but there was no way she could accept. "Last weekend was really busy, and if the beautiful weather holds, next weekend will be the same. I can't even afford to be late, much less leave town."

Griffin kept his gaze focused on the sailboats returning to the bay. "I understand. I've put you in a bind, and naturally you'd not want to harm Defy the World any further by being away."

While that was the truth, Darcy hated the slant he'd given it. "Eventually things will work out," she replied.

"I have no such faith, but still, I wanted to ask you. Sit still." He stood then sat behind her so she was cradled between his outstretched legs. He wrapped his arms around her shoulders and pulled her back against his chest.

"If I get the opportunity to play an encore or two, I'm going to play one of my own pieces."

That made the concert doubly important, and Darcy's heart sank. "Have you done that before?"

"No, but there are some excellent music critics in Seattle, and I'm anxious to hear their opinion of my work."

"So this is a major event for you," Darcy mused aloud.

"Yes, but if you can't be there, I'll just have to tell you about it when I get home. If you're still speaking to me. I've spent the day trying to figure out what went wrong this morning, but I'll be damned if I know," he confided softly in her ear.

He had the most seductive mannerisms, and Darcy wasn't immune, but she felt vaguely uneasy as well as guilty about missing the Seattle concert. She hadn't forgotten George's warning, and wondered if she wasn't just piling up more problems than Griffin could surmount. She covered his hands with her own and tried to sound reasonably sane.

"I shouldn't have gone snooping through your house," she said.

"Snoop all you like. I've nothing to hide. I told you the bathrooms were worth seeing, and they are. I always take a laptop with me, and I could send you an email or two while I'm away."

He'd changed the subject so smoothly, Darcy was simply in awe. She told him her email address and was confident he would remember it. She was going to have to be careful of everything she said when he might dredge it up later to prove a point. It was another reason to be wary, and she already had too many.

"Would you like to go whale watching Wednesday morning? Christy Joy and Twink are going out on Jeremy Linden's boat and want us to come along. It should be fun, even if we don't spot any whales."

"I get seasick," Griffin confessed.

Darcy turned to look up at him. "So do I, but we'll be out on deck with plenty of fresh air, and seasickness shouldn't be a problem."

"So you say."

Darcy was astonished to learn he possessed any weakness at all. "Do you get motion sickness when you fly?"

"Yes, but I have pills for it."

"Then take a couple Wednesday morning, and you'll be fine."

Griffin shook his head. "They make me kind of loopy, and I might fall overboard."

For a split second, Darcy wondered if he were refusing to come along to pay her back for missing the Seattle concert. It would be a petty way to get even, but she couldn't put it past him.

"I don't want you to get sick, Griffin, but when I tell you about the whales we saw, you'll be sorry you missed it."

"Probably, but I'll not be sorry I spent the whole voyage puking over the stern either. Besides, I'm flying up to Seattle Wednesday afternoon, and I can't really spare the time."

Now, Darcy was convinced he was paying her back. Rather than let him see her seethe, she just shrugged. "I imagine you do need to practice a bit."

"I'll have three days to rehearse with the symphony before the concert, so that should be enough. If it isn't, well, those critics I mentioned will have something new to report in their columns."

"You don't sound worried."

"I'm not, but I'll miss you. What do you want to cook for dinner tonight?"

Darcy looped her arms around his thighs. She'd never dated a man with his height, and it was nice to be surrounded with so much muscular male flesh. "Are you inviting yourself to dinner at my house, or asking me to come up to yours again?"

"Whichever you'd like. I'm the most agreeable of men."

"Except when it comes to boats."

"Oh, all right, boats are the exception, but at least I eat seafood. Let's just grab something at the little market we passed and eat at your place tonight."

Darcy rested her cheek against his upper arm. "It's getting chilly, but I'm awfully comfortable right here."

"So am I, but I'm hungry. Let's go." He slipped free of her grasp, rose and, with an easy scoop, lifted her to her feet.

Darcy took his hand and carried her shoes as they retraced their steps, but she made a mental note to keep track of how many times he discounted her suggestions to do what he wished. He might pamper her, but still, they did things his way. That was annoying, but at least she'd refused to abandon Christy Joy and go to Seattle.

"Where will you be performing next?" she asked.

"Budapest. Do you have a passport?"

"No, but—"

"Get one. Sooner or later, you're bound to want to come along."

Dazzled by the thought, Darcy tripped over a piece of driftwood and would have fallen had Griffin not kept her on her feet. The man was going to flit all over the world, but she couldn't be his traveling companion. That wasn't any contrived barrier either. It was simply the way things were, and what they spelled was disaster.

Chapter Seven

Griffin surprised Darcy by wanting to make soft tacos for supper. While she browned the ground turkey, he chopped and diced lettuce, tomatoes, olives, and sliced an avocado. After completing that chore, he grated a whole block of cheddar cheese.

"How's the turkey coming along?" he asked.

"I just added the spices, and it's sizzling nicely. The tortillas are warm, so the only thing left to do is slap the tacos together."

"Please, they'll taste so much better if we ease the ingredients into the tortillas slowly."

He winked at her, and she was certain he had something other than Mexican food on his mind. "My mistake, but I like things fast and hot."

"You ought to slow down and enjoy the moment," he cautioned more seriously.

"Oh, I enjoy myself immensely. I just slam my moments together, is all."

"Let's eat and argue later."

"Now where have I heard that before?" Darcy mused under her breath.

Her kitchen was so small they bumped into each other often, but it was far more entertaining than troublesome. "Would you put some ice in the glasses for soda, please?"

"I'll be happy to, ma'am."

Darcy observed in amazement as Griffin not only popped the ice from the trays, but refilled them and put them back in her freezer. She'd never expected to meet a man who would bother to refill her ice cube trays, and yet here he was. It made her heart flutter.

As soon as Griffin had poured the sodas, she ladled the meat onto the tortillas and handed them to him to assemble. "I can't eat more than two. What about you?"

"I'll start with four and count when I'm finished, but you should have enough salad stuff left to last you until I get back."

"I'll take care to make it last." Darcy carried her plate and soda out to the oak table, and Griffin followed. "Will the Seattle folks keep you as well-fed?"

Griffin sat and took a bite of taco and a sip of soda before he replied. "They'll try, but the company won't be nearly as interesting."

Darcy slouched down in her chair to run her toe up his leg. "Am I merely interesting? A history professor might be deemed an interesting companion."

"True. Perhaps it was a poor choice of words." Griffin was well into his second taco before he spoke again. "How's provocative?"

"Makes me wish we were in a restaurant where I could slip under the tablecloth to tease you a bit."

"Darcy MacLeod, you astonish me, but as long as you like me, I'll not complain." For the last hour, he had laughed so often there was no hint of the angry man who'd stormed into Defy the World that afternoon and demanded to take immediate delivery on an iron fish sculpture.

"What's not to like?" Darcy purred.

"You'll find out soon enough. Fortunately, I'll be gone fairly often until I complete this season's concert schedule, and you might actually learn to miss me."

Darcy pushed a bite of avocado back into her taco. She was still on her first while he was halfway through his third. He'd bought the groceries, however, and had every right to enjoy them. When he filled the whole house with his presence, it was ever so nice that he was again in a playful mood.

Although she still believed it was a good thing she couldn't accompany him on the Seattle trip, where surely she would be shunted aside and ignored by his adoring fans. "Do you usually take your women with you when you travel?" she asked, while attempting to appear fascinated by her taco rather than his reply.

Griffin wiped his hands on a paper napkin and reached for

another. "I don't have a posse of women. I already told you, the women I've dated have failed to grow any fonder of me while I've been away."

"None traveled with you?"

Griffin caught her gaze and held it. "No. You're the only one I've ever invited to come along."

Darcy was full and she pushed her second taco to the side of her plate untouched. "Why me, Griffin? What's so special about me?"

"Oh no, you're not going to pry that secret out of me. Aren't you going to eat that taco?" When she shook her head, he reached over and added it to his plate.

"That isn't fair," Darcy insisted. "You said no secrets."

"I didn't realize you were listening."

Darcy hung on his every word, but that would remain her secret. "Occasionally I take note of your ramblings."

Griffin shot her a highly skeptical glance, but kept right on eating. "I swear these are the best tacos I've ever eaten. You're an excellent cook."

"Thank you, but you did more than half the work."

Having finished his fifth taco, Griffin finally pushed his plate aside and again wiped his hands on a fresh napkin. "We're a good team."

"If an unlikely one."

"I disagree. Are you sure you won't come to Seattle with me?"

"Are you sure you won't go whale watching with me?"

"Positive. But before I forget, your sketches looked great, and I signed your estimate." He reached into his back pocket and pulled out the folded form. "Here you are. When can you begin?"

"I'll finish as much as I can while you're out of town. That way the noise and dust won't bother you."

"But I won't get to watch you work either. I'll have a key made for you, so if you want to go inside and take a nap or a shower, you can."

"That's very considerate of you, but—"

"But nothing. Use the house, live there if you like. Several lights have timers so it looks as though the house is occupied, but it would be better if someone were actually there."

"Your house is huge. I'd probably get scared staying there all alone."

Griffin straightened slightly. "I'll not have you staying there with one of your crew."

Darcy laughed at the absurdity of that threat. "They're a great bunch of guys, but there's no danger in that."

"That's a relief. Now let's do the dishes." He got up and carried their plates and glasses into the kitchen.

"Make yourself at home," Darcy called.

"I'll be glad to. Go lie down on the sofa and rest until I have your kitchen sparkling again."

"Griffin, really, it didn't sparkle in the first place."

"Of course it did. Go."

"Oh, all right." Darcy kicked off her flats and stretched out on the sofa. It was covered in a nubby dark green fabric that blended in perfectly with the profusion of house plants. She positioned a throw pillow beneath her head, yawned and closed her eyes.

She heard Griffin rattling around in the kitchen cleaning up and wondered if George was also giving him advice on how to score points with a woman. She covered a wide yawn and dozed a bit before Griffin sat at the end of the couch and began to rub her feet.

"You're either worn out, or bored witless. Which is it?" he asked.

Darcy wiggled her toes. He captivated her on every level, but he already thought too highly of himself, even if it was deserved. "Perhaps it's your constant need for praise rather than your frequent absences which sends women running."

Griffin gave her big toe a playful nibble.

"Ouch!" Darcy cried in mock pain. She tried to jerk her foot free, but he held on fast.

"Never insult a man within striking distance of your toes," he admonished.

At that bizarre comment, Darcy erupted in a fit of giggles. "That's the most ridiculous advice I've ever heard, but it has an endearing charm. Perhaps I can persuade Christy Joy to embroider it on a pillow for me."

"Just be sure you give me credit for the quote. You have such a beguiling laugh, Darcy. If I were smart, I'd say good night now."

"You're brilliant," Darcy reminded him.

"So I've heard, but it complicates my life rather than makes it any easier. Tell me what sent you running this morning, and I'll do my best to see it doesn't happen again."

His fingers were working such blissful magic on her feet, she feared she might tell him anything he wished to know. "My father was a colonel in Army Intelligence and retired last year. Maybe it was finding computers and maps in a room I expected to be empty that triggered old memories, but that room struck me as a spook's den."

"Spook as in spy? When would I have the time to engage in espionage, and for whom? Some secret cultural affairs society?"

He looked as perplexed as she and, with the benefit of a day's perspective, she felt extremely foolish. "Obviously I didn't stop to consider what your purpose could possibly be. I'm sorry."

"You're forgiven. Did your father discuss his work with you?"

"No, never, and I've no idea what he actually did. My folks now live in San Antonio where my dad and one of his army buddies have opened a private security firm."

"Body guards and high-tech security for millionaires, that sort of thing?" Griffin inquired.

"I believe so."

Griffin patted her calf. "What's his name?"

"Kieran MacLeod. Why, do you usually travel with body guards?" That he might actually require professional protection frightened her.

"No." Griffin chuckled as though the thought were absurd. "Lovers of classical music are big on decorum. They'd not rip the tux off my back nor yank out handfuls of my hair."

"Thank God."

"Yes, I'm grateful not to be adored to that extent, although I have had several women express an interest in having me serve as their sperm donor."

Darcy rose on her elbows. "You can't be serious!"

"Oh, but I am. You've doubtless heard of the sperm bank that offers their clients a range of Nobel prize winners as prospective fathers. Why not have such an enterprise that counts artists and musicians as donors?"

"Well, with so damn many artists and musicians sleeping around, it might be difficult to charge much," Darcy countered.

Griffin was too amused to be insulted. "That's undoubtedly a valid point in some quarters, but I'm no slut."

"There's no such thing as a male slut. Men who sleep with any woman who'll look their way are just called men. Which is totally unfair, but as you always say, we could argue that point later."

"Hey, I'm all for equality, so I'm on your side. Now I hate to end such an entertaining evening so early, but I really do need to practice at least the pieces I'll be playing Saturday night. I'll have to stay in tomorrow too, but I'll stop by before I leave Wednesday to drop off my key."

Darcy was badly disappointed that he seemed able to tear himself away without more than a twinge of regret. She wanted him to stay, and it pained her that he had such an excellent excuse to leave. Then again, only that morning she'd used work to justify running off and leaving him. She swung her legs off the sofa, stood and stretched.

"We each have professional commitments. I'll not fault you for keeping yours, if you'll not complain when I keep mine," she offered.

Griffin also stood and spread his arms in dismay. "Damn, I wanted you to be disappointed."

"I didn't say I wasn't devastated, but I don't want the Seattle audience to throw rotten tomatoes at you."

"Neither do I, but it's unlikely any of them will come laden with bags of spoiled fruit, and they won't be allowed to carry champagne flutes into the auditorium after intermission ends either. So even without chicken wire across the stage, I believe I'll be relatively safe."

Darcy walked him to the door. "I've never dated a man who owned his own tuxedo."

"I own half a dozen."

"Armani?"

"A couple, and others by designers who are equally fine, but they're just suits. They're not me. Why don't you call your dad, tell him you're seeing an itinerant musician, and see how thrilled he is."

While she wouldn't call her folks just yet, she found his down-to-earth sensibilities endearing. She reached up on her tiptoes to kiss him good night, and he responded with a playful sweetness rather than the passion she craved. She closed the door behind him and leaned back against it.

"Definitely too good to be true."

On her way to bed, she checked out the kitchen and was pleased to find it cleaner than Griffin had found it. He'd even swept the floor. Clearly his mother had raised him right, but she wasn't used to men who cleaned up after themselves so beautifully and, just like the strange computer-filled room, warning bells rang in her head.

Tuesday morning, Darcy met with her second client on Ridgecrest. Charlotte Peavey was a tall, willowy blonde, as was her daughter Michelle, the bride-to-be. The pair loved her ideas for picking up the peach tones of the bridesmaid's dresses in flowering shrubs and borders.

"Could you do all the flowers for the wedding?" Charlotte begged with clasped hands.

"Do you mean the bouquets, corsages and centerpieces?" Darcy inquired.

"Don't forget the boutonnieres," Michelle added.

Darcy had worked for a florist while in high school and at least knew the basics, but bridal bouquets were now works of art. It would be a stretch, but Christy Joy would be there to help. Still, she paused to look up at the Peaveys' sprawling modern home as she considered the surprising request. All glass and stone, the stark house sparkled in the morning sun, but in her view, it was in dire need of more elegant landscaping.

"I'd like to discuss handling the floral work with my partner before I give you a definite answer, but I'll get back to you before the end of the week. The yard will be no problem at all to transform, but I'll not promise anything I can't deliver."

"I wish bakers were as honorable," Charlotte replied. "We've yet to find one who'll prepare the wedding cake we envision for less than a thousand dollars."

Christy Joy baked delicious pastries, but Darcy didn't think her partner would want to attempt a wedding cake without a great deal of practice, and neither of them had any time to devote to their culinary skills.

"Sorry, we can't help you there," Darcy replied. "I'll prepare a formal estimate and bring it by for your approval tomorrow afternoon."

As she left the Peavey residence, Darcy couldn't resist driving on up the hill to cruise by Griffin's. As she rounded the curve, a silver BMW turned into his driveway and, appalled, she did a quick U-turn and headed back to Defy the World.

Apparently Ms. Randall didn't give up as easily as Griffin had expected. It was a quality any client would admire in an agent, and Darcy couldn't discount it in a rival. She absolutely hated feeling jealous. It was petty and mean-spirited, but jealous she was, and there wasn't a damn thing she could do about it.

Early Wednesday morning, Darcy joined Christy Joy and Twink on Jeremy Linden's sport fishing boat, the *Great Escape*. Christy Joy had brought hot chocolate and sticky buns, which they ate as Jeremy steered the powerful boat out of the harbor into the open sea. The sky was overcast, but just as the sun broke through the thick marine layer, they spotted a pod of California gray whales making their way south to Mexico.

"You brought us luck, Twink!" Jeremy shouted, and the little girl squealed with delight. He handed over the wheel to one of his crew and came to stand beside Christy Joy while he provided Twink with some fascinating facts about the whales.

Darcy hung on to the rail and observed the whales with equal wonder. She knew quite a bit about the marine mammals, but she was still impressed by the care Jeremy took to help Twink appreciate them. She also noticed how often Jeremy's gaze strayed to Christy Joy. It was clear the captain was more keenly aware of her than the whales, which made Darcy feel doubly alone.

They returned to the docks within the hour, finished up the hot chocolate and sweet rolls, and then Christy Joy took Twink to preschool. The brief cruise had been an exhilarating adventure for the little girl, and she skipped down the street at her mother's side.

Darcy thanked Jeremy again. She hesitated briefly, tempted to encourage him to pursue Christy Joy, but then thought better of offering the shy captain advice on his love life. She settled for a friendly wave as she reached the end of the dock, then walked along the Embarcadero to Defy the World.

It was still early, and she went into her office to straighten up before opening the nursery. Christy Joy had been eager to accept the challenge of creating the bouquets and floral arrangements for Michelle Peavey's wedding. Wanting to know the latest fashion in flowers, Darcy had bought a copy of a bridal magazine for inspiration.

George, however, took one look at the magazine lying on Darcy's desk, shoved back his hat and chuckled. "If you don't mind my saying so, it might be too soon to begin planning your wedding."

"It's not my wedding I'm helping to plan, George, so erase the smirk."

"Well, just who is getting married, then? Anyone I know?"

Darcy told him about the Peaveys' request and shrugged. "I'd like to do the flowers for the whole event, but this is probably a poor time to begin taking on new challenges."

"You have to take them when they come," George advised. "You can't just prepare yourself and expect one to fall into your lap."

"That's a good point."

"But on the other hand," George cautioned, "the flower shops in town might not appreciate your encroaching on their territory."

"Don't you think Mrs. Peavey has the right to hire whomever she chooses?"

"Sure, as long as Defy the World Tomatoes understands the risk."

"It's only one wedding. We don't plan to become full-time florists, so I doubt anyone will toss a flowerpot through our front window."

George nodded thoughtfully. "Just remember, problems have a way of snowballing."

Darcy just shook her head. She loved flowers, but wiring and wrapping their stems with florist's tape wasn't her idea of fun. "Thanks for your opinion, George. I haven't really made up my mind."

Griffin approached in time to hear that last remark. "Not

about me, I hope."

Darcy hadn't expected to see him so early. He was dressed in gray slacks, a navy blue blazer and a white oxford cloth shirt with a narrow blue stripe. The tip of a blue tie with tiny red accents peeked out of his jacket pocket.

She hadn't even brushed her hair since leaving the *Great Escape* at the dock and quickly combed her bangs with her fingertips. "While this may be an enormous shock, Mr. Moore, not all of our conversations here revolve around you."

George tipped his hat and scooted out of Griffin's way. "I'll see to the watering."

"Thanks, George." Darcy stood, but didn't think it was a good idea to kiss Griffin when anyone might walk by and glance into her office. "How did the practice go?" she asked instead.

"Pretty well, but I still had time to have a key made." He handed it to her attached to a key chain with a smiling plastic daisy.

"This is awfully cute, but I'll return the key just as soon as you get home."

"Whenever," Griffin replied. He pulled a small velvet box from his pants pocket and placed it in her hand. "This I want you to keep."

It was slightly larger than a box for a ring, but Darcy was still afraid to open it. She slid his key into her bib pocket, but then just held the gift in an awkward grasp. "What's the occasion?" she asked.

"Does there have to be one?" Griffin leaned against the doorjamb and folded his arms across his chest. "Go on, open it. I can only stay a minute, and I want to know what you think."

Darcy made the mistake of looking up at him, and he wore such an inviting smile that she couldn't think at all. "You'll only be gone a few days," she argued. "I don't need a present to remind me of you."

"Open it, or I'll open it for you," Griffin responded.

Pressured, Darcy took a single peek, saw the flash of diamonds, and slammed the lid shut. "Griffin!"

He laughed, cradled her hands with his and opened the box to show off a gold quarter note accented with pavé diamonds suspended from a fine gold chain. "I saw this a couple of years ago in Vienna, but I haven't had anyone I cared to give it to until now."

It was a stunning gift and, even knowing it was probably a mere trifle to such a wealthy man, Darcy's eyes flooded with tears. "If it came from Austria, I don't suppose you can take it back," she murmured.

He slipped it around her neck and fastened the clasp. "It was meant for you, Darcy, please don't cry."

She wiped her eyes with her fingertips. "I don't know what to say."

"Thank you will do for now. If you're inspired to be any more appreciative, it will have to wait until I get home."

"I really wish you'd been there to see the whales this morning. I missed you."

Griffin gathered her into a fierce hug. "Believe me, if I'd been there, it wouldn't have been pretty."

Darcy relaxed against him and hoped he wouldn't feel her heart doing flip-flops. Then she remembered she hadn't put on any pumpkin pie spice and feared after being out on a fishing boat, she might smell like a seagull. When he stepped back much too soon, she was sure she must.

"I'll be back Sunday afternoon, and I'll miss you too."

"Will you call me Saturday night? I want to know how the concert went. It's sure to go well, but I'd still like to hear the audience reaction to your composition."

"It might be awfully late by the time the applause stops," Griffin teased.

"Oh, I don't plan to stay up," Darcy assured him, "but my phone will wake me."

"I'll call," Griffin promised, and he gave her a good-bye kiss meant to linger in her memory the whole time he was away.

Once Griffin reached Seattle, he waited until most of the other passengers had left the plane before he rose from his seat. He yawned sleepily, grabbed his carry-on bag and tuxedo which had been hanging in the luggage alcove near the hatch. He made his way along the narrow ramp to the arrival area where families were hugging their loved ones and friends were being joyfully reunited.

Off to one side, a silver-haired limousine driver held a small placard with his name. Recognizing him instantly, Griffin walked over to him, and the driver took his bag.

"Good afternoon, sir. How was your flight?"

"I can't say. I slept through it," Griffin confessed and raised his hand to suppress a wide yawn.

"Then it was a good one." The driver kept up the friendly patter until Griffin was safely seated in the back of his limousine. As they began to weave their way through the airport traffic toward the hotel, however, the chauffeur dropped his jovial manner and became Griffin's Interpol link.

"The concert is sold out," he disclosed. "If your reviews are decent, Vaughn should appear soon."

Griffin responded with a succinct obscenity. "The critics love me, but Vaughn might be content to stay home, wherever that is, and listen to my latest CD rather than risk arrest at a public concert."

"You underestimate the man's arrogance," the driver warned, "probably because you share the same flaw. Are things still placid in Monotony Bay?"

Rather than react to the insult, Griffin glanced out at the passing traffic. "I'm seeing an unusually perceptive young woman who believes I'm tracking more than fan interest on my computers."

"You are. Dump her before she gets any smarter."

"Not an option."

The chauffeur stared at Griffin in his rearview mirror. "Keep your focus until Lyman Vaughn is no longer a threat."

"I agreed to do all that I could, but I'll not sacrifice my heart and soul in the process."

The driver responded with a mirthless laugh. "Forgive me if your budding romance just doesn't compare to the need to apprehend an arms dealer who may soon hold a garage sale to unload nuclear weapons."

"Spare me the gruesome threats. I'll do all I can to trap the conscienceless freak, but my personal life will remain off limits to your manipulations."

"Yes, sir, Mr. Moore, whatever you say, sir." The driver's voice dripped with a venomous disgust. "Just be on the alert for Vaughn. He could turn up Saturday night as easily as he could in Budapest."

"You needn't worry. I already see and hear far more than I

wish to. Pick me up at ten o'clock Sunday morning."

"Ten it is. You know how to reach me, should the need arise."

Griffin nodded and carried his own luggage into the exclusive hotel which catered to the few who could afford its luxurious accommodations and exquisite service. The drive there had left him tense and angry, but after an hour in the gym filled with the latest in exercise equipment, he had relaxed enough to play the Steinway thoughtfully placed in his suite. It was his own composition he rehearsed, however, rather than those planned for yet another sold-out concert.

Thursday and Friday, Griffin's rehearsals with the Seattle Symphony Orchestra went well, and Saturday night's concert was extraordinarily fine. In response to the crowd's enthusiastic pleas for an encore, Griffin made a brief announcement that he would be delighted to play one of his own compositions for them. He then gave such a spellbinding performance that at first he was greeted with a stunned silence; then the audience flew into frenzied applause that went on and on as they begged for still more. Griffin knew the value of a timely departure, however, and he bowed, gestured toward the orchestra and conductor, then left the stage to call Darcy.

"It went surprisingly well," he confided nonchalantly.

"That's wonderful! I'm so happy for you."

"Thank you. I'm sorry not to have time to say more, but I have to attend a private reception for major donors. Without you, it will be no fun at all."

The longing in his voice filled Darcy with guilt. "Let's have our own party when you get home. Have a safe trip."

Darcy hadn't been able to sleep before he'd called, and as soon as he'd wished her a good night, she punched her pillow. She couldn't help but wonder how many beautiful women in designer gowns would slither up to him at the reception. She could picture them so easily. They would be very blonde, or auburn-haired, supremely confident and so rich they would never have to leave a lover's bed to dash to work on time.

It was after four o'clock Sunday afternoon when Griffin

walked into the Defy the World nursery. Darcy had just rung up a sale of half a dozen cacti when she looked up and saw him moving down the crowded walkways with a long, masterful stride that sent astonished shoppers scurrying out of his way.

He'd sounded so blissfully relieved when they'd spoken last night, but now he wore an expression of such fierce determination that Darcy quickly handed the customer the cardboard box filled with cacti and left the counter. Fearing Griffin's reviews must have been horrid, she rushed to meet him.

Griffin took her elbows. "I can see you're busy, but can you spare a minute?"

Jeremy Linden stood within easy reach, and Darcy grabbed his sleeve. "Jeremy, you've been here a million times. Will you please show people there's a price sticker on everything? If there are any questions, call on George or one of the kids. I'll be back as quickly as I can."

The captain's eyes widened momentarily, but then he shrugged. "Sure, I can handle it. Take your time."

Griffin dropped an arm around Darcy's shoulders and steered her out the gate and down Embarcadero toward the beach. He stopped at the sea wall, sat and pulled her between his outstretched legs. He glanced away for a moment, then cleared his throat.

"I lied to you," he began. "If you want to walk away from me now without even knowing what it was about, I'll understand."

The man had a marvelously expressive face, but she'd never seen him this serious when he wasn't angry with her, which was deeply alarming. "If you've been married four or five times rather than only once, I don't want to know."

Griffin raised his right hand. "Once, I swear."

That was a relief, if a small one, but there was no mistaking his sincerity. "Why don't you just tell me what it was first, and then I'll decide."

"Fair enough." Frowning slightly, he set his gaze just above her right shoulder. "A couple of years ago, I played a concert in Zurich. The next morning, I was approached by an agent from Interpol, who explained they were after a particularly elusive arms dealer named Lyman Vaughn.

"He's apparently a bloodthirsty sort who would as soon rob and butcher a client as supply arms to him. He's enormously wealthy and attracts beautiful women by the dozen, but soon tires of them. One of his former lovers told Interpol that Lyman had a greater passion for music than sex, and she mentioned me as his favorite artist.

"Because he moves among the super-rich, Interpol hasn't been able to get an agent near him, but they believed our paths might cross. Should that occur, they hoped I would assist them."

Darcy had initially steeled herself for his outrage over a poor review. She was totally unprepared to think of him as a secret agent. "Did they expect you to off the guy when you met him?" she asked in a hoarse whisper.

The first hint of a smile snaked across Griffin's lips. "Piano wire has been used to strangle a man, but that would be rather obvious, don't you think?"

Darcy was too scared to appreciate his humor. "Is that a yes or a no?"

Griffin shook his head emphatically. "It's a no. As you've observed, I have an excellent memory of everything I hear. Ninety-five percent of cocktail reception chatter is just that, but there's always a chance that I'll overhear something useful to Interpol in the remaining five percent."

Darcy was completely confused. "Where was the lie?"

"You have superb intuition, my love. One of my computers is linked to Interpol. I'm not a full-fledged spook, by any means, but my computer set-up isn't as innocuous as I led you to believe."

Darcy focused briefly on a sailboat gliding across the bay. Like so many things, sailing required hard work, but from afar, it appeared effortless and serene. She wished just once her life would take on a similar sense of calm.

She was too shaken by the nature of Griffin's confession to know what to do, but she slid her hand up his shoulder and took comfort from his warmth. "All right, I'm still listening. What prompted you to tell me about Interpol?"

"I'm getting to that." Griffin pulled her closer still and took a deep breath. "My Interpol contact always appears as my limo driver. They have my concert schedule and, should they wish to speak to me directly, he just appears at the airport.

"He met me last Wednesday, and this morning, his limo was at the curb when I left my hotel, but my contact had been shot in the head."

"My God!" Darcy sagged against his thigh, and he caught her waist to steady her.

"That's what I said. The Seattle police assumed it was a botched robbery attempt, and I didn't tell them anything different."

"But won't they discover that the dead man was with Interpol?"

"He wouldn't have been carrying a badge, but I'll alert Interpol as soon as I get home. They'll send someone to claim the body."

"You came straight here?" Darcy had wanted him to be pleasantly surprised by how beautifully the landscaping was going, but now such a concern seemed utterly ridiculous.

"Yes. Someone obviously wanted my contact dead. You can connect the dots as easily as I can."

Darcy sure could, and she swallowed hard. "Whoever wanted him dead knows he was your link to Interpol."

Griffin nodded. "Right, which means I'm of no further use to them. Now you need to get back to work." He eased her away and stood. "I realize I've probably prompted more questions than answers, but it's all I know for now."

He took her hand and walked her back to the nursery, but Darcy was shaking so hard she could scarcely walk in a straight line. "Wait a minute, perhaps this has nothing to do with Interpol. Couldn't someone have shot a chauffeur, planned to take his place and kidnap you?"

"It's a distinct possibility. Just who do you think that kidnapper might be?"

Only one name came to Darcy's mind—Lyman Vaughn. She hadn't taken off the necklace he'd given her, and she touched the golden note for luck. She'd known Griffin was trouble, but she'd never dreamed just how terrifying that trouble could be.

Chapter Eight

Darcy forced herself to walk back into the nursery, but the last hour of business passed in a frantic blur. George locked the gate on his way out, and she stayed while Mary Beth ran the total for the day, but then she hurried home to shower. She doused herself in pumpkin pie spice, yanked on her new Levi's skirt and, hoping to elevate her mood, pulled on a yellow sweater.

Her hands trembled on the wheel as she drove up to Griffin's, but she made it safely. When he failed to answer the bell, she could have used the key he'd given her, but she quickly discarded the idea now that he was home. Certain he would be out in his Zen garden anyway, she raced around the side of the house and across the terrace.

The sun had already set, but Griffin was still seated on the bench, silhouetted against the sky's fading rosy glow. Darcy paused to catch her breath and approached him at a sedate walk rather than a desperate sprint. She sat beside him and reached for his hand.

"I'm scared to death," she confided in a breathless rush.

His voice was soft. "Then why are you here?"

She had an instant reply. "I thought you might need some backup."

The absurdity of that notion made Griffin laugh for the first time that day. "Thank you for the thought. The yard looks even better than your sketches, but you must have worked nonstop."

"Not quite, and we still need to build the arbor, plant the wisteria and suspend the fish. None of that seems important now, though."

"Oh yes, it does," Griffin argued. "I don't intend to look over my shoulder everywhere I go, nor will I turn my home into a fortress. Finish the landscaping, but take your time."

Darcy hadn't been sure what he would want to do, but she was grateful for the distraction. "Fine. The wood will be delivered in the morning, and the carpenter is scheduled for the afternoon. I plan to sink the posts in cement, but my crew can handle that chore."

Griffin nodded thoughtfully, then drew her hand to his lips and kissed her palm. "I told you the truth about Interpol for a reason, Darcy."

His touch again created a magical thrill that sizzled up her arm and twisted down her spine. She shivered with a chill unrelated to the coolness of the evening and struggled to find a lucid response. Tomorrow they would have known each other for two weeks. It was a mere blink of an eye, and yet for her, the time before they'd met had already begun to fade into insignificance.

"Did you really expect me to cut and run?" she asked.

"I'd hoped not, but it might be wise. Because of the concert tour, my life is heavily insured, but it doesn't follow that I'm not eager to continue living it.

"There's the outside chance that some crazy fool was trying to car-jack the limo, and that my contact's death had nothing whatsoever to do with me. I choose to think otherwise, however, and if I'm in danger, then anyone who spends time with me is as well."

Darcy didn't even want to go there. "You must have contacted Interpol. What did they say?"

"They're a coolly efficient bunch and merely advised me to remain calm. They'll investigate the Seattle shooting and replace my contact. The guy was rather abrasive, but I never expected to find him murdered."

"That must have been horrible."

Griffin reached over to pull her across his lap. "I'd rather talk about something else, if you don't mind."

"I don't want to talk at all," Darcy exclaimed.

"Better still," Griffin murmured as he dipped his head to kiss her.

He tasted of peppermint. His hand rested lightly on her knee, and he had such handsome hands that she wished men still wore fancy lace cuffs. There was something so very sexy about the delicacy of lace against a strong, masculine wrist. Yet she scarcely needed such tantalizing thoughts when she was in Griffin's arms.

She ran her fingers through his wind-ruffled hair. Shiny and black, it was as fine as silk and yet grew in a thick thatch. She'd never enjoyed merely touching a man as she did Griffin, and she drank in his deep kisses with a thirsty abandon. When he ran his fingertips up her inner thigh, she envied the piano on which he usually lavished his attentions.

"You smell absolutely delicious," he offered in an appreciative sigh. "If you'll only name your perfume, I'll buy it by the gallon so you'll never run out."

His lips tickled her throat, and she arched into him. "I told you, it's my own concoction." He would surely recognize the scent at Thanksgiving, but until then…

He kissed her with increasing passion, and she wound her arms around his neck to hold him tight. He was rubbing her now, tracing gentle circles over her bikini panties. It felt so good, and she tried not to squirm. Perhaps the thrill of his touch was no more than a trick of chemistry, but when combined with his own artistry, it felt indescribably good.

"You have the most extraordinary hands," she moaned against his mouth.

"Is that all?"

In Darcy's view, he also had an insatiable need for praise, but damn it all, he deserved every word of it. His fingertips brushed bare skin now, and she was sorry she'd even bothered to wear panties when they were only in his way. He touched her with such an easy grace, now delving deep to smooth his path with her own inviting wetness.

He stroked her toward bliss, creating a shimmering surge that coiled through her, winding tighter and tighter around his fingers until he deepened his kiss to send her crashing over the edge in tumultuous waves. The blinding ecstasy seared her heart and left her lying limp across his lap, perfectly sated and wonderfully relaxed.

Griffin waited a minute, then stood with her still cradled in his arms. He walked back into the house and upstairs to his bed where he laid her down gently, and slowly removed her sweater, then her skirt, her lime green bra, and last, the matching panties.

"Do you wear such exotic lingerie beneath your overalls?" he asked.

Darcy propped her head on her hand and smiled. "Always."

"You're deliberately trying to drive me crazy, aren't you?"

"Crazy, no. Mad with desire, most certainly," she revealed in a husky whisper.

Griffin quickly discarded his sweatshirt and Levi's. He stretched out beside her and drew her into his arms. "Now it's my turn," he said.

Darcy rose to push him back into the pillows. "I'd say it's mine, but as always, we can argue about it later."

"Later's good," Griffin agreed, and he sucked in his breath as she sent a trail of teasing kisses down his chest to his navel. She circled the tender dip with her tongue to make him laugh, then moved lower to straddle his leg.

She needed both hands to grasp his erection and she sucked the velvet-smooth tip into her mouth. He grabbed her hair in such a hasty clutch, she paused to look up at him. "Should I stop?" she asked sweetly.

"Lord, no," he moaned.

Darcy licked him this time, swirling her tongue around the sensitive ridge of his cock. She felt him shudder and moved lower to lick his balls and, with an exquisite delicacy, drew first one and then the other into her mouth. She knew just where the slight pressure of her fingertips behind them would intensify his pleasure and used it as she again drew his cock into her mouth.

He was too big for her to take deeply, but she knew how to use her hands to stimulate the whole length of his shaft until with a strangled gasp he shoved her aside. Then, with a swift lunge, he thrust into her. He fought for control, but he was too close to the edge to last more than a few hip-jolting strokes before he exploded in a fiery release.

Consumed by pleasure as intense as he'd given her, he collapsed across her. Deeply gratified to have pleased him so, Darcy welcomed the warmth of his weight. She wore a blissful smile when he rose to withdraw, but he was incensed and began to swear.

"I'm sorry. I didn't mean to go bareback," he claimed abruptly, and he shoved off the bed and strode into the bathroom.

Startled by the harshness of his tone, Darcy sat up. For a brief instant, she considered walking out on him, but when she heard the shower running, she chose to follow him instead. The glass-enclosed shower stall was large enough to hold half a dozen people and was already fogged by steam. She swung the door open and stepped in behind him.

"I'm on the Pill, and I'm positive a man who must be in peak physical shape to earn a living must also guard his health. So no one's been hurt here." She reached out to touch his shoulder, but he shied away.

He had his hands braced against the wall, and the water cascaded over his broad shoulders and sluiced down his back in a swift stream. "This time, maybe, but I won't let it happen again."

Darcy scooped the soap out of the soap dish and began to wash herself. The soap had a tangy citrus scent she recognized from his skin. "People are supposed to lose control during sex," she chided. "That's the whole point of it."

Griffin shot her a murderous glance over his shoulder. "I'm not a control freak. That's not what this is about."

His shampoo was on a convenient ledge, and Darcy helped herself to a dollop and massaged it into her scalp. "No, of course, not. You're angry about something else entirely, but I've no clue what it is. Unless, of course, you don't enjoy fellatio, or perhaps the way I perform it. That's easily solved. I won't do it again."

This time he turned all the way around and, even with his hair plastered to his forehead, his deep scowl should have terrified her; but she hadn't followed him into the shower to be meekly frightened away. She swiped a soapy hand across his hairy chest and grabbed hold.

"My God, Griffin, after the day you've had, how can not using a condom be all that big a deal?"

He continued to stare at her, his expression clouded with disbelief. "Aren't you angry with me?"

Darcy moved in close. "Had I wanted to stop you, you'd still be screaming. Do I even appear annoyed, let alone angry? I won't get pregnant. You won't catch anything from me, and I sincerely doubt that I'll catch anything from you. No crime has been committed here."

Griffin caught her wrists in a soapy vice. "You know damn

little about me. I could have slept with each of the women attending last night's reception."

"If you did, it's obvious by your present reaction that you used condoms."

His voice deepened with menace. "It wouldn't bother you if I slept around?"

"Of course it would bother me. But you insisted you were no slut, and I believe you."

"Why? You know how convincingly I lie."

Yes he did, Darcy thought, but it had been about something he'd undoubtedly been forbidden to reveal. "Don't think I'm not keeping score. I'll let you know when you reach your limit."

Griffin took her warning for the joke it was and turned to shove her under the running water. He laughed as she sputtered and squirmed, then reached around her to shut off the shower.

"You're so cool, I'll bet you've had sex in showers dozens of times," he observed.

Darcy slipped her hands around his waist. "I've done it, but never with you, and that's all that matters. Turn the water back on."

Griffin tilted his head slightly. "Didn't I just tell you I wasn't going to get carried away ever again?"

"Yes, and I believe you too, but let's face it, tonight the damage—and there's none I can see—has already been done."

"You're wrong, but that's definitely something I want to argue about later." He turned on the shower and adjusted the temperature to again bathe them in steamy perfection. They were all slippery, and it added enormously to the fun, but he kept his wits about him to again please her rather than himself alone.

Hours later, Griffin awoke in his own bed in a befuddled daze, but he recognized Darcy, wrapped in a black towel, her hair in savage spikes. She was seated in the doorway of the bathroom reading the Seattle concert review. The necklace he'd given her sparkled in the light and reinforced his conviction that it had been meant for her. He sat up and leaned forward.

"I swear, that is the sexiest thing I've ever seen."

Darcy looked around, apparently expecting to find something she'd missed. Perplexed not to discover anything new, she sent him a questioning glance.

"I'm talking about you, love. With your hair sticking out like a hedgehog's, you resemble some punk kid. But that you'd try to read the review without disturbing me, and wrapped in a towel, no less, is damn sexy."

"Maybe I'm reading the comics," Darcy responded coyly.

"No way, but the guy went overboard. The flattering comparison to the soaring melody of Beethoven's 'Ode to Joy' makes it sound as though I paid him."

Darcy sang the words of the familiar hymn, "'Joyful, joyful, we adore thee, God of glory, God of love'. Is that the tune?"

"That's it, and you have a lovely voice, by the way."

Darcy had re-read the review to be certain her own hopes were not magnifying the reviewer's praise. They weren't. It was as effusive as Griffin claimed.

"I've only heard you play once, but I'll never forget it. I didn't realize you had the same effect on everyone."

Griffin's grin grew rakish. "Let's hope, but haven't you listened to the CD you bought?"

Darcy would never reveal how often. "All right, sure, I've heard your CD, and while it's great, being in the same room with you is electrifying. Now it seems you show equal promise as a composer, which is saying a great deal. This is simply a fabulous review."

Griffin shrugged. "I thought so too, but the murder took all the joy out of it. You must keep everything I told you about Interpol a secret. I don't want the good citizens of Monarch Bay to fear an international crime syndicate is about to descend upon them."

"I won't say a word," Darcy promised.

"Good. There's a Wolfgang Puck pizza in the freezer that's calling our names. Let's go downstairs and eat."

Darcy tucked in her towel more securely and stood. She tossed the review atop his carry-on bag where she'd found it and looked around for her clothes. "Give me a minute to get dressed."

"No, that towel is most becoming. Aren't the designers

showing short, strapless gowns in their spring collections?"

"They may very well be, but I don't follow haute couture. This is a comfortably large, exquisitely soft velour towel, however, so I don't mind if that's all you're wearing too."

"Toss me one," Griffin called from the bed.

Darcy licked her lips. "Come and get it yourself."

Griffin came off the end of the bed and strode toward her, all six feet, two inches of virile male. "You may be petite, but you're definitely a handful, Darcy."

Darcy angled her gaze downward. "So are you, big boy."

He was brilliant, a masterful performer, and now apparently a gifted composer as well. That he was so handsome and charming, to say nothing of an extremely talented lover, was merely an added bonus. He was the type for whom most women would happily sacrifice their own identity. But for her, the mere thought was appalling.

She ducked by him as he entered the bathroom and waited for him out in the hallway. She struggled to find a better perspective where he was concerned, but as wonderfully attractive as he was, she still doubted they would be a couple for long.

Griffin quickly appeared with a clean black towel slung low around his hips and took her hand. "I figured out how to use the monster oven, but it seems a shame to fire it up for just the two of us."

"Look at it this way—it's also awfully late to invite the neighbors over, especially if you have just the one pizza."

"An excellent point," Griffin conceded. When they reached the kitchen, he took the pizza from the freezer, checked the directions on the box and set the oven to preheat. Then he leaned back against the counter and folded his arms across his chest.

"Did you mean what you said earlier about the whole point of sex being to lose control?"

Darcy laughed at his question. "It's wonderful to meet a man who not only listens to what I have to say, but remembers it."

"Thank you, but I'm not so easily distracted. Is sex just getting off to you?"

Darcy feared no matter what she said, it would be too

much, and she looked down at her brightly polished toenails. "No, I was merely attempting to make a point."

"Fine. What does it really mean to you, then?"

The man had a remarkable persistence, which she would have admired at another time. "Has it occurred to you that we've had some deeply personal conversations in odd locations?"

"You're not usually so evasive," Griffin observed with a slight frown. "Just answer me."

What Darcy really wanted to do was yank off his towel and flick his beautiful butt with it. She restrained the impulse for the moment. "With the truth?" she asked.

"Of course. We have a pact, remember?"

"Yes." Darcy shifted uncomfortably. "Well, the truth is, I flat out love men."

"Yeah, it shows."

He was smiling now, which she considered a vast improvement. "Good, but when it comes to sex, I'm also extremely particular about my partner. I've slept with you for the sheer joy of being with you and for no other reason."

Griffin studied her wistful expression and promptly judged it sincere. "That's the nicest compliment I've ever been paid."

"It scarcely compares to your latest review," Darcy protested. "Would you play what must be a masterpiece for me sometime?"

"Sure, I take requests." He slipped the pizza into the oven, reset the temperature and took her hand. "We've just enough time while the pizza bakes. Would you like to hear it now?"

"I'd love to." When they reached his piano, Darcy looked around for a chair, found none and sat on the navy-and-gold carpet.

She didn't really care what he played when watching him was so enjoyable, but after the first few notes, she was as captivated by the music as she was by the composer. Light and playful at the beginning, the composition gradually gained depth until it resonated with Griffin's own passionate fire, only to slow in the last passages until the haunting melody gracefully faded away to silence.

The piece was so incredibly beautiful it brought tears to her eyes and, fearful he would mistake her reaction, she hastily brushed them away. She kept a firm grip on her towel and, in an effort to regain her composure, took a deep breath as she rose to her feet.

"I'd like to applaud as wildly as your Seattle audience, but frankly, I doubt I have the strength. That was simply the most stunningly beautiful music I've ever heard. There appears to be no end to your talent."

"Well, let's hope not," Griffin responded. "I'm glad you liked it. I'm thinking of writing words and asking Andrea Bocelli to sing them on my next CD."

"Is it a love song?" Darcy asked, suddenly able to recognize a whole love story in the complex composition.

"Yes, but it could also be life with its bright beginning, dramatic middle years and anguished end."

Darcy swallowed hard. "I don't like that explanation at all. Is that how you see the course of love too, as beginning with promise, but doomed to a tragic end?"

Griffin responded by playing a series of minor chords. "It doesn't matter how deeply a couple might love each other. Eventually one of them will die and leave the other alone to grieve. Unless, of course, they're both killed in some senseless accident, which is scarcely a happy ending."

"If that's all you believe life has in store for us," Darcy warned, "you ought not to write lyrics. Just play the music and let the listener lose herself in her own dreams."

Griffin turned to face her. "There are only two things worth writing about, love and death. It's the juxtaposition of joy and sorrow that give that piece its resonance. Now let's see if the pizza is ready. I'm so hungry I may not make it back to the kitchen."

His dark comments reminded her of their very first conversation when she'd thought him so serious she'd wondered if he had a melancholy bent. Perhaps all creative artists did. Whatever his present mood, however, his opinion was deeply disturbing.

"I'm not really hungry," she told him. "I think I'll just go on home."

Griffin left the piano bench to take her hand. "Don't run off. Even if you're not hungry, we could discuss the meaning of life all night."

"You mean argue, which you constantly refuse to do, so

there doesn't appear to be much hope for a lively conversation. Besides, I have an early job. The man is my most important client, and I want to be at my best."

"If he's so important, he ought not to have to eat alone."

"Probably not, but I'm really just too tired to be good company, and I want to go home."

"You could sleep here," Griffin insisted.

Darcy stopped at the bottom of the stairs. "Thank you, but I'd not get any rest. Don't let your pizza burn. I'll get dressed, then tell you good-night before I leave."

Griffin didn't look pleased. "I'd really hoped the day would end better than it began."

Darcy raised her hand to caress his cheek. "It did," she swore convincingly, but she left with the same haste with which she'd arrived.

By the time she reached home, she'd come to the damning realization that while she might see the differences between them as too great to be successfully bridged, he must have always believed their affair would end badly. That was the real tragedy, in her view, but the only way she could prove him wrong was to remain with him forever, and that would require far more courage than she possessed.

Chapter Nine

Monday morning, Christy Joy caught Darcy before she left the nursery. "The way you dashed out of here last night, I was afraid something was wrong." She paused and smiled knowingly. "Or perhaps something is very right, and you were simply anxious to see Griffin again. If so, I hope you'll soon change his mind about our lease."

Darcy shuffled the orders on her desk and tried to find some innocuous way to admit everything had gone wrong without giving away a single hint as to why. She sank in her chair and managed a wobbly smile.

"Griffin is the most fascinating man I've ever met, or ever will. But I don't want to give up my dreams to live his, and yet, when I'm with him, it's difficult to believe anything else matters."

Christy Joy's brows dipped in concern. "It's not like you to get so deeply involved with someone this fast."

"No, it certainly isn't, but I should finish his landscaping job today, and that will give me some distance. I'm sorry I've no hope to offer about the building. Griffin is determined to put a recording studio here, and I'm afraid once he settles on something, he doesn't equivocate. He did offer to help us find a new location, though."

Now clearly disgusted, Christy Joy began to back away. "Try a little harder, Darcy. It's possible he's as fascinated with you as you are with him. Don't waste that advantage. I refuse to think about leaving here during the day, but after I've put Twink to bed, I end up in tears."

Darcy got up to hug her friend. Christy Joy was always so bubbly and sweet that it was easy to forget she could have problems too. Nothing compared to murder, however, and Darcy wasn't about to terrify her with that news.

Christy Joy returned the sympathetic hug with a quick squeeze. "I have to open the shop, but let's talk later. I realize your situation with Griffin is complicated, but I made the mistake of diving right into J. Lyle's life rather than building one with him, and I'm still paying for it. I'd hate to see you fall into the same abyss when it's so awfully hard to escape."

"I appreciate your advice," Darcy responded warmly, but she doubted she would have much more to confide later. She'd wanted Griffin, there was no doubt about it; but there was also no way to enjoy the spectacular beauty of a hurricane without being blown away.

The Range Rover wasn't parked in Griffin's driveway. While there were a great many places he could be that morning, Darcy had expected him to be there to watch them work, and his absence just didn't feel right.

She pulled his key from her overalls and entered the house through the back door. He'd wrapped the leftover pizza in foil and placed it in the refrigerator, but there wasn't so much as a glass or cup in the sink to indicate he'd been there that morning. The kitchen was too neat, and the house not merely quiet, but deathly still.

She ran up the stairs, throwing open the doors as she went. Griffin had made his bed and put away his luggage. There was a book currently on the bestseller lists by his bedside, but with no personal items to reveal the uniqueness of his personality, the room could just as easily have been a furniture showroom. Fresh black towels hung in the bathroom, and the window was open to draw in the sea breeze, but there were no toiletries in view.

While Griffin was away, she'd come inside to use the bathroom off the kitchen, but she hadn't prowled the house as she did today. Maybe it was always this immaculate, but again, she felt as though she were moving through a stage set rather than a man's home.

She paused at the door of the computer room. The computers emitted a soft whirring sound, and the printer was spitting out letters at regular intervals, but without the slightest inclination to read the correspondence, she hurried back downstairs.

Atop the piano there were neatly arranged piles of manuscript paper on which Griffin had begun transcribing his own compositions, but in her creative bursts she scattered her drawings and estimates all over the place. How could he write such beautiful music and at the same time be so damn organized?

She'd come to complete the landscaping, not to dissect Griffin's habits, but if something horrible had happened to him between the time she'd left him last night and this morning, the evidence had been erased with a frightening precision. She didn't dare report him missing when he might have gone to San Francisco for the day, or even down to Los Angeles.

That was the problem—he could be anywhere, but if he didn't appear, nor contact her by sundown, she was definitely going to alert the police. At worst, it would be a false alarm. Everyone would have a good laugh at her expense, but that was better than waiting for a pieced-together ransom note to arrive.

Construction of the redwood arbor was nearing completion that afternoon before Griffin arrived home. Darcy was relieved beyond measure, but she sucked in a deep breath and feigned a keen interest in the carpenter's work rather than rush to greet him.

He walked up beside her and let out a long, low whistle. "This looks even better than I'd imagined. It's a shame the original owners didn't have a superb landscape architect, because this house was just aching for an arbor and wisteria vine."

The carpenter paused to wipe his forehead on his sleeve. "You the new owner?"

Griffin introduced himself with his usual cordial ease, complimented the man on his work, then turned to Darcy. "Do you have a minute?" he asked, but he took her arm and steered her into the kitchen without waiting for her response. He shut the door behind them with one hand and drew her close with the other.

"I've found a building for you," he announced a second before kissing her soundly.

Startled, Darcy grabbed hold of him for support. His muscular arms felt like steel cable beneath her fingers. "Is that where you've been?"

"Do you actually expect me to account for my time?" He laughed with the same ready amusement as when she'd offered to provide him with backup.

Exasperated with his amused rebuff, Darcy stepped out of his embrace and leaned back against the counter. "No, of course not. Your time is your own, as is mine."

Even with Christy Joy's urgent reminder, she'd been worried sick that he'd been kidnapped, or worse, and hadn't once thought about their building. That oversight revealed a great deal about her priorities. After all the work they'd put into Defy the World Tomatoes, it was deeply unsettling.

"Just where is this building you've found?" she inquired abruptly.

"It's on Harbor Street near the off-ramp from Route 1. Tourists will be able to see it from the freeway. It was a market and has a huge parking lot which would be ideal for the nursery."

Darcy had only a vague impression of the site, but she wasn't impressed. "I know the place you mean, and the building, which is merely a warehouse, has been vacant more than a year. It's completely lacking in the intimate charm that's so much a part of our shop."

"Clever decorating will solve that problem. At least agree to see it before you make up your mind."

"It's on the edge of town," she pointed out. "We'd lose the foot traffic that accounts for better than half our business."

"Most tourists come up from Los Angeles on Route 1, don't they? They drive right by the site when they turn off for Monarch Bay."

"Right on by is more likely. I don't need to tour the building when the location is so poor. But it sounds as though it would be an ideal place for a recording studio."

Griffin's gaze narrowed. "Give it up, Darcy."

She clamped her jaws shut. His perverse insistence upon keeping a place that was like home to her and merely a space to renovate to him made no logical sense. Unless, of course, as she'd expected from the hour they'd met, he simply had to have his own way.

Griffin studied her deepening frown. "Don't go all dark on me. I have an excellent reason for reclaiming my building, even if I'm not willing to share it just yet."

"Harboring secrets again, Mr. Moore?" she challenged.

"Not a secret really, just a dream that I intend to bring into reality. Now I can see you're busy today, but when your work is finished here, I'll take you by the building on Harbor Street."

"From what I remember, it's big," Darcy argued, "and undoubtedly too expensive for us to lease. Or was cost a detail you failed to investigate?"

"I've not called the leasing agents for specifics, but if, as you say, the building has been vacant awhile, they should be willing to listen to all reasonable offers."

"Hasn't it occurred to you that the reason no one wants to lease the place is because people just zip by it on their way in or out of town?"

"No, I just think independent markets have a difficult time competing against the chains, but you have no state-wide competition. Will you at least tell Christy Joy about the place and get her opinion?"

Darcy shrugged. "Sure, I'll tell her, but you mustn't be surprised if her opinion is even worse than mine. She lives in the apartment above the shop. It's perfect for her and Twink, but I doubt that she'd want to call the back of a warehouse home."

"She'd not have to live there," Griffin stressed. "There are nice apartments just down the street."

"You just don't get it, do you? Even without considering the expense for her, neither of us has the time or energy to commute, even if it's no more than half a block. Christy Joy walks Twink to the best preschool in Monarch Bay, and still she's pressed for time. We also have clerks who walk to work, and being on the edge of town wouldn't work for them either."

Griffin leaned against the counter beside Darcy and folded his arms across his chest. "Can't you see how easily you could grow your business in a larger setting?"

"What I see is that you want us to move into a building we can't afford and tourists will fly right on by, in the hope our business will improve. Somehow that just doesn't seem like a smart plan to me."

"Has anyone ever commented on the fact that you're as

stubborn as your cacti?" he shot back at her.

She stepped in front of him. "I am not stubborn! I'm merely focused. And right now, I need to be outside. I'd like to plant the wisteria vine today, hang the iron fish and wrap up our work here."

Griffin pushed away from the counter. "What about the fountains?"

Darcy just shook her head. "You weren't actually serious about putting one in, were you?"

"Of course, I'm serious. I told you I might want two, remember?"

"Yes, but I didn't think you really meant it."

"Well, I did. The wisteria vine will be colorful and fragrant, but water cascading into a fountain provides soothing music." He took a step toward her and inclined his head. "Did I mention how glad I am to see you?" he whispered against her lips.

Darcy had been so worried about him, which she refused to admit, but she wouldn't apologize for rejecting the old market site. She would simply welcome his kiss and hope he'd see the wisdom of her argument later.

She expected only an affectionate hello, but when he pulled her into a fond embrace and unbuttoned her overalls, it quickly became apparent he had something far more intimate in mind. In one easy motion, he yanked the flower-bedecked garment and her lacy bikini panties down to her knees, picked her up and angled her face-down on the counter.

"Griffin! What are you doing?" she squealed, but she was more amused than alarmed by his sudden ardor, and her exclamation was tinged with laughter.

"You know damn well what I'm doing." He dropped his pants, stepped between her dangling legs and stroked the length of her cleft with the smooth tip of his cock.

Despite his haste, it felt so right to have him jammed between her legs. She braced herself on her forearms, but as she raised her head, she was appalled to find they were directly opposite one of the kitchen windows. Any second one of her crew might glance their way and realize exactly what they were doing.

"They're going to see us!" She stretched to catch hold of the cord on the mini-blinds, but it was just out of reach.

"Come back here," he urged in a husky drawl.

He was easing into her, inch by delicious inch, but she knew one glimpse of this wild sex on the counter and her crew would never stop teasing her.

"Can't you perform without an audience?" she hissed at him.

Griffin leaned over her back, caught the cord and jerked the blinds shut. "I need only you," he emphasized with a quick thrust that took him deep. He slid his arms around her, held her pressed against him and plucked her puckered nipples.

Balanced on the counter, she felt not only his strength, but his desperation to melt into her. It didn't matter where he'd been that day when he was with her now. She was frightened for him, not of him, and she twisted her hips to increase the friction along his shaft.

"That's it," he breathed against her nape, and he shortened his strokes to a playful flutter.

He filled her so completely that each time he began to withdraw she felt an aching loss and slammed her bottom back against his thighs. His breathing was quick and shallow, but his every stroke was calculated to carry her with him toward completion. When her climax at last spiraled around him in a heated gush, he rode the slippery wave one last time, then tensed and thrust deep. He held her as the most primitive of thrills shuddered through them both, then waited a long while to withdraw and put his clothes in order.

Had he not caught her, she would have slid right off the counter in a languid heap. Weaving slightly, she pulled up her panties and overalls then headed straight for the nearby bathroom. "Give me a minute," she called over her shoulder, but when she returned, Griffin was already outside on the terrace.

She struggled to adopt a carefree stride as she approached him, but two of her crew were grinning with what looked like rapt envy, and she feared even without an eyeful they knew precisely how she and Griffin had spent the last half hour. She nodded to inspire them to get back to work and looked up at Griffin.

"The ocean's roar is so loud here that I doubt you'd hear any gentle bubbling from a fountain. Let's go scout locations at the front of the house."

He gestured for her to precede him, but as they rounded

the corner, he caught up with her. "Don't you think your men already know that you're sleeping with me?"

"Not from me they don't," she scolded.

Griffin took her hand until they stepped out onto the circular drive. "I hope you're not ashamed of me."

His amused grin convinced her that was scarcely a concern. "No, I'm not ashamed of you, nor of anything we've done, but let's keep it private. Now what about placing the fountain in the center of the circular drive? You won't hear the sound of the water as clearly, but visually it'll be more interesting than flat against the house."

Griffin's gaze never left her face. "Sounds fine. When can you start?"

"First you'll need to select a design that will complement your home rather than detract from it. May I assume you'd consider a bust of Beethoven too obvious?"

"You may, but I rather like fat dolphins with water spewing from their mouths."

"They're popular, but I'll research the possibilities to give you a choice, but something classical rather than wildly modern would be appropriate. Once you've selected the elements, I'll hire contractors to handle the plumbing, cement and tile work."

"Great. Now since you don't appear eager to visit the property I described, when you wrap up here this afternoon, let's go on up the coast to the Monarch Inn for dinner. We might even spend the night there, if you like."

Darcy rested her hands on her hips. She still felt flushed all over and would have much rather been taking a long nap on his bed than beginning yet another argument. "This is Monday. I can't go tearing around the countryside as though I were on vacation."

"Why not? You have to eat and sleep somewhere."

"That may be true, but I can't spend every night partying with you."

Griffin leaned down to brush her cheek with a teasing kiss. "Sure sounds like fun, though, doesn't it?"

"You're incorrigible, but I didn't say I wasn't tempted. Could we postpone the visit to the inn until Saturday night?"

Griffin glanced off toward the mountains. "I'll be in Chicago for the weekend. I'm leaving Thursday morning. But isn't the weekend your busiest time at Defy the World Tomatoes?"

"Well, yes, but—"

"But you'll try to work me into your busy schedule?"

She straightened. "That's not fair."

"Isn't it? Tell me, when was the last time you loved a man enough to let him into your heart as well as your bed?"

Her first impulse was to slap him so hard the imprint of her palm would grace his cheek for a week. Refusing to resort to violence, she knotted her fists at her sides. "Damn it, Griffin, we've both got responsibilities, but I'm doing a whole lot more than merely accommodating you in my spare time."

Griffin straightened to his full height. "Accommodate me? Is that how you'd describe it?"

Now he was as angry as she was, and that hadn't been her intention at all. "No, it was simply a poor choice of words."

His expression didn't soften. "I explained why my marriage failed, but you've told me next to nothing about your relationships. I was hoping that if we got away from Monarch Bay you might open up, but if I'm wasting my time here, I'd appreciate your letting me know it now."

Darcy glanced at her watch. It hadn't been twenty minutes since he'd laid her on the counter like some delicious dessert and dived right in. The heat of the memory made her squirm, and she could hardly stand still.

"I don't know what's going on here, Griffin, but I don't like being pushed."

"Maybe it's what you need."

"What I need is to get back to work, but because you're so damn anxious to learn my secrets, I'll tell you one. I've never had a damn bit of luck with brown-eyed men. Lord knows there are plenty of them, but they have a nasty habit of just passing me right on by."

"I'd say we've broken that jinx," Griffin mused softly, "and if that's all you've got to confess, I'll consider myself lucky."

She opened her mouth and then shut it quickly. She would be damned if she would confess to falling in love with him when they were surely one of the most mismatched couples of all time. "I really should go check on the arbor."

She took a step toward the path leading to the rear of the house, but couldn't shake the uncomfortable feeling she was making a terrible mistake. She paused in mid-stride and turned to face him. "All right, let's go to the inn tonight. I can't promise to make any tantalizing confessions, but I've heard the food is excellent."

"It is," Griffin assured her, and he went inside to work on his compositions while she planted the wisteria vine she hoped would be a lingering reminder of their time together.

The Monarch Inn had been built during the 1920s in the ornate mission revival style to cater to tourists' fascination with California's colorful history. The dining room was softly lit by wrought-iron chandeliers and decorated with paintings of California's spectacular landscapes in heavy gold frames. Mariachis provided lively music on the weekends, but that night, a lone guitarist seated in a dimly lit corner strummed ballads as a romantic undercurrent to the guests' hushed conversations.

Darcy slid into the red leather booth and was grateful not to need a booster seat. She smoothed the skirt of her new black jersey sheath and tried to appear far more comfortable than she felt. It had been a long day, but she was so filled with nervous energy she was in no danger of falling asleep.

As always, Griffin had drawn considerable attention as they entered, and she'd overheard one couple whispering his name. The man had not only spectacular good looks, but a charisma that set him apart. When she'd been drawn to him at first glance, she couldn't fault others for showing the same weakness, but still, it made her feel even more petite than she actually was.

She opened her menu and scanned the evening's special selections, which all sounded incredibly good. "Do people often approach you in restaurants?" she asked.

"It depends on the restaurant," Griffin replied. "Would it bother you if they did?"

Darcy decided on the scampi and set her menu aside. "I don't know. It might if they wanted to sit and chat."

"You needn't worry that I'll invite anyone to join us. I want to be with you tonight."

She chewed her lower lip. She was badly worried she would spoil things by either saying too much, or too little. She almost wished a fan or two would stop by their table to keep him too distracted to focus on her. She took a quick sip of water and then had to grab for her napkin to blot the drip on her chin.

Griffin reached under the table to take her hand. "I meant for us to become better acquainted. I'm sorry I've made you so nervous."

She managed a smile and quickly changed the subject. "This place reminds me of an inn I visited with my parents in Europe. It might have been in Bavaria—the trips are all blurred together in my mind—but I remember the dark wood and the scent of candles."

Griffin surveyed the spacious room. "Yes, the inn fairly reeks of old-world charm. The cuisine, however, is deliciously modern."

Darcy's mind wandered as he gave their orders to the waiter. She hadn't thought about traveling with her folks in a long while, but she suddenly recalled waking up in a hotel room one night and hearing her mother's soft laughter from the adjoining room. She couldn't have been more than six or seven and, reassured by her parents' presence, she'd fallen right back asleep. Only now did it occur to her that they had probably been making love.

"Do you ever think about your parents having sex?" she asked.

Griffin nearly choked on his wine, and it took him a moment to recover. "Never. What makes you ask?"

"A vague memory of laughter," she replied. "My mother has always been such an enthusiastic person, always eager for whatever adventure my father cares to take."

"So she was happy being a wife and mother?"

"Yes, if she ever had any career ambitions, she never mentioned them, but I really do believe she's been perfectly content with her life."

"You'd not be equally happy with a family and world travel?"

His relaxed smile didn't fool her. The question was an important one, and she answered truthfully. "No. I would have married my college sweetheart if it had been. There, that's a confession for you."

"I'll agree only that it's an intriguing beginning. What was his name?"

She shook her head. "It doesn't matter now. He'd been in ROTC, planned to spend a few years as an army officer, then go into the Diplomatic Corps."

He nodded thoughtfully. "You would have had your mother's life."

"Precisely, and while it has been wonderful for her, the constant moves would have prevented me from practicing my craft as a landscape architect."

"It isn't really constant travel, though, is it?" he asked. "Aren't army officers stationed at one base or another for two or three years?"

She took a deep breath and exhaled slowly rather than shriek at him for that hint of disapproval. "Yes, that's true, but even in the States, I probably wouldn't have been hired by local firms when I couldn't promise how long I'd be there, and it would have been even more difficult to find work in a foreign country. Nor could I have built a reputation on my own planting gardens here and there all around the world."

Griffin nodded thoughtfully. "You didn't even give it a try?"

"You can't try on marriage. You either go into it with your whole heart, or not at all."

"In your view," he chided.

Darcy paused while the waiter served their salads, then jabbed her fork into the tantalizing mixture of crisp greens sprinkled with feta cheese, pecans and dried cranberries. "I'm really not so different from my mother. I just happen to want a career along with a family, and I want it in one place."

"So you broke this nameless fellow's heart?"

"No," she insisted through clenched teeth. "I shattered my own."

Griffin slipped his arm around her shoulders and gave her a comforting hug. "I'm sorry. I didn't mean to bring back such sad memories."

Before Darcy could respond, the woman who'd whispered Griffin's name as they entered approached the table followed by her husband. They were middle-aged, slender, expensively dressed and, from the width of their smiles, devoted fans.

"I do hope you'll forgive this intrusion, Mr. Moore," the woman began, "but I just couldn't leave without telling you how much we enjoy your concerts."

"We own all your CDs," her husband added.

Griffin slipped out of the booth to shake their hands. "Thank you very much."

The couple gushed praise for several moments, then turned to Darcy. "You look so familiar, dear," the woman exclaimed. "I'm certain we've seen you in a recent film, but I'm embarrassed to admit I can't recall your name."

"I'm Darcy MacLeod, and I'm part-owner of Defy the World Tomatoes, not an actress."

"Oh, then that's where I've seen you." Obviously disappointed not to have met a movie star, the woman turned back to Griffin. "Would it be too great an imposition to ask for an autograph?"

"Of course not." Griffin removed a card from his pocket and, after requesting the proper spelling of their names, he signed it for them. "Good night," he emphasized and sat.

The couple hurried away, passing the card between them, but Darcy was completely confused. "Did you just give them your home telephone number?"

"No, I don't give that out to just anyone." He pulled another card from his pocket and showed it to her. "All this has is my name and a list of CDs. It's shameless promotion, nothing more."

Darcy fiddled with her salad. She hadn't expected the couple to be as thrilled to meet her as they were to see Griffin, but the cool manner in which she'd been dismissed still hurt.

"I hated to disappoint them. Maybe I should have said I'd starred in the latest Pedro Almodovar film and given it some hot title like *Down to the Skin*."

Griffin laughed, then realized she wasn't kidding. "That does sound like one of his titles, but the fault was mine. I should have introduced you when they first approached us, but I just wanted them gone. I should have been more considerate. It won't happen again."

She stared him. "Do you actually plan to be seen with me again?"

Griffin had been about to lift a bite of salad to his mouth, but caught it in time. "Hold the jokes until we finish eating, please. Of course, I plan to keep seeing you. Unless you don't want to see me."

As if, she thought. "As long as you keep the blinds closed at

134

sensitive times, I won't mind."

Charmed by her nonchalance, Griffin gave her knee a playful squeeze. "You're going to need a passport."

"Why? I'll not have the time to travel with you."

Griffin winked at her. "One of these days, you'll make the time."

She could have argued, but it made little sense when she had the uncomfortable suspicion he was right.

Chapter Ten

Despite Griffin's prediction to the contrary, he'd fit in Darcy's bed, and quite comfortably, although they hadn't gotten much in the way of sleep Monday night. Tuesday he'd gone into rehearsal mode before leaving for Chicago, while she'd been inspired to rush his fountain to completion before he returned.

Certain he would go along with whatever she selected, she chose a trefoil over a simple circle and had it lined with a beautiful sea-green tile. She called a sculptor she'd admired, grateful that Griffin could afford the woman's exquisite work, and purchased a marble mermaid.

The enchanting figure was turned in a twisting pose, her chin nearly touching her right shoulder. Her crossed arms demurely covered her bare breasts, and water bubbled through her hands, clasped with da Vinci's graceful perfection, to spill into the base of the fountain.

Delighted with the whole installation, Darcy had photographed it for her portfolio and returned to Defy the World Friday afternoon to spruce up the nursery for the weekend. With lovely weather and plenty of tourists, the remaining time would pass quickly until Griffin's return, but she couldn't help but count the hours. She hummed softly to herself as she rearranged the white and pink cyclamen clustered beside the register stand.

"Where's Twink?" Christy Joy called. She scanned the walkways, then fixed Darcy with an accusing stare. "Isn't she out here with you and George?"

George immediately left his post at the cash register. "I'll check the pottery shed. Maybe she's playing inside."

Darcy felt certain she'd just seen the little girl skipping

along the paths. "Twink was here a minute ago."

Christy Joy shook her head. "I don't believe this. Either you've kept an eye on her or you haven't."

With the strength of an earthquake's first jolt, a burst of guilt-laced fear shot down Darcy's spine, but she refused to add to her partner's dismay and fought to respond calmly. "Twink's been darting in and out of the shop just as she always does. She can't have gone far."

George hurried back toward them, his face a mask of concern. "The shed's empty. Could Twink have gone upstairs to your apartment?"

"I'll look." Christy Joy hurried out the back gate and up the stairs. She unlocked the back door and nearly yanked it off the hinges as she entered. In a moment, she came back outside through the shop. "Twink's not upstairs. She's not in the shop, and she's not out here. I'm calling the police."

Darcy saw her own terror reflected in her friend's eyes and thought it a wise move. "You stay here, George, in case Twink turns up. I'll take a look on the street."

Foot traffic was light that afternoon, and a quick glance in either direction revealed no sign of the little girl. Hoping Twink might have gone back up the street to her preschool, Darcy broke into a quick jog. The Sunshine Nursery School was located in a buttercup yellow cottage that could have come right out of a Beatrice Potter tale, but after leaving earlier with her mother, Twink had not reappeared on her own.

Darcy sprinted on to the park where a small crowd had gathered to watch a chess match being played with the four-foot-tall pieces on the big outdoor chessboard. She circulated through the onlookers asking about Twink, but no one had seen a fair-haired little girl in the park.

Swallowing her dread, she forced herself to check the small adobe structure which housed the women and men's restrooms, but her voice echoed with a hollow ring through the empty stalls. As she came back outside, she tried to think where Twink might have gone, but the adorable little girl had always been right underfoot. She felt sick to her stomach and could only imagine how desperate Christy Joy must be.

She immediately thought of the sad ending to Griffin's beautiful composition, but she refused to consider his music appropriate here. She was positive children strayed all the time and just as often turned up within a matter of minutes. She had to believe Twink was all right, because the hideous alternative was simply too painful to contemplate.

She was out of breath by the time she returned to Defy the World, and a police car was already parked out in front. She shook her head as she passed George and went on into the shop where Christy Joy was clutching a photograph of Twink while she provided a tearful description of her daughter's clothing.

"I checked with the preschool," Darcy announced, her heart firmly lodged in her throat. "Mrs. Kelly would have called you immediately had Twink turned up there, and what staff she can spare is going out to look for her too."

"What about Twink's father?" the officer inquired. "Could she be with him?"

Christy Joy wiped away her tears. "He's a San Francisco attorney. He'd take me to court to win custody rather than snatch her off the street."

The police officer was a freckled young man with bright red hair. He frowned as he made a notation on the report form. "What about her friends from preschool? Does she ever go home with them?"

"She has," Christy Joy replied. "But their mothers would surely have called me if she'd arrived at their homes without our having made prior arrangements. I take good care of Twink, really I do."

"We all do," Darcy echoed, but she'd failed miserably that afternoon. She'd been so preoccupied with thoughts of surprising Griffin with the spectacular fountain that she'd been less than attentive with their customers, but she'd never dreamed Twink might slip away unnoticed.

"What about an Amber alert?" she asked.

"I'll ask the chief," the officer replied, "but with no license plate number or description of a car, freeway signs for an Amber alert won't be of much use."

Christy Joy sagged back against the counter. "Oh, please, don't tell me it's possible she's been kidnapped. You'd have noticed if a stranger had grabbed her, wouldn't you, Darcy?"

"Of course, I would have," Darcy insisted, but she was horrified to think how easily someone might have scooped up Twink while her back was turned. A target of opportunity, she believed it was called. Someone might have seen Twink playing alone, grabbed her and been gone before either she or George had noticed a suspicious stranger lurking nearby.

She feared she was going to be sick. "We'll find her," she vowed hoarsely. "Let's close early and we can conduct a store-by-store canvass."

Mary Beth came out from behind the counter. "I think I ought to stay here with Christy Joy," she offered.

With that decided, Darcy went out the door praying they would find Twink before nightfall. It was difficult enough searching for a small child in daylight, and she didn't even want to consider going out with a flashlight.

Christy Joy barely made it to the shop's restroom before becoming ill. She was terrified her precious daughter had been abducted by some sick monster who would abuse her and toss her tiny body on some filthy trash heap. She retched until she was dizzy and then, positive Twink deserved better, splashed cool water on her face and blotted it dry.

Mary Beth was pacing the front of the shop when she returned. "I swear I'll lie down and die if something's happened to my baby. None of this will mean anything if she's gone."

Mary Beth hugged her tightly. "She'll turn up any minute now. I know she will. She's such a sweet little thing, no one will harm her."

"No, that's only what you hope, but there are children who have disappeared and never been seen again, while others—"

"Stop it," Mary Beth ordered. "This is a very small town. Everyone knows Twink, and she's probably perched on a stool in one of the neighboring shops chatting happily with the owner."

Christy Joy bit her lip until she tasted blood. "I ought to call J. Lyle, but he'll just curse at me. Even if I don't call him, he's bound to find out that Twink was missing and he'll insist I'm unfit. What am I going to do, Mary Beth? Even if we find Twink, I'm sure to lose custody."

"Hush," Mary Beth replied. "You're only making it worse than it already is. I'll make you some tea."

Christy Joy shook her head, but Mary Beth insisted upon brewing a cup anyway.

Darcy had searched both sides of the street and was heading for the docks when she saw Jeremy Linden coming her way carrying Twink on his shoulders. Tears coursed down her cheeks as she ran toward them.

"Oh Twink, you had us all scared to death!" she cried.

Twink simply looked puzzled. "I went to see Jeremy."

Darcy had to grab on to the captain's arm for support. "You should have called us. We've been searching everywhere."

"I'm sorry. I thought it would take less time to walk her home than it would to look up Defy the World's number."

A police cruiser pulled up before Darcy could reply, and the red-haired officer who had taken the report on Twink climbed out. "What's your name, little girl?" he asked.

Twink straightened proudly. "Catherine Jennings, but everybody calls me Twink."

Jeremy swung her down off his shoulders, but kept hold of her hand. "I found her on my boat and was walking her home."

The officer shot Darcy a decidedly skeptical glance and reached for his handcuffs, but she stepped in front of Jeremy. "Captain Linden is a family friend. Twink went to see him without asking permission, but now that she's been found, we need to take her home to her mother."

The officer's glance never left Jeremy and he waited a moment too long to agree. "Okay, let's do that." He opened the rear door of his car and waited for them to slide inside.

"I'm sorry, I didn't realize—" Jeremy began.

Darcy raised a finger to her lips. "Let's concentrate on getting Twink home."

Once they were all seated in the cruiser, Twink bounced on Jeremy's knee. "Can you turn on the siren?"

"Not today," the officer replied. "We don't want to scare your mother any worse than she already is." He quickly reached for his microphone to radio in that he was on his way back to Defy the World Tomatoes with Twink.

Twink settled back against Jeremy's chest. "Am I in trouble?"

Darcy was too relieved to have found the little girl safe to want to see her punished. "You know better than to wander off, but you'll not do it again, will you?"

Twink played with the organdy apron on her pinafore. "I didn't get lost."

"That's not the point," Jeremy insisted. "Pretty little girls can't go wandering around the docks alone. I told you so, remember?"

Twink lowered her head. "Do I stink like fish?"

Darcy pulled the sweet child into her arms and hugged her tightly. "No, you smell absolutely delicious."

The police cruiser pulled into a parking place in front of Defy the World, and Christy Joy came running out to meet them. She plucked her daughter from Darcy's arms and muffled her tears in her shiny curls.

Jeremy left the car, but hung back. When Darcy glanced his way, he just shook his head. "Twink went to see Jeremy," she explained.

Christy gasped. "Oh, baby, you went all that way alone?"

The policeman cleared his throat. "Why don't you call your pediatrician and have him meet us at the hospital to check her over."

Christy's expression filled with confusion, swiftly followed by a sudden flash of horror. "Please, Jeremy, swear you didn't—"

Jeremy spread his arms wide. "What? No, of course not. I went up to the Scarlet Letter to pick up a book I'd ordered. When I got back, Twink was jumping up and down on my bunk."

The officer pulled a small notebook from his back pocket. "Captain Linden, was it? Better give me the name of your boat."

"The *Great Escape*, but no crime has been committed."

"Better let me be the judge of that," the officer replied. "I really think we ought to go on over to the hospital, Mrs. Jennings."

Christy wrapped her arms even more tightly around her daughter. "No, can't you see that Twink's fine? Thank you for your help, but you're no longer needed here."

Obviously disappointed, the officer waited until Christy Joy had carried Twink inside before he spoke. "She's in denial, but I've got your name, Captain, and you can count on my checking out your story at the Scarlet Letter."

"The time I paid for the book is stamped on the receipt," Jeremy exclaimed, "and it wasn't more than fifteen minutes ago."

"Doesn't take all that long to molest a child," the officer replied, but after regarding Jeremy with a final dark glance, he closed his notebook, got into his cruiser and drove away.

Darcy still felt sick, and Jeremy didn't look much better. "No one's accused you of anything," she assured him.

Jeremy shoved his hands in his pockets. "Christ, he didn't have to. Didn't you see the way Christy Joy looked at me?"

Indeed she had, and the unspoken accusation had stung her as well. "She was frantic about Twink."

"Sure, that's only natural, but suspicion's an ugly thing and damn hard to disprove."

Darcy again reached for his arm, but when he flinched she promptly withdrew. "We're all upset, but please don't imagine it's worse than it is."

Jeremy shook his head. "I'll not blame Twink. She's just a little kid, but whatever chance I may have had with Christy Joy is gone, and you know it."

Darcy hoped Christy Joy would see things differently tomorrow, but she was sadly afraid he was right. "I'll walk you back to your boat."

"Better watch out," he warned as he turned away. "No telling what people might be saying about me tomorrow."

Darcy fell in step beside him. She'd been so relieved to find Twink riding on his shoulders, but his dark prediction only served to reinforce her own guilt. "Look, I'm the one who should feel bad here. I didn't even notice Twink had disappeared until Christy Joy came looking for her."

"Somehow that isn't much consolation," Jeremy murmured under his breath.

The cool breeze off the bay chilled Darcy clear through, but when they reached his boat, she accepted his offer of a cup of coffee, then remained on board the *Great Escape* until she'd finished the last drop. She was ashamed of herself for asking to use the head so she could check out his bunk, but she was enormously relieved when the only evidence the blanket bore was a faint indentation left by a little girl's shoes.

Once home, Darcy slid down on the floor with her back braced against the sofa and hugged her knees. When she'd been a freshman in high school, four of the most popular seniors had been killed after a football game when their speeding car had flipped over rounding a curve. It had been a senseless loss, but it had served to warn the whole student body of how quickly tragedy could overtake them.

More than a dozen years had passed since then, but forever seventeen, the dead were frozen in her memory. They would have been laughing, singing along with taped music, never suspecting they wouldn't return home.

Twink had come home, though. The afternoon's whole frantic ordeal had been resolved in under an hour, but Darcy was still too badly frightened to relax. Twink could have been kidnapped, hit by a car or, making her way along the boats unnoticed, simply fallen from a dock and drowned.

They'd all been extremely lucky that day. No, blessed, she thought, but there was no relief in Twink's safe return. If only she'd watched Twink more carefully, then the whole terrifying episode would never have occurred. But had she never given Twink more than a bit of scattered conversation as she played in the nursery? she agonized.

Today's near-tragedy had simply been waiting to happen. They'd all been preoccupied, or shamefully careless, and dear little Twink could have been lost forever. Christy Joy would never have spoken to her again, and their ties to a thriving business would have been severed by blame and guilt.

Too unhappy to rise, Darcy remained seated on the floor until she was cold and stiff, but once in bed, she was too tense to sleep. The sunlit dawn brought plenty of tourists into Defy the World, but not a glimmer of peace.

Griffin debated calling Darcy Saturday afternoon, but, thinking that she would be busy selling cacti to tourists, he decided against it. Instead, he left a brief message on her voice mail, then closed his mind to all forms of distraction and focused on the evening's program.

Once it had begun, it was an effort to devote the necessary enthusiasm to the pieces he'd mastered years ago, but he strove to imbue them with fresh energy. When the concert was yet another triumph, he softly announced his intention to play the composition he'd debuted in Seattle. He heard a faint murmur roll through the crowd, but the audience quickly fell silent and listened in rapt awe until he'd gently tapped the final note.

He bowed through the deafening applause, but the person who mattered most was a half-continent away, and the concert hall's wide stage was a lonely place indeed.

Steeling himself to endure the reception with forced charm, he was badly embarrassed to discover his publicity photograph had been enlarged to cover half a wall. It was a handsome portrait, but he wanted attention focused on his music, not his movie star good-looks. He accepted a glass of champagne and nodded as though he were actually listening to the effusive compliments of the patrons who surrounded him, but he frequently glanced at his watch and counted the hours until his flight left for home.

Then a tall, slender brunette approached him on stiletto heels. Clothed in an elegantly cut black satin gown, she possessed a runway model's rolling gait. Her inky hair was pulled back in a chignon, and she reminded him of the line of guitar-strumming women in Robert Palmer's videos. He smiled at that thought and watched her mistake his expression for an invitation to move close.

"Your music is magnificent," she announced in the fluid French of a native.

"*Merci*," Griffin responded, and their conversation continued in French, effectively excluding the others gathered close by.

"I am Adriana LeMer, and I have a wealthy friend who wishes to engage you for a private performance," she confided softly. "He owns a magnificent chateau near Paris which boasts a piano worthy of your talent. How soon will you be available?" She cocked her head and leaned in to hear his reply.

It was not an infrequent request, but even when delivered with the haunting scent of expensive perfume, Griffin had no wish to oblige. "Unfortunately, my concert schedule is too full to permit a trip to Paris at present," he apologized.

She plucked a card from her low-cut bodice and slipped it into his breast pocket. "I think you will make the time for a million dollars. Let us know when you will arrive, and your plane will be met."

She turned away and disappeared into the crowd before Griffin could respond, but the brief encounter had been strangely unsettling. The world was filled with men who could afford to pay such extravagant sums to hear him play for an hour or two, and it was not unusual for such requests to come following a concert. Still, he was a man who relied upon his instincts, and he recoiled with a sickening dread as he withdrew her card from his pocket.

It held only a name, Simon Jordan, and a telephone number with a Paris prefix. He'd never heard of the man, but he suspected that Interpol would have. He was no longer excited by international intrigues, but others might find Jordan's offer sufficiently interesting to merit an investigation.

He took another sip of champagne and, after shoving the card back into his pocket, he wished an already too long evening would soon end.

Sunday evening, Griffin came through the nursery gate seconds before George locked it. He was carrying a bag from the Emperor's Palace and grinned at Darcy. "I sure hope you can leave now, because I haven't eaten all day, and if I have to hang around here, I'm liable to start nibbling the plants."

Darcy had been anticipating his return with as much dread as excitement. Now that he was here, she licked her lips and forced a shaky smile. "I'm all set." She wished George a good night, and he waved to them on his way out.

As soon as they passed through the back gate, Griffin pulled Darcy into his arms, hugged her tightly and lifted her off her feet. "The mermaid is almost as adorable as you are. Did you pose for her?"

"No," she exclaimed, doubting there was any resemblance between them. "But I'm glad you like her."

"I love her and, while I'd insisted upon a fountain, it was a nice surprise to find it all finished. It's proof you must have thought of me a time or two while I was away."

Darcy returned his eager kisses with a trembling enthusiasm and took his hand as they walked the short distance to her house. Her emotions had been in such awful turmoil since Friday, she had to blink back tears. She'd convinced herself she would surely regain her equilibrium once he returned, but her chest was still painfully tight.

She ushered him inside her home and quickly busied

herself setting the table. "Were you as pleased by the concert as the audience?" she asked.

Griffin laughed as he took the small cartons from the bag and opened them to find the walnut shrimp. "Not nearly, but then I hear myself play every day. They liked the new piece, though, and that made the trip worthwhile."

"I'm almost afraid to ask about the chauffeur."

"He wasn't a new contact, just a limo driver who wore cheap cologne."

Darcy slipped into her chair in time to glimpse a preoccupied frown cross his brow. "But still you look worried. Tell me what really happened."

Griffin shrugged, sat and spooned a generous helping of walnut shrimp onto her plate. "Well, there was one rather peculiar incident at the reception following the concert."

Darcy speared a shrimp, but couldn't seem to guide the fork to her lips. "Peculiar in what way?"

"A woman approached me. She was the kind anyone would notice in a crowd, but she was a little too perfect."

Fearing the worst, Darcy forced herself to make eye contact. "Are you trying to tell me that you slept with her?"

"No! I wasn't even tempted." Griffin leaned over and kissed her soundly. He summarized his brief conversation with Adriana LeMer, then began to eat.

"A million dollars is a staggering sum to refuse," Darcy exclaimed. "Do you ever play for private parties?"

"Sure. I've played for you, haven't I?" He winked at her.

"Yes, but if you send me a bill for a million dollars, I'll not pay."

"You needn't worry. But there was something about Ms. LeMer that was definitely off. I'll pass the card she gave me along to Interpol, but it's probably nothing more sinister than some rich music lover's extravagant whim. Now, what happened here while I was away?"

She didn't even know where to begin and, while she was still toying with the shrimp, she'd yet to taste it. In fact, she hadn't been able to eat much of anything in the last couple of days. She hadn't slept well either, and only a skillful application of makeup kept her resulting fatigue from being glaringly obvious.

The kettle began to whistle, and she excused herself to make their tea. She'd actually rehearsed a story to describe the Twink disaster, but that she couldn't shake her initial panic seemed absurd.

Her hands shook as she carried the mugs to the table. Griffin was serving the broccoli beef, but she doubted she could eat it either. "Nothing much happened," she lied. "It was another good weekend for us."

Griffin took a sip of tea. "What did Christy Joy say about the building I mentioned?"

She was grateful he'd changed the subject and added a piece of broccoli to the shrimp on her fork. "She wasn't pleased with the site either, and for exactly the same reasons. It's too large, the location is terrible, and it's probably too expensive, to boot."

"So she wants to keep looking?"

Her nerves raw, she blurted the truth. "No, she's pressuring me to convince you to let us stay where we are."

Annoyed, Griffin leaned back in his chair. "We've already been over that argument. The answer's no. Now I know you love walnut shrimp. Why aren't you eating?"

Darcy looked away. The table sat beside a window, but it was already too dark to see more than deep shadows outside. She refused to offer lame excuses for her lack of appetite, but if the weekend were any sample of what their life was likely to be, and she was positive it had been, then she would always have to handle the occasional crisis alone.

If it had been their child who was lost, no matter how briefly, would he be furious with her?

Since Friday, Christy Joy had been decidedly cool to her, and when her thoughts were as tangled as her emotions, she didn't need the additional burden of her partner's disdain. She gave up all hope of feigning an appetite and laid her fork across her plate.

"You're both making impossible demands on me," she complained, "and it's damned uncomfortable being stuck here in the middle."

"Somehow, I didn't think discomfort was the effect I had on you."

A teasing light glowed in his dark eyes, but she was in no mood to be cajoled out of her pain. "I understand you have an extraordinary talent, and you owe it to the world to perform, but it's difficult being left behind where anything might go wrong."

"I asked you to come with me. You wouldn't have had to sit in the hotel while I rehearsed either. Chicago is filled with interesting places to visit, museums and—"

"Yes, I'm sure it is, but that's not really the issue."

Griffin studied her downcast expression a long moment. "If the real problem is that you're already sick of me, then just say so. I can take it."

"No, it isn't that at all," Darcy cried. She wished he would pull her into his arms and hold her until she felt safe again, but she shrank down into herself, sending an unspoken message that she would rather not be touched.

"I wasn't gone that long, and I did call you," Griffin reminded her softly.

"Yes, thank you. That was very thoughtful of you."

"Thoughtful? You make it sound as though I were some distant cousin who calls occasionally to inquire about your health."

Darcy just shook her head. "I don't want to argue."

"Good, neither do I, but I don't know what the hell we're talking about here. Maybe I should just go home and when you feel like talking, you can give me a call."

Darcy nodded numbly. "Take the food, please. I won't be able to eat it."

"Then toss it out," Griffin responded as he rose from his chair. He leaned down to brush her cheek with a kiss, then paused on his way to the door. "Did you file a request for a passport?"

"No, but I thought about it."

"That's scarcely flattering, but it would still be a good idea for you to have one. You might actually want to travel with the next guy you meet."

Darcy braced herself, but he showed a great deal of restraint by not slamming the door on his way out. Her anguish got the better of her then, and she began to sob with hoarse gulps. She'd known nothing in life was ever certain, but with her once-trusted partner barely speaking to her and the man she cared about more determined to occupy a building than a place in her heart, tears were her only comfort.

Chapter Eleven

After another nearly sleepless night, Darcy awakened Monday morning to find a soggy coastal fog clinging to the ground. It was far too wet to burn off before afternoon and, contemplating a day as dreary as her mood, she pulled on a bright pink long-sleeved jersey and blue floral overalls to affect a spring-like cheer.

She made herself a poached egg on toast the way her mother had prepared them for her as a child and sipped tea while she ate her breakfast. She still had no appetite, but the nostalgic food offered a surprising amount of comfort on an otherwise bleak day.

After washing her dishes, she set a few of her philodendron out on the back porch to soak up the moisture in the air. She brewed a second cup of tea, poured it into an insulated cup and pulled on her bright green Defy the World windbreaker. As ready as she would ever be, she walked on over to the nursery, but her step lacked its usual bounce.

She entered her office intent upon ordering roses for the Peavey wedding. A couple of smaller jobs had come in last week, and they also needed her attention, but that morning her sketches were as distracted as her thoughts and she sent them sailing toward her wastebasket rather than attach them to her clipboard.

Mid-morning, George arrived carrying a bag of jelly donuts. He took one look at the faint shadows beneath her eyes and shook his head. "Now don't tell me you aren't hungry, because it sure looks to me as though you could use a good meal."

Ignoring his astute observation, Darcy helped herself to a donut, but after thanking him, she left the plump pastry resting on a napkin on her desk while she sipped the last of her tea. "I doubt we'll see a tourist all day in this weather," she mused aloud.

"Monday is never very busy, but it's good to have some extra time to clean up and restock after the weekend."

"Make a note of whatever is running low, and I'll call in an order."

"Looks to me like it's morale that's in short supply around here, and I expected you to be a happier girl once Griffin came home. Not that I'm prying into your love life, of course."

"Of course not," she replied, but the curious light in his eyes prompted a truthful response. "We didn't even make it through dinner last night before he got up and left."

George licked the last drop of raspberry jelly from his fingers, wiped them on a napkin, then leaned back against her door to get comfortable. "Then it's no wonder you're upset. I know you're an only child. Does Griffin have brothers and sisters?"

"No, but what's that got to do with anything?"

"Well, from what I read in Marge's magazines, it seems birth order might matter a great deal in relationships. Only children, as well as those who are the firstborn, are used to getting their own way. That works fine if they're paired up with someone who was a second or third child and is accustomed to going along with others. But when two such independent people get together, they just naturally butt heads."

Darcy nodded thoughtfully. "Yes, I can see where that might create a problem, but we have so damn many conflicts, and I can't blame them all on the fact that we're both only children."

"We could nibble away at those conflicts one at a time. What's your worst problem?"

"Nosy employees," she shot right back at him.

George waved aside her complaint. "Other than that."

Darcy shrugged slightly as she ticked off the list in her mind. "That he wants this building is right up near the top."

"Eat your donut," George ordered, and he waited until she'd taken a bite to respond. "We can blame the fact that he's a celebrity and people cater to his every whim, but that's too easy. What's the real reason he's so set on taking over this place?"

"He has plans to record here."

George appeared puzzled. "He could do that anywhere."

"That's my view exactly, but no, he insists upon having Defy the World's space in the universe for his own."

"Well, it is his own," George agreed, "but do you remember what I said about people sabotaging good relationships?"

"Sure. Do you think that's what he's doing?"

"Could be." George straightened. "Give it some thought."

"I've already exhausted myself on that score," she protested. "I think Griffin is simply a control freak who's going to push for every advantage. First he'll take our location, and if I'm still speaking to him, then he'll insist I travel with him. Every time I give in, he'll come up with some new demand. Nothing will ever be enough for him."

"That's a real dark prediction, little lady."

"You don't know the half of it," she replied sadly. "Now, I'm not paying you for therapy. Let's rotate the stock in the pottery shed and see if we can't sell some of the largest pots this week."

"I'll get on it, but right now I'm going into the shop with the rest of these donuts. I hope you'll remember I offered one to you first, though."

"I'll make a note of it on my calendar," she responded, but her pencil remained on her desk. She leaned back in her chair and closed her eyes. She wanted to concentrate on business, not Griffin Moore, but seconds later when she made the attempt, he was standing not two feet away. Startled that she might have conjured him up, she bolted to her feet.

"What are you doing here?"

"Sorry, I didn't mean to startle you. I came to pay for the fountain," he responded calmly. "You left your bill on the kitchen counter, remember?"

Darcy rubbed her palms along the side seams on her overalls. "Sure, but there was no need to rush."

"Wasn't there?" he asked softly. He took a check from his shirt pocket and handed it to her.

Being careful not to brush his fingers, she took it, then sat at her desk. "Wait just a minute, and I'll write you a receipt."

"I have all day."

His voice was dark honey, smooth and sweet, but her hands shook as she wrote out a receipt. For a panicked moment, she felt as though she might suffocate with him crowding her office, but she shook it off and signed her name.

"Tell me something," she asked without daring to look up at him. "What prompted you to buy this building in the first place?"

After a brief hesitation, Griffin slid his hands in his pockets and began to pace the cramped aisle beside her desk. "You want the truth?"

"That was our deal, remember?"

"All right. At the time, a press release claimed I was here for a short break in my concert schedule, but I was completely burnt out. I couldn't face another ten to twenty years of constant practice and performance where the city and orchestra would change, but audiences would expect me to remain exactly the same. I couldn't stand the thought of being frozen in my prime like some succulent strawberry.

"I happened upon this building, saw the for-sale sign and bought it for a studio that same morning. It didn't matter to me that it might take a couple of years to fulfill all my contracts. From the moment I bought this beautiful building, it became a lucky charm, a solid reminder that I could escape the frantic demands of fame and just write music. I didn't even care if I was a colossal failure as a composer. I just wanted to give it a shot."

He turned to face her. "I'm sorry it's not a more entertaining story."

Darcy handed him the receipt. "So our building is merely the embodiment of a dream you've already begun to realize? You've proven you can write incredibly beautiful music from your home, but you could do it anywhere, in your Zen garden, or down on the beach. The music is in you, Griffin. Don't you trust your own talent? Your genius?"

Griffin responded with a sly smile. "It's really too soon to categorize me as a genius."

"Not from the review I read it isn't."

"That was just one man's opinion."

She rose to confront him. "One extremely knowledgeable and respected man," she reminded him. "What did the critics say in Chicago?"

Griffin glanced away as though the subject tired him. "They were equally enthusiastic, but that doesn't make them infallible."

"Now you're being a prick!"

Griffin laughed off the insult and reached out to draw her close. "It isn't like you to mince words."

Darcy batted away his arms. "Back off."

Griffin raised his hands and stepped aside. "Yes, ma'am. Now, is my account paid in full?"

For one terrible instant, Darcy couldn't recall what account he meant. She'd done her best to score a point for her side, and if all he could think of was his bill, then she'd failed miserably. "Yes, it is."

"Good. Please feel free to list my address on your résumé."

Darcy watched him turn and walk away. As always he moved with more than a little swagger, but she twisted in a slow turn and sank into her chair. The man had no good reason for keeping their building other than he just damn well felt like it. Even if he were a genius, he was too lost in himself to consider her feelings. She knew she should consider herself lucky she'd seen through him this soon.

But she sure didn't feel lucky. She just ached clear through.

Griffin managed to hold on to his temper until he reached his Land Rover, but after climbing in he slammed the door shut and let fly with a string of curses in an impressive variety of languages. A week ago, he'd spent a fantastic night with a warm and loving woman, but why hadn't that delightful creature welcomed him home? Maybe if he'd had presents delivered to her every day while he'd been away, she might have been happier to see him. But he hadn't thought he would have to buy her love.

Wouldn't it be inappropriate to send flowers to a landscape architect? he grumbled to himself. She made her own intoxicating perfume, so that was out. He'd already given her a diamond necklace, and he suddenly recalled that she'd been wearing it last night and again this morning. Maybe she'd never taken it off.

Still, something was definitely wrong. She wanted the blasted building. She'd made no secret of that, but if he extended her lease, what would she want next? He'd never understood how women think, and perhaps they simply didn't bother.

Maybe they just followed their feelings and flitted from one lover to the next without giving their actions any more thought than a butterfly gave to a rose. Monarch Bay had been named for the beautiful black and orange butterflies that spent part of each year on California's coast. It was pure instinct that led the graceful insects, but what compelled Darcy to give him grief?

There were people who would kill for a fraction of the talent he possessed, but no one seemed to care much for him as a man. That was such a depressing thought he drove home and composed the darkest, most painfully difficult piece he could manage. He doubted there was another pianist alive who could play it, or even want to, and that brought a perverse satisfaction all its own.

By midnight, the pervasive fog had become rain. Griffin had always enjoyed the sound of water trickling along the roof and splashing into the pebbled pools at the bottom of the gutters, but the next morning he wandered through his near-empty house and longed for the sun.

His telephone rang, but he ignored it. He'd sent Interpol a description of the woman who had approached him in Chicago, but hadn't monitored his computer for a reply. He took an umbrella and went out to check for erosion along the cliff at the edge of the Zen garden, but it was solid rock and wouldn't wear away in a thousand storms.

He drove into Monarch Bay to work out at the gym and overheard an off-duty fireman mention sand bags, but it meant nothing to him. It wasn't until he started back up the hill that he noticed the streets were filling with water. Thinking it would all just run into the sea, he went on home and added to the darkly threatening piece that flowed to the keyboard straight from his splintered heart.

Jeremy Linden pulled his hat low and went out for a walk through town, but, unwilling to risk a chilly reception at Defy the World Tomatoes, he walked right on by without stopping in to say hello. He went instead to the Scarlet Letter to sip coffee and browse the latest magazines.

Nothing appealed to him, though, not even Karen, the tall, slender clerk. Whenever he came into the bookstore, she usually caressed his arm in passing, or let her fingertips linger across his palm while she counted out his change. She was attractive, and quite pleasant too, but he couldn't help but recoil from her touch. She seemed not to notice, however, which he supposed was a good thing for them both.

But that morning Karen didn't even meet his gaze, let alone flirt with him. It was disconcerting at first, then he wondered if she'd heard that he'd found Twink on his boat. The weekend had passed with no mention of the incident from anyone, and he'd been relieved to think it had already been forgotten. Now he wasn't so sure.

Concerned people might actually believe he harbored a yen for little girls, he left the Scarlet Letter and swung by the post office to pick up his mail. It was the usual assortment of bills, flyers for things he didn't need and appeals from several worthy causes which had included still more address labels. He shoved the bills into his hip pocket and tossed the rest into the trash bin on his way out.

Cold and wet, he had his head down as he headed for the docks and would have run right into Christy Joy had she not stepped out of the way and called his name. She carried a ruffled pink umbrella and smiled as though she were actually glad to see him.

"You shouldn't be out in this rain," he blurted.

"Neither should you," she replied, "but I'm glad I found you. I didn't mean to sound so ungrateful on Friday, but I was terrified something awful had happened to Twink, and I completely forgot my manners. Will you forgive me?"

Jeremy glanced up at the thick clouds overhead. "Are you saying you came out in the rain just to apologize to me?"

Christy Joy appeared puzzled. "Why is that so difficult to believe? You did me an enormous favor, and I was unforgivably rude, although I do hope you'll forgive me."

"Sure, but let's get out of the rain. We could go back to my boat, or would you rather stop in at one of the tourist traps?"

"Is that the way you regard Defy the World?" she asked.

She looked more hurt than insulted, and Jeremy cursed under his breath. "No, of course not, but you don't serve coffee either, do you?"

"No, but I prefer tea."

"I've got some, or hot chocolate is good on rainy days."

"I would absolutely love some hot chocolate." Christy Joy took his arm and fell in step beside him as they made their way along the docks.

Jeremy took her hand to help her aboard the *Great Escape* and hurried her into the galley. He nodded toward a convenient hook. "Hang up your coat, and I'll heat the water."

He'd given them a complete tour of the sleek fishing boat the day they'd gone whale watching, but Christy Joy had been too busy keeping Twink out of mischief to observe as much as she did now. "It must be wonderful to have everything so neatly stowed and yet within an arm's reach," she observed.

Jeremy set a measuring cup filled with water in the microwave before he turned toward her. "That's one way to look at it, I suppose."

"Is there another?"

Jeremy had never been alone with her, and it took him a long moment to realize she appeared to be completely at ease. He was a jumble of nerves and feared it must show. He shrugged off his coat and hat and ran his hands through his damp hair as he stalled for time and something to say.

"It's like living in a well-organized closet," he finally replied, "but not everyone likes things so damn cozy." The microwave chimed, and he mixed a cup of hot chocolate for her and heated more water for his own.

Christy Joy slid into the bench behind the small built-in table. "Well, obviously you do. Did you grow up on a boat?"

Jeremy chuckled at the thought and shook his head. "No. My dad was killed in Vietnam, and my mom raised me in an apartment in San Diego. So I grew up by the sea and graduated from the Merchant Marine Academy. I wanted to own my own boat rather than remain an officer on a cruise ship and so here I am, sitting out a rainy day waiting for the next charter."

"Somehow I can't quite picture you cruising the Caribbean in a fancy white uniform."

Her tone was playful, and Jeremy couldn't help but smile. "Well, it's been a few years, but my uniforms still fit. It's not a bad life, but I'm happier here."

"Are you really?" Christy Joy took a sip of her hot chocolate and licked the foam from her lips. "Aren't you ever lonely?"

Jeremy couldn't stifle a chuckle. "That all depends. Are you trying to proposition me?"

Christy Joy laughed with him. "It's awfully tempting, but I really should get back to work."

"You can't have much business today."

"None, actually, but there's always plenty to do." The galley had an inviting warmth which made confiding in him easy and, without making a conscious decision, she revealed how disappointed she was that they might soon have to move.

Jeremy was so startled he barely caught himself before he sloshed hot chocolate down the front of his shirt. "I've seen Griffin around, but I didn't realize he was such a—"

"Don't say it." Christy Joy stood and carried her empty cup to the sink. "Calling him names won't help anything."

"Might make you feel better," Jeremy offered. When she glanced up at him, he longed to lean over and kiss her, but she turned away to get her coat and the moment was lost. "I'll walk you back to Defy the World."

"No, stay here where you're warm and dry," Christy Joy argued.

"I can get warm and dry later," Jeremy insisted, and while he felt he'd missed the only chance he might ever have to kiss her, he took her hand as he walked her back to her shop, and she gave his fingers a gentle squeeze as she said good-bye.

Christy Joy shook out her coat and dropped her umbrella into the stand beside the door. She'd called her clerks first thing that morning and told them not to come in, and the shop was so quiet she waited until she reached the register to speak to Mary Beth.

"Captain Linden brews a mean cup of hot chocolate, but you were completely wrong about his being attracted to me."

Mary Beth made a final computer entry and then swung toward her. "Impossible. The man nearly drools when he comes in here."

"Maybe the candle fragrances make his mouth water, but we were alone on his boat for fifteen minutes or so, and he was no more than friendly."

Mary Beth pursed her lips thoughtfully. "That's a shame. I'd assumed he was just waiting for the right moment to make his move, and now you're disappointed. I'm sorry, but I still believe he has feelings for you. Maybe he was just so surprised to see you that he couldn't think straight."

"Right." Christy tidied up the ribbons behind the counter and sorted the little gift cards into the proper categories. "I'll grant you that it's an intriguing possibility, but I haven't been on a date in years, so even if Jeremy had asked me out, I would have been too flustered to accept."

"Then you ought to rehearse that scene in your mind so you'll be ready with a lucid response when he does get up his courage and asks for a date."

"Visualize it, you mean?"

"If it works for sports figures, why wouldn't it work for you?"

"I could probably think of about a million reasons if I put my mind to it, but right now, I'm too worried about the rain. How long do you suppose it can last?"

"I don't know what the record is for Monarch Bay. Do you want me to call the weather service?"

"No, I'd rather not know. Let's just keep busy and maybe the time will pass quickly." It had to, she thought, because it cost far too much money to keep Defy the World open with nary a customer in sight.

Wednesday morning, Darcy didn't even consider dressing in bright colors. She pulled on an old pair of Levi's, a black turtleneck and a gray cable knit sweater. Without pausing for breakfast, she yanked on her rain boots and raincoat and left for the short walk to work.

Christy Joy was already in the shop making coffee and, while they hadn't discussed anything other than the miserable weather since last Friday, Darcy went on inside. "I called the kids before they left for school this morning and told them not to come in this afternoon. There will be nothing for them to do other than bail water, and I sure hope it doesn't come to that."

Christy Joy handed her a cup of coffee. "So do I, but it's raining too hard to walk Twink to school. She's upstairs watching cartoons, and later she can work on the new coloring books I'd saved for a rainy day.

"I just didn't expect this much rain, and the water is about to slosh over the curb out front. I wish we'd gotten some sandbags when we had the chance."

"I got them," Darcy replied. She leaned against the counter, cradled her cup in her hands and inhaled the coffee's rich vanilla scent. "If George makes it in, I'll have him help me move what stock we can away from the street. Then we'll place the sandbags across the front of the shop."

Christy Joy poured cream into her own coffee and stirred it slowly. "Let's hope that's enough. We haven't made fifty dollars in the last two days. We probably won't make a dime today, and if the shop floods—"

Darcy pushed away from the counter. "Then we'll have a big mess to clean up, but I'll get on those sandbags right now. Why don't you clear everything off the floor at the front?"

Christy Joy raked her lower lip through her teeth. "We don't have insurance to replace damaged stock, much less damage to the building. Do you suppose Griffin does?"

"I don't want to count on him for anything."

"What's going on with you two? We haven't talked since, well, since last week."

Darcy didn't want to use last Friday's awful fright as a reference point either and just shrugged. "Let's worry about Griffin later. Right now, we've got problems enough with the rain."

She took a last drink of coffee, pulled up the hood on her raincoat and went out into the nursery to fetch the sandbags. They were piled in a wheelbarrow, but it was too heavy for her to either push or pull. She grabbed the topmost bag, headed through the nursery and carried it around to build a makeshift dam in front of the shop's door.

The chilly rain had dampened her clear through by the time she'd shoved the third bag into place. She turned to gauge the progress of the water along the curb and saw a hazy figure approaching. She stepped under the awning and waited for him to pass.

Jeremy stopped when he reached her. "It looks like the storm drains are getting clogged with debris. I thought you might need some help."

Darcy wished the same thought had entered Griffin's mind, but she managed a bright if slippery smile for Jeremy. "I sure could. Would you mind carrying sandbags?"

"Not at all. Just tell me where they are and I'll stack them for you. That way one of us can stay dry."

"No, I don't mind working. It's better than just wringing my hands." She led him to the wheelbarrow, which Jeremy promptly wheeled out front. They completed the low wall in a matter of minutes, but Darcy kept glancing out toward the street.

"Water's pouring off the mountain as fast as it falls from the sky," she moved in close to confide. "This corner lot is terrific for business, but with water coming at us along the front and down the side, we may be in for a very long day."

"Well, at least we don't have to worry about the shop sinking out from under us," Jeremy teased, "and I'm used to getting wet."

"You're also a very good sport." They surveyed the nursery stock, and began moving plants in five gallon cans away from the front. Darcy went into the pottery shed to grab a broom and found water running across the floor. The structure had been designed to provide shade rather than security, and it was no wonder rain was seeping under the wall from the side street, but the sight was still unnerving.

Jeremy came up behind her and looked over her shoulder. "That doesn't look good," he said.

"No, but maybe we can use plastic bags of potting soil as sandbags and divert the water away from the shed. Let's give it a try, at least."

"Good plan."

Jeremy reloaded the wheelbarrow, then pushed the ten and twenty-five pound bags around to the sidewalk. It took them awhile to stack the bags at the proper angle to deflect the water, but they were satisfied they had done some good. Ready for a break, Darcy led the way inside the shop.

"George just called," Christy announced. "His street's flooded, so he can't come in. Mary Beth won't be here either. It's nice to see you, though, Jeremy. The coffee's fresh, so help yourself to some. I need to run upstairs for a minute to check on Twink."

"Thanks. Take your time." Jeremy shrugged off his coat,

looked around for a place to hang it, then draped it over a stool near the counter. Water dripped off the cuffs and hem to form a soggy puddle on the tile floor. "Now I need a mop. Do you have one handy?"

"Let it go," Darcy replied. "Has it ever rained hard enough for the buildings along Embarcadero to wash away?"

"Not that I know of, but I've only been here a couple of years."

"That's reassuring." Darcy poured them each a cup of coffee, but before she could raise hers to her lips, Christy Joy came running down the stairs.

"There's water pouring in through the roof upstairs. Fortunately, the leak's right above the bathtub, but what if that whole side of the roof gives way?"

"We need a tarp," Jeremy suggested. "Don't you have some out in the nursery?"

"Yes," Darcy responded, "but I won't have you crawling around on our roof in the rain."

Jeremy chuckled at her rebuke. "If it weren't raining, there would be no need to get up on the roof."

"No, Darcy's right," Christy Joy agreed. "We'll have to call Griffin and let him send someone over to fix the roof."

It wasn't a call Darcy was eager to make, but she reached for the telephone and punched in his private number. He answered on the third ring, and just hearing his voice made her knees weak. She leaned into the counter for support and, fighting for a business-like tone, she provided a brief description of the problem.

"I'll be right there," he answered.

"No, wait. You shouldn't drive down the mountain in all this rain. The road will be awash in mud and rocks and—"

"Careful, Darcy, I'm beginning to think you might care what happens to me."

"Well, of course, I care. Just stay put and call someone who does roof repairs. That's all I need."

Griffin nearly purred in her ear. "Let's not get into your needs just now. I'll see you in a minute."

He hung up before Darcy could mount another argument. "He says he's coming down here, but he's just as likely to go flying right off the mountain on the first curve."

Jeremy nodded toward the clock. "Let's give him twenty minutes. If he isn't here, we can call the police and ask them to check the road."

Darcy could so easily imagine a black and white car with lights flashing also plunging off the road that she just shook her head. "I think I'm going to be sick." She ran back toward the restroom and even then barely made it.

Jeremy sent Christy Joy a sad smile. "Is she sick because he's coming here, or because he might not make it?"

"A little of both, I'm afraid, but Griffin will get the roof fixed and that's all that concerns me right now. No one's likely to be out shopping this morning. Would you mind if I went back upstairs to look after Twink?"

"Not at all. Looks like you were rearranging things. What can I do to help?"

He'd yanked off his cap, his hair was plastered to his head and his cheeks were pink from the chill, but for one wild instant, Christy Joy felt like asking him for his best kiss. It would have been an outrageous request and certainly would have shocked him, but as she turned away, her only worry was that he might refuse.

Chapter Twelve

Griffin had been lost in his new composition and hadn't realized how hard it was raining until he went outside where an icy blast of watery wind greeted him with a rude shove. Head down, he braced himself as he ran to his Land Rover. Now convinced Darcy's warning was well-founded, he eased the sturdy vehicle down the driveway and out onto Ridgecrest at a slow crawl.

He wiped the condensation from the inside of the windshield with the back of his leather glove, but the effort improved his vision only marginally. Fortunately, he knew each subtle curve and wide turn into town, so while it was a slow, harrowing trip, he made it without sliding off the hillside. He parked next to Darcy's truck, then tramped through the water coursing across the rear of the nursery to enter the shop through the side door.

Her attention riveted on the clock, Darcy gasped as Griffin was ushered in on a chill gust of wind. Clad in a red and black plaid Pendleton coat, black cowboy hat, Levi's and boots, he resembled a character out of an early Clint Eastwood western more than a concert pianist. Nevertheless, he looked awfully good.

"I was going to call the police if you weren't here in another minute," she exclaimed.

"I'd no idea I was expected to speed down the hill after the warning you gave, but if anyone is in need of rescue, it appears to be you with the leaky roof. Care to show me the problem?"

Darcy gestured toward the stairs, then led him up to Christy Joy's bathroom. Twink wanted to come in too, but Darcy sent her downstairs to wait with her mother. "It's dripping through the plaster, and we don't want the whole ceiling ruined."

The room was painted a pale aqua and Christy Joy had sewn a colorful valance for the window from a bright aqua fabric splashed with tropical fish. There were aqua towels and a basket of bathtub toys balanced on the side of the tub. Darcy couldn't help but think how different the charming room was from Griffin's gleaming art deco tiled bath.

He watched the water drip into the tub and nodded thoughtfully. "Might just be that the gutter is clogged with leaves, and that's left water to pool on the roof. I can probably fix that myself."

"You're not serious."

He flashed a disarming grin. "I doubt clearing leaves from a gutter is beyond my capabilities. Of course, even if it alleviates the problem, once the weather clears, I'll still have to hire someone to repair the damage. For now, you must have a tarp or two lying around the nursery."

She sagged back against the door. "Yes, but you're not going up on the roof."

"Why not? I can put a ladder on the porch by the back door and climb right up."

Darcy shook her head. "There's too great a risk you'll fall."

Griffin moved in close. "It's my building, Darcy, and if I want to dance on the roof, I'll do it."

"Not while I have the lease," she replied coolly.

He laughed at her resolve. "Better check the fine print. I'm responsible for repairs, and you can't prevent me from doing them myself."

Darcy chased him down the stairs. "Griffin, you're being totally unreasonable. If the wind caught you, you'd go sailing right off the roof and—"

Griffin paused on the bottom step and turned to look back up at her. "And what?"

Before Darcy could finish her sentence, Jeremy broke in. "I'll give you a hand if you want to stretch a tarp over the leak. We'll need something to weight it down, but the potting mix bags seem to be holding up pretty well."

Remaining on the stairs, Darcy clung to the rail. "You don't have to show off for me. If we're just going to use a tarp, I'll call a couple of the guys from my crew to come over and do it."

"Why bother them when the captain says he'll help me?"

Darcy's eyes narrowed. If he thought she would wrap herself around his knees and beg him not to endanger his life, he was dead wrong. She raised her chin. "Fine, go ahead and do it. The fire department is just down the street, so the paramedics should be able to respond in less than a minute."

"Think we'll need them, Captain?"

"No, I've crewed on sailing ships in worse weather than this. Putting out a tarp will be a snap."

Twink was seated at the small table coloring a giraffe. She looked up as the men went out the side door. "Where are they going?" she asked.

Christy Joy sat with her daughter. "They intend to fix the roof, honey. They'll be back in a minute."

Darcy sat on the steps and rested her head in her hands. "Now do you see how difficult it is to reason with Griffin? Once he decides to do something, he doesn't even blink, let alone change his mind."

"That can be a good quality," Christy Joy murmured. She reached out to comb Twink's curls with her fingers. "Are you hungry, baby, would you like some lunch?"

"Hot dogs?"

"Coming right up. Would you like one, Darcy?"

"How can you think about food? Lightning could hit Griffin and Jeremy, and they'd be fried before they hit the ground."

"My, what a pleasant thought. Why don't you come upstairs with me, Twink? I'll need some help spreading mustard on the buns."

Twink left her coloring to bound up the stairs behind her mother, while Darcy went to the front of the shop to check her makeshift dam. It appeared to be holding, but water was now up over the curb and lapping toward the building. She didn't want to imagine Griffin clinging to the roof like some fool monkey, but she could only stare out at the rain, unable to imagine anything better.

"You know this is a damn fool stunt, don't you?" Jeremy asked.

"Oh, hell yes. That's half the fun."

"Fine, as long as you know what you're doing."

Griffin adjusted the angle of his hat, but the rain still splattered his face. "I wouldn't go that far," he replied, but the wind swallowed his words.

Jeremy had nearly tripped over the ladder earlier and led Griffin right to it. Carrying it, they grabbed a folded tarp and made their way up the back stairs only to find the landing was too narrow to set up the wooden stepladder safely. What they needed was an aluminum extension ladder that would reach the roof from the ground, but there was none handy.

Griffin nodded toward the eucalyptus towering over the rear of the building. "Go get the bags of potting soil. I'll climb the tree to reach the roof, and you can toss everything up to me from here."

"Are you just plain crazy?"

"No, I simply relish a challenge." With a quick step up, Griffin balanced himself on the porch rail, reached out for a wildly swaying branch and, with a lunge, caught it.

Jeremy watched in disbelief as Griffin swung himself up into the tree. In the rain-choked light, the pale trunk of the eucalyptus had a ghostly pallor. The curved leaves lashed at the pianist with gray-green claws, but he merely laughed and waved.

"I'll get the potting soil," Jeremy yelled, and he ran back down the stairs to fetch half a dozen bags.

When he returned, Griffin was already lying flat on the roof and scraping leaves from the clogged gutter. When it was clear, he reached down for the tarp. Jeremy got a firm grip on the porch rail and flung the blue bundle toward the roof. Griffin made a grab for it, but missed, forcing Jeremy back down the stairs and out the gate to fetch it from the alley before it was washed away.

On their second try, Griffin caught the tarp, but the wind tore at the edge to unfurl it in his grasp. The plastic-coated canvas snapped him with a cruel slap, and he had to fight for control. "Better toss me the bags of soil to weigh it down as I lay it out," he shouted.

Jeremy took care with his aim and Griffin caught each one without trouble. The challenge was then to spread out the tarp and anchor it with the potting soil before he became so tightly wrapped in it he would careen right off the roof in a grim parody of a burial at sea. Griffin saw that calamity as a real risk, but stretched out to make the best use of his own weight. They were soaked and chilled clear through by the time he was satisfied the tarp would remain in place for the duration of the storm.

While they'd worked, the wind had shifted direction, and the eucalyptus now had a nasty twist to its sway. Certain he ought to have given more thought to how he was going to get down before he got up on the roof, Griffin edged carefully over to the slant above the back door. He thought he could drop off and hit the landing, but with the wind and rain a factor, if he missed, he would be in for a painful cart-wheeling fall down the slippery stairs.

"Get out of my way!" he ordered Jeremy and, shutting out all thought of a poor result, he turned to drop his legs off the roof and jumped down onto the landing below. For one dreadful instant, the porch seemed to tilt under him, but as he fought to regain his balance, Jeremy grabbed his arm and flung him toward the back door.

When he caught his breath, he turned to express his gratitude. "Thanks for your help."

Jeremy moved in close, grabbed Griffin's soggy lapels and spoke in a vicious whisper. "Now that job's done, let's get things straight between us. You hurt Darcy and Christy Joy, and I'll make falling off a roof look like a pleasure cruise."

Griffin had been trained in hand-to-hand combat of a savagery Jeremy could not even imagine, but he chose to shrug off the captain's threat rather than respond with violence. But first he locked his hands around Jeremy's wrists and pressed down hard.

"Those two don't need your protection, and it was Darcy who dumped me, not the other way around. But that wouldn't concern you, would it? As I see it, the only problem we've got today is the rain. Understood?"

Jeremy responded with a grudging nod and, when Griffin released his hold on him, he dropped his hands to his sides. "You've not been here long. You don't know how hard those two have worked, and Defy the World won't survive this storm."

"It's just a little rain," Griffin argued. "Everything will dry out."

Jeremy swore a particularly foul oath, a favorite among

sailors. "It's kept the tourists away, and they aren't making a cent. Hell, I can't either, but I don't have their overhead."

Cold, Griffin hugged his arms across his chest. "You needn't worry. If they get behind in the rent, I'll not evict them."

"Not until September, you mean."

Unwilling to debate his plans, Griffin leaned toward the stairs, but before he could take a step, Christy Joy opened the door behind them and drew them in.

"Are you all right?" she asked. "I heard you thumping around on the roof, and the water has stopped dripping into the bathtub."

"Then our mission was a success," Griffin assured her. "As soon as it stops raining, I'll have the roof repaired properly and the eucalyptus at the back of the property trimmed so its leaves won't clog the gutters again."

Slipping by Christy Joy, he headed on down the stairs. Darcy was waiting at the bottom. Twink was again at the children's table drawing a blue whale. They were both watching him with a wide, curious gaze. "Anything else you need?" he asked.

"Not right this minute, but they've just run a news bulletin on the radio. A mud slide has closed Highway 1 five miles south of town."

"I hadn't planned on driving down to LA this afternoon anyway," Griffin replied.

He just doesn't get it, Darcy swore under her breath, but as she paused to censor her response for Twink's benefit, the power failed and the shop disappeared in the resulting darkness.

Griffin pulled Darcy close. "Does this happen often?"

In spite of being cold and wet, he was as solid as a door, and she didn't struggle against him. "Not until today it hasn't."

Twink giggled. "This is cool."

"Just stay put, sweetheart," her mother called. "Darcy, there's a flashlight behind the counter. Can you find it?"

"Just give me a minute," Darcy offered quickly, but rather than release her, Griffin tightened his embrace and dipped his head to capture her mouth for a long, slow kiss that erased all thoughts of flashlights from her mind. She had to grab his coat to steady herself before she finally pushed away.

"You're all wet," she scolded. "You'll get sick for sure."
"No, I won't. I'm never ill. Now let's find that flashlight."

At the top of the stairs, Jeremy stood with his arm loosely looped around Christy Joy's waist. Her curls brushed his check and, filled with longing, he leaned closer to drink in her subtle perfume. Even with the storm, enough light seeped through the windows for him to make out her profile. She appeared perfectly relaxed as she waited for Darcy to provide some light, but he had to force himself to keep breathing. Now he envied Griffin his shameless bravado, but before he could emulate it, Christy Joy turned toward him, slid her fingertips along his cheek and raised her lips to his.

Her kiss was feather-light and yet somehow so delicious that he simply had to have more before she grew convinced he was the stupidest man ever born and shoved him down the stairs. He didn't just brush his lips tenderly across hers either. He kissed her as though she were his own dear wife and he hadn't been in port in years. He didn't stop until he felt the flashlight's beam cross his face, and even then, he couldn't step away.

Darcy hadn't meant to interrupt such a tender moment and quickly aimed the flashlight toward the shop. "Let's light some of the scented candles until the power comes back on. Come on, Twink, help me find some tall ones."

But rather than move, Twink sat staring up at her mother with a narrowed, suspicious gaze. Then she bolted from her chair, dashed up the stairs, and on past Christy Joy into their apartment.

"Oh, God, I'm sorry," Jeremy moaned.

"She'll get used to it," Christy Joy responded, and she gave him a hasty kiss before she followed her daughter.

Jeremy remained at the top of the stairs, grateful Christy Joy hadn't shown Twink's speed as she'd left him, but nevertheless certain he'd caused her another problem she didn't need. Then he sneezed.

"God bless you," Darcy cried. "You see, I knew you two were going to get sick, and now with no heat, it will probably turn into pneumonia."

"Don't be such a worry wart," Griffin chided. "There's a box of long matches here. Which candles shall we light, the strawberry or jasmine scented?"

Darcy reached for one with a subtle vanilla fragrance. "Let's begin with this one. Come on down here, Jeremy. There are towels in the bathroom behind the register, and you two ought to at least make an attempt to get dry. Don't think about leaving either, because you wouldn't be safe with all the streets flooded."

Griffin removed his hat and resisted the temptation to shake like a dog before peeling off his coat. "Am I safe here?" he whispered.

"For the time being," Darcy replied. "I'm sorry we don't carry any men's pants, but our extra-large sweatshirts ought to fit you."

After stifling another sneeze, Jeremy made his way down the stairs. "No, you ought to save them to sell."

"Well, I sure don't see anyone clamoring to buy anything today," Darcy countered. "Which color do you want?"

"I don't suppose you carry black?" Griffin asked.

"No, this is a nursery, you big dolt, and we stock several shades of green along with blue, purple, yellow and pink."

Griffin couldn't help but laugh at her sudden show of temper. "I want whatever color you have so we can wear them together and look like we're on the same team."

Darcy thrust a dark green sweatshirt into his hands. It was of excellent quality and would keep him warm. Across the front, the words Defy the World Tomatoes were embroidered over a bushel basket of vine-ripened tomatoes. It was a colorful logo and, while they sold more T-shirts, they did a steady business in sweatshirts as well.

"How about you, Jeremy, what color would you like?"

"Better give me that same green, and I'll pay for it."

"Nonsense, you've been working here all morning. A free shirt is the least I can do. Go on into the bathroom and dry yourself off before putting it on."

"I'll give it a try," Jeremy promised, but he waited until she'd handed him a lit candle to go.

Griffin carried another vanilla candle over to the counter and set it down. He dropped his coat and hat onto a stool and then pulled his flannel shirt off over his head.

Darcy tried to avoid staring at his muscular torso, but

failed miserably, although she hauled her glance to a halt at his belt buckle. She watched him dry his hair on his shirttail and, after pulling on the sweatshirt, re-comb it with his fingers. Not surprisingly, he'd given little thought to grooming and yet still looked better than most men did on the way to a job interview.

"Twink appeared real upset to see her mother kissing Jeremy. Hasn't Christy Joy dated much?" he asked.

Startled by his question, Darcy responded with a shrug. "No, she hasn't dated anyone since her divorce. Like most kids, I suppose Twink hopes her parents will someday get back together."

"Is it a possibility?"

"Not unless J. Lyle forced Christy Joy back with threats of a custody suit."

"Is he that heartless?"

Griffin was leaning against the counter, apparently sincerely interested in her response, but she shared her partner's fears, compounded by the certainty should J. Lyle press for custody, it would be entirely her fault. Seized by a desperate desire to confide in him, she described the terrible afternoon when Twink had disappeared.

"If J. Lyle ever found out Twink had walked down to the docks alone and gone on one of the boats, he wouldn't hesitate to use it against Christy Joy," she swore.

Griffin nodded and exhaled slowly. "Why didn't you call me when it happened?"

She angled away from him. "I didn't want to bother you when I was sure we'd find her."

"And if you hadn't?"

Afraid she would insult him no matter how she phrased it, she chose her words with special care. "Well, there would have been no point in calling you then either. You couldn't have done anything from Chicago."

"I could have offered some moral support, and a call would have kept me from walking right into a buzz saw when I got home. Damn it, but I knew there was something wrong, and you didn't give me a clue as to what. That wasn't fair."

"Perhaps not," Darcy sighed, "but it wouldn't have been fair to call and scramble your emotions just before a concert either."

He straightened. "Do you honestly believe I give a damn

about a concert?"

She'd tried her best, but anger still shone in his dark eyes. "Perhaps not, but your fans surely do."

"I'm touched you're so considerate of their feelings, but I sure wish you gave a damn about mine."

Before she could respond, Jeremy left the bathroom to join them. Eager to escape Griffin's ire, Darcy walked up to the front door to look out. "The water's reached the sandbags, and if it keeps raining this hard, the place is bound to flood."

What Griffin heard was not merely a quick diversion, but a heartbreaking weariness that made him regret being so sharp with her. "Why don't you go upstairs and take a nap on Christy Joy's couch? The captain and I can handle the shop."

Darcy remained by the door. "No, I couldn't sleep."

Griffin walked up behind her and rested his hands lightly on her shoulders. "Just think of us as part of your crew. You don't mind ordering them around." He took her hand then and led her to the stairs. "Just give it a try. Go on."

The candlelight gave the whole scene an eerie otherworldly glow, and to escape his dark gaze, if for no other reason, she gave in. "All right, but if the shop floods, you must promise to call me."

"Sure." Griffin watched her slowly climb the stairs and couldn't help but wonder when she'd last had a good night's sleep. His stomach began to rumble and, distracted by hunger, he doubted any of Monarch Bay's fine restaurants made deliveries by boat. Then he realized they wouldn't have any power to cook either, which was another problem he couldn't solve.

Christy Joy rubbed her daughter's back, but Twink had thrown herself across her bed and stubbornly refused to acknowledge her mother's presence. Rain pelted the window, but the faint ray of light falling across the braided rug only made Christy Joy feel more disheartened. Twink and the shop were her whole world, and she was ashamed to want still more.

"I know you were shocked to see me kissing Jeremy, but honestly, sweetheart, he's such a nice man, and when I had the chance, I just couldn't resist."

172

Twink rose slightly. "You kissed him?"

Pleased to have piqued her curiosity, Christy continued, "Yes, I sure did. He's so shy that I was afraid he'd never kiss me, and I was really curious about how he'd kiss."

"Is he better than Daddy?"

J. Lyle definitely knew how to kiss, but Jeremy had responded with a passion she'd never tasted with her ex-husband. "That's a tough question. Daddy's awfully good."

"Then why don't you love him anymore?"

She and J. Lyle had separated when Twink was only two and a half, but she'd expected her to raise some tough questions soon. Now she wished she'd prepared some answers which would make sense to the dear little girl.

"We hadn't known each other long when we married, which was a mistake, but we were lucky enough to have you right away. I had such fun being your mommy, and I began thinking about opening a wonderful shop where I could sell all sorts of pretty things. Your daddy didn't want me to work, though. He insisted that I spend my time entertaining clients and attending all the wonderful parties in San Francisco.

"So you see, except for you, we just didn't want the same things. Neither of us was happy, and we can be much better parents apart."

Twink's lower lip was still stuck out in a defiant pout, but she didn't ask another question and, relieved, Christy Joy stretched out beside her. "Let's rest for a little while. Maybe when we wake up, the power will be on again, and we can make some popcorn."

Twink snuggled against her mother, and in a moment she was asleep, but Christy Joy was wide awake. She and J. Lyle shared custody of their daughter, but he'd never made more than an occasional visit to see her. Still, when she'd left him, he'd been furious and sworn that she would come to regret it. It had been more threat than prediction, and she feared if he could have a hand in forcing that regret, then he would gladly use Twink to do so.

Her head began to ache, and she got up to take some aspirin and saw Darcy asleep on the couch. She covered her with a quilt, then went on downstairs.

"Are you hungry?" she asked the men. "I can make some sandwiches."

"That would be great," Griffin replied.

"I don't want to be any trouble," Jeremy hedged. "Or any more, at least."

"No, it will give me something to do other than wring my hands. Just give me a minute."

Jeremy watched her climb the stairs. She was dressed in a pretty pink jumper as though she'd expected to deal with customers all day. "Christy Joy," he called softly. "Better put on something warm."

She waved to him and disappeared into her apartment, and he turned to find Griffin eying him with an indulgent smile. "What? It's cold in here."

"It sure is, and I'd go out and get us some coffee, if there were shops open. What we need is a generator."

"I've got one on my boat, but by the time I walked back here with something I'd cooked, it would be cold."

"With a little more rain, you may be able to moor the *Great Escape* down at the corner."

"How'd you know the name of my boat?"

Griffin made a point of knowing things, but he hadn't been showing off. "Darcy must have mentioned it when you took her out whale watching." He turned away to look out the side door on the nursery, where the water was streaming around the plants placed near the building. "My memory just naturally collects odd bits of trivia."

"How's it look out there?"

"Terrible. What's the weather report for the next few days?"

Jeremy paced the shop's center aisle. "More rain. It's been such a mild spring. That just makes this storm all the worse."

"It will blow over eventually," Griffin offered. They'd been clearing shelves and moving stock to the rear of the shop, but now he wondered if they shouldn't be carrying things upstairs. "They have some expensive computer equipment. If we can't keep the water out, that ought to go upstairs first."

"Sure," Jeremy agreed. "I suppose the water could reach the counter. Just how solid is this building?"

"I asked that question myself before I bought it, and it's very well built. The wood on the exterior is there for show."

"Good, because I sure wouldn't want the roof to cave in on us."

"Now you sound like Darcy, and worry never changes anything."

"Which is probably a good thing," Christy Joy added on her way down the stairs with a tray laden with sandwiches. She had two bottles of water in the pockets of her pink ruffled apron. "I hope you don't mind wheat bread. It's all I buy. I had plenty of cold cuts, but I'll make peanut butter and jelly if anyone wants it."

"This is fine," Griffin assured her, and he helped himself to a ham sandwich and a bottle of water. "I'll just take this up front where I can keep an eye on the storm."

"Yeah, you do that," Jeremy encouraged.

Christy Joy had changed into a pair of Levi's and a pink sweater. She sat on the stairs and looped her arms around her knees. "I ate earlier with Twink. Come sit here beside me."

Jeremy sat on the same step, but he kept his distance. He took a bite of his ham and cheese sandwich, had trouble swallowing and had to wash it down with water. "Look, about earlier—"

"Don't you dare apologize. I kissed you first, not the other way around. It was wonderful, by the way."

Her smile was so very lovely, Jeremy wished he could have kissed her all day. "Yeah, I thought so too, but obviously Twink didn't."

"Twink's only four and, while she is very bright, it's natural that she'd be confused. I've told her only good things about her father, you see."

"That's very kind of you."

"It's not merely kind, it's smart. I don't want her to grow up disliking men."

"You needn't tell me any painful stories."

"I realize that, but let me say my ex-husband never expected me to make a success of Defy the World. He gave me a generous settlement, but still, he thought I'd do poorly at running a business, spend the money foolishly, and beg him to take me back."

"He didn't know you very well, did he?" Jeremy took another bite of his sandwich. It was the best he'd ever eaten.

"He didn't know me at all," Christy Joy confided softly. "But then, he wasn't the man I thought him to be either. Oh, I knew he was ambitious, but ruthless is a more accurate term. His law practice didn't leave much time for a wife and family, but when we were together, he expected a perfection I had no desire to achieve. So rather than become his version of a Stepford Wife, I left him. It's not an insult he'll ever forgive."

Christy Joy paused and, while Jeremy nodded thoughtfully, he offered no insight of his own. Nor did he volunteer any regrets over any of his past relationships. She knew him to be quiet, but his silence now provided ample evidence that she'd said too much. Embarrassed, she rose hastily to her feet.

"I'm sorry. I didn't mean to burden you. Please excuse me, I need to check on Twink."

She hurried up the stairs before Jeremy could swallow a mouthful of sandwich and assure her she was wrong. His appetite gone, he finished the sandwich anyway rather than waste the time and money it had cost her to make it.

When she'd visited his boat, he'd greeted the fact that she'd confided her fears for Defy the World's future as a sign she really did trust him. Now it seemed that she'd changed her mind, and he didn't understand why.

He could just make out Griffin's silhouette against the front window. That guy was so damn slick, while he was about as smooth as a scrap of sandpaper. The candle on the counter had begun to sputter, but when he rose to find another, he spotted a trickle of water inching across the floor.

"Griff, get back here," he yelled.

Griffin was at his elbow in an instant. "I didn't think we were in much danger of flooding from the side. Come on, let's go back outside and see what we can do to divert the water from the building."

"Maybe we can use another tarp and some plants to block the door."

Griffin yanked on his coat and hat. "Let's hope so, or we'll just have to lie down in front of the door and block it ourselves."

Jeremy's shout pierced Darcy's restless dreams, and she rolled off the couch, tripped and bumped her knee hard on the floor. By the time she recovered from the sharp burst of pain and hobbled down the stairs, the men were already outside. Even in the dying candle's faint glow, she saw the water pooling near the counter and understood where they'd gone.

They'd all been so concerned about the front of the shop flooding, clearly they hadn't given enough attention to the nursery side. "Oh damn!" she cried, for if water was backing up into the nursery, then her office was sure to flood. Terrified she might already have lost all her work, she tore out the door without bothering with a coat.

Chapter Thirteen

When Christy Joy had first approached her about going into business together, Darcy had begun keeping a journal to record their hopes and dreams as well as their practical concerns. Those initial discussions had led to the creation of a well-defined business plan. There had been no question of trust between them, but they'd still taken the precaution of hiring an attorney to draw up their partnership agreement.

Darcy's copy was in the file cabinet in her office, but before she could reach it, Griffin grabbed her and lifted her clear off her feet.

"You're likely to drown out here. Go back inside."

"But my office—"

"I'll see it doesn't flood. There's a dip by the door into the shop, that's why the water's leaking under it, but there's a step up into your office so it's in no immediate danger."

"Well, maybe not immediate, but—"

Griffin put her down at the side door. "As soon as you're inside, we'll block off this door and come back inside from the back stairs. Just leave everything to me, Darcy. I won't let you down."

She nodded numbly, went back inside and got the mop to clean up the water that had seeped inside. Once she'd finished, she kept a close watch, but whatever Griffin and Jeremy had devised was working, and there was no more evidence of the torrent outside.

The front was also still dry, but with constant checking the next hour passed in a watery blur. When Griffin and Jeremy finally came back inside, she was seated at the children's table with her head resting on crossed arms. She sat up at the sound of their voices, but couldn't bring herself to rise.

Griffin sat on the stairs. "There were firemen at the corner laying out sandbags, and we talked them out of a few. The water's still rushing right through the nursery, but we've banked the flow toward the center and away from the building. The pottery shed is definitely leaning, but with any luck it won't collapse and we can shore it up once the rain stops."

Darcy eased back slowly in the small chair. "If we had any luck at all, the rain wouldn't have lasted more than an hour or two."

"Don't get all excited, but the sky appears to be clearing."

"I'm too tired to get excited about anything," she murmured and put her head back down on her arms.

"Why don't you go on home and sleep for a couple of hours?"

It was a very tempting suggestion, but she couldn't leave. "No, I'll stay here."

Christy Joy had been coming down the stairs every few minutes to check on things and had offered her one of the sandwiches, but her stomach was tied up in knots. She doubted she was being of much use to anyone, but at least she was there. When Griffin bent to kiss her cheek, she sat up in surprise.

"Sorry, I didn't mean to disturb you. You just looked so sweet, I didn't think you'd mind."

His lips had been cool against her cheek, and now she was positive he was going to be sick. "Take off your coat and hat, and I'll give you another sweatshirt if that one's wet."

"No, thanks, it's still dry. What about yours, Captain?"

Jeremy was seated on the top step. He just shook his head. "I'm fine."

"Neither of you is fine, and you know it," Darcy insisted. "Maybe we can heat some water over scented candles and make you some tea. How did people keep warm before they had electricity?"

"They lit fires, but that's not a good idea in here," Griffin responded with a deep chuckle.

"No, it sure isn't, but maybe I can talk the landlord into putting in a fireplace."

Griffin laughed again and removed his hat, gloves and coat.

"I hear the guy's totally unreasonable, so I doubt he'd go for it."

Jeremy laughed with them, then sprang to his feet when Christy Joy appeared at the top of the stairs. "How's Twink?"

"She's asleep, which is a good place to be on such a rainy afternoon."

"I agree, and it's nice being on dry land too."

He sure didn't look dry, though and, forgetting her earlier disappointment in his reticence to confide in her, Christy Joy brought him a towel and tossed one down to Griffin. The telephone rang in her apartment, and she hurried to answer before it woke her daughter. When she returned, she was near tears.

"That was J. Lyle. He heard how hard it was raining here and that the power had gone out. He wanted to make certain Twink was all right. I assured him she was snug in her bed, but he went on a rant about a cold, dark apartment. He said he was on his way to get her and hung up."

Darcy left her place at the children's table and started up the stairs. "Please don't be upset. He probably won't be able to reach us in this weather."

"You know J. Lyle, he'll rent an amphibious vehicle if he has to, but he'll be sure to arrive in a few hours."

Jeremy reached out for her hand and gave her fingers a fond squeeze. "Doesn't Twink ever visit her dad?"

"Sure she does, but those are scheduled visits, unlike today, which he'll undoubtedly describe as a damn rescue."

"How big a guy is he?" Griffin inquired.

"He's six feet tall, one hundred-eighty pounds, and he runs and belongs to a gym. What are you thinking, that you'll just punch him out?"

"That could get messy," Griffin offered, "but it will help that there're two of us."

Christy Joy just shook her head. "He'll call you Popeye, Jeremy, I can hear it already."

"It won't be the first time, but I've always been rather fond of Popeye and don't regard it as an insult. Of course, if you'd rather I weren't here when he arrives, I'll wait in Darcy's office until he leaves."

Christy Joy slipped her hand from his, sat on the top step and hugged her knees. "Wouldn't you rather return to your boat? At least there you could make some hot soup and have a bunk to lie down."

"What, and miss out on all this fun?" Jeremy sat beside her and gave her a hug. "No, ma'am, I'm staying right here."

Darcy looked toward Griffin, who was observing her with a curious glance, but he made no such cheerful declaration, and she was too proud to let him know how much she liked having him there. His presence was a comfort until a rumbling blast of thunder shook the whole building.

"That was too close!" Christy Joy cried.

"I thought you said it was clearing up," Darcy reminded Griffin.

"I meant it at the time, but clearly weather forecasting isn't an exact science."

Darcy left the stairs to check the front door but the situation hadn't worsened. She strained to see the shops on the opposite side of the street, but there wasn't so much as a candle's glow from any of them. Maybe their owners were working frantically in the dark to prevent flooding, but there was no evidence of it from where she stood. She was about to turn away when Griffin came up behind her.

"Do you think we're going to end up sitting on the roof like those poor flood victims in the Midwest?" she asked.

"Probably not."

His voice was softly reassuring even if his words were not. "Well, I wish we had an inflatable raft handy just in case."

"Darcy, look at me."

She swallowed hard before she turned toward him, then still had to force herself to look up. There was barely enough light for her to see him clearly, but he looked too serious to mistake his mood.

"I meant what I said about playing on the same team," he whispered, "and I wasn't simply referring to sweatshirts. I'm looking for a lot more from you. Is it just this building that holds you back?"

"Is that a trick question?"

Griffin drew in a deep breath. "I'm doing my best here, Darcy. Help me out."

That Griffin Moore would even make an appeal for sympathy made it difficult to form a coherent reply. "Let's not do this now, please. I'm too tired to think straight on any subject, let alone one as important as this."

She was still wearing the pretty quarter note necklace he'd given her, which was far more revealing than her hesitant excuses. He leaned down and kissed her lightly, pulled her into his arms and rested his cheek against her shiny dark hair.

"All right, we'll postpone that discussion, but for now, I've realized this is a poor location for a recording studio. It's not been difficult to move your stock to the back and, if we need to, we can carry the bird houses, garden angels, ceramic fountains and all the other cute stuff upstairs. The electronic equipment I'd planned to install for recording would be next to impossible to move, to say nothing of the concert grand I'd intended to buy."

"You could put everything upstairs," Darcy murmured against his chest. While he sounded sincere, she refused to get her hopes up only to have them shattered with the first ray of sunshine.

"No, there's not enough room. I'd have to be on the ground floor, and this rain has proven that's simply not practical."

"Storms this bad don't come along often."

"It would only take one to ruin a significant amount of work. I'm not willing to take that risk. I'll extend your lease another year, or five, if you like. What do you say?"

Darcy snuggled against him rather than admit it might already be too late to save Defy the World with the losses they'd sustained that week alone. Perversely, she wished he'd chosen to extend the lease simply because he loved her far too much to crush her dreams. Still, whatever his reason, she was too grateful for his change of heart to quibble over the cause.

"I'm overwhelmed. Give me a minute or two to get used to the idea, and then I'll thank you properly."

Griffin grasped her shoulders and took a step back. "Have you eaten anything today?"

"No, but—"

"Either go upstairs and make yourself a sandwich, or go back to sleep on the couch."

"I don't recall putting you in command here."

"You did when you called me this morning. Now look, if you're too tired to think, you're much too tired to put in any more work, should your help be needed."

He was right, of course, and a wide yawn stopped what would have been only a token argument at best. "Maybe I could do with another little nap," she agreed reluctantly. It seemed as though she'd merely lain down when hours later J. Lyle woke her with a frantic pounding on the backdoor.

Christy Joy ran up the stairs with the flashlight to let him in. He was dressed in a trench coat and hat, and wrestling with a black umbrella. He pushed past her to drip water in a splattering oval all around them.

"I had to park the car a couple of blocks away and walk into town. A policeman tried to stop me at the corner, but when I explained why I was here, he told me that you'd reported Catherine missing last week. Why wasn't I called before the police?"

Christy Joy fought not to cringe under his accusing frown. "We found her almost immediately," she swore. "Really, there was no need to upset you."

"Oh no? How did you expect me to react when I finally found out about it? Never mind, it's plain you'd no intention of ever admitting you can't keep track of our daughter."

Darcy had been a bridesmaid at their wedding and seen J. Lyle on several occasions since. He'd never been one of her favorite people, and now she liked him even less. While fair-haired and blue-eyed, he was as striking an individual as Griffin. Unlike Griffin, however, who appeared largely uninterested in his remarkable good looks, J. Lyle made a point of dressing as well as any *GQ* model. She couldn't even imagine him in a pair of Levi's.

Upset by how rumpled she must appear, she stepped out of the apartment just as Twink bounded up the stairs and leapt into her father's arms.

"Catherine! I'm all wet," he scolded. He set her down quickly and pushed her away. "You're coming home with me. Help your mother pack your things."

J. Lyle recognized Darcy standing in the shadows and nodded curtly. "Why make yourself miserable here, Christy Joy? You and Darcy should come home with us."

"Thank you, but no," Darcy replied.

Griffin had heard more than enough and, seeing how easily Twink had distracted her father, he climbed the stairs and extended his hand. "Good evening, I'm Griffin Moore."

At first startled, J. Lyle's expression slid from pinched spite into a relaxed grin. "It really is you, isn't it?" He pumped Griffin's hand warmly. "I attended one of your concerts last year in San Francisco. Transcendent is the only way to describe the whole experience. I've bought several of your CDs. I had no idea you lived here in Monarch Bay."

Darcy caught Christy Joy's eye and shook her head. Her ex-husband was doing his best to schmooze Griffin, but he would have overheard the way J. Lyle had greeted Christy Joy and Twink and not been pleased by it. Expecting the worst, Darcy held her breath.

Rather than respond to J. Lyle, Griffin looked to Christy Joy. "Would you like to send Twink home with her father for a few days while we clean up here?" he asked.

Christy Joy rolled her lower lip through her teeth. "If you're sure you'll have a safe trip home, J. Lyle, it might be best."

"Well, of course we'll have a safe trip," he assured her. "My Mercedes is a big, solid sedan and less than a year old. I brought along a car seat too."

"All right then," Christy Joy murmured softly, and she took Twink's hand to lead her back to her bedroom to pack a bag.

"I can't tell you how surprised I am to find you here, Griffin," J. Lyle continued. "How long have you known my wife?"

"A few weeks," Griffin explained. "I'm seeing Darcy."

J. Lyle's eyes widened slightly, and his glance again swept Darcy's sleep-spiked hair. "Really? I wouldn't have thought, but then, who you date is no concern of mine."

"No, it most certainly isn't," Darcy interjected sharply. "It can't rain much longer. When the power returns, we'll have the shop cleaned up in no time. We can come up to your place to get Twink, or would you rather bring her home yourself?"

"When the time is right, I'll bring her back to Monarch Bay," J. Lyle responded smoothly.

His response was too vague to please Darcy and, perplexed, she wondered what had happened to Jeremy. She quickly decided it was just as well if he stayed out of sight. Of course, she would have been happier had the captain punched out a few of J. Lyle's sparkling white teeth, but had he risked it, the smug attorney would surely have sued in an effort to take his boat and livelihood.

That was what she really disliked about J. Lyle—there was

a hint of a threat in his every word. Except for his fawning attempts to impress Griffin, he'd been as thoroughly disagreeable as always. How he'd ever remained pleasant long enough to win Christy Joy's heart was a mystery.

Twink rejoined them carrying a pink Barbie suitcase. She was wearing a slick pink raincoat over her overalls and a pink rain hat. She appeared to be happy to be going off for a visit at her father's home, but the door had barely closed behind them when Christy Joy burst into tears.

"I'm sorry," she choked out. "I know he'll take better care of her than I can here in the dark, but I miss her already."

Jeremy climbed the stairs with a slow, deliberate step. "I didn't want to make more trouble for you than you already have, but I swear if I ever hear that son-of-a-bitch speak to you in such a disrespectful tone again, he'll think Popeye was a wimp."

Christy Joy pulled a tissue from her pocket and dabbed her eyes. "Please, Jeremy, I appreciate your gallant offer, but you mustn't touch him or he'll squash you with a lawsuit he'll drag out for years just to bleed you dry."

"It would be worth it to teach him some manners," Jeremy swore.

Christy Joy shook her head. "Oh no, it wouldn't. Now is it my imagination, or is the rain finally slacking off?"

Griffin went by her to peer out the backdoor. "It's still raining, but not as hard. If you have anything left to make sandwiches, let's light a few more candles and have ourselves a party."

Darcy doubted any of them felt in a party mood, but forty-five minutes later they were seated on the rug around Christy Joy's coffee table toasting marshmallows over jasmine candles. They were using wooden skewers, and it took forever, but it only added to the general silliness of their mood. Darcy marveled at how easily Griffin had teased a smile from Christy Joy and, once he'd accomplished that feat, Jeremy had broken out in a grin.

Darcy consumed only half a cheese sandwich and quit eating after dripping a single gooey marshmallow into her mouth. "Damn, but these are good."

"Thank you, ma'am," Griffin replied. He had two marshmallows on his skewer now and turned them slowly over the flame. "This is as close to camping out as I care to get, but it's gratifying to have my clumsy efforts rewarded."

Christy Joy licked her fingers. "I wish we had some chocolate bars and graham crackers to make 'smores. Remind me to stock up on some, Darcy, so next time the power fails we'll be ready."

"Will do. Oh by the way, Griffin's decided to extend our lease. Do you want to go for another year or five?"

"What?" Christy Joy shrieked.

Jeremy cocked his head and regarded the pianist with a decidedly skeptical glance before nodding. "That's real good news."

"I'd kiss you, but Darcy might object," Christy Joy added. "I'm not going to ask why you've changed your mind, but it's really appreciated."

"You're welcome." Griffin winked at Darcy. "I had my reasons."

Clearly he preferred to let Christy Joy and Jeremy believe love had prompted his generosity, and she was too relieved they weren't bailing water to reveal the truth. "Is there enough light to play cards?" she asked instead.

"Sure," Jeremy responded. "I've always loved Go Fish."

He was joking, of course, and they all knew it. "You guys finish the marshmallows first. I want to check the doors."

Darcy's knee complained a bit as she rose to her feet, but she walked out smoothly. She grabbed the flashlight and carried it downstairs to survey the shop, but the floor was still dry. Grateful, she remained by the front door and scanned the street. It was so dark now she could no longer see the water flowing past, but only hear a sizzling rush.

Within minutes, Griffin joined her. "I don't like J. Lyle," he whispered softly. "What's your take on him?"

Darcy leaned back against him and, when he unsnapped the button on her Levi's, her breath caught in her throat. She had to force herself to inhale deeply to respond.

"He has a nasty streak a mile wide, and while I wouldn't dream of saying as much to Christy Joy, I'm afraid he might not bring Twink back."

Griffin slid his hand inside her panties and down over the flat hollow of her stomach. When he reached the triangle of curls, he tugged gently, then parted her clef. He teased her inner lips with a fluttering touch before bracing her hips against his thigh and plunging a finger deep inside.

He nuzzled her ear. "Maybe I should have let him think I was dating Christy Joy."

She felt herself growing wet and reached back to encircle his thigh. "Not a good idea."

He withdrew to stroke her clit with her own slippery wetness, then slid two fingers up inside her. "Still, it might have made him think twice about questioning their custody agreement."

His erection was impossible to mistake, and she writhed against him to supply some distracting friction. "No, when he slants everything to his advantage, we ought to stick with the truth."

"Which is?"

It was on the tip of her tongue, but as her inner muscles began to quiver along his maddeningly playful fingers, the thought was lost. He was simply too good at turning her insides to hot cream, and she thrust down on his next stroke and came with a sudden shudder.

She grabbed hold of his wrist to prevent him from withdrawing before the last tingling bit of ecstasy faded, and he cradled her in such a tender grasp, she felt as though she were floating. It really wasn't fair, she mused silently. No man should have such remarkable gifts, but at least he used them beautifully.

Jeremy sucked Christy Joy's fingers into his mouth to catch the last taste of marshmallow. "The power ought to fail more often," he murmured against her palm.

His lips tickled her skin, but despite the good news from Griffin, she'd never felt less like laughing. Jeremy's hair had dried in boyish curls, and she smoothed it softly with her free hand.

"I didn't send Twink away for this," she whispered.

Jeremy straightened with an ungainly jerk. "Do you think I'm taking advantage here?"

"No." He appeared incredulous, and she caressed his now

beard-roughened cheek. It had been so long since she'd touched a man, and she promptly withdrew her hand rather than appear pathetically needy.

"Well, you'd be right," Jeremy confessed. "Twink's adorable. Anyone would love her, but do you ever leave her with a sitter and go out on dates?"

Christy Joy sat back. "When no one's asked me out, I haven't needed a sitter."

"Sorry, my mistake. Let's go out to dinner just as soon as the weather clears."

"As long as I can sleep a couple of days first, I'd love to have dinner with you. Then I'll make supper for us here. I'm really a good cook when the power's on."

"I'm sure you are, but are you certain you want to commit to a second date before we've been out on our first?"

She glanced toward the doorway. "I'll risk it. What do you suppose has happened to Griffin and Darcy?"

"Just this," Jeremy whispered before his lips met hers.

She froze for an instant, then relaxed against him. His kiss was absolutely luscious, and she was positive this was unlike J. Lyle, no trick of technique, but sincere affection. Determined not to break his heart while hers was scarcely whole, she broke away.

"Please, I've been numb for so long, and—"

"I know numb," he responded. "But the first time I saw you, well, let's not even go there."

His smile had turned shy and, while flattered, she wouldn't press him for more. "You must have been very handsome in your cruise ship uniforms. I'll bet the female passengers trailed after you like ducklings."

He laughed at her compliment. "That they did, but I built up quite a tolerance to them. They were just out for a good time on their vacation and regarded me as one of the specialty items on the menu."

"But you weren't?"

"No, ma'am, I have my standards, but that wasn't true for all the officers, and many were more than willing to fulfill an attractive passenger's fantasies."

"I've never been interested in casual affairs," she confided. "But it's desperately difficult to really connect with someone."

His smile turned teasing. "That all depends. How am I doing?"

She hadn't imagined Jeremy could be so charming, and it was easy to respond truthfully. "Very well, actually. I just need a little time. I hear footsteps on the stairs, so I better find the cards."

She rose with her usual grace, and Jeremy licked his lips rather than drool. Her ruffled pinafores hid the length of her legs, but he couldn't wait to have them wrapped around him. But for now, he was happy just to keep her company.

The foursome played gin rummy until they could no longer count the spots on the cards. Then they made a last check of doors and windows for leaks and, finding none, treated themselves to peanut butter and jelly sandwiches with apple juice.

Darcy was relieved to have made it through the day with no major disasters, but even cradled beneath a blanket in Griffin's arms on the couch, she couldn't doze off while the wind slammed the eucalyptus tree against the roof with strange syncopated thumps.

Griffin shifted positions so often it was clear he wasn't resting comfortably either. While opposite them, Christy Joy, who hadn't invited Jeremy into her own bed, was nevertheless stretched out beside him on the rug. The pair had barely finished arranging their blankets and pillows before they'd fallen asleep.

When Griffin leaned around her to put out the last candle, Darcy whispered, "I haven't stayed up this late since college."

"It's been a while since I partied until dawn too," Griffin added.

"I was up studying," she emphasized. "Have you ever had to work hard to learn anything?"

After a long silence, he confided softly, "I'm not much of a cook."

Darcy clamped her hand over her mouth rather than laugh and wake their companions. "You can read, that's all cooking requires."

"There's a lot more to it than simply assembling ingredients. That's why some chefs are better than others. They rely on an originality and flair that I lack."

"Is that your only flaw?"

He hugged her tight. "The only one I'll admit."

For the remainder of the night, they teased each other with softly spoken questions and entertaining, if not downright silly, replies. When the rising sun finally lit the apartment with a pale yellow glow, the wind and rain were gone, and the water had begun to recede in the alleys and streets.

Anxious to check on his own home, Griffin coaxed Darcy to her feet. "Let's take the day off to allow the last of the water to run into the sea, and work straightening up here tomorrow. By then the power ought to be back on, and the clean-up will be a whole lot easier."

Christy Joy was already awake and, hearing their voices, she rolled out of her tangled blanket and led them out to the stairs. "Jeremy doesn't look as though he'll wake before noon, so taking today off is fine with me. I'll call George, the clerks and the kids to let them know we won't be needing them today. Why don't you two go on home?"

Darcy had seldom heard a better suggestion, but when Griffin walked her to her door, he followed her right inside. "Grab some of your lacy lingerie and a change of clothes. You're coming home with me."

"I don't think that's such a good idea. Neither of us got any sleep last night, and—"

"That's all we'll do then," he promised, but when they reached his house and found the hill still had power, they made a detour through his spacious shower.

This time Griffin shampooed Darcy's hair, but when she began to spread soapy foam over his chest, she inspired the predictable erotic result. "Looks like you've got more than sleep on your mind after all," she responded.

"I would have been fine if you'd just kept your hands to yourself."

"Around you? Never." But she had to grab for his shoulders as he lifted her off her feet. Parting her thighs, he entered her with a single, slick slide, and she wound her legs around his hips to hang on. Steam billowed around them, as though they were making love in a warm, spice-scented cloud.

He kissed her deeply and slid a hand between them to rub her in time with his thrusts. Riding that shimmering thrill, she bent her head to nip at his shoulder. He quickly caught her mouth again and shoved her back against the tile. For a long, breathless moment, he held her hips still, then with a final deep lunge, he carried her along with him into a release so intense he had to grab for the shower head to remain on his feet.

Also overwhelmed with an aching pleasure, Darcy slid from his embrace, left the shower enclosure and caught a thick velour towel on her way to bed. Still dripping wet, she flopped across the towel and, with no more than a satisfied moan, fell asleep.

Equally sated, Griffin paused to rinse off the soap bubbles before leaving the shower. He wrapped a black towel around his hips, then hesitated at the doorway. He planned to join Darcy for a very long nap and then start over right where they'd left off, but first, he had to check for messages from Interpol.

Just as he'd suspected, they were provoked with him for not remaining in contact, but he refused to offer what would have been a totally insincere apology. His monitor filled with a photo-montage of the woman who had introduced herself as Adriana LeMer in Chicago. Some were posed, as she was indeed a haute couture model, while others were candid shots taken in a variety of European cities.

Only the last photo interested Griffin, for it showed her walking along a Paris street hand-in-hand with Lyman Vaughn. He didn't need any further interpretation from Interpol's experts to recognize Simon Jordan and Lyman Vaughn were one and the same.

That meant he had no choice about playing the private concert in Paris, but far more troubling was his promise to Darcy not to lie.

Chapter Fourteen

Hunger woke Darcy shortly after noon. Nearly a forgotten sensation, it took her a moment to place the gnawing emptiness for what it was. She dimly recalled a late night peanut butter sandwich, but now she could almost taste a turkey dinner with all the trimmings.

She turned and found Griffin, his head propped on his hand, observing her. He was clean shaven, his hair combed, but clad only in a towel.

She yawned and whipped the bedspread up over her bare backside. "Why didn't you wake me?"

Griffin reached out to caress her cheek. "I needed the time to think."

Alarmed by his solemn mood, Darcy sat up and twisted the cream-colored bedspread across her breasts. "Look, if you want me to leave, I'll just go."

Griffin shook his head, reached for her and whispered against her lips, "No, this is what I want."

His kiss was sweetly insistent. He traced her lips with the tip of his tongue, then angled kisses along her jaw and down her throat to the soft hollow where his necklace lay. He licked her collar bones, then slid lower to peel away the bedspread and suckle at her breasts.

Blissfully distracted, Darcy arched her back to lean into him. She wound her fingers in his hair, then spread her hands across his shoulders as he moved lower still.

With an easy shift of position, he moved between her legs, slid her knees over his shoulders and dipped a finger into her slit to smooth the way before he began to tease her with his tongue. He lapped gently, then slipped inside her with quick jabs. All the while, he caressed her thighs and breasts with a feather-light touch.

Darcy raised her arms above her head to grasp the headboard and rolled her hips to move with him. He reached up to pinch her nipples, and she flexed her inner muscles to slow his strokes. That he was always such an adoring lover was a constant thrill, and her slow smile spread wide as she plotted how best to return the favor.

In no rush, he paused frequently to allow the delicious sensations he created to subside before he again brought her close to the inevitable peak. Her appreciative moans inspired him to shift his position again to tease her sensitive folds with the smooth head of his cock. He rocked above her, intent upon satisfying them both, and when her breath came in short grateful bursts, he thrust deep and rode the ripples of ecstasy shooting through her until they overflowed into him as well.

Locked in his arms, Darcy lay in a languid daze until she felt him stir. Then she blew softly against his ear and whispered, "If making love gets any better, I sure hope you know CPR."

Griffin propped himself on his elbows and looked down at her. "I assume that was a compliment, but you're a powerful inspiration."

Darcy would have said he was awfully tempting himself, but a puzzling shadow crossed his smile and stopped her. "You've got more than sex on your mind. Are you sorry you offered to extend our lease?"

"No, not at all. We do need to talk, though, but not here." He rolled off the bed and rewrapped his towel low on his hips. "You get dressed first, and I'll check the kitchen. There has to be something we can eat."

He was the most direct individual she'd ever known, but he'd glanced away as he'd spoken, and she knew instinctively that something was wrong. She rose on her knees and called to him before he reached the door.

"Hey, did you bring me up here just to say good-bye?"

Griffin rested his hand on the doorjamb. "If you think that was a sample of my good-byes, then your thinking's so muddled you need breakfast worse than I do. Now hurry up and get dressed."

Rather than point out he was again being evasive, Darcy

entered the bathroom, but she hadn't been fooled. Her heart fell as she realized how swiftly he might demand something from her in exchange for the new lease. Appalled to be so cynical, she took her time getting downstairs.

When she entered the kitchen, Griffin was peeling an avocado and nodded toward a glass of orange juice on the counter. "Help yourself. I meant to buy some tea for you, but I can't remember when I last went to the market. But even without much talent as a chef, I've enough here to make us another passable omelet."

"Anything with avocado is fine with me." Darcy didn't really care what he made when he looked so damn good half-dressed. She took a sip of juice and pulled up a stool. "Tell me what's bothering you. I promise not to pitch a plate at you."

"That's a relief." He took the carton of eggs from the gleaming refrigerator and set them on the counter. "I have to play that private concert in Paris after all, and I hate to go away again so soon."

"You have to play the concert? Why? Oh Griffin, do you have money problems too?"

He laughed at her question and began to crack half a dozen eggs, drop them into a stainless steel mixing bowl and toss the shells into the sink. "Why don't you grate some cheese? Then maybe you can listen without leaping to such ridiculous conclusions."

Darcy found the block of cheddar and grater easily enough, but she still wasn't happy. "Look, this house has to have cost you a fortune, and you're cutting back on your concert schedule. It's only logical that you might have to watch your expenses."

"All right, I'll concede the point, but if you'd stop interrupting me, maybe I'd have a better chance of explaining clearly."

"I once dated a psychologist who accused me of interrupting him when all I meant to interject was a polite comment to assure him I was listening. It was obvious to me then that what he really wanted was a worshipful audience, not a conversation, and I refused to return his calls."

"Fine, you've warned me. There's a timer on the stove. Shall we set it for a couple of minutes each and take turns?"

Darcy sent him a deeply resentful glance. "Where's the

omelet pan? I'm going to whomp you upside the head with it."

Ignoring her request, Griffin pulled a whisk from the utensil drawer and attacked the eggs. "Am I supposed to have a special pan to make an omelet? Can't I use any old frying pan I have handy?"

Darcy glanced around the spotless kitchen. "I doubt you have anything here more than a couple of months old. Which is beside the point, of course. Just tell me why you feel you must play the private concert in Paris and be done with it."

Griffin shook his head. "I should get dressed first. It wouldn't be proper to come to the table without a shirt."

"This is your house, Griffin, you can make clothing optional if you choose."

"Not when you look so pretty in that lavender sweater." He set the bowl of eggs on the counter and backed away. "It won't take me but a minute to dress. Add whatever you want to spice up the eggs."

"Another diversion," Darcy muttered under her breath, but she found a bell pepper and onion in the refrigerator and began browning them in a pan. She'd never cooked on a commercial-size stove, and it was somewhat intimidating. Still, the bell pepper and onion were browning nicely by the time Griffin returned in Levi's and a blue chambray shirt.

"That smells awfully good already," he said. "Why don't you fix the omelet? I'll set our places at the counter."

"Fine, but first, is there any bread for toast?"

Griffin found a loaf of wheat bread he'd tossed in the freezer, pulled out four slices and buttered them. "I hate to go away again," he murmured softly. "But I'll make every effort to get back as quickly as I can."

Darcy moved the pan off the fire. "I'm unlikely to forget you in a week or two, but that's not your real worry, is it?"

Griffin slid the bread into the toaster oven and turned the dial. "Let's eat and then talk. Maybe you don't need the strength, but I sure do."

Giving in, Darcy replaced the pan on the fire, gave it a minute to reheat, and then poured in the eggs. When they began to set, she added the avocado slices and grated cheese.

"An omelet pan is hinged in the middle to make flipping half over a cinch, but it isn't all that difficult to do it with a pancake turner."

Griffin paid close attention as she gave a quick demonstration. "You've eaten one of my omelets. Short of dropping it on the floor, once you've got it cooked, does it really matter how it looks when it hits the plate?"

"A chef in a fancy restaurant would be big on presentation and undoubtedly shriek at your question, but I'm with you. This will taste as delicious as it smells, and that's what matters."

Griffin set their places and, as soon as Darcy had split the omelet between two plates, with his the far more generous portion, he added toast and carried them to the counter. He ate half of his before she'd swallowed more than a single taste.

"I'm going to buy a generator for your building," he said between bites of toast. "And lay in a supply of food, so the next time there's a storm, you'll be able to make more than a sandwich."

"I didn't realize you were so hungry."

"Don't say anything to Christy Joy. We were lucky she could feed us what she did, so I'm not complaining. I just want to plan ahead is all."

He opened a fancy jar of orange marmalade, and she spread some on a slice of toast and insisted that he take her second piece. She doubted he was all that concerned about emergency preparedness, but finished the rest of her breakfast before giving him another nudge toward the truth.

"Why don't we let the dishes soak and go on out to your Zen garden to talk?"

Griffin shrugged. "Sure, just let me grab a beach towel to dry off the bench."

The ground was soft beneath their feet, but the sun was shining brightly now and drying up the scattered puddles. Griffin laid the towel on the bench, took Darcy's hand and pulled her down beside him. "I flat out love this view," he said.

He was gazing out at the ocean, but she was concerned by his preoccupied frown. "Tell me why this trip to Paris is different from all the others."

He slid his thumb across her fingers. "The woman who approached me in Chicago is a known acquaintance of Lyman Vaughn. The card she gave me had the name Simon Jordan, but that's probably the alias he's using this spring."

Alarmed, Darcy sat up straight. "He's the arms dealer

Interpol is tracking, isn't he?"

"That's the man. Apparently he feels secure enough in his Paris chateau to invite me to perform."

She gripped his hand between both of hers. "Wouldn't his friends be criminals too?"

"That all depends on how you define the word. There's a worldwide demand for arms, and dealers see themselves as businessmen who are entitled to make a fair profit."

"At the expense of innocent lives," Darcy cried.

"In their view no one is innocent, and they are merely supplying a valuable commodity, but I wish Vaughn had contacted me before I'd met you."

"Wait a minute, when your chauffeur was murdered in Seattle, wasn't your first thought that Vaughn must have linked you with Interpol, and that you'd be of no further use to them?"

Griffin brought her hand to his lips and kissed her lightly. "Yes, but it was merely a theory and, with no suspects in the crime, there's no way to know what really happened. Besides, if Vaughn had had a man killed to get to me, he'd not have failed. The mere fact that he sent an attractive woman to issue an invitation makes it unlikely that he had anything to do with a murder in Seattle."

The gray-green sea stretched before them as far as the eye could see. The waves were high in the storm's wake, and hundreds of surfers would be streaming into Monarch Bay. While it didn't follow that great numbers of tourists eager to buy Defy the World's goods would follow, at that moment, Darcy couldn't make herself care.

"I'll go with you," she exclaimed. "If we appear to be lost in each other, then Vaughn and his buddies won't be wary, and you'll be able to gather whatever information Interpol needs."

Griffin pulled his hand from hers to raise his palm. "Wait a minute, let me get this straight. When I asked you to come to Seattle and Chicago with me, you refused to consider it. Now you're eager to go to Paris, which won't be simply fun, but dangerous?"

"Yes! What about our being a team?"

He shook his head. "That's different. I don't want you anywhere near Lyman Vaughn."

"Well, I don't want you near him either."

Griffin studied the stubborn set of her mouth. "The answer's no, Darcy. I'm going alone."

Her glance narrowed slightly. "People have emergencies all the time, so there must be a way to get a passport in a hurry." She rose and took a step toward the house. "Come on, I need to get back to town."

Griffin rose with a weary stretch. "Fine. It will take me a few days to arrange the trip, so I'll still be able to come into Defy the World tomorrow to help clean up the nursery."

"No, you needn't bother. I'll just hire some of my crew for the day." She started for the house, but he quickly caught up with her.

"I don't want to fight with you over this. Go ahead and request a passport, and I'll be happy to take you on my next trip. But I won't take you to Paris."

Unwilling to argue when the matter was settled in her mind, Darcy insisted they wash their dishes. Then she hung up the dish towel and crossed her arms over her chest. "You told me Vaughn travels easily among society's elite. If that's the case, then he can't be murdering people right and left. He would have to behave as a gentleman, not merely dress like one."

"Whether or not he's ever fired a shot himself isn't the issue," Griffin replied, swiftly becoming exasperated with her. "We're not talking about some courtly Mafia don, here. The man is pure evil. He prides himself on manipulating world events, and then he capitalizes on the very chaos he's created."

"You mean he'll start a war just to sell arms?"

"Yes, and to both sides. It's only a matter of time before he gets his hands on nuclear weapons, and terrorists are already among his best customers. Let me put it this way, I want to get in and out without having you there to distract me."

His sense of urgency warned Darcy of a danger he had yet to explain. "You swore that you just passed along information. Is that true, or do you perform an even more valuable service for Interpol?"

"Such as?"

"Come off it, Griffin, you know what I mean. You joked about piano wire being too obvious, but once you're inside Vaughn's chateau, does Interpol expect you to kill him?"

Griffin stared at her, the fury in his dark gaze easily read. "I'm going to say this one last time, no, I'm not an assassin, nor have I ever been. The world is filled with evil men. How many could possibly be such big fans of mine that I could get close enough to kill them? Damn few, I imagine, and even then, if every time I played a concert for a dictator, he died, I'd soon run out of plausible alibis."

"That's why you need me," Darcy announced proudly.

"You've seen too many James Bond movies, sweetheart. All I do is play the piano."

"Like hell, but we can argue later. Just give me a couple of days to secure a passport before you book our flight."

"Why don't I just strangle you now and be done with it?"

Darcy braced herself against the counter. "You're too well-known to travel alone. At the very least, you ought to travel with a body guard."

"Oh Christ. Do you expect me to hire someone from your father's firm?"

"I just want you to take me. My karate might be a little rusty, but I'd certainly have the element of surprise on my side should you need a quick defense."

Griffin couldn't help himself. The thought of her defending him against anything other than a pack of marauding Munchkins was so incredibly goofy he simply had to laugh. "I'm glad you finally want to travel with me, elated in fact, but no, you simply can't come with me to Paris."

Darcy reached out to poke him in the chest. "What about this angle? Let's say Lyman Vaughn never heard of Seattle, but somehow he suspects you're tight with Interpol. If you show up with an adoring girlfriend, it will be plain that you're simply a concert musician out to have an entertaining weekend, rather than a talented snitch with something to hide."

Surprised by her logic, Griffin relaxed his stance and shoved his hands into his hip pockets. "That's very good. But if I wanted a sidekick, I'd take one from Interpol."

"What makes you think Vaughn doesn't have a dossier on all their agents? No, a pro just won't do, and together, we'll be so thoroughly convincing he'll have no clue what you're up to. Let's just do it, Griffin, and then you can retire from the world of international intrigue to write beautiful symphonies."

"I think you're the one who needs to be whomped upside the head. But for now, I'll just take you home."

"Promise me you'll think about it," Darcy stressed.

"Oh, yeah, I can promise you that. I'll think of little else."

Darcy hadn't been home five minutes before she made a quick trip to the post office to pick up the form for a passport. An hour later she'd had photos taken and put the request for rapid service in the mail. It had been an easy process compared to the battle to accompany Griffin which still lay ahead.

When she finally entered the nursery, she found an even worse shambles than she'd anticipated. She sat on an overturned bucket to decide where to begin and was still prioritizing jobs in her mind when George climbed over the sandbags at the corner and pulled open the gate.

"Lordy, what a mess!" he called.

"My sentiments exactly, but we'll have my crew here tomorrow to slick things up real quick. Any damage at your place?"

"The roof sprang a leak over the dining room, but Marge had wanted to redecorate the room anyway."

Darcy rose and set the bucket aside. "So it's not a disaster then?"

"No, and a decorating project will keep her out of mischief for a while. You look a whole lot happier than I expected. What did I miss?"

Darcy didn't describe how frightened they had been during the storm. She just gave him the good news about the lease. "Griffin made it sound as though the weather had influenced his decision, and maybe it did. But whatever his reasons, the pressure's off for a while. We'll still have to make certain Defy the World looks great before the next batch of tourists arrive, but I think we will."

George focused his attention on the pottery shed which was definitely listing toward the shop. "Sounds like Griffin Moore is just full of surprises. You gonna marry him?"

Darcy responded with a playful punch to his shoulder. "Get out of here! Isn't a year the absolute minimum a couple should know each other before they start talking about marriage?"

"That's what I read in Marge's magazines, but you ought to know your own heart. What are the man's chances?"

Taken aback by the question, Darcy felt her cheeks fill with a bright blush. "Ask me again next summer. For now, I haven't even told my parents that we've met."

"Seems like that call is a mite overdue, Missy."

Darcy agreed, and that night she called home, but when her father answered, she didn't even know where to begin. So she talked about the storm, and Defy the World, and asked about his growing security business before finally admitting she'd met a man who jokingly described himself as an itinerant musician.

"His name's Griffin Moore," she added breathlessly. "Perhaps you've heard of him."

After a mumbled exchange, Darcy's mother came to the telephone. "Your daddy's just shaking his head. Did you say you were dating Griffin Moore?"

"Yes. Is Daddy upset?" Darcy held her breath. Her parents occasionally attended a concert, but she doubted they were such great fans of classical music that they would be privy to any distressing information about Griffin.

"Stunned is a better word, honey. Last week, the PBS station here reran one of Griffin's concerts from Carnegie Hall. I couldn't help but notice what a handsome man he is, while your father thought I should close my eyes and just listen to the music. It's silly of him to be jealous after all these years, isn't it? Is Griffin as nice as he looks?"

"Yes, he certainly is." But Darcy found it far easier to explain that Griffin owned their building than to describe how she felt about him. "I hadn't called in a while, and I didn't want you to worry."

"We know you're busy, sweetheart, but thank you so much for calling. I'm going to rush right out tomorrow and buy one of Griffin's CDs. You tell him we're big fans and say hello to Christy Joy and Twink for us."

"I'll do that. Let me talk to Daddy again, will you please?" Her father cleared his throat as he picked up the telephone. "I don't know that I can take any more surprises. Let me sit down."

"Oh, Daddy, I just have a question. Have you ever heard of Lyman Vaughn?"

"Good God, Darcy, please tell me you aren't dating him too."

"No, but you have heard of him?"

"Of course. The elusive bastard is on every most-wanted list in the civilized world. As for the uncivilized half, he's up for Man of the Year. I sure hope he's not vacationing there in Monarch Bay."

"No, I was just curious. Thanks, Daddy, I'll call again soon."

Darcy remained by the telephone long after they'd said good-bye. She was proud of herself for at least introducing Griffin as a topic, but she knew she could have revealed a lot more. She hadn't been this interested in a man since college, and his celebrity was the least appealing thing about him. Were he a physician or engineer he would be equally attractive, but she hadn't made that clear.

She'd just dropped his name, a tantalizing tidbit, rather than confess she was falling in love. Besides, it was much too soon to speak of love, and she'd not be the first to say the word either.

She did care, though, an awful lot, and maybe she hadn't taken Griffin's warning about Lyman Vaughn as seriously as she should, but her father's disgust with the man had been chilling.

There was no way she could allow Griffin to face Vaughn alone. Focusing on Paris, she went into her bedroom and took a good look at her wardrobe. She doubted overalls were popular in Paris that spring, but Monarch Bay had some nice boutiques. Maybe over the weekend she could shop for a few classic pieces which would not only travel well, but make Griffin proud.

When Griffin arrived at Defy the World Friday morning, three men he recognized from Darcy's crew had already shoveled away the debris, swept the asphalt clean and were arranging the plants.

"Looks like there isn't much for me to do out here. What about inside?" he asked Darcy.

"We're doing okay, but come on into my office." She led the way and leaned back against her desk.

"I owe you an apology. You told me Lyman Vaughn was a dangerous man, but I didn't really appreciate just how bad he is until my dad told me that—"

"What?" Griffin shoved the door closed. "You asked your

father about him?"

He looked horrified, and Darcy had expected him to be pleased that she'd begun taking the danger Vaughn posed more seriously. "Yes, but you needn't worry. I didn't tell him why I was interested in Vaughn."

Griffin shook his head. "Let me get this straight. I asked you—no, insisted—that you respect my privacy and not repeat our conversations to anyone. Does any of that sound familiar, or have you completely forgotten your promise?"

Darcy recalled that particular discussion vividly as well as the weight of his cock in her hand. "No, not at all. I left your name out of it. Well, perhaps that's not exactly true. I did tell my folks that I'd met you, but I didn't believe that had to remain a secret."

Griffin raked his fingers through his hair in a vain attempt to grab hold of his temper. "That's just great. 'Hi, Dad, I met Griffin Moore, and by the way, who's Lyman Vaughn?' In other words, you linked us in his mind. I'll bet you anything you name that he's already repeated your question to his partner."

"Stop it!" Feeling trapped, Darcy moved away from her desk, but with Griffin blocking the door, there was no way to escape him.

"I wish you'd looked half as panicked when I told you I'd be going to Paris," Griffin continued. "Now right this minute you're going to call your father and tell him that under no circumstances is he to mention my name or Lyman Vaughn's to anyone. Then call your mother and do the same."

Darcy opened her mouth to argue, then realized this was probably the only way to undo whatever harm had been done. The intelligence community was acutely sensitive to rumors and a single mention of Lyman Vaughn from a security firm in Texas might snowball into widespread interest that would swiftly reach the arms dealer's ears.

She called her father's office and, relieved to hear his voice, repeated Griffin's message. "This is really important, Daddy. I shouldn't have said anything about Vaughn, and you mustn't either."

Then she called her mother, who was delighted to hear from her again so soon, and quickly agreed to be as silent as her husband. Feeling very foolish for having involved them, Darcy hung up and turned to Griffin, who was still eying her coldly.

"I wasn't trying to sabotage your mission," she swore. "I simply wanted more information. Now, what else can I do?"

"Frankly, you've done more than enough already. But at least half the fault is mine. I never should have mentioned Interpol, let alone Lyman Vaughn."

"We agreed to tell each other the truth, remember?"

"Yes, and it was obviously a mistake. Look, I'll find someone to repair the roof and trim the eucalyptus. Then I'll give you a call when I'm home from France."

While he no longer appeared close to a murderous rage, she wasn't pleased by his aloof stranger act either. "Wait a minute. You think I've blown your cover, and you're going anyway?"

"The subject is closed, Darcy."

"No, it is not. Neither of us is the most forthcoming individual ever born, but at least we were both trying. Or at least I thought we were. You're acting as though I'd deliberately screwed things up, and that's not what happened at all. Were you hoping that I'd run the first time you mentioned Interpol?"

Griffin swore in French, but his meaning was perfectly clear. "Do you honestly believe I'm grabbing for an excuse to stop seeing you?"

"No, I'm not that insecure, but I can't bear to have you mad at me."

She looked so contrite Griffin didn't doubt her remorse, but neither could he overlook how careless he'd been. "I really like the fact that you're a spontaneous person who runs with her instincts. It makes for great sex, but there's a whole lot more at stake here. Let me sort it out on my own."

"Do I have any choice?"

"No, but I will call you when I get home."

He swung the door open and walked out before she could tell him that she'd heard that one before, but this time, she felt truly abandoned.

Chapter Fifteen

Christy Joy had requested a couple of days to sleep before they had dinner together, but by Friday afternoon, Jeremy couldn't wait any longer to see her. He was surprised to find the sandbags gone from the front door, the shop open and Mary Beth behind the counter. If he hadn't known better, he would have believed the week had been as balmy as any other.

"Hi, Captain," Mary Beth called as he entered. "I'm glad to see you didn't go down with your ship in the storm."

"Impossible, I float like a cork. Where's Christy Joy?"

"She went to the market, but she'll be back in a minute. Want to leave a message?"

Jeremy couldn't think of a thing he'd care to say or write for Mary Beth to pass along. "No, thanks, just tell her I stopped by."

He wandered on out to the nursery, where Darcy and the men were stacking pots outside the shed. "Need another hand?" he asked.

"Thanks, but what I really need is to call the carpenter who built the arbor up at Griffin's. He'll be expensive, but he'll be able to really repair the shed, while all we can do is prop it up."

"Won't Griffin foot the bill? After all, you are his tenants."

Darcy glanced away. "He's leaving for France, but I'll try to find a time to discuss it with him."

"Come on, he'd do just about anything to please you," Jeremy offered with a ready grin.

After the scene they'd suffered through that morning, Darcy harbored no such romantic illusions and promptly redirected their conversation. "I'm going to mark everything down and have a gigantic clearance sale out here. Do you have time to help change prices?"

"Sure, just show me where to begin."

Darcy put him right to work. She was grateful to be able to keep busy rather than dwell on the mess she'd made with Griffin. They hadn't known each other long, so despite Jeremy's optimistic assurance, she doubted she'd built up enough good will to win his forgiveness. Especially when in his view she'd carelessly jeopardized the security of the free world. But at least she could whip the nursery into shape.

Jeremy was relieved to have something useful to do so he wasn't just hanging around until Christy Joy arrived home. When half an hour later she parked in the back, he hurried out to help her carry the shopping bags upstairs.

Once they had everything inside, she began fumbling through her groceries to sort them and put them away. "We were lucky the power came on before everything I had in the freezer was ruined. Not that Twink and I eat a great deal, mind you, but I seemed to have run out of everything."

Jeremy reached for his wallet. "Let me pay for some of this. After all, Griffin and I ate more than our share while we were here."

"No, I wouldn't think of it," she insisted, "not after all the hard work you put in."

He slid his wallet back in his pants, but he still felt he owed her. "Thank you, but it was my pleasure. Now we talked about having dinner, would you rather wait until tomorrow night?"

Christy Joy stacked the soup cans in the cupboard before answering. "I know we talked about going out, but—"

Jeremy's heart fell. "You've changed your mind?"

"No, not at all, and it would obviously be easier to go out while Twink's with her dad, but she called me last night before she went to bed, and I don't want to miss talking with her."

Relieved she hadn't just shown him the door, Jeremy reined in his grin before it became reckless. "The restaurants are all open late on the weekends. We could go out after Twink calls."

"Thank you, that's so sweet of you, but would you mind terribly if we just ate here tonight?"

"I could bring take-out, then you wouldn't have to go to any trouble."

"You're no trouble, Jeremy, and I'd really like to cook for you. Not that it isn't fun to cook with Twink, but it's been ages since I fixed dinner for a man. I'm sorry, does that sound pathetic?"

"Not at all, although when you consider how long it's been since a woman invited me to dinner, I'd say we're even in the pathetic department."

Christy Joy laughed with him, then looked up at the clock. "How does seven sound to you? If it's too early or too late—"

"Seven is fine. Isn't there something I can bring?"

She thought for a minute then shook her head. "No, I have everything I need. Now I have to get back to work."

"Yeah, me too, I'm marking down plants for the sale Darcy's planning." He walked her down the stairs and with each step regretted missing a chance to kiss her.

Mary Beth watched Jeremy's cool salute as he cut through the shop for the nursery and was too intrigued to keep still. "Looks like I missed more than a leaky roof here on Wednesday. What's up with you and Jeremy?"

Certain there had to be a few things to mark down, Christy Joy scanned the shop. "Don't rush me, I'll let you know when I figure it out."

"What's to figure? He's a hunk and owns his own boat. That makes him quite a catch in Monarch Bay and, from what I've seen, he's already caught."

Rocked by that possibility, Christy Joy had to swallow hard. "Right now, I'm too worried about getting Twink back home to obsess over a man."

"Well, you needn't obsess over him," Mary Beth scolded. "Just enjoy him because it's plain he's set his sights on enjoying you."

Christy Joy just shook her head and got busy looking for items to put on sale. But when she opened the door that night and found Jeremy standing there in his white uniform holding a big bouquet of pink roses, he looked so good it was all she could do not to burst into tears.

"My God," she sighed. "I can't help but pity those poor tourists you wouldn't...well...entertain?"

Jeremy was amused by how quickly she'd censored what had obviously been her first thought. He handed her the roses. "They got over it, but there is something about a man in a uniform, isn't there?"

"Well, you look awfully good in yours." Christy Joy had always thought him nice looking, but the dazzling white uniform accented his deep tan and sun-streaked hair, while it also brought out the vivid green of his eyes. Desperate for a distraction, she showed him where to set his hat, quickly found a crystal vase and carried the roses into the kitchen.

"But the real question is, are you comfortable?"

Jeremy tried not to laugh. "Isn't it the woman who's supposed to excuse herself to slip into something more comfortable?"

Christy Joy was wearing one of her favorites, a pink gauze dress in a tiny floral print liberally trimmed with lace. "I'm as comfortable as I'm likely to get, thank you, but if you want to remove your jacket, go right ahead."

Jeremy had debated long and hard before donning his uniform, but seeing as how it had obviously had the desired effect, he planned to stay in it. "No, thanks, I'm fine. Need me to toss the salad or something?"

"I swear you're the most helpful man I've ever met." Christy Joy carried the roses into the living room and set them on the coffee table. "Thank you so much for these. They're just spectacular. Darcy is landscaping a yard up on Ridgecrest with plenty of roses for a June wedding. Somehow I let her talk me into doing the flowers for the ceremony, but roses are so pretty by themselves, that I may just tie ribbons on a dozen for the bridesmaids and use them in crystal vases for the reception."

"What about the bride's bouquet?"

"That's going to be another challenge entirely, but Darcy knows how to wire flowers, and she'll help me."

"You two are a good team."

"Yes, we are, aren't we?" Christy Joy risked glancing toward him again, but as the resulting heat flooded her veins, she wished she were holding a lace fan. "Is it too hot in here for you?" she asked.

"Not at all, but I'll open the window if you like."

"Yes, thank you." Christy Joy wiped her palms on her skirt and wondered how she was going to survive the evening when he looked good enough to eat, and she knew precisely where to begin nibbling. Amazed by how tempting that thought truly was, she hurried back to the kitchen.

"Would you like some wine?" she called.

"If you're having some," he replied.

"Oh no, I don't dare drink while I cook, or I'll end up tipsy for sure."

Jeremy leaned against the doorway and crossed his arms over his chest. He couldn't recall the last time he had heard anyone even mention the word, and it sounded delightfully old-fashioned coming from her. "Then let's wait and not risk it."

"Would you like a soda then, or water?"

"No, I'm fine."

He was too damn fine in her opinion, but she managed to remove the potstickers from the oven, slide them onto a plate and carry them back out to the living room. She placed them atop a neat stack of *Victoria* magazines on the coffee table.

"I buy these frozen and they're absolutely delicious. Please try one."

Jeremy waited for her to sit on the sofa, then slid in beside her. He speared a potsticker with a toothpick, rested it on a napkin for a moment and then popped it into his mouth. The delicate shrimp-filled hors d'oeuvres were incredibly good, and he quickly took another.

"These are terrific," he agreed.

Pleased he was so appreciative, Christy Joy took two herself. "Other than to drive to the market, this is the first opportunity I've had to sit all day. I love owning my own business, but this week has been even more exhausting than most."

"Do you have any vacation time planned?"

"Are you kidding? Our whale-watching trip was my vacation for this year. At least we won't have to relocate in September, but if Highway One doesn't reopen soon, I don't know what we'll do."

"I know what you mean. I had a group cancel a charter for tomorrow because they can't get through from LA. They rescheduled, which is great, but I hate to just sit on the dock and twiddle my thumbs."

"I can't imagine your ever being idle."

Jeremy took another potsticker and chewed it slowly. "Well, I do a lot of running in place."

"Is that good exercise?"

Jeremy waited until she'd swallowed a bite of potsticker before he replied. "It was a metaphor, Christy Joy. I'm thirty-seven years old and I captain a boat that's never out of port for more than a day or two. Sometimes it's difficult to convince myself that I'm making much progress."

Christy Joy was mortified not to have understood him, but she was relieved he was in such a relaxed mood and apparently didn't care. "I thought you loved your boat."

"Don't get me wrong, I do, but sport fishing is just that, a sport. I'm not making any sense at all here, am I?"

"No, I understand completely. You sense something's missing, that there ought to be something more to life."

"Exactly." Jeremy drew in a deep breath and released it slowly. "Is owning Defy the World all you'd hoped it would be?"

"It's a lot more work than I'd anticipated, but mostly it's what I expected. Still..."

She glanced toward him and found him studying her as closely as she'd regarded him earlier. "Twink is such a special little girl, and I feel guilty for wanting more."

Jeremy knew precisely what he wanted and leaned forward. This wasn't the first time they'd kissed, but it felt just as tentative and sweet until she melted against him. Then all he could think of was how good she tasted and smelled. He kept right on kissing her as he pulled the bobby pins from her hair and sent her curls tumbling all around them.

Christy Joy was so lost in him she could scarcely breathe let alone think, and when the telephone beside the sofa rang, she jumped as though she'd been stung.

She gasped. "That must be Twink."

Jeremy reached around her to lift the receiver and handed it to her. He got up then and took a few paces away. The apartment wasn't large and, believing she would like some privacy, he walked into the kitchen. He opened the oven door and peeked in at the chicken breasts baking in a rectangular pan.

A bottle of rosemary and thyme marinade sat on the counter, and if the chicken tasted half as good as it smelled, it would be the best he'd ever eaten. There was a pot of brown rice on a back burner and a plate of asparagus ready to be steamed in the microwave.

He'd known Christy Joy would be a good cook from the attention she lavished on detail in her shop. She was a treasure in every way, but he was smart enough to realize she might be looking for more than a Popeye clone in a man. He could taste how much she liked him in her kiss, but was that enough?

Ten minutes passed before Christy Joy came breezing into the kitchen. "Twink and her dad are going to the zoo tomorrow. I'm glad he's giving her some much needed attention, but I couldn't pin him down as to when he'd bring her home."

"If you want to go up and get her, I'll be happy to go with you."

Christy Joy pulled on a pair of oven mitts, removed the pan of chicken and set it on a trivet. Then she remembered the asparagus and slid it into the microwave. "Thank you, but for the time being, I don't want to upset J. Lyle any more than he already is."

"You're a beautiful woman. He has to know other men will appreciate that fact."

Blushing slightly, she took the rice off the stove and fluffed it with a fork. "Thank you. Intellectually he might agree, but he still believes that I'll 'come to my senses' and return to him."

Jeremy struggled to make his question sound casual. "Is that even in the realm of possibility?"

"No. What he wants is a Barbie doll wife he can trot out to impress his partners and clients, not someone like me who's always up to her knees in one project or another and far too busy to keep having acrylic nails redone. Believe me, it was a spectacular mismatch, and if we'd not had Twink so soon, I'd not have stayed with him as long as I did."

"Then J. Lyle will have to get used to me, or another man, being with you sometime. What's the J. for?"

"John, which he claims is far too common to use. He's a gifted attorney, there's no doubt about it, but he's never made a decision without first considering his own self-interest. Now let's just forget him for the rest of the evening, please."

"That's fine with me." Jeremy stepped out of her way as she prepared their plates, then he carried them to the small dining table at the end of the living room. It was covered with a yellow-and-blue tablecloth, matching napkins and set with sterling silver utensils with a floral design. The blue water glasses were already filled, and he again refused the offer of wine.

Christy Joy removed a tossed salad from the refrigerator and then swore, "Oh, damn. I forgot to heat the rolls."

"We don't need them," Jeremy assured her.

"I know, but I wanted everything to be perfect." She sat and filled his salad plate with a generous scoop of green salad topped with cherry tomatoes, avocado slices and croutons.

He winked at her. "Relax. It was already perfect when you were serving peanut butter and jelly sandwiches."

She spread her napkin across her lap. "If I'd known that, I'd not have tried so hard to impress you tonight."

He reached for her hand and brought it to his lips. "I'm already impressed." He released her to take a bite of chicken and murmured appreciatively, "This is every bit as good as it smells. Thank you for doing this. I know a dozen ways to prepare fish, and it's so nice to have something else."

She also thought everything tasted especially good and attributed it to the charming company. Jeremy was not only handsome, but helpful and sincere, traits sadly lacking in J. Lyle, and she made a hasty vow not to compare the men any further. After a few bites, she thought of her daughter.

"I don't want to put up obstacles, but I'm worried about leaving Twink to go out on dates. One of our clerks has offered to babysit, and I could leave her with George and Marge, but when she spends so much time either in preschool or with a sitter..."

"I understand the two of you are a package deal," Jeremy replied. "I'm also sure there are a lot of things the three of us could do together. But let's not get ahead of ourselves. Let's just have a good time tonight."

"Yes, thank you for being so sensible. I'm afraid I like to line up problems and then check them off, but the worst problems, like Twink getting lost, can't ever be foreseen."

Jeremy wasn't sure how to respond to that ghastly reminder. He reached for a forkful of salad, but barely tasted it as he chewed. He glanced toward Christy Joy, who was still eating as though she hadn't just lobbed a grenade into the middle of the table, and realized she didn't blame him for the incident at all.

She looked up and caught him observing her. "I know I talk

too much, but you really seem too good to be true. If there's something important you've not told me, I wish you'd reveal it now."

Jeremy sat back in his chair and took a sip of water. "You mean if I have four illegitimate children with four different women, you'd like to know?"

"My God, you don't really!"

He laughed at her shocked expression. "No, not even one, but no one expects guys in the Merchant Marine to be saints. I pulled my share of wild stunts in foreign ports, but there aren't any I recall clearly enough to share now. Which is undoubtedly a blessing."

Christy Joy could so easily imagine him being a cocky twenty-one and avoiding arrest by mere seconds. "You've not served any time in jail, then?"

"Nope, not a day, and insanity doesn't run in my family either."

"That's certainly a relief," Christy Joy teased. "It looks as though the two of us are downright normal."

"Normal's good."

Christy Joy reached over to catch his hand. "Then why am I so scared?"

That she would admit to being afraid caught him by surprise, but he squeezed her fingers and managed a smile. "Maybe you just need a little time. I'm willing to take things real slow."

"I thought you were just shy."

"Well, that too."

She released his hand and continued eating while she gave her options some serious thought. J. Lyle had been so damn smooth. They were married before she'd realized there was nothing beneath his glossy veneer except another thick layer of gloss. It was her own emotions she doubted, not Jeremy's, and that realization made everything clear.

"Maybe the danger is in being too cautious," she announced suddenly. "Maybe we ought to just jump right in."

Jeremy nearly choked, but caught himself before launching into an uncontrollable coughing fit. "Wait a minute, are you suggesting what I think you're suggesting?"

Christy Joy felt her loose curls brush her shoulders as she

nodded. "I sure am. I bet you'd look twice as good out of that uniform as in it, and you needn't worry, I bought a box of condoms at the market."

Jeremy nearly lost it right there. He didn't know whether to laugh or cry. Then he thought he might be the first in his family to be institutionalized that very night, but with Christy Joy so unexpectedly inviting him into her bed, he just couldn't get his thoughts to run in any coherent direction.

"Wait a minute," he finally begged. "Could we at least finish this wonderful dinner first?"

"Of course, you'll need your strength."

She looked so incredibly sweet, but now Jeremy suspected that she'd be a tiger in bed. He couldn't even hold on to his fork with that possibility rolling around inside his head. He tossed his napkin on the table and shoved back his chair.

"Oh hell, come here."

Christy Joy rose and moved to his lap. She looped her arms around his neck and then bent her head to suck his earlobe. "You see why I don't dare drink wine?"

He didn't care if she never drank anything other than milk when she made such enticing suggestions cold sober. He framed her face with his hands and kissed her long and hard. "You're absolutely right," he breathed out against her lips. "We've waited too long as it is."

She reached for the shiny brass buttons on his jacket and thought of all the lonely tourists who had gone back to their staterooms alone. When he shrugged off the coat, she yanked his undershirt off over his head. His tan reached to his waist, and his chest was covered with thick, blond curls. She leaned down to lick a leathery nipple, and he stood with her still in his arms.

"That's it, lady. Where's your bed?"

She waved him toward the rear of the apartment, and he quickly strode past Twink's toy-filled bedroom to hers. The walls were the pale pink of dawn, and the bed was covered with a white crocheted spread dotted with ruffled pink roses. There were matching pillow shams topped with more ruffled pillows in pastel prints. It was a feminine bonanza, and he couldn't wait to climb in.

"Did you make the spread?" he asked.

"Sure did. It took me almost a year, but it's pretty, isn't it?"

"Yes, but not nearly as pretty as you." He set her down, then tried to figure out how best to remove her dress.

"Wait a minute," she urged. "Let's fix the bed first." She grabbed for the pillows, flung them aside and peeled the crocheted spread down to the foot of the bed. With another quick yank, she pulled back the pink blanket to reveal white ruffled sheets adorned with tiny pink roses.

Jeremy was afraid he'd fallen into a fantasy she might end long before he was ready, but she came back to him and reached for his belt buckle. He slid his hands over hers. "Wait a second. I've done this before, and my shoes have to come off first."

"Good idea." She kicked off hers then raised her brows.

Jeremy sat on the side of the bed to untie his shoes. He was suddenly so clumsy his fingers felt the size of bananas, but he finally freed his feet and ripped off his socks. He'd expected to take her out to dinner on Saturday nights, to hold her hand in the movies and spend weeks getting to know her before she would let him anywhere near her bedroom. Now he wondered if anything he'd ever imagined about her was true.

When he stood, Christy Joy slid her fingers through the crisp curls on his chest. "You have a really nice build, and I'll bet it doesn't come from workouts at the gym."

"Never joined one," Jeremy mumbled before wrapping his arms around her tight. He kissed her hungrily and lifted her clear off the floor.

That he could have kept so much passion under wraps all the months he had done little more than wave to her amazed her now. She ran her hands over his broad back, then slyly went to work again on his belt buckle. "I sure hope you're not wearing Sponge Bob Square Pants boxers," she teased.

He grabbed her wrists. "And if I am?"

"I'm going to keep them to sleep in."

He rubbed his forehead against hers. "I'll buy some tomorrow."

"What makes you think I'll let you leave here tomorrow?" Christy Joy had him out of his pants and boxers before he could think of a reply, and then she shoved him back on the bed. She removed the box of condoms from the nightstand, tore it open, then set it back down where he could reach it.

"Just get comfortable," she urged in an enticing whisper. "I want to try something."

Jeremy managed only a strangled gasp before she climbed over his outstretched legs and lowered her head to brush her tousled curls across his hips. He was already hard and when she sat up to wrap her hands around his cock with a slow spiraling grip, he feared he was about to embarrass himself, and badly.

"Christy Joy, wait—"

She flicked him with her tongue, then sucked him deep, and he was positive she'd been reading more than *Better Homes and Gardens*. The sensation she created was more intense than anything he'd ever felt, and that this was the same beautiful woman he'd longed for for months made it even better.

An instant before he was completely undone, he grabbed for her curls. "Stop," he begged hoarsely.

Christy Joy sat up and brushed her hair aside. "Am I hurting you?"

"No, yes, clear to my soul," he gasped. "Now let's get you out of that dress."

She raked her nails up the inside of his thigh as she moved off the bed and felt him shiver. "You're ticklish. I like that in a man."

"Whatever you want, baby."

Christy Joy giggled as she slid her dress off over her head. Her lace-trimmed slip followed. She worked too hard to have much appetite, so she was thinner than she'd once been, but she still had nicely rounded boobs. She'd worn a sheer bra not expecting to remove it, but she unhooked it slowly just to make Jeremy wait. Then she remembered the stretch marks and turned off the overhead light. The night light cast a friendly glow up the wall by the door, but it wasn't enough to reveal more than she wished to show.

Jeremy came off the bed to roll her panties down over her hips and, eager to taste her, he ran his fingers along her slit. He pulled her close and kissed her, then twisted to pull her back down on the bed under him. He pushed a finger up into her, then withdrew and licked it clean.

"God, you taste good," he moaned before nuzzling her breasts.

J. Lyle had loved the feel of her mouth on his cock, but he'd never gone down on her. She knew Jeremy would, though, and arched to thrust her nipple deeper into his mouth. His fingers dipped into her again, then traced teasing circles around her clit. She slid her knee along his hip, then spread her legs to invite more.

His next kiss tickled her belly button, and she squirmed and laughed. "If I'd known sailors were this good, I'd have joined the navy."

"It's just us captains, love," he corrected.

He shifted positions again, and then his tongue found her clit, already swollen in anticipation. She grabbed a handful of his hair to press him closer still and tried not to pass out from the thrill. She felt him twist two fingers inside her core and rolled her hips in time with his gentle lapping.

When the pleasure he gave bordered pain, she slapped her hands over her mouth rather than scream out loud, but she'd never felt anything half so good. Her cream flowed over his hands, and he drank it up hungrily. This was what sex was meant to be, she thought numbly, absolutely spectacular and completely exhausting.

He sat back for a moment, but before she could utter a soft moan of complaint, she heard him tear open a condom. Utterly limp, she reached out with a graceful stretch to draw him back down into her arms. He nudged her legs apart with his knee, then settled himself between them. He entered her with a first shallow thrust, and she shoved down to meet him, then wrapped her legs around his hips.

He braced his weight on his arms and lay still. He was big, but her muscles contracted around him, welcoming him as he eased deeper still. He couldn't recall the names of most of the women he'd slept with over the years, but he'd never found such an amazing fit. It was like coming home and, glorying in it, he withdrew only an inch, then reclaimed the full length of her.

She reached for a pillow to muffle her moans, but she felt every sweet stroke clear to her toes and out to the tips of her fingers. "You feel so good," she murmured breathlessly.

Jeremy licked his lips, tasted her, and withdrew a little farther before again plunging deep. He longed to make the magic last all night, but when she bucked beneath him, he was lost. He swallowed the scream that would have brought the neighbors running and, had he died right there, it would have been worth it.

When he could again breathe deeply enough to focus his eyes, he lay collapsed upon the bed and Christy Joy was gently combing his chest hair. He caught her hand and drew it to his lips. "Let's catch a flight to Las Vegas and get married tonight."

She hugged him with her whole body. "That's a great idea, but Monarch Bay doesn't have an airport."

"Oh yeah," he mumbled. "I don't think I can stand and walk anyway."

With their limbs so closely entwined, she didn't even want to move. "I'm so glad we didn't wait," she whispered.

"I've waited since that first morning I walked by your shop and saw you standing outside."

"I noticed you too, but I thought you were just lonely."

He wound his fingers in her curls and pressed her cheek against his chest. "I didn't realize I was until I saw you."

Christy Joy bit her lip in a futile attempt to hold back her tears, but they splashed on his chest before she could catch them. "I'm sorry, but everything has happened so fast, and yet, not nearly fast enough."

Jeremy squeezed her tight. "Wait a minute, I'm sure I proposed to you a moment ago, and you didn't give me an answer."

She ran her hand over the smooth skin of his hip and down his hairy thigh. "Right now, I doubt either of us is thinking clearly."

Jeremy pulled himself up slightly. "Is that a no?"

"No. I want to wake up in your arms and tell you then."

He settled back down beside her. "Sounds promising."

"Sure is," she murmured, and she fell asleep imagining them as a family with Twink, but it was J. Lyle's angry frown that cursed her dreams.

Chapter Sixteen

Saturday morning, Darcy drove up to Ridgecrest to check the Peaveys' yard for storm damage. Both Charlotte and Michelle greeted her warmly and after a brief tour of the yard, Darcy assured them no previously unforeseen work would have to be done in preparation for the wedding.

When Darcy returned to her truck, she glanced up the hill toward Griffin's home. She could also justify running a quick survey of his property, but at present, she couldn't face another of his righteous tirades.

"Artistic temperament, my ass," she grumbled under her breath.

Her mood was still dark when she entered the shop, but Christy Joy greeted her with an ecstatic smile. "Did you just win the lottery?" Darcy asked.

"Better than that. Come on upstairs with me for a minute." She promptly led the way at a bouncy jog.

Darcy followed with a slow, deliberate step. By the time she reached the top of the stairs, her partner was already in her living room waiting for her.

As Darcy entered, Christy Joy giggled and held out her left hand. "What do you think of this pretty ring?"

Darcy gaped at the impressive heart-shaped diamond. "I'm too dazzled to think. I assume Jeremy is the man?"

"Oh, indeed he is. Last night, we spent what was easily the best night of my life together. And this morning, as soon as the jewelry stores opened, he left to buy me an engagement ring."

Darcy tried to be happy for her best friend, but it was a challenge with her own heart aching. "I've always liked Jeremy, but he's never struck me as the impulsive sort."

"No, he certainly isn't, so I took it upon myself to inspire him."

"Good for you. Do you love him?"

Christy Joy shrugged. "What's not to love?"

"That's not what I asked."

Christy Joy twisted the gorgeous ring on her finger. "Yes, I do. He's everything J. Lyle isn't. Look, Darcy, Jeremy is so sweet, and I decided to go for it the way you did with Griffin. Hasn't that tactic worked out well for you?"

Darcy didn't know where to begin on that one, but she hadn't forgotten that Griffin had sworn her to secrecy where he was concerned. "I went for it all right, but mind-blowing sex doesn't send everybody to the altar. I'm real happy for you two, though. Have you set a date?"

"No, but we both want it to be soon."

"Wonderful, then you can practice on your own wedding bouquet before you make one for Michelle Peavey."

Christy Joy laughed as they went back downstairs. "I thought of that too. Now, with the sun shining, let's hope we make some money today."

"Amen to that, sister," Darcy replied, and with her smile firmly fixed in place, she went out to the nursery and got to work.

The tree trimmer arrived before noon, and the crew Griffin had hired to repair the roof swiftly followed. Darcy was still trying to decide what to do about the potting shed when the carpenter she'd meant to call for an estimate parked in back.

He greeted her with a cheerful smile. "Mr. Moore asked me to fix up the shed better than new and send him the bill."

"I'd planned to call you too, but thanks for coming so soon. We've emptied the shed, but if anything is still in your way, just let me know."

As the carpenter got to work, Darcy toyed with the possibility that Griffin was sending all the help to please her rather than merely to maintain his property, but she quickly dismissed the view as delusional. She stayed out in the nursery rather than mope in her office, but the pretty sunshine failed to raise her spirits.

The day crept by and while she hadn't been dating before she met Griffin, spending a Saturday night alone now was a discouraging prospect. She had a couple of frozen entrées in her freezer, but neither held any appeal. She made some microwave popcorn instead, and sorted through her collection of DVDs for something humorous and grabbed "Galaxy Quest", a hilarious Star Trek spoof staring Tim Allen and Sigourney Weaver.

She'd just settled down on her sofa with the bowl of popcorn balanced on her stomach when the doorbell rang. Annoyed by the interruption, she turned down the sound on her television, set the popcorn aside and answered the door.

Griffin was standing on the steps, dressed in gray slacks and navy blue blazer. His maroon tie matched the narrow stripe in his white shirt. A mere hint of a smile tugged at the corner of his mouth. "I thought I'd stop by before leaving for Paris."

Darcy stepped aside to invite him in, but decided for once to keep her mouth shut and let him bury himself. That she looked frazzled after a day of work while he looked so damn cool was unfair, but then nothing had ever been equal between them.

Griffin studied her implacable expression a long moment and then reached into his coat pocket and withdrew a passport. "If you'll promise to remain at the hotel while I play the private concert, then you'll need this."

Darcy quickly brushed her salty hands on her overalls, took the passport and opened it to find the photograph she'd submitted. "This should have been sent to me. How did you get hold of it?"

Griffin walked over to the coffee table and grabbed a handful of popcorn. "Does it matter? I have to be at the airport in San Francisco by midnight, and you either want to go with me or you don't."

Darcy understood why he would insist upon her remaining in the hotel, but she was disappointed he couldn't trust her to behave herself around Lyman Vaughn. "You can't treat me like a pet Yorkie and toss me a dog toy when you go out."

"Of course not. I didn't plan to lock you in our suite. You could go shopping, tour the Louvre, entertain yourself however you please. Just don't argue with me about attending the concert, and don't say what I want to hear now, if you intend to do exactly as you please once we've arrived in Paris."

She licked her lips and glanced up at him. "Why do you want me to go along? As I recall, you take sedatives for a flight, so you won't need my company on the plane. If we won't be together in Paris either, then what's the point?"

"The flight's in the middle of the night, so you'll probably be sound asleep too," he stressed. "As for Paris, I didn't plan to just fly over and then catch the return flight home. It won't take more than a few hours to plan and give a concert for Monsieur Jordan, whether or not he turns out to be Lyman Vaughn. Then we can do whatever we please together."

"Would you recognize Vaughn on sight, or does he frequently change his appearance?"

"I've not met the man, but he looks the same in all the surveillance photos I've seen. He's in his fifties, five foot ten, one hundred seventy pounds, silver hair, green eyes. He favors finely tailored suits, and if he passed by you on the street, you'd probably assume he was an attorney or businessman on his way to an important meeting."

"He has no distinguishing marks, no mole on his cheek, or a tarantula tattooed on his neck?"

"No, what did you expect, that he'd be seven feet tall with flaming red hair?"

"No, I suppose it's only movie villains whose looks are extraordinary." Darcy focused on her pink socks. "Still, you don't really need me along when you could find agreeable company in Paris without much effort."

"Without any effort at all," he countered smoothly, "but she wouldn't be you."

Darcy risked a peek at his smile, and her knees turned to butter cream. "Would that matter?"

"Yes. I'm sorry about the way I blew up at you yesterday. I know you meant well, and we'll just have to hope no harm was done."

The threat of unexpected tears stung her eyes, and she quickly blinked them away and turned her passport in her hands. She hadn't had time to go shopping, but she might be able to get by with the few good things she already owned and add to her wardrobe in Paris.

Of course, when Griffin planned to walk into a lion's den, being concerned about her clothes was ludicrous. Then again, if she somehow managed to stay with him, he might be injured protecting her. She would never forgive herself if he suffered even the slightest harm because of her.

"Okay," she agreed softly. "Give me a minute to call Christy Joy. Then I'll toss a few things in a bag and be ready to go."

"You might want to shower."

She looked down at her rumpled overalls. "Do you honestly believe I'm too great an idiot to come up with that on my own?"

"No, I was teasing you, Darcy."

Unconvinced of that, she left the room without responding, but she'd meant to take a shower and wash her hair right after calling her partner. Only Christy Joy didn't answer. She might be out with Jeremy, or the pair could be having too good a time to come to the telephone. Either way, Darcy was forced to record a hastily conceived message, but she was amazed not to feel a crushing guilt for leaving the country on such short notice.

When had her priorities taken this alarming shift? No answer appeared while she showered and, once out, she hurriedly towel-dried her hair and dressed in her black Levi's, boots and black sweater. While she usually went without earrings, she put on small gold hoops which went nicely with her diamond note. She returned to the living room pulling a wheeled travel bag filled with lacy lingerie and little else.

Griffin was watching Galaxy Quest and laughing between bites of popcorn. She was surprised a man as sophisticated as he would enjoy it as much as she did.

"Just stop the movie and we can watch it when we get home," she suggested.

"Great, I don't want to guess how it ends." Griffin rose from the sofa with an easy stretch, carried the now empty popcorn bowl into the kitchen, and set it in the sink. "You ought to leave a few lights on to discourage burglars."

"Right, like I've got any valuables to steal," Darcy shot right back at him.

He came forward to take her bag. "All right, I know you're capable of running your own life. Just tell me to shut up if you like."

"I think I just did." Darcy grabbed her trench coat from the closet and caught a quick glimpse of herself in the mirror by the door. With her gamin hairstyle and black apparel, she might pass for a French girl. If she just kept her mouth shut, which, as always, would be the greatest challenge.

She nearly snorted on that one, and had to quickly take a deep breath. She checked to make certain her passport and keys, and then with a few lights burning, she followed Griffin out the door.

Darcy had flown since childhood with her parents, but they'd never traveled first class. She was surprised to discover there was so much room between the wide seats that a man of Griffin's size could stretch out and be comfortable. She would be able to curl up as though she were still on her own couch.

While the plane was taxiing out on the runway, Griffin pulled a vial of pills from his pants pocket and asked the stewardess for a glass of water. "I hate to do this, but the alternative is too ugly to contemplate."

"You couldn't be ugly if you tried," Darcy scolded.

"That's just it, I refuse to try." He swallowed a couple of pills, finished the water, then requested pillows and blankets for them both.

He was already yawning by the time they had the pillows comfortably tucked beneath their heads and the blankets stretched across their laps. He reached for Darcy's hand, laced her fingers in his, then brought them to his lips.

"You know what I love best about you?" he murmured.

"I didn't think you loved me at all," she responded, but she sat forward eager to hear it. Unfortunately, before he could answer, his lashes fluttered, his eyes closed, and he was sound asleep.

"It's Sleeping Beauty who's supposed to be lost in dreamland," she whispered, "not the handsome prince."

She closed her eyes as the engines roared in take-off, but once the flight was underway, the couple seated across the aisle kept her awake. Their voices were low and teasing and, while she couldn't catch their exact words, it was plain they were lovers bent on enjoying every minute of their trip. She envied them and patted Griffin's hand.

She wondered if he'd been about to say that he loved her eyes, or maybe just her lacy lingerie. She refused to push the thought any further, however, when by the time he awoke, he'd undoubtedly have forgotten he ever mentioned the word love.

He'd raised the armrest between their seats and pulled her hand into his lap the way he had the one time they'd gone to the movies. The first time, she corrected mentally. Then afterwards she'd seen him almost jump the poor clerk from the Song and Dance music store. Now she understood why he'd been so quick to not only expect, but ward off an assault. She shook her head. What else was he hiding? She'd expected so damn little of him then, and yet amazingly he'd kept pursuing her.

Maybe beauty really was in the eye of the beholder. Either that, or the pumpkin pie spice, which she'd packed, was even more potent than George had promised. Whatever the reason, Griffin really cared for her, and she was scared to death she might lose him.

The stewardess paused beside Griffin. "May I bring you anything?" she whispered.

It was a long flight, and Darcy wished she could sleep too. "Some hot tea?"

The stewardess returned with a small silver teapot filled with hot water and a fancy assortment of teas. Darcy thanked her, slid her hand from Griffin's to select orange spice and took several of the delicate sugar cookies being offered.

The couple across the aisle was sipping wine and now snuggled so close they occupied a single seat. Darcy drank her tea and slid closer to Griffin's comforting warmth. The evening had begun on such a lonely note, but with an enticing invitation from Griffin, it had become surreal.

After saying no to her first love, a man she'd adored but simply couldn't follow around the globe, she'd shoved all thought of men from her mind and dived headfirst into her career. Then Griffin had strolled into Defy the World Tomatoes, under what now appeared to be false pretenses, and she'd felt such an intense attraction there'd been no time to warn her heart.

Now look what had happened, she mused. Prior to meeting him, she hadn't missed a single day of work for Defy the World, but she'd just blown her perfect attendance record and was still precisely where she wanted to be. Maybe it was possible to have it all, she thought sleepily, but so much depended on Griffin that she dared not dream past Paris alone.

She set her empty cup on the tray, this time pulled his

hand into her own lap, and fell asleep.

After speaking with Twink by telephone, Christy Joy and Jeremy had gone out for a walk. They had strolled around town, marveling at how quickly merchants had cleared away the storm damage, then stopped for ice cream. Because her bed was so much more comfortable than his bunk, they'd returned to her apartment to continue where they'd left off that morning, but Christy Joy checked her messages first.

She had to replay Darcy's breathless farewell three times to make certain she understood it before she sat back and looked up at Jeremy. "She didn't say when they're coming back, did she?"

"No, she sure didn't, but you know they will."

"This isn't like her at all." Christy Joy remained on the sofa, picked up one of the throw pillows and gave it a playful punch.

"I don't have a charter for the next few days, so I'll come over and help George with the nursery."

"Thank you, I'd like that, but when I invite you up here for lunch, you'll know I won't have food on my mind."

Jeremy sat beside her and pulled her into a fond hug. "That sounds awfully good, but let's make certain J. Lyle doesn't walk in with Twink before we climb the stairs."

Christy Joy leaned in to kiss him. "You're right. Tomorrow, I'll pin him down as to when he intends to bring Twink home, and if it isn't in the next few days, I'll go and get her."

Jeremy kissed her again. "We'll go get her, and I won't give a damn if he calls me Popeye when I've won the girl."

Christy Joy savored his next kiss and then sighed, "Honey, why don't you start calling me Olive Oyl."

For a couple of hours, Darcy slept fitfully, but then awoke with a start. Their amorous neighbors were now sighing softly with a rhythm that convinced her there was a whole lot more going on under their blanket than hers.

It hadn't been their near-silent lovemaking that had awakened her, though. It was the sudden awful realization that should their plane experience any difficulty during the flight, she might not be able to wake Griffin. She'd actually seen a television program containing tips for surviving a plane crash in the sea, but it hadn't included advice on how to rescue an unconscious man twice her weight.

She was sorely tempted to give him a good shake just to see if she could wake him. "God, Darcy, get a grip," she mumbled under her breath. She'd never been given to panic attacks. Well, withdrawing her savings to open Defy the World Tomatoes had taken an enormous burst of courage. But she'd countered that anxiety with the exhilaration of achieving her dreams before she turned thirty.

Now she was just scared and there was no joyful happenstance to balance her fright. She toyed with the diamond note. It was a spectacular reminder of the man seated beside her, but she felt strangely disconnected from her own life.

How in the world was she going to remain in Monarch Bay, placidly replanting gardens, if Griffin continued jetting around the globe consorting with master criminals to pass tips along to Interpol? Equally worrisome, how was she to help grow Defy the World's business if she neglected it to accompany him?

Griffin was such an extraordinary man, perhaps he deserved a woman whose mission in life was to dote on him. But she had too many goals of her own to become his devoted shadow. Of course, that was a feeble complaint on a night when she'd willingly accompanied him on his latest adventure.

She tried to breathe deeply and relax, but the engines' deep hum was far from comforting. Too antsy to remain in her seat, she crawled over Griffin and went to the restroom. She splashed her face with water and peered into the mirror. With a slight pout, she did look like a sultry French woman, but inside, she felt like a deer caught in headlights.

"Darcy, wake up," Griffin urged softly. "We'll be landing in a few minutes."

She opened one eye and was surprised to find he'd been awake long enough to shave and comb his hair. "Why do you look so damn fresh while I feel as though I've been turned inside out like a sock?"

"Modern medicine," he replied, "and I've also learned how to clean up real quick so I don't have to be awake too long."

Darcy yawned and stretched, then sat up straight. "Couldn't you use your sedatives to knock out Lyman Vaughn?"

"Slip him a Mickey, you mean? I suppose I could, but I doubt he'll be alone, and his companions might become suspicious."

"Yeah, I suppose they would, but please keep it in mind just in case you need an escape plan."

"Believe me, I file all your ideas." Griffin stood to ease her way out into the aisle. "You'll want to fix your makeup before we land."

Darcy slipped by him and noted the couple who'd kept her awake were asleep, snuggled in each other's arms.

It took a while to go through customs, but just as Griffin had predicted, a chauffeur holding a placard with his name awaited them. He was a sandy-haired young man with sparkling blue eyes and a ready grin.

"I hope you had a pleasant flight," he greeted them in softly accented English. "My name is Antoine, and it is my pleasure to welcome you to Paris."

The chauffeur was a personable young man, not the shifty-eyed fugitive from the law Darcy had feared they might encounter; but that didn't alleviate her worries about what might await Griffin later.

As Griffin replied, Darcy covered a wide yawn. It was still morning to her, but early evening there in Paris. As the other passengers hurried away, she clung to her lover's hand.

"I usually stay at the Hotel Meurice in the Tuileries Quarter," Griffin explained. "The staff is discreet, and they provide excellent service. Do you know of it?"

"Certainly, sir, it has a wonderful reputation," the young man responded.

"Good. I'd like to take Ms. MacLeod there before we go on to Monsieur Jordan's."

"As you wish, it is not out of our way." Antoine took Darcy's bag and led the way to their limousine. He stowed their luggage in the trunk, then opened the rear door and made certain they were comfortably seated. "The bar is fully stocked, and I'm told the DVDs are quite entertaining."

Darcy gave Griffin a startled glance. "DVDs?"

"Don't worry. Porn doesn't appeal to me."

"Thank God," she replied, but she leaned forward when a second man in a dark uniform slid into the seat beside the driver. The glass partition behind the front seat was raised, and she couldn't hear what passed between them before the limousine began to roll.

Griffin pulled her back beside him and patted her hand. "Don't worry, my pet. I'm sure the speaker is on here in the back seat, and should you have a request, they'll hear your every word."

Darcy understood his warning and did her best to appear totally unconcerned. But certain something, if not everything, wasn't right, her heartbeat quickened to a wild thump. The traffic was thick around the airport and, with dark tinted windows, the limousine seemed to float among a sea of lights. She wasn't fooled, however, by the deceptive calm.

She could only cling to the belief Simon Jordan, or Lyman Vaughn, must be a great fan of Griffin's to offer a million dollars to meet him and hear him play. She tried to concentrate on that aspect, as it would surely guarantee his safety, but she was still terribly afraid.

"I wish we'd arrived earlier so that we could see something of the city," she remarked breathlessly.

"You've been here, haven't you?"

"Yes, but it was so long ago I don't recall much except for the Eiffel Tower and Arc de Triomphe."

"We'll make it a point to see everything in the guide books before we go home," he replied.

They'd been traveling perhaps twenty minutes when he sat forward slightly. "Antoine, we appear to be going in the wrong direction. Are you lost?"

"You need not worry, sir. I know the city."

The speaker lent the chauffeur's voice a slightly metallic ring that alarmed Darcy as much as Griffin's complaint. While she couldn't tell east from west in a strange city at night, apparently he could. Thinking there still might be time to flee, she checked the doors, but the interior handles had been removed and there were no controls for the windows. She raised her brows and pointed, but Griffin merely nodded. Apparently he'd already noticed the limousine had been rigged for kidnapping.

When they continued on the same route, Griffin knew Antoine hadn't merely mistaken the location of the hotel. They were headed somewhere else entirely. He addressed the chauffeur in French this time and, while Darcy couldn't understand his words, there was no mistaking his displeasure.

"I can assure you, Mr. Moore," Antoine responded in English, "that Monsieur Jordan's hospitality is far superior to that of the Maurice, but the hotel will be informed to hold your reservation until you arrive."

Darcy watched Griffin shake his head, but now that the choice had been made for her, she would simply have to deal with her fears. She rose to sit on her knees and, with a sparkling giggle, threw her arms around his neck and pressed her mouth close to his ear.

"Don't worry," she whispered. "I'm going to play real dumb."

Griffin laughed as though she'd offered something else entirely. "Not in the car, Darcy, absolutely not. Now turn around and behave yourself."

She licked his ear. "What fun is that?"

"I'd no idea you'd enjoy having an audience."

"I thought chauffeurs were paid to ignore what's going on back here."

"No one is that well-paid," he argued, and he swatted her bottom and forced her back down beside him. "There's a good girl."

He looped his arm around her shoulders in a relaxed embrace, but he was furious with himself. It was his colossal arrogance that had landed his darling Darcy in this awful predicament and, determined to get her out safely, he hugged her more tightly.

"The French countryside is very beautiful. Because you know the names of every shrub and tree, I imagine you'll see a great deal more than I will on our way back to Paris."

Darcy squeezed his thigh. She was uncertain if he were signaling her to keep her eyes open for landmarks so they could retrace their route, or if he were merely chatting to calm her nerves and fool their silent escorts.

"Yes, I especially want to visit Versailles again," she responded gamely. "The palace is so very beautiful, but I'd really like to concentrate on the gardens this time."

"I'll take you there," he promised.

She hoped they lived that long. At least she'd memorized the license plate number while Antoine, if that were really his name, loaded their luggage in the trunk.

"I'd hoped to spend tomorrow shopping," she complained petulantly. "France has such wonderful designers. I hadn't expected to be stuck out in the provinces."

"I know." Griffin sighed regretfully. "I'll make it up to you, but at least you'll have an opportunity to hear me play again."

"Oh, honey, you're so handsome in your tux, I only hear every other note," Darcy gushed. If they hadn't been in such a fix, she would have enjoyed teasing him.

Griffin shot her a skeptical glance in a clear warning not to go overboard. "I'll set the program after speaking with Monsieur Jordan, but I'll try to include at least one of your favorites."

Darcy's smile froze, but she was relieved not to be forced to name one. She played his CD all the time, but she hadn't memorized the names of the pieces. Then she realized she did have a request.

"I love your own compositions best. Will you play one of them?"

Griffin rewarded that bit of flattery with an enthusiastic kiss. "That's my girl."

Darcy wished that were enough, but she was so anxious it was all she could do not to bounce on the seat like a toddler. When Antoine at last slowed the limousine and turned into a long, curving road, she was so desperate to get out of the car, she feared she might leap out the moment the door was opened and run off into the woods, or whatever terrain lay beyond the road. She would never leave Griffin, though, so she quickly erased a quick escape from her list of options.

Griffin gripped her knee as the luxurious car slowed to a halt. "Just let me run this show," he whispered. As soon as Antoine opened the rear door, he burst through it.

"Where's Jordan?" he shouted. "I was invited here, but I won't tolerate the shocking lack of respect you've shown me thus far."

He reached back into the rear seat to help Darcy out beside him. He laced his fingers in hers and pulled her close.

Antoine appeared to be unconcerned by Griffin's reproach, while his companion, a big, bear-like man in a matching uniform, came around the front of the car and fixed them with a malevolent stare.

They were parked in front of an enormous chateau whose huge central structure was flanked by generous wings. It was well-lit, and the soft, dove-gray exterior had been freshly painted. The flowerbeds on either side of the driveway contained a splendid array of roses in a variety of hues.

The magnificent estate had the pristine beauty of a movie set, but when the front door opened and a man came toward them, Darcy recognized him instantly from Griffin's description of Lyman Vaughn. Only rather than affect the confident swagger she'd expected, he moved slowly, as though he hadn't slept in days. He was dressed in a white silk shirt and gray slacks rather than a suit, and his preoccupied frown failed to lift as he greeted them.

"Please forgive my impatience, Mr. Moore. It was so good of you to accept my invitation, and I apologize for whatever inconvenience I may have caused you." His hushed voice contained a slight lilt, as though he might possess Scandinavian roots. "My only child is desperately ill. She has been attended by the world's finest physicians, but they can do nothing more. While she cannot escape the inevitable, her fondest wish is to meet you."

Griffin nodded slightly. "I'm so sorry, I had no idea you even had a daughter. I wish Miss LeMer had spoken of her illness when we met in Chicago."

"Yes, I should have directed her to do so, but none of us realized how little time Astrid had left."

When he included Darcy in his glance, Griffin provided the introductions, and she extended her hand. "I hadn't expected to be here tonight, Mr. Jordan. I hope I won't be in the way."

"Of course not, my dear. I wish there were time for you both to rest after your long flight, but it would be best if you were to warm up a bit on our piano, Griffin, and play for us before we shared a late supper."

"Is Astrid strong enough to make requests?" Griffin inquired. "I'll tailor my performance to suit her tastes."

"Chopin is one of her favorites," Jordan replied. "But come, let me introduce you to her. She'd hoped to one day be a concert pianist herself, but sadly, that is not to be."

Griffin kept hold of Darcy's hand as they followed Jordan

up the walk. He had only enough time to shoot her a dark glance, but the defiant tilt to his chin warned her far more was required than a tender show of sympathy.

She pressed his fingers quickly. They might be unable to confer for hours, but she understood this was Lyman Vaughn. That a man who dealt in death on such a vast scale should lose his daughter in so tragic a manner was a form of justice, but she prayed they would be safely back in Paris before he unleashed the full force of his grief.

Chapter Seventeen

Astrid's hospital bed was placed in the center of the cavernous living room. Her head was swathed in bandages, her skin as pale as her crisp white sheets and her eyes as clear a green as her father's. Fluid from an IV bottle dripped into the needle in her left hand. She raised her right gracefully in greeting.

"Griffin, this is such a thrill." Her hushed voice held only a faint trace of a French accent.

Griffin introduced Darcy, then took Astrid's hand and brought it to his lips. "The pleasure is mine, mademoiselle. What may I play for you tonight?"

Darcy stood back as Astrid requested several favorites, and then just as quickly changed her mind and mentioned others. She had a great many favorites it seemed, and Griffin approved of each one.

The exquisitely furnished room was decorated in shades of misty blue. There was a concert grand at the end of the room, but the focal point was a large painting of dancing nudes which Darcy thought was probably an original Matisse. She wasn't surprised Lyman Vaughn lived in such splendor, but she doubted he'd done more than hand over a suitcase filled with his ill-gotten gains to an interior designer.

In contrast, Astrid was touchingly innocent, and also completely unable to make up her mind as to what she wished to hear. She looked no more than sixteen and was so terribly thin, her eyes were huge and now glistened with a sheen of tears.

"I've made so many lists," she apologized, "but then Papa brought me your latest CD, and I love it so, that became the music I wanted to hear you perform. But then, there are all my former favorites as well. How does anyone choose?"

"Perhaps Astrid would enjoy one of your own compositions," Darcy suggested softly. "Why don't you begin with the one you debuted in Seattle?"

"You're writing your own music?" Astrid gasped in surprise. "Why didn't anyone tell me, Papa?"

"If I knew, I must simply have forgotten, dearest," he replied.

Darcy thought it was more likely that Astrid had been one to forget, and she left the girl's bedside to take a seat closer to the piano. She'd seen a housekeeper near the door as they'd entered, and a petite blonde in a nurse's pale peach smock and matching pants now approached Astrid's bed. She checked her IV, and then, with a nod to her father, left the room. Lyman Vaughn remained at the foot of his daughter's bed, his hands tightly clasped on the metal frame.

They'd seen only two men, Antoine and his heavily muscled companion. If Vaughn had no other bodyguards about, then Darcy thought she and Griffin should be able to get away without encountering much in the way of resistance. If she got her way, they'd split as soon as he'd played his final note, even if they had to steal the limousine to make their getaway.

"I'll play all evening if you like," Griffin promised, "but let's begin with the piece Darcy mentioned. Listen closely, because I'll ask your opinion afterward."

"I'm sure it will be marvelous," Astrid replied, clearly adoring him.

"That is my hope," Griffin assured her. He walked to the piano, pulled out the bench and sat. He played several scales, and then paused. "You had the piano tuned for me?"

"Of course," Vaughn stated. "If it isn't tuned to perfection, I'll send for the technician immediately."

"No, it's fine for the most part, but the bass needs a bit of work. I have a tuning hammer with me. Would you mind if I used it?"

"No, not at all," Vaughn exclaimed. "Do whatever you must to be satisfied with the sound. Your things have already been taken up to your rooms."

"It won't take me long," Griffin replied. "Darcy, come with me so you'll know where everything is."

The housekeeper came forward to show them the way. She was a tall, slender woman with close-clipped gray hair. Her black dress was as severely tailored as a military uniform, and her black oxfords made an audible thump as she climbed the carpeted stairs. She did not once smile, nor make any welcoming gestures. Darcy kept still until they'd been shown to adjoining rooms in the east wing. In San Francisco, Griffin had had to explain the use of the tuning hammer, which was actually a small wrench, to security, so she'd known he'd packed it. She was just amazed that he wanted to tune the blasted piano when she was so desperate to leave.

As soon as the solemn housekeeper excused herself, Griffin crossed his room and opened the doors overlooking the garden at the rear. "It's a lovely night. Come on outside with me," he called as he stepped out on the balcony.

When Darcy followed, he pulled her into a fierce embrace and whispered in her ear, "I'm sorry everything's gone wrong. The whole house is probably bugged, so be very careful what you say even when we're alone. I'll get us out of here as quickly as I possibly can."

Darcy reached up on her tiptoes to kiss him, but his response was no more than a quick peck. Disappointed, she stepped away and followed him back into the room.

Griffin unzipped his garment bag. "As long as I'm up here, I might as well change into my tux." He tossed her his shirt and a box containing diamond studs. "Put those in, will you please?"

He stepped into the bathroom to change his trousers and shoes, but she was shaking so hard she still had one stud left to place when he returned. "These are beautiful. Did they come from an adoring fan?"

"Yes, but he wasn't my type." Griffin quickly pulled on the shirt and fastened the pleated front and cuffs with the sparkling studs. "What? Do you think I should have returned them?"

"Well, I suppose that all depends on what this generous fan expected in return." Darcy almost hoped someone was listening in to this exchange.

"He claimed his intention was to reward my genius, which made it difficult to object." He stepped back into the bathroom to use the mirror to tie his bowtie.

When he was ready, Darcy held his jacket. Once he'd slipped it on, he grabbed the tuning hammer, and they hurried back down the stairs.

Astrid's eyes lit up when she saw him. "You look almost too handsome," she complimented.

"Thank you, but I believe I play better when I'm properly dressed."

Darcy had thought his music spectacular when he'd been dressed in no more than a towel. She kept that delicious memory to herself and paced in front of the fireplace while Griffin made what to her untrained ear were nearly imperceptible adjustments in the pitch of the bass keys. Then when he sat and repeated the scales, she was amazed the piano actually had a richer tone.

"Even I can tell that's better," she exclaimed without thinking.

"You're not a music lover, Miss MacLeod?"

Lyman Vaughn had come up behind her so silently she hadn't noted his approach over the thick oriental carpet, and a horribly uncomfortable sensation crept up the back of her neck. It was all she could do to stifle an obvious shudder.

"I do love music," she assured him, "and most especially Griffin's, but no one would describe me as an expert."

"Then you should concentrate on simply planting beautiful gardens," Vaughn remarked casually, and he moved away to place a silver-tinted side chair with a blue-and-silver striped seat closer to his daughter's bedside.

"I've no name for this yet," Griffin announced, "and it may yet prove to be part of a longer work."

As he began to play, Darcy hastily retook her seat, but she could scarcely breathe. Griffin hadn't mentioned her profession when he'd introduced her, and yet Lyman Vaughn had commented on her area of expertise as though he were intimately acquainted with her background. She doubted that he'd stumbled upon the information about her in his effort to contact Griffin either.

If he knew so much about her, was he also aware of Griffin's link to Interpol? If he were, then this wasn't simply a risky performance for a man who wouldn't blink at murder. It was a carefully laid trap.

She struck a more relaxed pose as though her only concern was to fully appreciate the brilliance of Griffin's artistry, but she hadn't truly drawn a relaxed breath since they'd left home. The setting was elegant and Griffin's performance bold perfection, but their host sickened her. She didn't understand how Griffin could lose himself so completely in his music that the danger surrounding them simply faded away.

She envied him his detachment and glanced toward Astrid. Her heart ached for the frail girl. She didn't appear to be in any pain, but even without any specific details, Darcy imagined her suffering from the fright of an original diagnosis, through delicate brain surgery, and perhaps several bouts of excruciating chemotherapy. Apparently all to no avail.

By the time Griffin reached the melancholy strain which signaled the close of the magnificent piece, Darcy deeply regretted requesting such a moving selection. She reached for the tissue in her pocket. Astrid was blotting away her tears on a lace handkerchief, while her father's expression remained unchanged.

Griffin held the final note, and Lyman Vaughn began to applaud enthusiastically. "I'm not surprised you've begun to compose, but I had no idea you'd be so extraordinarily gifted in that regard. Have you recorded that piece?"

"No, I plan to wait until I've enough original music to fill a CD. What did you think, Astrid?"

"It's lovely, but so poignant. Not that music shouldn't evoke sorrow, but I can't help but be curious as to your thoughts when you wrote it. Were you nursing a broken heart?"

Griffin glanced toward Darcy. "No, I was inspired by the changing seasons and the rhythms of life."

Astrid considered his comment a long moment. "Then perhaps it isn't sad at all, but merely flows like the tides."

"Yes, but I need a title which won't be confused with Debussy's 'Le Mer'. Now, you mentioned Chopin."

Astrid murmured her delight as Griffin continued with his usual effortless grace. He looked up frequently to smile at her, and her face filled with a pretty blush. When he completed the piece, she made a request, and he continued without pause.

He played for an hour before Vaughn rose. "I can't thank you enough for coming here, but you must be hungry. Perhaps you could play for us again after supper."

"It's always a pleasure to play for such an appreciative audience." Griffin stood and came forward. "May we dine here so Astrid and I may continue to discuss her favorite music?"

"I can't eat real food," she explained regretfully. "But I would love your company."

"Of course," her father exclaimed. "We'll dine right here. Excuse me while I inform my staff of our change in plan."

Astrid was such a charming girl, and clearly infatuated with Griffin. Darcy got up to walk around but stayed clear of the hospital bed so as not to intrude on their conversation. She tried to appear interested rather than simply snoop when she approached the dancing nudes, but Matisse's bold signature could be read from several feet away.

She kept her eye on the doorway to prevent Lyman Vaughn from sneaking up on her again. Other than the remark on her profession, he'd done nothing untoward, but she didn't expect him to show his true colors until he'd gotten everything he wanted. Still, she felt as though she were calling upon an executioner who just hadn't bothered to don his black hood.

Regardless of how talented a cook Vaughn might employ, she doubted she would be able to chew a single bite. She decided to cut up the food and slide it around her plate to rearrange it, then scolded herself silently for worrying about hurting the feelings of an arms dealer or his cook.

A tall gray-haired man in a dark suit, who could have been the housekeeper's twin, carried in a set of decoratively painted gold stacking tables. Lyman Vaughn followed and directed him to place them around Astrid's bed. The servant made several trips to set their places, then returned carrying side chairs with pale blue tapestry seats which appeared to be from the dining room.

Darcy chose a chair on the opposite side of the bed from Griffin and Lyman Vaughn. When both concentrated on Astrid, she was grateful to be forgotten. She'd been well-aware that wives and girlfriends of celebrities were often pushed aside by adoring fans, but this was her first experience with anything even remotely approaching that predicament.

Prior to their arrival, Griffin had wisely insisted she occupy herself elsewhere, but despite the tragedy of Astrid's situation, this was still a valuable preview of what traveling with him would be. People would be courteous—even master criminals had manners, apparently—but in any gathering of Griffin's fans, she would be shunted aside.

To think of her own comfort while Griffin charmed a

terminally ill fan was more self-centered than she cared to be. But what were her choices? She could sit there like a lump and hope the time passed quickly. She might pretend they were at the home of some legitimate businessman, where eventually her presence might be noticed. Or she could concentrate on plotting their escape from this well-decorated chamber of horrors. The third option held the most appeal.

Their first course was served by a young man in a white chef's jacket. He mumbled something in French to Vaughn, then served them bowls of lobster bisque. Darcy meant to take only a polite sip, not that anyone would have noticed had she lapped it up like a cat, but the soup was so creamy and delicious she left only a spoonful pooling at the bottom of her bowl.

The china had a gold rim and a pale blue band. Their utensils were heavy sterling silver, and the crystal was delicate perfection. That they each had their own small table was unavoidable that night, but Darcy imagined Vaughn's dining table must be at least twenty feet long and lit with highly polished antique candelabra.

She glanced up at Griffin, and he looked her way and winked. She didn't understand how he could be in such high spirits. The dark-suited man, the butler, perhaps, returned to pour wine, but she took only water. Her hand shook so badly she could barely bring the goblet to her lips, alcohol would have undone her. Griffin, however, entered into a lengthy conversation with Vaughn and his daughter on the merits of various French wines as opposed to their California counterparts.

Their next course was Dover sole amandine. Vaughn assured them the fish had been flown fresh from England that morning. Now expecting a huge meal, Darcy limited herself to two bites, but the sole was also delicious. She rested her fork on the side of her plate and tried to breathe deeply rather than continue to obsess over their dangerously bizarre situation.

The conversation again turned to music, and Darcy was relieved no one expected her to contribute anything. She made a mental note to study the lives of Griffin's favorite composers in an effort to become more knowledgeable. Of course, if they didn't make it home, her ignorance would no longer be a problem.

Depressed by that gruesome thought, it took her a moment to come up with something positive. Finally she settled on her gratitude that Griffin had chosen to play the piano rather than the bagpipes. Not that he wouldn't look smashing in a kilt, but it would have been impossible to pretend a true affection for that peculiar instrument. She could well understand how the Irish had terrified enemies in battle with their pipes, but believed a battlefield was where they belonged.

The white-coated young man returned with their entrée and this time spoke at more length with their host. Darcy couldn't follow their exchange, but hoped it pertained to the food rather than anything more sinister.

Griffin noted Darcy's confusion. "He's describing the pheasant as particularly fine."

Darcy recalled eating pheasant once in Germany. She sampled a forkful, and it almost melted in her mouth. There were also artichoke hearts, tiny new potatoes and dinner rolls as flaky as croissants.

One look at Lyman Vaughn suppressed her appetite quite effectively, but she sampled everything in an attempt to keep up her strength. By the time they were served a crème caramel for dessert, she was sleepy, and she feared she'd made a big mistake to swallow even a bite.

Griffin rose with care so as not to overturn his small table. "This has been one of the best meals I've ever eaten, but if I'm to stay awake long enough to play something else for you, I'll need some fresh air. Darcy, come with me out to the garden."

Darcy nearly sprinted through the french doors leading to the terrace. Night had fallen, but the garden's gravel walkways were well-lit. She reached for Griffin's hand and led him along a rose-lined path to a majestic marble fountain. The entwined figures of the three graces stood in the center. They were ringed by half a dozen fine sprays that splashed over their feet and filled the shallow pool. Confident they wouldn't be overheard, she still pressed close to share her news.

"Vaughn knows I'm a landscape architect. Could he have also discovered your ties to Interpol?"

Alarmed, Griffin abruptly pulled her around to face him. "Tell me exactly what he said."

Darcy repeated their brief exchange verbatim. "If he's been snooping around Monarch Bay, then we should assume that your cover's blown."

"Maybe, maybe not. We were out of the room for several minutes, and he could have done a quick Internet search then. If anyone typed your name into Google, what would they find?"

Darcy hadn't even considered that possibility. "Defy the World Tomatoes has a web site where I'm listed as the landscape architect."

"I've seen the web site," Griffin offered. "It's a good one."

"Thank you, Mary Beth and Christy Joy designed it, but I think that's a long shot."

"Well, for now, I'm not willing to assume anything, except for this."

He bent to kiss her, wrapped his arms around her waist and, when he straightened, her feet left the ground. It was a possessive kiss, an abandoned assault on her senses that went on and on until they were both dizzy and in need of air. When he finally released her, she slid down his leg to find the ground.

When she caught her breath, she poked him in the chest. "I'll agree this is a wonderfully romantic garden, but we'll be damn lucky to get out of here alive. Let's just steal the limo and go right now."

"No," he responded in an urgent whisper, "that would arouse far too much suspicion. We're going to wait and pretend that we love it here."

"Easy for you to say! You've got your music to distract you. I keep thinking how despicable Lyman Vaughn is, and poor Astrid breaks my heart, but—"

"I've not been thinking about the music," he confided softly. "I've been remembering the other concerts I've given for the terminally ill. Most have been in hospitals, but a few were in private homes. Music has the power to lift people out of their pain, momentarily at least, but it can't defeat death. Now, what I'm hoping is that we can give Astrid a few hours of peace, and then get out of here first thing in the morning."

"If Vaughn knows the real reason you're here, he won't allow you to leave," Darcy argued. "We need to get out tonight, and if not now, then just as soon as Vaughn has gone to bed."

He shook his head. "I didn't want you involved in this, but now that you are, you'll do as I say."

"And if your strategy gets us both killed?"

Griffin chuckled under his breath. "Then I'll admit to having made a disastrous miscalculation, but at least we'd be together for all eternity."

"Well, that's a comfort!" she fired right back at him. She moved closer to the fountain and dipped her hands into the cool water. "Fine, I'll do what you say, but you've got to promise me this is your last bit of intrigue."

"Darcy—" he warned.

"No, let's not argue. Just go on back inside and play some lullabies so Vaughn and his whole household will fall asleep."

Griffin dropped his arm around her shoulders as they started up the walkway. "Fine, I'd already planned to play something soft and sweet for Astrid. It's amazing that even monsters can father nice children."

"Where's her mother? If my child were dying, nothing could keep me away."

"Let's not ask that question."

"Do you honestly believe Vaughn would admit to storing her body in the freezer?"

"Darcy, I'd no idea you were this cynical."

The complaint hurt, but only because it was true.

By the time they reentered the house from the terrace, all evidence of their small dinner party had been cleared away. The nurse had returned and was fussing over Astrid, but Vaughn quickly intervened.

"Tonight, my daughter needs nothing more than time to appreciate our guests," he assured the pretty nurse, but she did not look pleased as she withdrew.

"What's your favorite piece, Griffin?" Astrid asked.

He moved to her bedside to answer. "I try not to have favorites, because then I play them too often and swiftly tire of them. The opposite is equally true—if I'm not fond of a particular composer, then I neglect his work. Of course, I can then count on being invited to play his most beloved concerto for some prestigious event, and it's difficult to prepare in time."

"But you make everything look so easy," she exclaimed.

"Thank you, but you must remember how many years it took me to reach this level of technical proficiency, and how difficult it is to maintain."

"I'm so sorry," Astrid apologized. "I didn't mean to insult you."

Griffin leaned down to kiss her cheek. "You haven't in the least. Now let me just surprise you this time."

Darcy returned to her comfortable chair, but she resisted becoming complacent. Instead, she wondered what had happened to the burly man who'd ridden there with them from the airport. Was he out patrolling the grounds, perhaps hoping they would make a break for it so that he could use them for target practice?

The butler wasn't heavy, but he looked tough as a whip, and she sure didn't want to go up against the housekeeper. Or the chef, who was undoubtedly an expert with knives. Antoine didn't pose any grave threat, nor did the nurse, but that still left Lyman Vaughn, who might use anything from a handgun to high voltage to defeat someone who got in his way.

Her job, of course, was simply to dote on Griffin and let Interpol handle Vaughn, but not even Griffin's marvelous music could soothe her fears. Fortunately, after paying him a wistful compliment on his second piece, Astrid drifted off to sleep during the third.

Vaughn rose from his chair to lean over the bed, but satisfied she was resting comfortably, he crossed to the piano. "The wire transfer was completed before you left San Francisco," he assured the pianist. "But this evening you have given my daughter a gift beyond any price. I will be forever in your debt."

Griffin rose and stepped around the bench. "It was a joy to me as well. I'll play for Astrid again tomorrow. We can find our rooms, so we'll bid you a good night."

"Good night," Vaughn responded, and he quickly returned to his daughter's bedside.

"I'm surprised you didn't bring any music," Darcy offered, believing the question safe to ask while they were still within Vaughn's hearing. "What if Astrid had requested something you didn't know?"

Griffin shot her an incredulous glance and taking her elbow, escorted her up the stairs. "There are thousands of pieces of classical music written for the piano and, frankly, a great many deserve to be forgotten. Others are universally loved. Those are the ones I expected her to request, and she did."

"Has no one ever arranged for a private concert and then asked for a piece you hadn't played?"

Griffin led her into his room, then paused to turn the key in the lock before continuing on into her room, where he also secured the door. He shrugged off his coat and draped it over the chair at the desk.

"I generally confer with my host on the content of the program so I'll have sufficient time to prepare, but occasionally I receive a last-minute request for something obscure."

"What do you do?"

Griffin pulled her close. "I do what women often do with other men—I fake it."

He nuzzled her throat and tickled, and she couldn't help but laugh. "Obviously over-confidence never poses a problem."

"No, not when I have such good reason to be self-assured." He slid his hands to the small of her back and pressed her close to whisper, "You're doing great."

His room was decorated in a deep forest green, hers in pale pink. The four-poster bed was covered in a thick pink satin comforter, but even with a charming setting and Griffin in a playful mood, she'd never felt less like making love. She gave his lower lip a playful nip.

"Have you ever had sex on a balcony?" she asked.

"No, but this is the perfect night to begin." He stepped away to open the french doors to the wrought-iron balcony that ran between their rooms. He drew her outside and tugged on his tie to remove it.

"Don't worry," he whispered. "I'm not in the mood either."

Darcy thought better of revealing in any other circumstance he was all she needed to be in the most romantic of moods, but that night she was relieved not to have to give a performance that might be taped. She snuggled against him and took comfort from his strength.

"I'm so tired," she said in her normal tone. "It was a long flight, and even if it is still daytime for us, we ought to try and get in sync with France."

Griffin rested his hands on her shoulders lightly, then gave her a long, slow kiss. "Come on, let's sleep in my room."

But once they reached the bed, he grabbed the extra

pillows and shoved them down under the covers to create believable models of them asleep. He then gestured for her to follow him into the bathroom where he turned on the water in the bathtub and added bubble bath.

"Play with me awhile," he invited with a charming smile.

"Are you crazy?" Darcy rested her hands on her hips.

Griffin removed his shirt and hung it up on the hook behind the door. "No, but you're as jumpy as a flea, and I want you to be able to sleep. I'll stay awake and keep watch."

"Fine, but what will you do if an intruder appears?"

Griffin's smile spread wide. "He'll never know what hit him. Now come on, the surf's up."

A bath did sound awfully good, and Darcy peeled off her clothes down to her lacy lavender lingerie before she turned away and glanced up at him through her lashes. "I usually read in the bathtub. I sure hope I won't be bored."

"It's highly unlikely," Griffin responded with an amused chuckle.

The bathroom had a soft green marble floor and matching walls. The towels were pale green, as was the huge tub. The fixtures were gold and included a handheld showerhead which resembled an antique telephone. An assortment of expensive shampoos and conditioners were placed on a convenient shelf behind the tub.

Darcy waited until Griffin had turned off the water to cast her lingerie aside and climb into the tub. She slid down under the bubbles and covered a wide yawn with both hands. She closed her eyes and sighed softly. "Promise you won't let me drown."

"I'll make a passable lifeguard."

Adrift in her own tiny sea, Darcy didn't hear him remove his clothes, and she was startled when he slipped into the tub behind her. "Not in the mood?" she observed slyly.

"Hush, just close your eyes and relax," he cajoled, and he began to massage the tension from her shoulders.

She dipped her chin to her chest. "That feels so good, but I wish we were anywhere but here."

"We'll be gone by noon tomorrow." He reached for the coconut-scented shampoo and poured some into his palm. "Let me wash your hair." He rubbed the creamy liquid into her scalp with slow circles. "Still think I have great hands?"

"They're as incredible as the rest of you, but my head is still full of bees."

He slid a bit lower and pulled her back against his chest. "I know that feeling, but this should help." He picked up the showerhead and turned on a warm spray to rinse her hair. "This is really fun. Tomorrow, let's not leave the hotel."

Seated between his outstretched legs, she could feel his erection cushioned against her bottom. It would be so easy to turn, take him deep and ride him until he begged her to stop. She ached with the temptation to lose herself in him, but she wouldn't risk their lives for a brief burst of pleasure when it would leave them too sated to be mindful of the danger that might lurk right outside their door.

He was so damn spoiled, but neither his extraordinary talent nor well-deserved celebrity would save them if Lyman Vaughn wanted them dead. "That might as well be Ted Bundy, or Jeffrey Dahmer, or even Adolph Hitler, for that matter, sitting downstairs. I can't do this."

She grabbed hold of the tub and nearly vaulted over the side. She wrapped herself in one of the enormous towels and walked into her room to dress for the horrible eventuality she feared was mere minutes away. She was still sorting through her bag when Griffin entered, already dressed in a pair of black silk pajama bottoms.

He circled to face her, then placed a fingertip on her lips and mouthed the words, "Trust me."

Darcy rested her palm over his heart. The beat was slow and steady while hers was all aflutter. "This is just another performance for you, isn't it?"

Uncertain what she meant, Griffin frowned. "With you, never. Go to sleep. I'll wake you in the morning."

Darcy turned away to lock the door leading to the balcony. Then she tossed him his jacket from off the chair. Next she wedged the back of that same chair beneath the doorknob to block the door leading to the hall.

It was all she could do to barricade the room, but she wasn't satisfied it was enough. "Sweet dreams to you too."

Griffin just shook his head and walked back into his room, but it was difficult to console himself with the fact that he had been provided with a great deal of undercover training, which she lacked. It was no wonder she couldn't be as cool-headed as he was under stress, but what rankled most was that she didn't trust him to protect her.

Later, they would have to tackle the huge problem she'd created by asking him not to work for Interpol again. Depressed by that thought, he followed her example and shoved a convenient chair under the doorknob to block the door to the hall. Then he went out on the balcony to scan for vines that would provide a man with a convenient ladder. He was relieved to find none. Several potted plants had been set on the balcony, but no foliage reached it from the ground.

With Astrid so eager to hear him play again, he believed they were safe. He was also an extremely light sleeper, but he sat in the corner across from the bed, intending only to rest. If anyone were so stupid as to slip into his room, they would be fooled by the pillow-stuffed bed for the split second it would take him to react. Uncertain whether or not he was merely picking up on Darcy's fear or reacting to his own sense of danger, he rested his head against the wall and hoped the night would pass as quickly as the day.

Chapter Eighteen

Darcy dozed fitfully and, each time she awoke, the night surrounded her with familiar sounds: the crickets' rhythmic chirping, the fountain's bubbling rush and the occasional hoot of an owl.

But the soft scrape of a flowerpot being edged aside on the wrought-iron balcony sent her bounding from the bed. She tiptoed through the bathroom to Griffin's room, but remained in the shadowed doorway until she found him pressed against the wall. His attention was riveted upon the balcony doors at his left, which she thought he'd been crazy to leave slightly ajar.

Her heart was in her throat, and a silent scream circled her whole body. A shadow crossed the french doors, and then a man slipped between them into the room. He took a step toward the pillowed figures in the bed, then waited a long moment before taking another step closer. Only a pale sliver of moonlight leaked through the open doorway, but Darcy saw the glimmer of a blade clutched in his hand.

She was certain Griffin saw it too, and on the man's next stealthy step, he came away from the wall with a flying leap and kicked the would-be assassin in the temple. She covered her ears, but it was too late to muffle the sickening crack of a shattered skull, and she was certain the man was dead before his body bounced on the rug.

She quickly crossed the room to hit the light switch. The burly man who'd accompanied them from the airport lay sprawled beside the bed, the glow from the overhead fixture reflected in his blank stare.

"Damn, but you're good," she swore softly.

Griffin turned away to open the french doors wide, then he

came near to whisper, "Save the compliments, just help me roll the guy off the balcony."

That someone could still be listening unnerved her all the more, but she replied just as softly, "Why? He's already dead."

Griffin drew her outside. "That he is, but if he's found splattered on the ground rather than in my room, no one can say we had anything to do with it."

That made sense to her, but Griffin had to do most of the lifting while she grappled with the dead man's legs. Limp, he presented an awkward burden, but once they'd hoisted him to the railing, he rolled right on over and landed with a hollow thud in the flowerbed below. Griffin snatched a tissue from the bathroom to lift his knife from the rug and tossed it down to him.

Darcy drank in the night air rather than shriek with what they had done, but had they been in that bed sound asleep in each other's arms, they might very well be the ones who were dead. Refusing to dwell on that awful possibility, she moved to the end of the balcony. The window was open in the room next to hers and, while it must have taken a good stretch from the window ledge, she could easily see how the man had climbed onto their balcony.

"I heard him brush by one of these pots," she said.

"Yes, so did I. I'd checked to make certain no one could come up from the garden, but I should have noticed how close the windows are here on the second story. I did listen to your warning, though, Darcy, and I was ready."

"You sure were, but now what?"

"Now I'm going to be the one doing the hunting." He pulled her into a fond embrace and brushed her lips with a light kiss. "I want you to stay here."

She put her hands on his bare chest to push away, but he continued to hold her tight. "The next man might have a gun, and if he kicks in the door and takes me hostage, then Vaughn could force you to do his bidding."

"Not if he can't find you, and you needn't remain here."

"Look, was I in your way just now?"

"No, but—"

"But nothing. We've got to stay together. Why don't we just get the hell out of here?"

"Don't think I'm not tempted to take you by the hand and run all the way back to Paris, but this is the closest I've come to Lyman Vaughn, and I won't allow him to slip away."

"Shouldn't you contact Interpol and let them handle it?"

"It's not as easy as dialing 911, but they should already be close."

Darcy clung to that hope, but she felt sick clear through. Her only consolation was that they hadn't been jumped while they were in the bathtub and left to float in blood-tinted water.

She slid her hands up his tightly muscled arms. He had enormous talent, the looks of a god, and struck with a cobra's lethal force. It wasn't her usual idea of a winning combination, but she would definitely make an exception for him.

"It looks as though I was right. Vaughn must know about your extracurricular activities, or he'd not have sent one of his men to kill us. But it also has to mean that he's got a mole at Interpol, doesn't it?"

Griffin's eyes narrowed slightly as he considered the possibility. Deeply disturbed by it, he released her and took a step back. "He could."

"Well, why else would he want us dead?"

"Excellent question, but we've got to act now rather than debate the issue until the next thug arrives."

"Fine, I'll stay out of your way, but I'm not staying here. Your size gives you a greater range, but I really do know karate."

Griffin rested his hands on the balcony rail and gazed out into the night. He appeared to be weighing his options, found very few and reluctantly straightened. "With Astrid so ill, I may be able to strike a bargain with Vaughn. Just let me do all the talking."

"Yes, sir." Expecting the worst, she was already dressed in her black Levi's and a pale pink T-shirt and, after a quick kiss to seal the deal, they moved through the bedroom and shut off the lights. Griffin led the way into her room where he removed the chair blocking her door and cracked it open.

The hallway was dark and silent. Unable to sense the presence of anyone near, they stepped out holding hands like two children creeping toward a haunted house on Halloween. Both barefooted, they made their way silently down the hall to the top of the stairs. Lit by a crystal chandelier, the steps were clear, if not inviting.

"The house is too quiet," Darcy whispered. "Could they all have gone?"

Griffin shrugged and glanced at his watch. He'd reset the time when they'd landed, and it was now two a.m.. "Vaughn may still be with Astrid. If that's the case, keep a close watch on the foyer behind us, and also on the french doors to the terrace."

"You've got it." Darcy wiped her damp palms on her pants and prayed Vaughn and his whole entourage had vanished. But when they reached the bottom of the stairs, they heard him speaking softly to his daughter.

Griffin made a quick check of the library and dining room on the opposite side of the foyer and, once assured they were empty, he entered the living room with a confident stride. "I hate to bother you, but I'm afraid someone's fallen from the roof."

Lyman Vaughn was seated at Astrid's bedside, leaning forward, arms braced on his thighs. His hands were clasped between his knees. He regarded Griffin with a distracted nod then turned back toward his daughter.

"I'd rather not be disturbed," he replied.

Darcy moved out from behind Griffin to gain a better vantage point. A single lamp placed near the hospital bed left the rest of the well-appointed room in deep shadow. Hoping the darkness kept them from becoming easy targets for a sniper stationed in the garden, she left the rest of the lamps unlit.

Griffin gave her a quick thumbs up sign, then continued in a considerate whisper, "I doubt the poor soul lying in the flowerbed wants to be disturbed either, but someone should notify the police. I'd have handled it myself, but I'm not sure of our location. I haven't seen a telephone, and I didn't bring my cell phone with me."

Darcy had expected Griffin to kick the chair right out from under Vaughn, and she was impressed that he'd instead chosen to play innocent for Astrid's sake. The ailing young woman was curled up on her side with one of Griffin's CDs pressed close to her heart. She wore a sweet smile as though she were enjoying a lovely dream.

"If the man is dead," Vaughn replied wearily, "the authorities can be notified in the morning."

"Then you do have a telephone?" Griffin asked pointedly. "I'm unfamiliar with your home. Would you please come and show me where it is?"

"Tomorrow, after breakfast."

"The person who fell from the roof must be in your employ. Doesn't he deserve more respect?"

"You're becoming tedious, Mr. Moore. Take Ms. MacLeod into the kitchen, make yourselves a nice snack and go back to bed. We'll deal with the dead tomorrow."

Griffin spread his hands wide. "I wouldn't want to inadvertently eat something the chef might plan to serve for breakfast. Come to the kitchen with us, and we'll look for his menus."

"I had absolutely no idea you two were so helpless." Vaughn rose, paused to massage the stiffness from his neck, then leaned down to kiss Astrid's cheek.

It was a touching gesture, but when he straightened, he'd pulled a 9mm Glock from beneath the mattress. "My daughter is very fond of you, so I'm going to lock you both in the pantry where you may eat anything you please. My chef will release you in the morning. Come over here, girl."

Darcy stayed put. "Mr. Jordan, really, we didn't mean to be pests, but that's no way to treat your guests."

"Obviously I disagree. You've given the concert, Griffin, so there's no further need for this ridiculous charade. You know who I am. It took longer than I'd hoped to bring you here. I should have sent Adriana to Seattle instead of that lumbering fool you claim just fell from the roof. Well, good riddance."

"Wait a minute," Griffin interjected. "Are you admitting to having my chauffeur killed?"

"No, of course not. Octavio was told to see you received my invitation, but unfortunately, when he approached your limousine, your chauffeur recognized him. You know the rest. Now, I do not enjoy repeating myself. Ms. MacLeod, march."

When he motioned with the weapon, Darcy trusted Griffin to move with lightning speed and, pretending to be completely flustered, she gestured wildly as she took a step toward him. "Mr. Moore and I are barely acquainted, and I've no idea what happened to some chauffeur in...where?"

Without waiting for an answer, she spun to her right and caught Vaughn in the kneecap with a bone-jarring kick.

Knocked off his feet, he juggled the automatic pistol as he went sprawling.

Griffin fell on Vaughn and pinned him down. He grabbed for the gun with one hand and used the other to slam the arms dealer's head into the floor. Even with blood gushing from a cut above his left eye, Vaughn still fought fiercely to break Griffin's hold without losing his grip on the weapon.

Darcy danced back out of the way and did a frantic search for something small but heavy enough to strike Vaughn over the head. Before she found one, he arched his back and, still struggling for control of the gun, shoved the barrel into his mouth.

She screamed, "He's going to shoot!"

With a sickening jolt, Griffin gasped the horror Vaughn intended, and dove to the side a split second before he fired. Blood and bits of brain splattered the wall near the bed, but only a few drops sprayed across Griffin's shoulder.

Thoroughly disgusted, he sat back and fought to catch his breath. "Son of a bitch," he swore. "He meant to take me with him and right in front of his own daughter."

Darcy gagged and clapped her hand over her mouth, but even with all the commotion, Astrid lay perfectly still. While Darcy's ears continued to ring from the gun's loud report, the darling girl hadn't even flinched.

"Griffin," she called fearfully. She reached over the bed rail to feel for a pulse in Astrid's neck, and her skin felt unnaturally cool. "I think she may have already been dead when we came in."

Griffin shoved himself to his feet, came to the bed and searched for a pulse in Astrid's wrist. Her hand was limp in his grasp, and he laid it down gently. "She was such a sweetheart." He sighed.

"Yes, she was, but where is everyone else? Why didn't anyone come running when they heard the shot?"

"If we're lucky, they cleared out hours ago."

"The body count is now up to three, and you're relying on luck?"

"Good point." Griffin stepped over Lyman Vaughn's legs to pick up the gun. He checked the clip, then clicked on the safety. "Come on, let's search the house and make certain we're alone."

"I hate to leave her here with him." Darcy stroked Astrid's

pale cheek in a tender farewell, but before she'd reached Griffin, the front door flew open and half a dozen heavily armed men rushed in.

Dressed in black with helmets and body armor, when they saw Lyman Vaughn's body and Griffin holding a gun, they halted in midstride. A stocky man with intense dark eyes waved the others off toward the rest of the house and greeted Griffin in French.

Relieved some apparently friendly forces had finally arrived, Darcy shoved Vaughn's chair around to the end of the bed and sat. She wondered what Vaughn could have been saying to Astrid when they'd entered. He must have known that she'd died in her sleep, but he'd been dry-eyed. She'd known Astrid only a single day and had been touched by her death. How could her own father have been immune from that pain?

Griffin handed the Frenchman Lyman Vaughn's Glock, knelt by Darcy's side and took her hands. "Interpol agents followed us from the airport. Lucien just assured me that if we hadn't left here by noon today, he and his men were coming in. But you were never here, do you understand?"

She could smell Vaughn's bloody corpse, and it would become an indelible memory. "I don't care what the 'Le Swat' team leader says. I'm never going to forget this."

"No one expects you to." He placed a kiss in her palm and folded her fingers over it. "But you mustn't tell anyone you visited this house, nor met Lyman Vaughn. In his obituary in the French newspapers, he'll be referred to by the alias Simon Jordan and described as an internationally known financier."

"Will they also report that he fell from the roof?"

"No, I imagine there will be a discreet reference to health issues and suicide."

Fluent in English, Lucien nodded in agreement. Unconcerned with gathering evidence at the crime scene, he shoved the Glock into his belt, removed his helmet to wipe his shaved head with a handkerchief, then replaced it.

He continued to observe Darcy with a suspicious gaze, but if this were his idea of a timely rescue, she definitely thought he needed a new watch. "You're worth a dozen of him, you know," she whispered to Griffin.

"Thank you, but I must have your word on this. You're not to tell Christy Joy, nor your parents, nor, God forbid, write a tell-all book about this and give an interview on the Today Show. I'm sure you can understand why."

"Of course, the freedom of the civilized world depends on my keeping quiet, so you can tell Lucien here he won't have to take me around back and shoot me."

"Darcy! None of us would ever harm you, but Vaughn has associates who kill for sport, and you don't want to be on their radar."

"What about you?"

"No one will know I visited this estate either. I'll readily admit to being in Paris this week, and the register at the Hotel Meurice will prove we stayed there. It was a brief pleasure trip, nothing more."

"And what about Astrid? She ought to have a funeral, and who else will give her one?"

Griffin turned to Lucien. "What do you know of Astrid's mother? Will she claim the body?"

The Frenchman replied in heavily accented English, "No, she was a French cabaret singer, regrettably without much talent, who perished in a traffic accident when her daughter was five. She and Vaughn were never wed, and Astrid was schooled at a convent near here. She did not live with her father until she fell ill last year."

"But they seemed so close," Darcy protested.

"He visited her from time to time," Lucien added. "They were not strangers."

"Perhaps not, but still—"

Griffin squeezed her hands. "Vaughn was a consummate performer, and we saw what he wished us to see."

"Well, you can bury him in the garden if you like, but I want a real funeral for Astrid, and a grave in a nice cemetery with an angel on the headstone. Perhaps the convent could arrange it."

Griffin looked up at their companion. "Will you contact the Mother Superior and make such a request? She should know which mortuary to call."

"I will see to it personally. Gather up your belongings. We will take you to the Meurice and let you know when and where the funeral is to be held."

"Wait a minute," Darcy asked. "What about all the others—

256

Antoine, the nurse, the butler and housekeeper, and the chef, who was supposed to let us out of the pantry? What's happened to them?"

Lucien's wide mouth crimped in a brief smile. "They left here little more than an hour ago. We intercepted their van. They have been detained and for just cause, I assure you. They have all been involved in Vaughn's crimes."

"I doubt the nurse was in on any arms deals," Darcy argued.

Lucien shot Griffin a warning glance, and the pianist was the one to reply. "Don't worry so, she'll not be sent to Siberia, but it wouldn't be to her advantage to admit that she'd been in Vaughn's employ. Another job will be found for her, and a respectable one this time."

Darcy had one last question. "What's happened to the beautiful Adriana? Why wasn't she here?"

Anxious to finish his work, Lucien shuffled his feet. "From what we have observed, Vaughn kept his daughter separate from his mistresses. But you need not worry that Adriana will seek you out to avenge his death. She was arrested last night in a sting operation in Zurich which led her to believe she would be collecting a payment for stolen weapons."

Griffin rose and pulled Darcy to her feet. "There, that's enough. Come on, let's pack up, go to the hotel and finally get some sleep."

"We can't leave Astrid here with strangers," she responded sadly.

After the night they'd had, Griffin did not feel up to arguing. "Lucien, will you please contact the Mother Superior immediately? Apologize for waking her, but when you explain Astrid has died, she should forgive the lateness of the hour and provide the necessary information. The doctor's name will be on Astrid's medications. Contact him to sign the death certificate."

Lucien nodded stiffly and left them to complete the calls.

"We'll stay until the mortician arrives," Griffin assured Darcy, "but I've got to clean up and get ready to go. I don't want you sitting here within sight of Vaughn's carcass. Come upstairs with me."

"No, please, I'll sit closer to the piano where I did earlier and wait with Astrid here."

"I won't be long," he promised and hurried out of the room.

Darcy sat in the comfortable upholstered chair and rested her head against the back. She heard Lucien talking with his men and, after taking a few quick photographs, they zipped Vaughn into a body bag and carried him out of the house. A few minutes later, two of the men returned with sponges, a mop and pail and began cleaning up the mess.

Darcy covered a wide yawn and closed her eyes, but the hideous images that greeted her kept her wide awake. Griffin soon appeared wearing Levi's and a black sweater. He paused to kiss the top of her head and then went to the piano and began a piece she instantly recognized as his.

She'd regarded his other composition as melancholy, but this one was even darker in mood, and far more intricate and intense. It sounded as though he'd written it while being ravaged by some horrendous loss. Spellbound, she listened with such rapt attention she failed to notice the men who had stormed the house had gathered in the foyer. When Griffin struck the final chord, they broke into respectful applause, but she had to hold back tears.

"You didn't care for that piece?" he asked her.

"What's it called, 'The Garden of Doom'?"

"I've not titled it yet, but I like that. Would you mind if I used it?"

"Not at all, but I hate to think of your being that unhappy."

"I'm all right now that you're speaking to me again."

Thinking the impromptu concert over, the men continued their search of the dwelling and, alone with Griffin, Darcy left her chair and crossed to the piano. "If that's the type of music I inspire, then we ought to go our separate ways before your career suffers irrevocable harm."

"Impossible. Besides, it's important for a composer to have both range and depth." He patted the bench. "Sit here beside me while I play something for Astrid."

Still unnerved, Darcy sank beside him, but her spirits rose when she recognized Chopin's Polonaise. It was a thrill to watch Griffin's graceful touch upon the keys, and the music flowed as though the notes leaped to meet his fingertips. Seated so close, she was surrounded by the beautiful melody, but that his own music was so desperately sad still disturbed her.

The first time she'd seen him on the path at Defy the World, she'd suspected he might have a melancholy bent. Then he'd flashed a smile that had made it impossible to think at all. She feared her thought processes were still muddled.

She drew in a deep breath and tried to float on the beauty of the music. Later, she moved back to the comfortable chair, and he was playing one of Chopin's sweet nocturnes when two white-suited men arrived in a hearse.

Griffin left the piano to greet them, while Darcy stood at the foot of the hospital bed grateful all evidence of Lyman Vaughn's death had been so skillfully erased.

"Griffin, please tell them not to remove the CD from Astrid's hands. We should have looked for her clothes. Do you suppose she has any nice things here?"

"I doubt it if she'd been sick for a year, but we'll buy her something new." He took the morticians' card so they would know where to have the clothing delivered, and then insisted that Darcy come upstairs with him to pack rather than watch them take Astrid away.

She held his hand tightly as they climbed the stairs. She'd been frantic with worry when they'd arrived at the chateau, and now she felt completely drained. "Thank you," she murmured softly, "for being the man you are."

Griffin tried to take that as a compliment, but he was not entirely convinced that it was.

The Hotel Meurice was located on the Rue de Rivoli. Beautifully restored with fine replicas of the original furnishings and decor, it was described by guide books as among the city's grandest hotels. Darcy didn't even want to know the cost of Griffin's spectacular suite overlooking the Jardin des Tuileries when it was so far above anything she would ever be able to afford on her own.

Her jaw dropped when she saw the baby grand piano. "Do all the suites have pianos?" she asked.

"No, but I stay here because they have this one for me."

Darcy gazed out at the garden below, and beyond it, she glimpsed the Siene. "You're a bigger celebrity here in Europe than at home, aren't you?"

Griffin came up behind her and rested his hands upon her shoulders. "Well, let's just say the Europeans have a longer tradition of classical music and therefore a more enthusiastic appreciation for classical musicians."

"That's very diplomatic of you."

"How else can I be?" He began to knead her shoulders gently. "I could play 'Great Balls of Fire' and you'd swear it was Jerry Lee Lewis banging on the piano. Would you like that better?"

Darcy dipped her head to encourage his touch. "I'd really love to hear that, but rather than outrage the hotel, better wait until you get home."

Griffin wrapped his arms around her and hugged her tight. "I'm sorry everything turned out so badly. I don't know how I could have been so stupid as to think Lyman Vaughn would allow me drop you off here before I met him."

"You are never stupid," she scolded. "Perhaps no one could have successfully predicted what he might do."

"Thank you for being so forgiving, but it was a colossal blunder that could have cost you your life. I'm still furious with myself—that's why I played 'The Garden of Doom'—but I didn't mean to depress you."

Darcy turned in his arms. "We're both here, in what has to be one of the world's most beautiful hotels. I know I'll cry all the way through Astrid's funeral, but for now, please, let's not be maudlin."

Griffin kissed her deeply rather than agree, but he'd been shaken clear to the marrow by how narrowly they'd escaped death that night, and not merely once, but twice. Darcy had been the best of partners, but what woman would remain with a man who exposed her to that level of risk?

One who loved him, perhaps, but he doubted even Paris with all its magic would be enough to help him win her heart.

Chapter Nineteen

Griffin gave Darcy a last brief kiss, then stepped back. "Are you hungry? I could call room service to send up some breakfast."

"The sun's not even up yet." She paused to cover a wide yawn. "Besides, I didn't sleep more than ten minutes at the chateau, and I know you didn't sleep either. Can't we just go to bed?"

"If you like." He moved into the suite's bedroom, ripped off the heavy brocade spread and dumped it on the floor at the foot of the bed. Then he peeled away the blanket.

Darcy followed him into the bedroom in time to see him shuck off his clothes and toss them onto a gilded chair. Still wearing his sexy silk boxers, he climbed into the king-size bed. He punched the pillow, stretched out and looked ready to sleep the day away.

She thought he'd probably expected more from her, but she had absolutely nothing left to give. At least he hadn't sneered openly at her lack of interest in him, but then he always behaved as a gentleman should even if he had to grit his teeth while doing so.

Clearly he had incredible self-control, which probably had a lot to do with his success. On the other hand, she felt about as secure as a bit of dandelion fluff and was in real danger of flying apart in the next breeze.

She went into the bathroom which was all mirrors and pale marble streaked with gold. The towels were a pale cream, and there were two cream-colored French terry cloth robes waiting for them on brass hooks behind the door. She ran a bath, poured in plenty of scented bath salts and tossed in her pink lingerie to soak while she bathed.

She felt like a princess surrounded by such opulence, but then she imagined most women who dated Griffin must feel like Cinderella. She relaxed in the tub until the water cooled to tepid. She used the fancy hand-held showerhead to wash her hair before she left the tub and thought she just might be relaxed enough to sleep all day too.

She didn't want to sleep nude, though, and pulled on a lavender nightgown that was more lace than silk. She no longer recalled where she'd bought the sinfully soft garment, but this was the perfect place to try it out. She slipped into bed beside Griffin and envied him the ease with which he'd fallen asleep.

She gazed up at the beautiful plasterwork on the high ceiling and tried to shut out all thought save those of sleep. But each time she closed her eyes, the gunshot roared in her ears and the terrifying blood-drenched scene flashed in her mind. Tears began to spill over her lashes and drip down onto her pillow. She turned away and used both hands to muffle her sobs rather than disturb Griffin.

He still felt her tremble and rose slightly. "Hey, everything's all right now."

He turned toward her, drew her back against his chest and curved his whole body around hers. He searched his mind for a comforting phrase, a line from a beloved poem, a scrap from memory, but he came up empty. All he could do was rock her gently and blame himself for bringing her along on the worst trip of his life.

When Darcy finally cried herself to sleep, he continued to cradle her in his arms while he dozed on the edge of sleep. She didn't stir until afternoon, and he came fully awake the instant she sat up.

"Feel better?" he asked.

"I'm sorry. I didn't sleep well on the plane, and by the time I get used to the time change, it will be time to go home. Could we go out into the Tuileries garden? I doubt we'll find a Zen garden in the park, but there should be benches."

"Sounds great, but I have to call room service and order something to eat while we dress, or I'll faint before we get downstairs. Don't tell me you're not hungry either."

She wasn't, but it had been so long since they'd eaten, she knew she should be. "Nothing too fancy, please, maybe just a turkey sandwich and iced tea. Would they make it on a croissant, or do the French only eat them for breakfast?"

"Who cares what they prefer? They're paid to prepare whatever their guests request." Griffin grabbed for the telephone without leaving the bed, and Darcy went in to use the bathroom first. When she came out wearing her denim skirt and chambray shirt, the young man from room service was just closing the door. Griffin walked by in his Levi's eating a piece of cheese.

"If you can wait a couple of minutes to eat, let's take everything down to the garden," he suggested and swung the bathroom door closed.

Their food had been delivered in an elegant gold box, and Darcy opened it to find turkey sandwiches on buttery soft croissants, a selection of cheeses and gorgeous fruit tarts. She used the plastic knife to slice off the curved end of a sandwich and carried it over to the window to enjoy the view while she ate. Paris was such a lovely city, and she absolutely refused to allow Lyman Vaughn to ruin it for her. She was embarrassed to have cried so hard she'd bothered Griffin and told him so when he joined her.

"Don't be silly," he cajoled. "If it weren't so damn unmanly, I would have wept myself. Lucien called to say the funeral's set for tomorrow afternoon. The shops here are closed on Sunday, but the boutique in the hotel should be open, and we need to buy something for Astrid. Then let's go down into the garden and pretend we came to Paris just to enjoy the sights."

"And each other?" Darcy added coyly.

"Exactly." He grabbed the gold box, and she carried the drink containers.

The shops in the hotel were expensive, but Griffin didn't even check the price tag when Darcy spotted a pale pink dress trimmed in lace. He added a pink scarf to cover Astrid's bandages, then asked to have their purchases delivered to the mortuary early the next morning.

As they exited the Meurice, Darcy had to make a conscious effort not to dwell on Astrid's sad fate, but just as she'd hoped it would, the sight of the Jardin des Tuileries sent her spirits soaring.

The young families who frequented the garden on the weekends had already pushed their charges home in their strollers, but the wide paths were still crowded. Veering off toward the left, Griffin led the way to a shady bench beneath a chestnut tree.

"Will this do?" he asked.

"Perfect." Darcy took a sip of tea. "The last time I was here, I didn't even know there was such a thing as a landscape architect."

"Eat," Griffin insisted. "I don't want you to waste away before we get home."

"There's very little danger of that," she assured him, but the turkey sandwich was delicious, and she consumed another third of hers while Griffin finished all of his.

"I'll bet you know who designed this garden," he said. "Tell me about him."

"I thought you wanted me to eat."

"Tell me between bites."

"All right, if you insist. André Le Notre was the royal gardener to Louis XIV, and he also designed the garden at Versailles. We have a beautiful view from the hotel, but from here you can see how the flowing patterns of the low boxwood hedges and flowers create a living tapestry. The trees lining the walkways were planted to provide shade and frame the magnificent view.

"In the seventeenth century, when this beautiful garden came into being, people believed as we do that walking was healthy exercise. I love the idea that a tree Le Notre planted has been enjoyed for generations."

"Yes, that's what I love about music. We can enjoy it long after the composer is gone. It's very peaceful here, isn't it?" Griffin reached for another piece of cheese.

"Isn't this where they had the guillotine?" she asked.

He winced. "Actually, it was just outside the gates, but I'd hoped you'd overlook that portion of the Tuileries' history."

She patted his thigh. "It's peaceful this afternoon, which is all that matters to us. I must have been a bird or squirrel in a previous life, because I love being outdoors. I'd shrivel up and die in one of Dilbert's cubicles."

"I always get a laugh out of Dilbert in the comics, and I've never worked in an office. In fact, I've never even had a job."

"Never? Not even in high school? Oh, never mind, you

didn't attend high school, did you?"

"No, I spent my teens either practicing the piano or studying with tutors, so I missed the whole experience. But I've never met anyone who longed to repeat it."

"Thanks for keeping the conversation light. I'm so grateful you're not the type who just clams up and broods."

Startled by that unexpected compliment, Griffin was appreciative nonetheless. "Well, thank you. Are you going to eat the last part of your sandwich?"

"Why don't you finish it? I want to try one of these gorgeous little tarts."

"You could be described in the same way, you know."

She laughed with him and then nibbled the blackberry tart. The buttery crust broke away with gentle pressure, and the sweetened fruit was superb. "Oh, this is heavenly."

"I love the way you lick your fingers."

"I'm sorry, I know enough to use a napkin." Darcy had two in her lap, so she really had no excuse.

"No, I mean it." Having eaten the rest of the sandwich, Griffin took a bite of the strawberry tart and nodded his approval. "The French have raised baking to an art form, haven't they?"

Darcy swallowed the last blackberry. "Yes, indeed. They do everything here with great flair." Over his shoulder, she spied two handsomely dressed young men pointing their way.

"Fan alert," she whispered. "There's a couple closing in on us. It looks as though they're working up the courage to ask for your autograph. Makes me appreciate how rock stars' wives must feel."

"I'm sorry, but at least I've never been mobbed like Sting. If they actually speak to me, I could tell them regardless of whom they believe me to be that they're mistaken."

"That would be dishonest," Darcy warned, "and unworthy of you."

"True." Griffin reached for her waist, pulled her across his lap and kissed her soundly. "There, did that discourage them?"

Darcy smoothed the hair at his nape as she surveyed the curious pair. "No, both men look as though they'd like to line up for kisses themselves."

"Let's get out of here." He set her on her feet, and she

wrapped the leftover cheese in a napkin and shoved it into her purse before helping him toss their trash into a nearby container.

"Let's just walk until we're too tired to go any farther," she suggested, and they set out to explore before the pair observing them could say bon jour.

Four hours later, they had toured the Latin Quarter to the level of exhaustion, and Griffin drew Darcy into a cafe on the Boulevard St. Michel. They chose a table in the rear where they were unlikely to be overheard and began with an appetizer of escargot.

"We used to order these every time we went out to dinner in Germany." Darcy sopped up the garlic butter with a toast point then picked up the tiny fork to pluck another snail from its shell. "I'd forgotten how good they are."

"You see, there are advantages to travel." Griffin was having such a good time watching her eat, he'd consumed only two snails while she was on her fifth.

"Speaking of travel, whatever happened to your trip to Budapest?" she asked.

Becoming decidedly uncomfortable, Griffin shifted position before responding. "I hate to admit this, but I just plucked Budapest out of the air in an effort to inspire you to apply for a passport. If you'd really like to go there, I'll arrange it."

"You can do that, just flit around the globe whenever you choose?"

"It takes some planning to work around my concert schedule, but yes, I can. We can."

Darcy wiped her hands on her napkin and sat back. "And if Interpol has another request?"

"They contacted me because Vaughn was a music lover. I doubt my particular talents will be needed again anytime soon."

"I'll take that as a yes."

"This operation was a nightmare, so let's not argue about what I may or may not do in the distant future."

"All right, but I'm sorry not to have been more help."

Griffin reached across the table to catch her hand and gave her fingers a loving squeeze. "You saved my life, Darcy. I was running out of excuses to lure Vaughn away from Astrid, but I didn't expect him to draw a gun. That was obviously poor planning on my part, but you not only drew his attention, you kicked his legs right out from under him. Then if you hadn't yelled a warning, I'd be going home in a pine box. I ought to request a medal for you."

"Don't bother. If I can't brag about how I won it, there's no point in owning one."

"True, but still you deserve one. Vaughn didn't anticipate your being so damn fierce. Thank God, I did. That's what I told you on the plane, wasn't it? That I love your spirit most?"

"No, you fell asleep before you completed the thought." She glanced toward a nearby couple who was leaning close to carry on an animated conversation in French. She couldn't understand a word of their exchange, but their teasing smiles made it plain they were lovers. She took a sip of Perrier. "Won't we have to give statements to someone?"

"No, Lucien handled it." Griffin watched her attention wander around the dimly lit café. She'd suddenly become vitally interested in everything, it seemed, except him.

"I didn't mean to spook you," he apologized. "I'll be patient. Maybe I'll grow on you."

"If you hadn't grown on me, I'd not have sweet talked you into bed. I'm not in Paris just to see the sights either."

"There, that's what I mean," he teased. "It doesn't take much to get your back up."

"And you actually find that appealing?" she asked incredulously.

"Oh hell, yes." He leaned toward her. "When I turned sixteen, my mother sat me down and told me that I was not only a good-looking kid, but bright and talented as well. She warned that everything would come to me so easily, I'd probably not appreciate it. She was especially adamant that I not take advantage of the women who'd be drawn to me."

"Isn't that the type of talk a father usually has with his son?"

"I've no idea, is it? My dad was probably in court pulling some poor kid's ass out of the fire. But regardless of who gave me that particular bit of advice, I remember the main point, which was if I expected everything to just naturally come my way, I'd never learn how to go after what I wanted on my own."

Darcy nodded thoughtfully. "Your mother's a wise woman, but hasn't it occurred to you that being the chick magnet you are, you might be overly susceptible to a challenge?"

Highly amused, Griffin tried not to laugh. "I've never thought of myself as a magnet for anything other than lint, but you're a lot more than a challenge, Darcy. You're a very exciting woman."

"Yeah, all the hot chicks go to work in overalls."

His gaze brightened. "Don't discount what you wear underneath."

What she couldn't discount was that she was no different from all the other women who'd adored him on sight. She'd just hidden it better than most to avoid being totally humiliated when her chances with him were slim to none. She'd never confess how easily he had gotten to her before he had spoken a single word.

"Every time I try to talk about us, you get awfully quiet, Darcy. That worries me. Do you want to spend the rest of your life alone?"

"No, but we don't always get what we want, do we?"

The waiter arrived with their entrees, and Griffin let her end the conversation for the moment, but he was determined to wring at least one word of affection from her before they flew home.

His lamb chops were so good he wished he'd asked for a double order, while Darcy was merely picking at her curried chicken. "You mentioned avoiding red meat. Do you eat lamb?" he asked.

"No, they're much too cute."

"They're also delicious. How about pork?"

"No, not since I saw *Babe*."

"Piglets are awfully cute, I'll agree, and apparently quite intelligent. I know better than to ask about veal, but you're fine with fish and fowl?"

"Yes, and I love snails, lobster, and crab."

Griffin took a sip of his Burgundy. "But you don't care what I eat?"

"No, not at all. That's your business. You've not made fun of me."

"And you appreciate that?"

Darcy gestured with her fork, then caught herself, and laid it along the edge of her plate. "Yes, I'm very grateful. Now what is it you're really after here?"

"Just a kind word is all. I'd hoped that you'd stumble across something you liked about me."

She rolled her eyes. "When other women spew a fountain of compliments, I think you'd be glad I give your ears a rest."

"You're right, of course. Just as my mother warned, I've been spoiled by cascades of lavish praise, while you stubbornly refuse to accept compliments graciously." He butted his fists together. "I'd say we pull each other toward the center. Such perfect balance is difficult to find."

Darcy paused to take another bite of chicken. "Maybe we could borrow the chalkboard they use to list their daily specials and chart all our differences over dessert."

"Sure. That sounds exciting."

"You excite too easily."

"Perhaps that's what you like best about me."

Darcy was about to respond with a suitably sarcastic reply when a car backfired out in the street. Her knife slipped from her grasp, clattered against her plate and brought disapproving glances from several of the café's patrons.

She wiped her hands on her napkin. "I'm sorry. I shouldn't be so jumpy."

"Of course you should. We can't pretend nothing happened last night."

She drew a deep breath, but it didn't ease her mind. He had lain in wait for a man rather than allow them to be stabbed in their sleep. They would have killed a second man if he hadn't committed suicide right in front of them. Then dear little Astrid had died. It was all more than she'd been prepared to face.

"I thought pretense was our only option," she responded wistfully.

"I'll show you another when we get back to the hotel."

Darcy shook her head. "It's a good thing you're the one with the dick, because I sure couldn't get it up tonight."

"Darcy!" Griffin fought to contain his laughter to a deep chuckle, then had to use his napkin to muffle the sound. "That's another thing I love about you. No one talks to me the way you do, and I'm so sick of fawning women."

"Well, no one's ever mistaken me for Bambi. But just for the sake of argument, what if I were to fall madly in love with you and pay you effusive compliments all day long?"

When she quickly focused on her plate rather than wait for his reply, Griffin was hit with a blinding glimpse of the obvious. "Oh, Darcy, how can you believe that I'd ever tire of you?"

She shrugged. "It could happen."

"Yeah, and a piano could fall out of the sky and crush us both while we're out sightseeing tomorrow, but it's highly unlikely."

Darcy hadn't meant to reveal so much and, badly embarrassed, she toyed with her food rather than argue. Up until now, she'd met a lot of boys masquerading as men, but here was Griffin, the genuine article, and she was terrified she wasn't nearly woman enough for him.

She looked as though she were about to dive under the table to avoid him, and Griffin couldn't bear to watch her squirm. "Would you like to call Christy Joy when we get back to the hotel and see how things are going at home? Or maybe you'd like to call your parents."

Relieved he'd changed the subject, Darcy nodded. "Thanks. Maybe I will, but you better tell me what to say so I won't get us both into trouble again."

"Okay, but I don't suppose there's any hope of your saying any flowery stuff about me."

She almost hoped he would write out some audacious script, because when it came to describing him, she had no clue where to begin.

Griffin took his time taking Darcy back to the Meurice. The evening was cool, but not too cold to be out for a walk. The glittering lights were beautiful, and he hoped the exercise would help her sleep. While she made the telephone calls from the bedroom, he sat at the piano and played Debussy's "Le Mer" very softly.

Darcy waited in the doorway until he looked up. "Everyone says hello. I was afraid J. Lyle might want Twink to stay in San Francisco, but he called Christy Joy this morning, admitted he couldn't keep up with his little girl and promised to bring her home today. I'd like to buy her a present while we're here."

"Sure. Does she like dolls?"

"Not really. She'll probably skateboard and play soccer in a couple of years. She likes to draw and color, but as her father discovered, she's a very active little girl."

A teasing light sparkled in Griffin's dark eyes. "Let's buy her a drum."

"Easy for you to say. She'll not be banging on it in your house."

"It was just a thought." He was tempted to ask if she wanted children, then realized how poorly she'd react and thought better of it. "How are your folks?"

"Fine, and once I mentioned we were in Paris, they reminded me of the time the three of us were here together. No one asked any questions I couldn't answer with the truth."

"That's a relief," he replied. He played another few bars of "Le Mer", and then paused. "I've been thinking about what you said this afternoon about having been a bird or squirrel. Do you really believe in past lives?"

"If being a squirrel qualifies, but let me ask you something. Do you feel any different than you did as a child? I realize our bodies age, but the part of you which is most you, your spirit or soul, do you feel your inner self aging?"

He played a final chord and left the bench to lean back against the piano with his arms casually folded across his chest. "No, but all the time you hear people say, 'I'm eighty, but I don't feel a day over twenty. It's just seeing an old man in the mirror that's a shock.'"

"Yes, that's precisely what I mean, and if our spirits don't age, why would they die?"

"Excellent question. Philosophers and theologians may have debated it for centuries, but you've convinced me it's true."

Appearing skeptical, Darcy came toward him. "Are you saying that your experience supports my theory, or are you simply trying to be agreeable?"

"Your theory makes perfect sense to me," he swore. "I told you I was never really a child. But it sure would be helpful if we could remember what we'd learned in our last life so we'd not have to start from scratch every time we're born."

"Maybe if we remembered, we might mourn for what we'd lost and ruin our chances for happiness in this life."

"A valid point, and this whole line of inquiry will give us something new to contemplate while we sit in my Zen garden."

"Yes, I can imagine post-it notes stuck all over the back with questions worthy of further thought."

"When we get home, remind me to leave post-it notes and pencils out there with the rake."

"Will do." She leaned against him. "This was a lovely day, thank you."

He ran his fingertip along her cheek. "It's not over yet, is it?"

In response, she unbuttoned his shirt, laid her ear upon his chest and listened closely. "Hmm, your heart's still beating. That's a very good sign we might hope for more."

He wrapped his arms around her to press her closer still. Her reticence to say she cared for him when she gave affection so freely confused him completely. She'd claimed to be very particular about her partners, so he knew she didn't just love sex. She had to care for him too, but he wished she'd just come out and admit it.

He swung her up into his arms, carried her into the bed and dropped her in the middle. "Where's that lavender nightgown?" he asked.

"You like it?"

"*Oui.* You look delicious in lace, but first, let's take that bath you jumped out of last night."

After being out all afternoon, she did feel a mite gritty. "That sounds wonderful. Give me a minute and I'll fill the tub."

She entered the bathroom and looked through the bottles of salts, bubble bath, creams and perfumed oils. Then, throwing caution to the wind, she turned on the tap and added some of each to the tub. She quickly slipped off her clothes and opened the door before climbing in.

Griffin paused at the doorway where the combined fragrances nearly bowled him over. "Are you daring me to go to bed smelling good enough to eat?"

"I sure am." Darcy flung a handful of soapy bubbles at him.

"You're on." Griffin kicked off his loafers. He couldn't understand how any woman could be so invitingly playful one minute and maddeningly aloof the next. If she kept it up much longer, she might run the risk of his drowning her in some fancy bathtub. Then he remembered how they'd used the shower at his house.

"What are you laughing about?" she called.

"Private joke," he insisted as he slipped into the tub behind her. He reached around her to roll her soapy nipples between his fingers and thumbs.

She relaxed against him and looped her arms around his thighs. "I've long been of the opinion that adults don't have nearly enough time to play."

"You're just full of opinions today, aren't you? Fortunately, I agree. We're a little old for a sandbox, but could we suspend a swing from the wisteria arbor?"

Darcy wiggled her bottom against his erection. "One we could use together?"

"Sure, although I do have exposed beams in my bedroom. Maybe we ought to put it in there."

"I'd say that all depends on what you intend to do in your swing."

Griffin traced a meandering trail from her breasts down over her flat stomach to the soft nest between her legs. "I can think of several amusing pastimes."

As he described them, his faint accent turned each word into the most enticing possibility. She floated on his honeyed whispers as much as his knowing touch. He knew just where to lightly graze her skin, and where to apply gentle pressure. It wasn't just his great hands she loved, though—it was all of him.

"Of course, the motion of the swing should make every sensation more intense," he added.

Darcy let her head drop back on his shoulder. "I like the way you think."

He pulled her across his lap to kiss her, but kept up his intimate massage. Next, he dipped his head to draw a tightly puckered nipple into his mouth. He sucked and licked until her whole body grew warmer than the water.

She reached up to lace her fingers in his hair, and he bit her lightly. "Let's get out of here," he whispered.

He slid her forward, rose, and lifted her to her feet as he pulled the plug. He watched the water swirl around her legs before he helped her from the tub. "You have the cutest little feet." He grabbed a towel and rubbed her dry. "Oh, hell, you're cute all over."

Darcy laughed with him until he eased her down on the bed and began to suck on her toes. "Griffin!" she screamed. "Stop it, that tickles!"

"Really? I thought it was supposed to have a more erotic effect."

"Do other women like it?"

"I wouldn't know. I've never tried it with another woman."

"Good." She bent her knee and patted her exposed thigh. "Lay your head here, and I'll do the same with you."

"Well, this is France," he murmured as he lay down alongside her in the classic position for *soixante-neuf.* "But with your mouth on me, I might not be able to do a very good job on you."

"Don't worry, I'll give you an A for effort," she coaxed.

"Did I mention that I love the way you tease me?" His head comfortably pillowed on her thigh, he slid his tongue along the length of her slit and gasped as her hands tightened around his cock. He inhaled deeply and found her own delicious scent mixed with that of the bath oil. He parted her folds with his fingers to caress her clit, but when she drew the tip of his cock into her mouth, he couldn't concentrate at all.

In a matter of seconds, he pulled away. "That feels so good you've got me completely distracted." He rolled off the side of the bed. "Here, kneel on the bed in front of me."

Darcy grabbed a pillow to support her head and shoulders and angled her bottom toward him. He had her so hot she didn't care what position he chose, but when he slid just the head of his cock in and withdrew, she shoved back against his thighs. He might love being teased with words, but she didn't like being teased to the edge of climax and abandoned.

Griffin understood what she wanted and entered deeply on his second thrust. Filled, her inner muscles caressed him, drawing him down until he was buried so deep he came with quick, pistoning spasms. He felt her orgasm spiral around him, milking him dry and, when he collapsed beside her on the bed, neither of them wanted more.

Chapter Twenty

Monday dawned overcast and cool. Griffin described it as a perfect morning to visit the Louvre, and Darcy agreed it would be an excellent distraction from what lay ahead that afternoon.

As they viewed a splendid portrait of Louis XIV by Rigaud, she couldn't help but think the king looked utterly ridiculous showing off his white-stockinged legs while his torso was so heavily draped in his fleur-de-lis embroidered royal robes.

She looked up at Griffin, who was again wearing his navy blazer and gray slacks. "I can't even imagine you dressed like that."

"Thank God. He looks rather like a drag queen, doesn't he?"

"Imagine how many tailors it must have taken to sew such elaborate garments. Then there were the ancient Greeks, who just wrapped themselves in sheets and spent their time discussing the meaning of life in such depth we're still quoting them."

"You're saying it's a matter of priorities?"

"Definitely, but I didn't mean to dawdle here when there's so much to see."

"We needn't visit every gallery this morning," Griffin assured her. "We can come back another day, or on our next trip to France."

He sounded as though he sincerely believed they'd tour the world together, while she feared harboring such a wonderful dream would only magnify her heartache when they parted. Her spirits plummeting, she was grateful when a guide with more than a dozen tourists in tow approached them to ask if Griffin were the famed concert pianist.

He nodded and greeted them. *"Bon jour."*

Chastising herself to get a grip, Darcy strolled away to view the next painting while Griffin answered the groups' questions in both French and English. He signed autographs in their guide books, then quickly broke away.

"Let's go find the Mona Lisa," he suggested and again took Darcy's hand.

"It must be nice to have such an adoring public."

He winked at her. "It's not nearly as nice as being adored in private."

She understood precisely what he meant, but when she had such a good time with him, she didn't resent being interrupted by the occasional fan. The morning passed all too swiftly, and neither cared to stop for lunch.

Lucien met them at the hotel with a Mercedes sedan for the drive to the funeral. "The Mother Superior told me that Astrid was one of their favorite students. Quite naturally, they have all been praying for her and are deeply saddened by her death. The Reverend Mother was overwhelmed by your generosity in paying not only for the funeral, but in providing for the continued operation of their school as well."

Darcy squeezed Griffin's hand and whispered, "Did you give them all the money Lyman Vaughn paid you?"

"Yes. I certainly don't want it, and it's rather fitting, don't you think? Besides the IRS is used to my giving large sums to charity, so they'll not quibble over the amount."

She swallowed hard. "You routinely donate a million dollars to charity?"

"Of course. Do you know how many worthy causes there are?"

She shook her head. "Thousands, probably."

"At least. I've been very lucky, Darcy, so I share it. I only wish I could do more to make the world a better place."

For a brief instant, Darcy wished that he possessed some disastrous flaw, but he really was Prince Charming and, as usual, he made her proud.

The convent where Astrid had been schooled was located in a quiet village south of Paris, and for the majority of their journey the highway paralleled the banks of the Seine. Once outside the bustling city, the countryside was draped in such vibrant shades of green, Darcy sat back to enjoy the view. More than an hour passed before Lucien turned the car into the gravel parking lot beside a small Gothic church. The adjacent convent lay behind a high, ivy-shrouded wall.

There were only two other cars parked off to the side, and Darcy supposed they must belong to the priest and nuns. "It doesn't look as though there will be any other guests," she mused aloud.

"If there are, please remember their faces," Lucien advised.

"Whom did you expect to attend?" Griffin inquired softly.

"Astrid's physician, perhaps, or her friends' parents."

Lucien shrugged his thick shoulders. "I will tell you about the physician after the service. As for parents, I believe many of the convent's students are orphans. Would you care to wait inside the church? I will inform them of our arrival."

The gravel crunched beneath their feet as they made their way up the path. While Lucien disappeared around the side of the church, Griffin grabbed the worn brass handle and pulled open the heavy oak door. Inside, the stained glass windows tinted the candles' dim light with rainbow hues, but Astrid's rose-draped casket stood out clearly in front of the altar.

"You thought of the flowers too, didn't you?" Darcy asked.

Griffin took her arm to escort her to a front pew. "We couldn't have a funeral without flowers."

"I agree, but the white roses are spectacular. It was very thoughtful of you."

He responded with a raised brow, as though she should have discovered how considerate he was long before now. He slid into the pew after her and left room for Lucien to join them on the aisle.

Darcy sat back and wondered what it must be like to grow up in such a close-knit community. She'd changed schools and friends so frequently that she had no real sense of the permanence which pervaded the incense-scented atmosphere. Suddenly feeling very alone, she reached for Griffin's hand and curled her fingers over his.

Lucien soon arrived, and next, the nuns, still preferring their traditional habits, filed in with their charges. The girls ranged in age from five or six through their teens and were dressed in neatly pressed navy blue uniforms. Many were weeping pitifully into their handkerchiefs.

One of the sisters sat at a pump organ, but it took vigorous effort on her part to bring it wheezing to life. Darcy didn't recognize the somber hymn, and she thought it a shame they had not asked Griffin to play. Then she promptly dismissed the idea, for not even a man as gifted as he would be able to coax beautiful music from such an ancient instrument.

Sharing her thoughts, he leaned over to whisper, "Yes, I'll buy them a new organ too."

The priest was a sandy-haired young man who broke down and wept before he had completed the funeral mass. Although Darcy couldn't follow his lengthy remarks in French, the little girls and nuns were all nodding as though he were paying Astrid an appropriate tribute.

What she recalled was Astrid's delight in meeting Griffin, and how attentive he'd been to the frail young woman. With her classmates sobbing throughout the funeral, Darcy had to keep mopping away her own tears, while Griffin and Lucien sat silently absorbing the waves of sadness flowing around them without any visible sign of emotion.

As the service drew to a close, Lucien checked his watch, and Darcy leaned forward to speak. "We needn't stay for the burial if you haven't the time," she whispered.

Griffin appeared relieved. "I'd rather visit the grave when the angel headstone is in place, but I should speak with the Mother Superior before we leave."

Lucien and Darcy waited for him outside by the car. When he caught up with them, Lucien drew him aside. "Please excuse us a moment, Ms. MacLeod," he begged and addressed Griffin in French.

Darcy dried the last of her tears, but when Griffin reacted to Lucien's confidence with an anguished cry, she rushed to rejoin them. "What wrong?" she asked.

Griffin looked sick and recoiled against the Mercedes. "Tell her."

Lucien did not look pleased to have to repeat his news, and his hushed tone failed to lessen the shock. "Astrid's physician questioned the suddenness of her death. Tests revealed evidence of a morphine overdose."

Stunned, Darcy reached for a plausible explanation. "Could

the nurse have mistaken the dosage?"

"No," Griffin exclaimed through clenched teeth. "Vaughn did it himself after he'd sent the nurse and the others away and dispatched Octavio to kill us. Do you remember what he said, 'We'll deal with the dead tomorrow.' Clearly he knew more than one person had died."

Appalled, Darcy grabbed hold of Lucien's sleeve. "Vaughn murdered his own daughter?"

"Yes, it appears so, but we'll never know whether or not he also intended to take his own life."

"No," Darcy whispered. "I'll bet he meant to leave us dead and walk away." Her own anguish was mirrored in Griffin's stricken expression. They'd been grateful to escape a life-threatening ordeal unscathed, but now Astrid's murder would haunt them forever.

"That's it, Lucien," Griffin swore. "Tell Interpol I quit. I'm not contaminating my life another second with men like Lyman Vaughn. Let's get out of here." He yanked open the car door and helped Darcy inside. Once they were underway, he moved away from her toward the door and focused on the passing scene.

She didn't feel like talking either, but she hadn't expected him to book a flight home as soon as they returned to the Meurice. They had to gather their belongings quickly to leave for the airport, but when Paris had lost its magic, home was the perfect place to be.

On the flight, Griffin floated on his sedative-induced dreams, but Darcy was again too anxious to rest. She understood why the full force of the weekend's horror had hit her lover so hard, but because she'd been with him every step of the way, she wished he hadn't withdrawn from her so completely.

With the nine-hour time difference between France and San Francisco, even after a long flight, they landed in the late afternoon, close to the time they'd left Paris. Certain it would be wasted energy, Darcy made no effort to lift Griffin's spirits on the drive down the coast. Instead, she stared out at the fog-veiled highway and wondered if he would fill his next composition with near-palpable despair.

He left the motor running in the Land Rover while he walked her to her door. "Give me a few days to sort everything out," he asked.

"Take all the time you need." Darcy reached up to brush his cheek with a fleeting kiss and hid her disappointment when he offered no affectionate gesture in return.

She unlocked her door and made it inside before the flimsy dam holding back her tears cracked wide open. She left her suitcase in the middle of the living room, turned off the lights she'd left burning and went straight to bed. It wasn't until the next morning that she realized how little she could tell her friends about their trip.

George was watering the plants when Darcy came breezing into the nursery. "I didn't expect to see you back so soon. How was your trip?" he asked.

At the airport, Darcy had bought a bag of fanciful building blocks cut from slender tree limbs for Twink, but now she was sorry she hadn't brought George a present too. "I had a really good time in Paris," she confided truthfully. "But I don't think I'm cut out for the jet set."

"Why not? I'll bet Griffin travels first class."

"Yes, he sure does, but plane travel is still awfully wearing. Now I've got to get busy on the landscaping for the Peavey wedding. Can you handle everything out here?"

"Sure, we've been doing just fine. Christy Joy will tell you we had a good weekend."

Darcy waved to him and went on inside. Both Christy Joy and Mary Beth were standing at the counter and gaped in surprise. "We didn't expect you to come home so soon!" Christy Joy cried.

"Griffin had only a quick trip planned," Darcy hedged. "But a person could spend years in Paris and not see it all."

Christy Joy was still admiring her beautiful engagement ring, and she turned her hand into a ray of sunshine to catch the sparkle. "Are things heating up between you two?"

Darcy refused to admit they'd heated up to scalding only to cool down to an Arctic chill. "Let's not even go there," she replied. "I've a present for Twink. Did she get home all right?"

"Yes, but she's already at school." Christy took the bag of unusual blocks and peeked inside. "Aren't these clever. Twink will love them. Thank you for thinking of her."

"I thought about you all, but unfortunately, we left before I had time to shop for more presents."

Mary Beth laughed. "I didn't expect a Dior gown, but it's nice to have you home. Let me show you the figures for the weekend."

Darcy feigned an interest she didn't feel, but she was pleased their profits were up since the storm. She kept busy all day, but as George got ready to leave, she walked him to the gate.

"If someone asked for a few days," she began, "how many would you assume that would be?"

George tucked in his shirt and adjusted his hat. "Are we talking about one of your clients, or Griffin Moore?"

"What difference does it make?"

George chuckled and rested his hand on the gate. "Griffin, then. He'd probably consider a few more than a couple, but less than a week. Is that any help?"

"Yes, thank you. That's what I figured too."

"I wouldn't worry, he always turns up," George advised.

"Thanks." She understood how men needed their space, but as she locked up for the night, she still felt uneasy. Griffin definitely had a dark side, but she doubted he'd slide into it so deep that he couldn't climb out. Still, regardless of his inner turmoil, she couldn't spend half the week terrified she'd lost him.

Then she remembered their conversation about leaving post-it notes on his bench. The days were lengthening, and if she hurried, she'd be able to plaster the bench with love notes without invading his privacy. Or at least that was how she saw it. She grabbed a pack of yellow notes and, with a flower pen tucked in her bib pocket, she set out for Ridgecrest.

Unfortunately, she hadn't counted on the wrought-iron gate being closed. Unwilling to allow such a minor detail to ruin her plans, she parked on the street. She checked for traffic, found none, and then used the gate's coiling floral design for footholds. She quickly pulled herself up and over and then sprinted past the bubbling mermaid fountain.

When she rounded the side of the house, she heard Griffin playing the same series of notes over and over again as though the sequence weren't quite right. Whatever his problem, it was a pretty tune rather than some wretched dirge. Encouraged, she skirted the terrace and crossed the Zen garden.

Her first note simply said she loved him. After slapping it on the bench, she added one to praise the passion he poured into his music. She also loved the sparkle in his dark eyes when he teased her, as well as the gentleness of his touch. She loved his smile, and the confident way he moved. She loved how he listened to her so attentively and remembered everything she said. She loved that he took her seriously. She loved his intelligence and how handsome he looked in a tux.

She wrote I love you a couple more times and added them to the flurry now adorning the bench. With the light rapidly fading, she dashed back around to the front of the house rather than let him catch her writing sappy love notes in the dark. If the audacious stunt worked as she hoped, he ought to be inspired to drive right down the hill to her house.

If it didn't, she sure didn't want to be home alone waiting for a call that would never come. So, she sat on the fountain wall, trailed her fingers in the water and waited. Now that it was too late to remove the notes, she was afraid they would all sound impossibly silly, but damn it all, every single one had been sincere. She really did love him, and it was high time she got out of her own way and stopped sabotaging their future.

Griffin had kept his eye on the angle of the sun and, eager for the serenity of the sunset, he left the new melody unfinished and went out to the Zen garden. At first, he thought the wind must have littered the bench with scraps, but then he recognized the small yellow squares for what they were. He laughed as he peeled them off and read them in the gathering dusk.

He hadn't shaved that morning, nor combed his hair, but on the off-chance Darcy might be waiting in her truck, he didn't want to waste any time cleaning up. He jogged down the driveway, and when he found her at the fountain, he looked down at the handful of notes.

It was the first time she'd ever seen him at a loss for words, but she still had a few. She got up and walked to him. "I didn't plan on hanging around, but when you finish sorting out everything, I don't want to end up being something you've sorted out."

"Oh, Darcy, you're an absolute treasure." He pulled her into his arms and hugged her tight. "Come on, let's catch the sunset."

Certain being regarded as a treasure was a promising sign, she fell in step beside him. He was dressed in his gray sweats and looked as though he'd just rolled out of bed, but being with him always tugged at her heart.

"I should have thought of it sooner," she apologized. "Then maybe I could have written more original notes."

When they reached the bench, Griffin shoved the post-its into his pocket and pulled her down across his lap. "These were fine, but there's no rule that says you can't do it more than once, is there?"

"No, I suppose not, but the next time it won't be much of a surprise."

"Are you kidding? With you, it's bound to be." He nuzzled her neck playfully and held her clasped in a fond embrace until the sunset had turned the whole sky a heavenly pink.

"I'm sorry you were worried," he whispered. "After we learned how Astrid died, I was afraid you might decide I was more trouble than I'm worth. So rather than crowd you, I backed off to give you some time to think."

Amazed he could be so damn clueless, Darcy blamed herself for not sharing the love overflowing her heart. She framed his face with her hands and kissed him sweetly, but she couldn't help teasing him. "What? And miss having my work featured in the *Architectural Digest*? Or was that just something you made up, like Budapest?"

"Do you see what I mean? You're the most unpredictable woman I've ever met, and it's another thing I love about you."

"Nice evasion, but I really don't give a hoot about the *Architectural Digest*. I just care about you."

"You're the coyly evasive one, but thank you, the feature story is real. I'll show you the confirmation letter. Give me a couple of minutes to clean up, and we'll go out to dinner."

"No one else gets to see you looking this scruffy, and I like it. Let's stay right here."

He raked his fingers through his hair. "You actually like this?"

She slid her hand under his sweatshirt and tickled his ribs. "I love you in a tux or nothing at all. I understand why you'd want to impress your public, but you don't have to slick up for me when I'd love you in a clown suit."

His smile grew wide. "All right, we'll stay here. Would you call this a romantic spot?"

"A lovely Zen garden overlooking the sea? Yes, it's wonderfully romantic."

"Good, because I want you to remember this." He moved her off his lap to the bench and got down on one knee. "Darcy MacLeod, I love you with all my heart and soul. I don't want to spend another day without you. I've already cut way back on my concert schedule. I intend to write and record right here in Monarch Bay, so you needn't worry I'll be away from home more than I'm here. As for Defy the World Tomatoes, it's a brilliant concept, and I hope you go nationwide."

He paused to take a deep breath and then plunged ahead. "Will you do me the great honor of becoming my wife?"

His proposal was so completely unexpected, she was flabbergasted and just stared at him, unable to do more than gape witlessly.

"Would you like to think about it?"

He'd already made it plain they'd have a real home, and the last of her reservations dissolved in a flash of pure bliss, but she managed only a strangled gasp.

He took her hands in his and squeezed them lightly. "I didn't mean to send you into a catatonic trance. Should I call the paramedics?"

Finally able to suck in a deep breath, she threw her arms around his neck. "All this time, I've been telling myself none of this is real. But you are for real, aren't you?"

He fluffed her hair. "Just because I've a closet full of Grammys doesn't mean I'm not as real as the next guy."

Darcy pulled back slightly. "You've won Grammys for your classical recordings?"

He nodded. "Sure, lots of them, but they give them out before the televised awards, so you've never seen photos of me in *People Magazine* hugging whoever's hot that year.

"Let's go shopping for your ring in the morning. Then I want to take you home to Atlanta to meet my folks. Your parents could come from Texas, and we could be married there. Would that be all right with you?"

She raised her hand to beg for a minute. "Just let me catch my breath." Looking back, it seemed as though she'd boarded a roller coaster that first day he'd walked into Defy the World Tomatoes. It had been an incredible ride, and she didn't want it to ever end.

"I'm doing the flowers for a June wedding down the street," she finally replied. "Then Christy Joy and Jeremy want to get married, but if you can give me a couple of months to pull everything together, I'll marry you in Atlanta or Fresno or Katmandu, wherever you like."

Griffin stood and pulled her into his arms. "Thank you. Now let's go inside before we start celebrating, get too wild and roll right off the bluff."

Darcy looked out toward the sea where the waves shimmered with the last of the light. "We're going to have to put up a railing here so that when we turn the Zen garden into a sandbox it won't be dangerous for the kids."

Griffin swung her up into his arms. "We'll have beautiful children."

She could so easily imagine their girls being tall like him and the boys barely grazing five feet that she began to laugh. Together they would always have laughter and such beautiful music she couldn't wait to say, "I do".

About the Author

To learn more about Phoebe Conn, please visit www.phoebeconn.com. Send an email to her at phoebeconn@earthlink.net or join her Yahoo! group to join in the fun with other readers as well,
http://groups.yahoo.com/group/phoebeconn.

CPSIA information can be obtained at www.ICGtesting.com
Printed in the USA
LVOW12s1441020813

346027LV00002B/230/P